## The Stallion

'I have to be strict, you see,' said Nadine. 'My brother requires it of me. Everything has to be perfect. It's all a matter of self-discipline.' The voice was as languorous and decadent as her pose.

'I see,' said Penny. So...she thought, Nadine influences Alistair's life. For a moment Penny wondered if there was something decidedly unhealthy in their relationship. If that was the case, then she could easily win her wager to win the prize stallion. It could even be easy if those recently dormant and dark feelings that were racing through her body were anything to go by.

**By the same author:**

Eye of the Storm
Runners and Riders
Like Mother, Like Daughter

The Stallion
Georgina Brown

Black Lace books contain sexual fantasies.
In real life, always practise safe sex.

This edition published in 2008 by
Black Lace
Thames Wharf Studios
Rainville Rd
London W6 9HA

Originally published 1995

A catalogue record for this book is available from the British Library.

*www.black-lace-books.com*

Typeset in TheSerif by Palimpsest Book Production Limited, Grangemouth, Stirlingshire
Printed and bound in Great Britain by CPI Antony Rowe, Chippenham, Wiltshire

Distributed in the USA by Macmillan, 175 Fifth Avenue,
New York, NY 10010, USA

ISBN 978 0 352 34199 0

3 5 7 9 10 8 6 4 2

# 1

What Ariadne told Penny was a challenge, and one she could not help but rise to.

'You'll get his backing,' Ariadne said, tossing her blonde mane whilst cupping her breast. From there, she ran her hand over her narrow waist and down over her curving hip. As the hand caressed, her body moved to meet it, undulating appreciatively as if it belonged to someone else. It was an alluring gesture, inviting, yet evidently self-gratifying. 'But you won't get him,' she added, almost as an after-thought.

Ariadne's eyes seemed to be avoiding her own and for a moment Penny detected an air of insincerity rather than disappointment. Ariadne hated rejection.

Penny raked her fingers through her own hair, which was dark and glossy, and a crowning compliment to the rich cream-iness of her skin. At the same time, she asked herself what she'd let herself in for by signing a contract with Alistair Beaumont. The answer was easy. Showjumping cost money. Everyone sought out a wealthy backer nowadays, and he'd made her an offer she couldn't refuse. Besides that, Beaumont was handsome in that classic masculine way that silk shirts and well-cut clothes do heaps to accentuate.

There was, of course, Mark to consider. She lived with Mark, and in the heady days and weeks of early passion, had convinced herself that she would stay with him for ever. So she'd loitered in a comfortable rut until the feeling of being stultified had crept up on her. Suddenly, the urge to move on had become irresistible.

Ariadne had helped her get Alistair Beaumont's backing and she was grateful for it. This extra wager on the side added a little spice to the basic business of securing sponsorship in a very competitive sport.

Penny had known Ariadne since childhood and had once caught her giving one of her own brothers fellatio whilst her other brother pushed his immature but responsive penis into her golden-haired cleft from behind. They knew each other well, though Ariadne consistently niggled Penny that she did not know herself well enough; that there was more to her than met the eyes.

Penny had taken little notice. She was beautiful, successful (so far), and now she had won the backing of Alistair Beaumont. In addition, Ariadne's wager had intrigued her. What was there to lose in rising to it? Besides, at the end of it, Ariadne's black stallion would be hers. Not that Ariadne would miss this most beautiful animal. Ariadne had a lot of things, in fact, that had seemed to accumulate since leaving Alistair Beaumont's stables. And that was how Penny herself had got his support – Ariadne had arranged it for her.

High breasts, blonde hair and long legs were attributes Ariadne possessed among many others. Penny did not resent that. She'd known Ariadne a long time, regarded her as beautiful, knew she was demanding and also had a particular penchant for intrigue and an abnormal appetite for men. Not that Penny could condemn that. She was very fond of them herself.

'It's a bet, then,' said Ariadne. 'If you can strike it with Alistair, you've won Daedalus – one stallion for another. If not, your horses are mine.'

Penny agreed. The very thought, that Alistair had resisted

the temptations Ariadne had in plenty, intrigued her. From what her friend had told her, her benefactor only watched others making out. The very thought filled her with an obsessive determination she didn't know she had.

Sponsorship in showjumping was hard to come by, and when someone like Beaumont made an offer, any rider had to sit up and take notice. Horses cost money to keep, and with entry fees rising all the time, there was not one successful showjumper who didn't have the backing of a double-glazing company, a building firm or a multinational corporation.

The very first time she'd seen Beaumont, she'd liked the look of him. Power and wealth gave something extra to a man that made him more alluring. He responded to his wealth, lived up to it, moved like a cat and had eyes that darted over her body like naked flames. Like a moth, she was attracted to those flames. She'd only seen him clothed, but the body beneath the misted blue of an Armani sweater, tailored breeches and high leather boots seemed hard and well formed.

Ariadne had done a season with him. She didn't explain why it was only one season, so Penny took it that her failure to seduce Beaumont must be the reason for her not staying. Failure with regard to men was not something Ariadne took kindly to.

'Everyone rides hard, everyone plays hard, but not him,' Ariadne explained in a voice that edged on sulkiness. 'He stands, watches everything you do, as though he's looking through your clothes – that sort of thing.' She lowered her eyelids in her usual sultry way and leaned closer. 'He watches everyone else making out. He likes watching.' And she smiled in a catlike way.

And you loved it, Penny thought as she felt the hot breath from Ariadne's red lips not far from her neck. 'A voyeur? Is that what you're telling me?'

Ariadne tossed her hair and let it fall unbridled over her bare shoulder. She nodded.

'Then our wager's on? No backing out?' Ariadne asked with a wicked gleam in her eyes. 'You've seen my new stallion. All yours if you get Alistair Beaumont.'

Penny eyed her friend before answering. 'No backing out,' she said at last.

No backing out, she thought to herself. She had not backed out then, and she had not backed out today. Her interview with Alistair Beaumont had started off in an ordinary way: name, career to date, etc. Then he had asked her just how important it was for her to receive his backing and what she was prepared to do to get it.

'Anything,' she had replied.

He'd taken her at her word, and here she was wearing nothing but shoes, a pair of sheer chocolate-coloured stockings and a crisply frilled, but scanty, suspender belt – all, thankfully, covered by the soft opulence of a cashmere coat. Beside her walked Alistair Beaumont.

'How does it feel?' he asked in a husky, sensual voice. His steel-grey eyes did not leave the mix of shoppers and lunch-time office workers ahead of and around them.

Somehow Penny didn't want to say anything. What she was doing, what was happening to her, was something solitary, for her enjoyment alone. Her very breath caught slightly before release. She yearned to moan her ecstasy, but couldn't. She was in a public place, and although the thought of going public excited her, she kept her pleasure to herself though her eyes sparkled and her skin tingled. Her sex was tantalised and she relied on a rising breeze to cool the heat that burned between her legs and would not be fully quenched.

'What do you mean?' Her voice was provocative, yet hushed

and as soft as the coat lining that caressed her naked body and teased her senses.

'Exactly what I said. Describe it to me.' He did not raise his voice. Still he did not look at her. 'Well?' he demanded.

'I'm trying to think,' she replied, determined to take her time and enjoy what she was experiencing despite it being at his suggestion.

She took a deep breath and thought about how she felt – and not just with regard to her nakedness beneath the swishing coat. That was something to be relished as no more important than thick cream on coffee cake.

This was something she hadn't expected, and was incomparable to anything she'd ever done before. She could not forget that Alistair was walking at her side. He was a presence, a presence much appreciated, and, judging by the looks of secretaries bustling by on their lunch-time breaks, much admired.

Ariadne had admired him, too. Ariadne had wanted him but, according to what she'd told Penny, had not got him. Why should she succeed where Ariadne had failed?

'You still haven't answered,' she heard him say.

'Erotic.' It was the first word that came to mind. How else could she describe what she was doing, what she was thinking? Delicious shivers of excitement and sensual pleasure made her nipples grow and become almost painful with their need for touch. Wetness oozed from the warm lips that nestled provocatively between her silky soft thighs. 'Very erotic. Arousing!'

She stressed the words. Now it wasn't just a question of needing his sponsorship for her highly expensive sport. She had a wager to win, and what a way to win it.

So, he was a man who liked to watch. Surely something of what he watched would arouse him until he had to take her, had to give in to his own sexuality and bury his cock deep within her inviting cleft.

Beneath the cover of her coat her hips swayed as she tried to elicit the last ounce of sexual turn-on from the cool silk lining. She trembled and, as if taken by the chill waters of a mountain torrent, all her inhibitions seemed to flow away. Feelings and emotions she had never known seemed to bubble to the surface. She knew that in the past she had kept them hidden and had disguised her secret desires and outright fantasies with a brittle veneer of what she chose to call feminism. It had not been an honest term, she told herself, for what she was feeling now belonged solely to her, and no matter what this man might be getting from her experience, she was getting more.

'That's not a very good description,' she heard him say. 'I said describe it to me.'

There was demand in his voice now. She sensed his need to draw her own personal feelings out of her; savour the sweet juice of arousal in his mind via her voice. But it wasn't his experience. It was only hers. Those new emotions told her that; those new desires would show her.

She tossed her hair and looked at him sidelong, the soft darkness of her lashes briefly alighting on her creamy cheeks. The dark-pink lips of her wide mouth smiled.

Beneath the impenetrable barrier of her coat, her nipples erected against the coolness of the silk lining, her buttocks quivering as though caressed by the fingertips of an unseen lover. Her skin shimmered with the feel of it. Her nerve ends tingled as though charged with a feather of electrical current. She buried her hands deep in her pockets and nestled her chin down into the collar.

'It's very difficult to do ... here.' She licked her lips as her eyes flitted over the faces of the crowd. Those that did look her way she knew were only taking in her good looks – the dark hair, the dark-blue eyes – not what she was; not how she was underneath. They could only imagine her flat belly, her silky thighs and the heart-shaped tangle of dark curly hair that nestled between them, hiding an awesome thirst that had need of quenching.

She wore stockings, chocolate against the milky creaminess of her skin. Her calves were taut and ankles slim above the black straps of her high-heeled shoes.

She was shapely, she was sexy, and she was loving every minute of this. As she walked, she could feel the movement of the black, lace-edged suspender belt and the whispering rasp of sheer stockings as her thighs brushed one against the other. She relished the heightened sensation of vulnerability that encircled her exposed sex. There was nothing else between her and public outrage – except for her coat.

'No one can see,' he said suddenly as if reading her thoughts. 'Only you and I know what you look like beneath that coat, but only you know how it feels. Describe it to me. I want to share it with you.'

His sigh filtered into her thoughts. She licked her lips and looked at him sidelong again. She studied the crisp, dark eyebrows and the thatch of dark hair. He was handsome. She had to admit that. But distant, somehow remote. His eyes stared straight ahead.

'I want to know exactly what you feel,' he said somewhat impatiently.

Impatience, she thought, was only to be expected. Alistair Beaumont was a man of influence; a man of money who was used to giving orders and used to having them obeyed.

Choosing her words carefully, she formed her answer. So much depended on them. She took a deep breath and licked her dry lips. 'Hmmm,' she murmured as the cool silk caressed her skin. 'The silk is very cool, very smooth. It's rubbing my nipples. They've grown bigger. They're stiff, almost painful.

Cold air is circulating between my legs. I can feel it disturbing my pubic hair.'

Poetic, she thought; my words sound poetic. She was aroused by them as well as pleased. Funny, she thought, that no matter how cool the air, my cleft is still hot – still moist, demanding.

Her voice was husky and low. Her own words excited her. Within her body, the bud of passion that sat so secretly among lips of pink flesh was reminding her of its existence; reminding her of the effect her lurid thoughts could have on it. Fleetingly, she glanced at the other people who hurried along the pavement. She voiced what she was thinking.

'What would these people think if they knew; if they could see?'

She glanced swiftly at this man who could use his money to back her expertise, and perhaps extend her sexual experience *and* give her ownership of a thoroughbred stallion who had covered more than twenty mares already this year. She uttered a silent prayer that he would confirm his decision today.

Her body bristled with anticipation as draughts of cool air caressed her slim thighs, but did nothing to cool the heat that burned between her legs.

'They see nothing. They hear nothing.' she heard him say. 'Go on.'

Somehow, she knew what she had to say next, what he wanted her to say. The words seemed engraved somewhere inside her along with the birth of her new desires. Her body trembled when she answered.

'It excites me, as though I have some kind of power over them. I am doing something that is strictly taboo, that they would condemn me for. Yet I am doing it. Despite them, I am doing it.'

She did not add that he, too, was one of them. Perhaps he thought this gave him power over her, as though she were doing it purely for his enjoyment. She wasn't. This was for herself.

Will this one small act be enough to gain his body? she asked herself. Had Ariadne refused to do this, yet still got the sponsorship for her showjumping season but not the man to go with it? No, she told herself. Ariadne would not have refused. There had to be more to this.

He cleared his throat, turned and smiled at her. 'That's very good to hear, my dear. Very good indeed. I think you might be exactly what I'm looking for.' One arm reached out and curved around her back as he guided her through the midday crowds towards the bank. An ordinary occurrence. Something people did every day. But not dressed as she was. Not attired only in shiny stockings, a crisp, black-lace suspender belt and a cashmere coat.

'How else does it make you feel?'

The silk lining, that had only lightly trembled against her bare back and taut, rounded bottom, now slid over it from the touch of his arm. She clenched each pearlike orb of her rear, one against the other. It was hard to suppress the urge to thrust forward. Her legs and secret lips parted as she extended her stride to take in the two steps up to the door of the bank. Before very long her love juice would begin to flow, and then . . .

He repeated his question.

She took a deep breath before answering. 'In need.' It was an honest exclamation, but one offered in a hushed gasp, secret and meant for nearby ears only. Briefly, she caught sight of his smile. She returned it and knew instantly that she had won his sponsorship for the coming competitive year, and everything else that went with it.

Eyes bright and heart beating with excitement, she watched

him as he made his way forward along the roped-in queue over the dappled cream of the cold marble floor.

For his age, Alistair Beaumont was a good-looking man. Nearing late forties, dark hair only faintly streaked with grey, and a deep cleft almost dividing the strength of his square jaw.

He was well built; not that of the over-zealous athlete or weightlifter, but a smooth firmness coupled with confidence in his own good looks, his own good body. He was of average height. His status was otherwise. There was nothing average about that. His clothes cried out what he was. His shirt crisp Sea Island cotton; his jacket Highland wool in a neat, checked pattern; trousers of purposely faded green, countrified English casual, yet obviously made by some Italian fashion house.

Alistair Beaumont looked wealthy and was wealthy. He had no real need to be here today queuing with the common herd. There were more than enough people in his employ, beholden to his benevolence, to send off on the mundane errands of life.

But today, Alistair George Beaumont had an ulterior motive. Today it seemed he had put her to the test. If she was as committed to her career as she said she was, then she would do it. What would she do, he had asked her, to gain his backing? Anything, she'd told him, absolutely anything. And she'd meant it.

She'd been living with Mark a while now, and he hadn't been entirely happy about her joining the Beaumont yard. They'd ended up rowing about it. Bitterness had erupted where once there had only been deep words of undeniable lust and passion. She would be leaving him, and now he accepted that.

A fleeting self-consciousness made her raise her hand to push back the thickness of her bouncing hair, not quite brown, and not quite black, but as rich in colour as the darkest brandy. Her hands felt cold even though they had been sat in her pockets during their walk.

She looked at her long fingers. Fine, slim, but very strong when they were inside a riding glove, exercising the most energetic showjumper or three-day eventer. Yet so expert, so exciting when they were caressing the muscles and equipment of a yearning lover, wielding the crop or whip that was so important in the training of either.

Her blue eyes gleamed as she thought of the member that hand had only lately released. Mark, back there at her own stable yard waiting for her, waiting to see if she would gain what she wanted. He would be petulant, perhaps. If she was successful, he knew he would be losing her. Her time with Mark had been good, but now it was basically over. All the same, she would miss him and that rich, ripe cock that reared so subtly in her hand when she squeezed his balls, or playfully tweaked at the bulbous end and poked her fingernail into the weeping opening. But she had to move on. So far in her life she had not found precisely what she was looking for.

'You're incorrigible,' he'd told her. 'Restless. Nothing's ever good enough.'

Was she? That wasn't the message she was receiving from these volcanic upheavals she was feeling inside. As yet she didn't fully understand them. She only knew that after today, a day she'd spent sauntering half-naked through a shopping precinct in a large city, she would never be the same again.

As she watched for Beaumont's return, Penny shifted her long limbs slightly. Moistness dripped in pearl-like droplets from the dark hair that nestled between her legs. Vaguely, she felt it run like quicksilver down her inner thigh and wished suddenly for a hot tongue to lick it all the way back up to her yawning opening. Once there, the tip of a hot tongue could poke inwards, lick slavishly around the satin pinkness of her vulva before entering and plugging the gap for a brief moment before something more substantial was inserted.

As she savoured her thoughts, she pivoted slightly on one heel, the soft whiteness of her inner thigh nudging gently against the thick bush of her ticklish pubes.

A bank clerk ogled her from behind the thickness of his glass screen on which was written FOREIGN EXCHANGE in big green letters. She smiled at him. He blushed and bent his head.

'All done,' said Alistair at last, sliding his cheque book into the inside pocket of his well-cut tweed jacket. He smiled as he said it. She smiled back. To those around, an ordinary enough passing of pleasantries between two good-looking people. But to her, and, she guessed, to him also, there was an undercurrent of understanding. Instinctively, she knew she had passed the test. His sponsorship was hers, her commitment was his, and her excitement at what was to come overwhelmed both.

Back at his office – with just the two of them in a room with very high windows and very thick carpets – he became suddenly withdrawn. It was as though he wanted her out of the building as quickly as possible. This was something she did not understand and was not prepared for.

Slightly peeved by his sudden lack of interest in her, she dressed slowly, turning boldly in front of the full-length windows which stretched from gold and white ceiling to lush, blue carpet. By doing that, she knew she would better catch the light on her breasts and belly.

But Alistair had picked up a pen, and appeared to be concentrating on the sheaf of papers that came into view once he had opened the brown-leather letter folder on his desk.

His desk was big and incredibly baroque – the size of a dining table to most people, and a substantial barrier between him and her.

Only the decorations inlaid in maple and gold leaf within the pattern of the desk testified that he had any interest at all in that process which humans have abandoned themselves to since time immemorial – lovemaking.

Satyrs with outsize phalli chased blatant nymphs, their buttocks round and presented more for penetration than in fearful flight.

One nymph, prominently displayed in the centre panel of the huge desk, was accommodating one satyr in her mouth, whilst another she rode, his hands spread like forked twigs over her breasts, nipples gripped vicelike between finger and thumb. Another satyr came from behind, his phallus already half-hidden between the cheeks of her pear-shaped bottom.

The nymph looked strangely bloated, as though all the fluid that had, and still was, spurting into her was filling her veins, seeping in a frothy mass just beneath her skin.

Penny was stunned. Not by the leering satyrs and willing nymphs, but by Beaumont not throwing her on that plush, blue carpet and taking what she was only too willing to give.

She was deeply disappointed but made an enormous effort not to show it. She had been so sure he had wanted her and she had been wet and ready for him.

Her disappointment stayed with her all the way back down the wide, sweeping staircase and through the green-and-white decor of the enormous reception hall, which was big enough to take a fair-sized orchestra.

His behaviour had confused her and given her a slight feeling of insecurity. Didn't he like her body? She couldn't believe that. Her body was good, perhaps even beautiful. Men had told her that – many men. And what was the purpose of making her walk through the streets like that? It must have aroused him; in fact, she was sure it had. His eyes betrayed his desire even though she detected no evidence of an erection behind the sharp-cut fly of his trousers.

Of course, she could have made the first move, yet somehow she had instinctively known it would not have been welcomed.

Never mind, she told herself as she swept out of the wide front door and between the Palladian columns, white yet sparkling slightly pink in the late autumn sun, time is on my side. I'll be back, and I'll be successful.

Now the wager seemed even more attractive than it had been. Now it wasn't just a case of acquiring Ariadne's prize stallion; it was also a case of massaging her own damaged ego.

On the drive home, she wound the window down. Her face was pink and her mouth dry as she fought to control the mix of arousal and confusion resulting from her experience with Alistair Beaumont.

She could have pulled over in a lay-by or some grassy incline on the way home, whipped off her knickers and brought off an orgasm all by herself, but she didn't. She needed a man, and Mark was back at her own stables.

The pent-up desire, the aching need, would be all the more exhilarating, all the more spurring to their mutual satisfaction. And anyway, she did have something to celebrate.

# 2

'You had to do *what*?' Mark was incredulous; and, although aroused by her statement, more than a little jealous.

She avoided looking at him. She hated it when he was jealous, but no matter what rules had been laid down at the beginning of their relationship, this was the one emotion he did have difficulty dealing with.

Mark tried not to show possessiveness, tried not to let his own masculine needs dominate hers. But he was a failure at it. That was why, at times, she just had to lay down the law, remind him that he didn't own her, would never own her, and that she still had a great many things left to do in her life.

However, so far she'd mentioned nothing about her wager with Ariadne and the stallion. That, she decided, would only complicate matters. Why should she give him a false impression that her entry into that very exclusive establishment was purely to acquire the stallion?

She smiled to herself, ran her hands through her hair and openly admired her tawny reflection in the full-length bedroom mirror. She raised her arms, piling her long dark hair up on to her head. Her nipples pouted round and dark towards the mirror and her breasts lifted as if inviting willing hands to feel their softness and test their firmness.

Tonight she needed a man. Through half-closed eyes, she looked sidelong over her shoulder and took in the effect her confession had had on Mark. Her eyes dropped to the fruitful response which was already pressing against the crotch of his jodhpurs. Too much pressure, she supposed, smiling with satisfaction as Mark unzipped.

'You heard me,' she repeated in her most alluring voice, knowing that its sound and what it was saying would make him want her; make his prick swell painfully against the hard steel of his zip. 'I walked to the bank with him, clad in little more than my coat. It was arousing,' she said, lowering her voice until it was little more than a soft purr and as smooth and dark as her hair.

Lips parted and an incredulous look in his eyes, Mark got up from where he'd been sitting on the pine-ended double bed they'd often shared. He pulled his trousers off. He stood naked, hard, his skin bronzed and hairless, each muscle standing in divisive relief from its brother.

With unbridled longing, his hot lips nuzzled against the concave space between her neck and shoulder. His blond hair, usually tied back with a thong of black leather, fell forward so its ends brushed lightly across her breast. 'I heard you.'

The sweetness of apple shampoo mixed with fresh sweat in his hair filled her nostrils and loins with desire.

Eyes closed and mouth open, her hips began to move in a slow rhythm, swaying back and forth and from side to side, her buttocks sliding against his rising hardness and the crispness of his pubic curls.

His chest was warm and firm against her shoulder-blades. The slight roughness of his hands caressed her skin as they travelled round her body and cupped her breasts. His lips suckled at her shoulder.

In the mirror she could see his eyes sliding down over the reflection of her body. He would not resist her, not like Alistair Beaumont.

Remembering Beaumont made her want to frown, but she controlled the need to do that. Being reminded of failure was not welcome. Penny, like Ariadne, didn't like failure. It haunted her dreams and threatened her own confidence.

Tonight, she decided, she would rage with desire, devour Mark as he had never been devoured before; and he would have her in every way he could have her. She was resolute about that, very resolute.

Purring with desire, her eyes too travelled over her own body. She enjoyed the view, loving the unison between sight and senses as her hips undulated in gentle waves. In response to both, she parted her legs slightly, and her nipples rose, blushing with the dark-pink heat of deep-seated need.

I look good, she told herself, and her smile was more for her reflection than for him. I look really good, she repeated in her mind. Her eyes saw what men saw: lean ribs and waistline dividing neat, round breasts from slim hips. A nest of hair, dark as midnight, bridged the top of her thighs like a thick wedge of soft moss that entices touch.

With a whispering progress, his hands slid from her breasts to her stomach, then arrowed in a deep 'V'. She sighed with pleasure as his fingers tangled in the satin softness of her pubic hair and dipped tentatively into the rising pool of fluid.

Very gradually, a plush pinkness of velvet peered from amid the cluster of hair. She groaned and opened her legs a little more, tilting her hips so both he and she could see her clitoris swell like the head of a tiny flower.

'I want you,' he murmured, his words drowned in the rapidity of his own breathing.

'I want you to want me,' she breathed back at him. 'I want you to want me so much, you beg me to touch you, to suck you, to take you in.'

'You're beautiful,' he stuttered, hearing her, but apprehension stunting his words and making his penis swell more and batter against the base of her spine.

'Don't you think my little bud is pretty?' she asked him, toying with his thickening cock as it continued to beat its own tattoo against her firm behind. She tilted her hips some more, then put one foot up on a pink cushioned stool so he could see everything.

'Very pretty,' he murmured. 'Incredibly pretty.'

As if in a bid to capture the shy creature that blossomed so secretively, his finger ran through the mass of dark hair, then touched the rising tip of pinkness. It responded, twitching slightly. He withdrew, only to alight again with all the softness of a landing butterfly or a wandering moth.

She gasped her pleasure as one finger travelled along her welcoming slit, his other fingers rolling back the hot flesh of her labia. Each petal of her sex was outlined, its moist wetness drowning the progress of his finger before he buried it in her opening furrow.

Her muscles clenched against it, trapping it within her, drawing it further in.

Behind her, his breathing increased as her buttocks pressed back against him. With wicked determination, she rubbed them against his probing weapon; hot, pulsating as it fleetingly explored the cleft in her buttocks from its beginning at the base of her spine to its wider point near her anus and the sparse hairs along her perineum. Upwards through the division in her bottom; downwards, through her cleft; then upwards again in dizzying succession.

No longer able to contain her delight and her ardour, she turned to face him. Her pubic mound began to beat a slow rhythm against his velvet-sheathed hardness as her hips moved backwards and forwards.

'Was it that delicious?' he asked between strangled breaths. 'Walking through a crowded street with your pretty little bosoms bouncing around loose in your coat and no knickers?'

'And the breeze in my hair,' she mused, smiling mischievously up at him. 'My pubic hair!'

In obvious response, his fingers tangled in her pubic hair.

Although his white teeth flashed in a smile, she knew there was something else he wanted to ask.

She offered no relief to the curiosity he was obviously feeling. Withholding such information gave her a feeling of power. He was holding her, pressing his body tight against hers, and all the time wanting to know every detail of her interview with Alistair Beaumont.

Gradually she sank downwards, arms and hands held high above her before she ran them from his shoulders and down over his chest.

At last, her face was level with his pride and joy. How strong it looked, how richly purple the velvet-soft flesh; how vibrant and full of the force of life. The staff of life, she mused, the giver of all good things.

It pulsated with metronome perfection, its tip lightly touching her cheek, her nose, then her lips.

'So soft,' she cooed. 'So strong, yet so soft.'

As if in response to her soothing words, his cock-head glistened with the first pearl drop of sexual secretion. Tentatively, her tongue flicked, once, then twice, and the drop was gone, salty sweet on the tip of her tongue. His penis reared each time.

Both hands travelled over the sculpted perfection of his firm thighs – the sort of muscles that are so well formed and very hard in a man that rides horses for a living.

She could smell the warmth there, her breath disturbing the crisp hair that circled his cock and covered his balls in a sweet, dewy down so that it tickled her chin, her nose, her mouth, as her tongue licked tantalisingly over his cock. Above her, he moaned.

As one hand fondled the peachy softness that hung like ripe fruit between his legs, the other grasped the rising stem. It reared with delight as her fingers wrapped protectively around it. How hot it was. How soft, how strong!

For a moment her eyes marvelled at the contours of veins, ducts and arteries beneath the blushing purple redness. Then her mouth kissed its head, her tongue probing the opening and taking more of the salty pearl drops. Then her lips divided and sucked the first juice of his erection.

Up and down her head moved in constant rhythm, her lips sliding downwards, retreating, opening slightly wider before travelling back towards the base. As her head moved, so did her hands. One curved around the engorged muscle, her fingertips resting on the duct that would carry his release. Her other hand gently stroked the hanging testicles, tracing the outer softness and probing the inner hardness.

Sucking, kissing, she felt as if she wanted to eat it yet, at the same time, her own needs were rising; her own wetness was forming around the quivering centre of her sex.

Mark tangled his fingers in her hair and began to move her head up and down his shaft to suit himself. When his hand released her, she kissed the rearing head one more time before she got to her feet and followed him to the blue-and-white-striped *chaise-longue*.

He lay back on it, his legs dropping to the ground on either side. His shoulders filled the width of the seat. At the narrowest point of his body, his penis stood to attention, strong, proud and ready for action. Briefly, he stroked it.

As she studied his erection, her own hands busied themselves. One slid between her legs, anxiously rubbing at her demanding clitoris. The other rubbed at her breasts, gently manipulating first one nipple, then the other between one finger and her thumb. It was nice, but not enough. She knew what she wanted and, from familiarity, knew he did, too.

Even before the words were out, she guessed what he was going to say.

'I'm ready,' he said. 'Ride me.'

She smiled, her eyes bright and wide as she took in the beauty of the firm mount that awaited her. His dick was stiff and upright, standing proud from the prostrate body to which it belonged.

Just as if she were mounting a horse, she swung her leg across him. For a moment she paused, suspended above him, the head of his throbbing cock just reaching her and its tip touching lightly against her humid portal.

With one hand, she reached beneath her. Lightly, her fingers stroked the crown of his penis. How strong it was, how full of power standing so proud from its forest of pubic hair. It was hot, hard and full of blood and jerked appreciatively with each touch, each light caress. Pleasure purred from her throat as she rubbed it back and forth along the length of her dividing lips. They were wet and slippery with secretions that would coat his member like a silver sheath.

The friction of its journey from clitoris to vulva increased her breathing. She closed her eyes, relishing the experience of being over and above this man, and using his own body to satisfy her desires.

As her breathing quickened, she tweaked at one breast. Her head fell forward as her hand cupped her breast higher. With her tongue she licked at the soft flesh. She loved the feel of it, the silky gloss of her own skin. Moaning in selfish rapture, she slid slowly down to impale herself on him, her vulva sucking the man into her hot interior.

At first her movements were slow as her inner lips adapted to the intruder. Around its rim, her nerve endings tingled as their power increased. She clenched her buttocks and tightened her stomach knowing that he, too, would feel the constriction in her muscles. Below her he moaned, his breathing heavy and increasing in tempo as she rode him faster. Her breasts leapt, almost of their own accord, as she gasped her pleasure.

Suddenly, just as if she had dug her heels into her mount to spur him on, she increased her speed, bobbing up and down as if she had urged to a trot. On this mount, she was impaled. Faster and faster she rode, her pussy making a sucking sound as her juices increased to a flood.

Her head was back, her eyes still closed, her mouth open as she sucked the air. She imagined being out riding with the wind against her face. And all the time, impaled in place, at one with her mount.

She increased her speed and fell forwards, her hands either side of his neck. Their lips sucked at each other.

As her breasts swung back and forth, his hands held them, cradling and caressing them to steady their progress; his thumbs flicked at her risen nipples.

She felt his pelvis rise towards her; felt the first threads of her orgasm racing like a mass of electric currents to concentrate around one spot. Tension gathered there, congregated like high-voltage wires waiting to explode in one almighty burst of energy.

She was barely aware of his face, of his existence. Now he was just her mount, an aid to her own rising release. She had her own needs to satisfy.

As her release came, her voice exploded with satisfaction. She cried her orgasm to the ceiling, pinpoints of ecstasy like medals on her breasts and a violent sunburst between her thighs. With one last thrust she felt him tremble within her, momentous at first, his throbbing diminishing until he was spent. Then they fell and collapsed into a gasping heap.

Clasped together by a light film of sweat, they lay motionless.

On cue, his fingers began to feather downwards along the indentation of her spine. Her smile was hidden. She awaited the question that he had not yet asked.

'Did you go to bed with him?' He rushed the words, and she detected jealousy.

'Who?' She smiled as she said it, her mouth and her eyes hidden in her tumbling hair. There was a wicked satisfaction in keeping him in suspense. He had no right asking as far as she was concerned. He didn't own her. She was her own woman. She sensed his irritation.

'Him. Alistair thingummy.'

She smiled at his offhandedness with the name.

Half a sigh seeped from the corner of her mouth. It was hard to admit her disappointment, even to Mark.

'We didn't do anything very much.'

There was a pause. Again she knew what he was thinking, knew what he would ask next, but offered no crumb of knowledge to free him from his query.

'Suck? Hand job?'

She raised her head. Her eyes met his. They were blue like her own, but not fringed with the same dark lashes as hers were.

His mouth was twitching a little at each corner and he was frowning slightly. Suddenly she felt sorry for him. She was leaving him. He didn't want her to go, yet she had to. They were still friends and would remain so, but there was a world beckoning – a career in which she excelled. She had to go.

Gently she kissed the tip of his nose. She saw his nostrils dilate and knew he could smell himself – his sex on her lips.

She smiled suggestively, but in an affectionate kind of way.

'Nothing. Nothing at all. Not even a kiss. It was all very polite. Very businesslike.'

His bottom lip dropped open. He was as surprised as she had been.

But she didn't tell him that. It was irrelevant. Her path was marked out and she'd signed a contract. She couldn't go back on that. They both needed new pastures.

She turned on to her back and threw her arms above her on the pillow. She stared at the ceiling for a while and prepared herself for Mark's next question which she was positive would come.

'Do you think he's queer?' he asked tentatively.

'Typical!' She laughed.

In her experience, it was the first assumption in any strictly heterosexual male. Mark, she knew, would never turn down an opportunity to have sex with her or any other likely looking female and found it difficult to understand that someone else might not feel the same.

Nevertheless she thought about it for a moment before she answered properly. On reflection, she remembered the eyes of Alistair Beaumont when she had been removing her clothes. The steely grey eyes had become brighter as each article had left her shoulders and cascaded from her limbs.

'No.' Her voice was low, almost secretive. 'No, I don't think so.'

# 3

She felt no clinging affection or pangs of guilt about leaving Mark or the place where they'd lived together for nearly a year. Love had become a habit; and sex, although still enjoyable, was getting near that time where familiarity had replaced red-blooded passion.

Apprehension sapped her concentration as Gorgeous Sir Galahad, the chestnut gelding, and Flamboyant Flame, her dapple-grey mare, were loaded into the box. Soon all three of them, her and her two horses, would be in their new home.

Excitement had coloured her preparations since early morning. No matter how Mark might feel about her going, she could not hide her enthusiasm for joining the team at Beaumont Place. Facilities were the best there and, if what Ariadne had to say was anything to go by, the social life was pretty good, too.

Limbs stiff from an over-abundance of sex the night before reminded her that she would miss Mark's hard body covering hers. But, she told herself, he was not irreplaceable.

All the same, Beaumont's not taking her sexually still grated on her mind. There was a niggle inside that asked whether he had not thought her good enough for his taste. It rankled and made her feel slightly insecure.

And yet it seemed even stranger that he had not taken advantage of Ariadne. Who could fail to be knocked out by her apple-ripe breasts and available pussy? But now the wager was struck and her curiosity aroused, it didn't matter. Now it was up to her to rise to the challenge. What kind of man was it who could watch other people enjoying sex and not indulge himself, she asked herself? It didn't matter. She would do her best. She smiled to herself as she slid the bolt into the lock of the tailboard. Pleasant thoughts came to mind.

Perhaps, she thought, his tastes had become jaded, suffused with too much of the sensuous – a quality readily available to the man who could afford everything. Beaumont had a business empire that straddled the Atlantic, offices in London, Boston and New York, plus subsidiary companies in Australia, South Africa and South America. He was one of those men whose lives are dominated by their business interests. Yet still he found the time to fund the stabling, training and all the other costs incurred by those so unwise as to be immersed in the world of showjumping.

For the last time she looked around her old stable yard where mice had chewed through the wooden walls, and yellow-headed weeds pushed through the cracked concrete.

Goodbye to all this, she said to herself, looking one last time at the strident growth of the elder tree that had started as a rigorous sapling and was now taking over the yard, its virile roots splintering the concrete into smaller pieces. Strange, but she'd become almost fond of it, of all it represented. It was against its trunk that she and Mark had made love the very first time, its splintery bark scratching like blunt fingernails over her naked behind.

No matter. Mark and all this were behind her now, but she still managed a little smile for the man who had made her happy, and might even do so again in the future. Mark, like any rejected male, had put on a brave face, but she couldn't tell if he was sad or merely impatient to bury his regrets and his cock into her replacement.

She turned away. Like precious stones, she folded her memories away. Her life was about to take on a whole new course, even though she had some regrets about leaving his hard body and his very satisfying prick behind her.

The tailboard was finally bolted up. The horses nickered gently, snorting as they pulled hay from the temporary nets fastened inside. They sounded to her ears as though they were urging her onwards, telling her that pastures new – where grass was more numerous than weeds – would be welcome to their tender palates.

She turned back to Mark. Their goodbye was brief, though she did detect a hint of jealousy surge momentarily.

'Never mind,' she whispered as he nibbled a last time at her ear. 'Jackie will look after you.'

Over her shoulder, green eyes looked out from a mass of bubble blonde hair and full breasts strained against a black jersey. Jackie, her understudy for the past month, she guessed was already contemplating the pleasures to come now Penny, her rival, was out of the way.

Mark patted her bottom with as much pleasure as he did his prize stallion. Penny wriggled against it, savouring the pleasure for the final time. Then he helped her up into the rattly Bedford horsebox. His hand cupped one cheek of her bottom, which was tightly enclosed in her dark-blue breeches. Then his hand slid to the cleft in between as he pushed her up into the cab.

She wriggled against it and murmured with pleasure – after all, it might be some time before she got the opportunity to have some of that, though of course she had no intention of letting the grass grow under her feet.

'Hope this old crate gets us there,' she said as she turned the key.

'Last time,' he answered in an offhand, sarcastic kind of way. 'Mr Beaumont will no doubt have your new box already waiting for you with his company name emblazoned along the side. And all you have to do for it is your very best.' He smiled sardonically. Suddenly she knew she'd have to work hard not to miss him. Either that or swiftly find her own replacement – singular or plural.

As the engine sprang into spluttering life, she took a deep breath and put on her own brave face. She smiled down at him and winked.

'I will,' she said as she thought of Ariadne and everything she had told her. She was unable to control the spreading smile that made her cheeks bunch into pink apples. 'I most certainly will.'

Foot to floor, she pulled away, eyes straight ahead. On this occasion, at this moment in time, she could not look back.

Suddenly the seduction of Alistair Beaumont was of great importance, like going after a new trophy, a whole new wedge of prize money. A new life and new experiences beckoned. And now, she reckoned, she was ready for them.

'Alistair Beaumont, I'm coming for you,' she muttered to herself as the old horsebox rumbled out of the gate.

Built in warm, red brick at the latter half of the nineteenth century, the stable yard at Beaumont Place was entered through a curved archway surrounded by rich boughs of drooping purple wisteria.

The gravel crunched beneath the tyres as the horsebox came to a stop in the middle of the yard. Penny's eyes surveyed her new surroundings as she turned off the engine and pulled on the brake. Blank windows stared back at her. Those, she guessed, hid offices and storerooms behind their dusty facade. The other three sides were given over to loose boxes, a tack room and a hay store, numerous buildings all catering for the competitive world of equestrianism. At the far end of the enclosure was a large barn and next to it what looked like an indoor riding-school.

What a difference to her own place, she thought enviously, as her eyes took in the scene of gentlemanly opulence. There was no sign of neglect here; no sign either of lack of funding. Here there was money. Here also, she reminded herself, was Alistair Beaumont who was both a man worth waiting for and worth having. She remembered him from that day strolling through the lunch-time crowds, that classic patrician profile set on a firm neck and shoulders that bore both responsibility and confidence with easy geniality. Just thinking of him made her moist against the crotch of her white cotton knickers. He was a handsome man, besides being a powerful one.

In the middle of the yard was a fountain; perhaps of earlier construction, from the time of the Prince Regent when the main house was built. Around it was a circular trough into which a bronze cherub peed from a green copper spout. The water tinkled like light laughter, sparkling like falling diamonds into the dark greenness of the pool.

'Nice little guy.' She smiled to herself, referring as much to the cherub itself as to the appendage he so copiously peed from. It was bigger than normally associated with classic statutary, and certainly exhibited the sort of length normally associated with an aroused adult male rather than a rotund little boy.

So involved was she in studying the rich opulence of the stable yard and its buildings, that she did not at first notice Alistair strolling over to where she had parked. Her heart thudded and she ran her hands nervously over her slim hips. A fire ignited and simmered gently between her legs.

He looked as good as that day when she'd walked beside him through the streets with all the beauty of her body teased by the soft touch of the coat lining. His shirt looked to be silk, his pullover pure lambswool and his breeches and high brown-leather boots hand-made purely for his well-muscled frame.

But today, it wasn't just him that filled her eyes. He was not alone. A few steps behind him walked another man. He seemed with him, but slightly apart, and although Alistair still dominated her vision, she could not help but stray to this other presence, this very tall man with very blond hair that curled in satin drifts over his naked neck. Her breath caught in her throat, and a numbness stilled the flames that Alistair had ignited in her. This other man was beautiful in the same way that a woman is beautiful, or an angel, or even Michelangelo's David. His features looked almost sculpted. Angelic, she decided, was the best description. High cheekbones; high forehead beneath the luxuriant fringe of white blondness; wide mouth and profiled chin: all these gave the appearance of him being somewhat etherial. His eyes were brown and seemed to look straight ahead as though they were looking beyond her, as if there must be something else more profound than the red brickwork, the tangled wisteria or the yellow gravel of the stable yard.

It was strange, but even though she was still sat in the cab of the rattly old Bedford horsebox, she had the oddest urge to cover her breasts and her lower regions with her hands as if she were naked, as if he could see her bare flesh and it was somehow lewd for him to do so. It was almost, she thought, as if she were in church and he really was a creature etched in stained glass, complete with white wings and gold halo.

The feeling passed. She swallowed her sudden breathlessness and turned her attention back to Alistair. If he had noticed her interest in the man at his side, he did not mention it. He did not introduce him either. Mature lines that enhanced his character crinkled at the side of his bright, grey eyes.

On the mild breeze his aftershave wafted towards her, mingling tantalisingly with his most obvious maleness. Maleness was a smell she had always noticed. It was aftershave, it was sweat, it was wood smoke, damp grass, and even the faint trace of tobacco. Men had those smells, completely unlike the sweet and salty mix that women seem to have; bouquets of flowers mixed with female perspiration. Men most definitely smelt different from females, and the difference excited her.

His handshake was warm and sent shivers of expectation up and down her spine. His smile became even warmer and she thought it the sort you could drown in.

'Miss Bennet. So pleased to see you.'

She took the offered hand as she stepped down from the box. The palm was warm, the fingers firm. Just to look at him sent shivers of pleasure coursing like cold water down her spine and into the deep valley between the cheeks of her bottom. For the moment, the 'angel' was forgotten.

'Glad to be here,' she replied, breathless with enthusiasm. Her stomach was still knotted with excitement, her mind still tossing and tumbling the intrigues and stories she had heard about this place. She awaited an introduction to the tall man whose navy-blue jersey had a boat-style neckline that exposed the strength of his neck and the outline of his collar-bone. His flesh was tanned, as warm in colour as clear honey. He was not introduced. His eyes flickered over her for a moment, then stared guiltily ahead, and even though she smiled at him, he did not smile back.

The 'angel' tossed his head, throwing back the sleek blond fringe that covered his forehead. The rest alighted in soft waves around his bare neck.

Suddenly, she felt hot and her lips seemed dry. This man was something she had not foreseen. She could feel the blood pumping to her cheeks and knew they were becoming as pink as almond blossom. Lust oozed like honey in her hidden love-nest. She felt in great need.

But Alistair was speaking. With effort, she concentrated on what he was saying. After all, he was the man she had come for; the man who would pay her bills and fall to her charms if she played her cards right.

Alistair indicated the range of buildings around her, but made no obvious attempt either to introduce or bring the tall blond man into the conversation. Silently the man walked behind them – three paces behind – like some Oriental wife or harem eunuch. It was, she thought with rising curiosity, as though he were not there as a person, only as an item – something Alistair had paid for. All the same, he was beautiful to look at in his navy sweater and his pale-blue jeans. To see him move was enough for her to imagine what might be underneath.

But she listened attentively as Alistair spoke. His looks, even his voice, demanded her attention. The very tone of his voice and the smell of everything expensive and masculine held her attention. This, she told herself, was a man to behold and to have. In time, she said inwardly. In the meantime, she was still curious to know the name of this blond Adonis who walked three paces behind them. Would he introduce him soon, she asked herself, and what was his job around here?

'If you'd like to unload your animals,' said Alistair in that warm timbre of his, timing his words to almost half answer her question. 'Gregory will show you your stabling. After that,' he added, gazing at Gregory with an odd look of self-satisfaction and mild amusement, 'he'll show you your accommodation. He will also help you unwind. He's very good at that. I'm sure you'll have no trouble making yourself at home very quickly.'

A pained look followed the one of self-satisfaction on Alistair's face, but then it was gone. Penny couldn't fathom what its meaning might have been, so she didn't dwell on it. Instead, she looked at Gregory and smiled weakly.

When she turned again to Alistair, he had already half-turned his back on her. Like a schoolgirl, she felt she had been dismissed, handed over to a lesser staff member, though definitely a very beautiful one.

'I will no doubt see you this evening, Miss Bennet. At dinner,' Alistair called over his shoulder as he walked off.

'Yes. Yes. Of course . . . I wish you'd call me Penny,' she said as an afterthought.

He did not turn or acknowledge her call.

'Miss Bennet!' Gregory's voice caught her unawares and caused a weakness in her most energetic muscles. His voice was melodious; a rich mix of church organ and jazz clarinet.

'If you'll come this way,' he said as he unloaded her luggage and began to walk towards the eastern side of the yard. 'The stable-lads will take care of your horses.'

At the sound of his voice, two young men, barely twenty, strode out through the wide door of the main stable block where stalls were ranged in rows down one side.

She smiled at the stable-lads. They smiled back.

She followed Gregory, taking full advantage of the opportunity to run her eyes down over his broad back and tight behind. She started at the sleek blond hair that covered his head like a page-boy in some Renaissance painting. Her observations proceeded over the thickly classical neck and the masculine shoulders that rippled beneath the jersey, straining with the weight of her luggage. His stride was long enough to suit his legs, and his thigh and calf muscles seemed to fight against the stiff cotton of his washed-out jeans as though they were trying to escape.

Her room was on the third floor in a high tower that brooded at the eastern corner of the house. It looked older than the rest, perhaps a leftover from some Civil War battle.

The steps leading up were made from stone and wound between cold matching walls. Just for a moment, she wondered about the comfort of the accommodation allotted to her. Would it too be stone, unyielding and dankly cold like some tattered poet's garret?

She needn't have bothered worrying, she told herself, as a heavy wooden door, like something out of a medieval romance, opened on a room that she immediately fell in love with.

The room was circular, the ceiling high, its beams running from the top of the walls to a central apex. It was as though the room was a giant tent.

The bed was big and old, with heavy wooden posts of barley-sugar twists at head and foot. There was a fireplace with a real fire burning, thick tapestries lining the walls, and ancient, though expensive, rugs were scattered over the polished wooden floor like some giant patchwork quilt.

There was also a mirror – massive and enclosed within a dark wooden frame of intricate carving that stretched almost from ceiling to floor.

There were plenty of cupboards, plenty of writing space, a television and an en-suite bathroom. Some hotels she'd stayed in, she reflected, didn't have rooms as good as these.

'It's lovely,' she exclaimed with honesty as her bags hit the floor with a thump. 'Are all the rooms like this?' She watched him closely as she waited for him to answer. Her breathing had quickened. Was it the fault of the stairs or the study she had made of his body? He did not answer. He busied himself putting her things away; and watching him tear around her room like some manic chambermaid angered her.

So far she'd got precious little in the way of conversation

from Gregory. But it was worth trying again just to hear the rich mahogany of his voice.

'Do you ever talk?' she asked in a sudden fit of pique.

His back was to her, yet she was sure he must have heard.

'Damn you!' she yelled as he took three strides or so and disappeared into the bathroom.

Penny heard water running, then saw steam rising. It didn't take a Sherlock Holmes to realise he was running a bath.

'I didn't ask you to do that,' she called out. Either the taps were gushing too loudly or he was deaf or just plain ignorant. Still she got no response.

'What the hell!' she exclaimed, then sighed loudly. 'OK. I'll take up the offer. I'll have a bath.'

A bath was just what she could do with, anyway. This morning had been an early start, the journey had been long, and she could do with relaxing in hot water for an hour or so. Who cares who'd turned the taps on?

'Thank you,' she cried as loudly as she could. 'It's just what I need.'

Penny approached the bathroom door, then leant against the door surround.

'So this,' she said brightly, her eyes squinting for any reaction from him, 'is the bathroom.' He was bent over the bath, pouring something into the water from a long plastic bottle with a very interesting neck. The water eddied in pink whirls of varying degrees as a result of the added essence before it formed small mounds of white bubbles.

As he didn't answer, she took the opportunity to look more fully at the bathroom. Pure white fitments with gold taps and fittings sparkled beneath deep-seated spotlights. Floor-to-ceiling mirrors covered one wall opposite the bath where steam rose from the streaming tap.

Automatically she undid the top two buttons of her blouse

as she walked back into the bedroom, her naked breasts sensitised as the input of air caressed them. In need of clean underwear, she unzipped a bag. A hand gripped hers and stayed its action.

'I'll do that,' he said crisply. 'You have your bath.'

There it was again, that voice that made her breasts tingle and her crotch moisten with fluid anticipation. His hand, including his fingers, was cool upon her arm.

Open-mouthed she took the opportunity to study his eyes, which looked at her with such strange intensity. This close, his face was even more beautiful, even more breathtaking. His eyebrows, she noticed, were arched and darker than his hair. His lips were sensuous and pinkly soft as though they could suck at her very soul.

His fingers released her and she felt their loss. Disinclined to argue, and having received no answers to anything she had asked, Penny sighed and slumped down on the bed. She was tired after an early start this morning and the journey itself. Why not let this man with the face of an angel and the body of an Olympian athlete wait on her?

Placing the toe of one boot against the heel of the other, she started to nudge the boot off her foot.

Without being asked, his legs straddled hers. Suddenly, she was lost in her own fantasies, her own lustful desires. There was his bottom, turned towards her face. His cheeks were rounded, the flesh tight and made of muscle rather than fat.

He tugged, his firm hands and strong arms struggling with the reluctant boots.

She let her head fall back and allowed her hair, which had broken loose from its black velvet band, to brush the counterpane. This was luxury. How could she not let him do this? There were his buttocks, open to observation, plus his muscular haunches curving down to tight knees and well-shaped calves.

She had a sudden urge to run her hand between those fine legs, to feel for the soft scrotum that lay so secret, yet so exposed, between his parted thighs.

An ache of wanting tightened her chest as she raised her head and studied his body. Dare she touch him? Dare she feel the most private part of this man who barely spoke to her, yet was so beautiful that he was almost a work of art?

But the moment passed.

Once one boot was off and lying in the middle of a dark red and blue carpet, the same strong grip was applied to the other.

'I'll get these cleaned,' he said, and promptly put them outside the door. Then he closed it and came back in. She hadn't expected that, but voiced no objection.

Penny rubbed her toes together. Oh well, she thought to herself, if that's the way it is ...

With urgent fingers she began to undo her buttons. She had an urge to catch him here, to expose her body so he had to say something, and had to stay to take her.

'I'll do that,' she heard him say.

Her own hands halted, and her mouth dropped open in surprise. This was something else she hadn't allowed for.

Now the fingers that had been so cool and long upon her arm were undoing her buttons for her.

'Please do,' she exclaimed in a breathless purr, her breasts rising suddenly higher in their endeavour to feel those cool fingers on her satin flesh.

Her senses were now flying around in wild abandonment. What would he do now? What did it matter? Whatever he wanted to do, she was game. He filled her eyes, this tall man who towered above her and had very cool fingers and a voice as warm as mulled brandy. She wanted him in any way she could.

When her blouse was open and her breasts exposed she studied his face. There was no change in his expression; no acknowledgement in the steady eyes that she was beautiful; no sign that he desired her.

It made her feel dejected somehow. As if to reassure her own self-esteem, she looked down at the two firm orbs of her breasts which thrust so invitingly towards his hands and his face. She arched her back. It made no difference. Nothing altered.

Her blouse was open, taken off her. She was naked to the waist. Her arms stayed at her side.

'Stand up,' Gregory demanded. There was no emotion in his face; no recognition that her breasts were now close to his own chest or that she was looking up at him longingly, wanting him to cup each bosom in his cool hands and to tantalise her crowning nubs with the tips of his fingers, the warmth of his lips.

She felt cheated, let down. What was wrong with her that this man ignored her most obvious invitation? Did he prefer blondes – those as Scandinavian in features as himself?

She thought of Ariadne, tall and blonde. Suddenly, she was jealous ... least, until he spoke again.

'Put your hands on your head. I will help you off with your trousers.'

'But I can do it myself ...' Penny began, then called herself a fool for doing so.

'Put your hands on your head,' Gregory repeated without looking at her.

Trembling slightly, Penny did as she was told. The music of his voice was irresistible. Her body wanted out of these dusty, sweaty clothes. Her body was warm. She wondered if his was, too, or whether his flesh was as cool and soothing as his hands.

Her sighs turning to pleasurable moans, Penny turned her eyes to the bathroom. Hot steam rose and curled out of the door, beckoning her to indulge; to submerge herself in its comforting heat and perfumed aroma.

Perhaps, she thought with rising excitement, he would join her. What a prospect – that sublime form squelching with her in the confines of warm water and rising suds.

His face was but a few inches from her now; his hands were on her waistband. Their eyes met, though his seemed strangely vacant, but still fired with an unusual intensity that turned up her toes and made butterflies dance in her belly.

'Are you taking yours off?' she asked, the hope in her voice and her eyes exceedingly obvious. She'd received no answers from him so far so she was surprised to hear one this time.

'No.'

His reply was abrupt. His eyes held hers, then dropped as he undid her waistband then the zip of her breeches.

He didn't seem to notice her staring at him, her eyes sliding down over the broad chest, his neat ribs, his waist and then the zip of his faded denims.

She was almost surprised to see a bulge. So far, he had made such a good job of avoiding her eyes, of keeping his conversation to the barest minimum. Yet he was aroused, but seemed disinclined to do anything about it. She wondered why, but said and did nothing.

As with Alistair she was disappointed but determined to let this particular man see her in all her unfettered glory, without shame ... and without pity.

There was something soothing about his dextrous fingers undoing her trousers and sliding them and her knickers down her legs. She almost swooned with joy as his hand dived between her legs to dislodge the crotch of her panties from her sweating slit. For a moment she thought she was going to get what she so badly desired and he so obviously wanted.

Desire spread in a cobweb cloud through her body and limbs once her creamy flesh, radiant with a mixture of health and sweat, was exposed. Her clothes lay discarded.

She watched as he picked them up and laid them on a chair near the door in a neat pile as though they were crisply clean rather than smelling of sweat and horses.

There was something annoying in seeing him give the clothes more attention than he had her. The annoyance threatened to bubble over. Even before she spoke, she knew he would hear it in her voice. But she'd had enough. She had to say something.

'Right! Now I'll take my bath.' She sounded imperious and meant to.

Tossing her head and holding herself as proudly as she could, she walked naked towards the bathroom. Perhaps now, she thought with a pang of regret, this man would leave, or take her, or do something!

Gregory followed her into the bathroom.

Penny stopped, turned and stared at him. Again he averted his eyes.

'Thank you. I can manage now,' she said, rolling her breasts with her hands for his and her benefit and very aware of all the other naked Pennys reflected back at her from the misted mirrors, and all the other rolled breasts and jutting nipples.

'Get in. Stand up and I'll sponge you down.' His voice was sudden, but she was so mesmerised by its tone and quality that she felt obliged to obey.

She hesitated just for a moment. Her thoughts roller-coastered between desire and pride. Who was this man who could tell her what to do? And why didn't he just fall on her, knead her breasts in his strong hands, lay her down and press his hard cock into her welcoming pussy? She had no answers. So she stepped into the bath and hoped for the best. She knew very well what she wanted that 'best' to be.

She began to moan with pleasure. Her skin glistened with soap bubbles as Gregory squeezed a well-lathered sponge across the round firmness of her breasts. The droplets of water and white foam tumbled like a mountain torrent down the gleaming slopes only to hang like imperfect white pearl drops from deep pink buttons.

She let her senses delight in this amazing experience. She and Mark had bathed together, but this wasn't some ordinary homely experience. Like a princess, she luxuriated in the warm water and towering bubbles. Like a slave, angelic beauty and masculine strength moulded into one, he stood over her, the sponge in his right hand following the exploring fingers of the left.

With mounting ardour, she watched wide-eyed as he took off his shirt. Now! yelled her mind. Now!

But nothing happened. That was all he took off. Feeling his way along the edge of the bath, he retrieved his sponge, and continued as before.

Her breath quickened as his hands explored and soaped her body. She was lost in pleasure, purring and moaning in alternate spasms. Anything he wanted was his. Anything at all. She had an overpowering urge to touch the tanned, hairless skin that so tautly covered the hard, lithe body.

'Put your hands on top of your head,' he said. Then he stepped backwards as though he had anticipated that she would try to touch him, to run her soapy fingers over his hard body.

'What . . . ?' she began, her words strangled by her racing breath.

'Do as you're told,' he repeated. 'Put your hands on your head. You are not allowed to touch me.'

With a moan of deep regret, she raked her eyes over the beautiful, boyish flesh that she longed to feel beneath her fingers, and cursed the heavy ache that hung like lead between her thighs. Now what could she do?

Strong urges wanted her to disobey, to run her fingers over that delicious form, the skin now glossy from the mix of steam and sweat.

Then she sighed. She would resign herself to whatever part she had to play. And if he wanted to act the part of the bathhouse slave, then so be it.

Tension dissipated and anxiety banished, she rested her hands one on top of the other on her head. Unsmiling, his face serious with intent, he came nearer. Now she could smell him, tangy, male and juicily desirable.

Tremors of sensation tingled throughout her body as the sponge was rolled down over her belly and in between her legs.

'Open your legs wider.'

Having no intention of missing such a golden opportunity, she did as she was told. The warm sponge and the diligence of his hands spread and rolled her plush nether lips until they hung with soap suds, thoroughly spread and thoroughly cleaned.

There was a pleasantness about it. Almost like satisfaction, she thought to herself – but not quite. Pink flesh much used and abused the night before felt refreshed and touched with new life.

She closed her eyes now. Better to savour that way and to fully absorb the tingling that ran over her skin and centred on her precious clit and blossoming nipples.

The hand that was not using the sponge travelled to her hip, his fingers soft and tantalising. His hand held her hip. He reached round, his fingers clasping gently at the taut flesh of one buttock.

'If you get down on all fours,' he said suddenly, 'I'll do your back.'

The request was irresistible. She got on to all fours. She wanted to do this; to feel her tension dissolve in the warmth and her sexual desire flood over her like a warm wave on a tropical beach.

The water reached her elbows. The furry mixture of sponge and soap loosened the muscles of her back and shoulders. She opened her eyes, closed them again and purred like a kitten. The hands travelled down over her back to her pink buttocks.

It occurred to her that Gregory did this for everyone new, and had probably done it for Ariadne. That made her jealous. Calm down, she told herself, use your self-control. Obviously this was routine, an act designed to put people at ease and promote mutual trust. And what could be better than sharing a bath? Didn't the Japanese do it anyway?

Suds circulated around her neck and dropped in white globules from her breasts. She murmured with surprised delight as the squidgy softness of the sponge was pressed in between her buttocks, the soap trickling down the deep crevice and through the channel that divided her legs.

Warmth, suds and softness invaded the wet folds of flesh. Her thighs opened slightly. Her head felt dizzy, her eyes closing as she revelled in the sweet decadence of doing nothing, of depending on someone else to cleanse and pamper her willing body.

She felt the long fingers, as delicate in their touch as any artist, spread her cheeks apart, expose her anus and press the sponge and its soapy issue into her puckered hole.

There was no stopping the moan of ecstasy that issued from her throat. She closed her eyes, threw discretion to the wind, and pressed her buttocks more firmly against it.

'I think you need more soap,' she heard Gregory say, his voice as melodious and beguiling as his looks.

'Whatever . . .' she replied through her moans of pleasure.

His hands ran down over her back. His fingers parted her buttocks. Something soft but basically hard was forced into her anus. She gasped, and realised the invader could only be the soap which was long and shaped more like shaving soap than bath soap. Its effect was incredible. Her muscles gripped as it slid gently in and out. Still moaning and savouring all that was being done to her, she arched her back and pressed herself on to it. This was the best bath she'd ever had.

'More,' she moaned, and wished that the soap was twice the size it was; that there was something bigger to push into her pulsating vulva which cried out for attention. Her clit also tingled with demand, entering the scenario like a star act stepping on to centre stage.

The folds of flesh that hugged the core of her sex began to open like the petals of a lotus in bloom, droplets of dewy essence mixing with the lather as her plump labia opened in anticipation.

'All finished,' she heard him say as the soap was withdrawn. Now her moans changed to groans.

'Don't stop!' she cried out, turning to glare at him. She would have begged longer, but something in his face told her that such pleas would not be welcome.

'Patience,' he replied. 'Acually I haven't quite finished yet. I have my orders.'

She wanted to ask him what orders. But her need to enjoy more of his ministrations was greater than her curiosity.

Disappointment filled her. She had a need for release, and if it wasn't for the fact that Gregory was with her and likely to do more, she would have slid her hand between her legs and tickled her tight little bud until she did come.

Quizzically she looked over the foam that sat on her shoulder and saw him take something down from off the wall.

Then she gasped as cold water sprayed from a hand-held shower hose washed the suds from her body. Goosebumps dimpled her tight flesh as the soft hands directed the water over her back. Streams of cold delicacy seeped between her buttocks and dangled in icy dribbles from her stiff nipples. She gasped, her skin tingling as the process was repeated until the shower was turned off.

'Cold water aids muscle tone.' Gregory's explanation sounded reasonable enough, but Penny did not entirely believe him, or rather she didn't want to believe him. She wanted to believe that he was enjoying this, too; that the sight of her naked form and opening sex tempted him. If it wasn't for the obvious bulge in his trousers, she would have questioned his gender. But she knew instinctively he was a man. His physique was beautiful, but decidedly masculine. And his smell was masculine. He was a man all right.

She considered his comment on muscle tone. The divide between health and sex had always been blurred. In the bath, it was sex that was on her mind, not sport.

'The soap's all gone,' he said, then switched off the cold water.

Catching her breath, she got out of the soap-filled tub and let Gregory envelop her in the softness of a thick white bath towel wrapped tightly around her by his sinewy arms.

'Delicious,' she murmured, closing her eyes and hugging the sheet to her. She was cocooned in it, glad of its warmth, of its softness, and even more glad to be so close to his body.

Wetting her lips with her languid tongue, she reached out and touched his glistening shoulder. He started and stepped back. The look in his eyes was impossible to read. There was defiance there, and also something resembling pain or fear.

'I'm sorry...' she said, in a broken voice. Puzzled and dis-appointed, she clenched her fingers into her palm, withdrew and let the towel that so warmly enfolded her slip from her grasp.

'It's not allowed,' he said, stepping away from her like he had earlier. 'At least, not yet.'

She stared, but bit her tongue. She was new here. She had to remember that.

Her body was dry now, aglow with the warm hue of the recent bath. Her breasts pouted proudly forward as though inviting his fingers. Very slightly, she opened her legs and was immediately aware of the sweet mix of musk and highly perfumed soap.

'Don't you want me?' she asked him plaintively, running her hands down over her breasts, the flatness of her belly, the forest of soft dark hair that flowered between her thighs.

She couldn't help but frown. His expression did not change; at least not in his eyes. His jaw dropped momentarily before he answered.

'Yes,' he suddenly said in a bright way that softened the hardness of his jawline. 'I want you to lie down on the bed.' He threw the last words over his shoulder in a more casual and offhand manner.

She didn't care about that. If he wanted her on the bed, he could have her on the bed. In fact, he could have her in any way he chose. She picked up the crumpled towel and made her way into the bedroom.

The thick green and red of the tapestry bedspread was rough against her back, and did nothing to subdue the heat of sexual desire that ran all over her body.

She lay her head on the crisp white linen of the pillow. Gently, she writhed her hips, rubbing one leg against the other in excited expectation.

She closed her eyes as the smell of lavender from the pillow assaulted her senses. Sensuality itself played havoc with her nerve ends.

Purrs of ecstasy escaped from her mouth as she raised one knee, then the other, so that the top of one thigh was always in contact with her aching clitoris.

Through narrowed eyes, she watched him re-enter the room and gasped with sheer lust when she saw he now wore only the briefest of coverings: nothing more than a posing pouch that hid his cock from view but nothing else.

'Why don't you take that off, too?' she asked through rushed breath.

Abruptly and without answering, he turned his back on her and became absorbed with something on the dressing-table.

She watched; licking her lips, rubbing her breasts, mesmerised by the view of his well-formed buttocks divided by the thin strip of material. She assessed the power of strong thighs and the incredibly detailed muscles in his well-honed calves.

He was totally hairless. His skin shone like soft gold in the subtle glow of the ornate lighting.

When he turned back to her, he was rubbing his hands together. Aware of the aroma of sandalwood, musk and wild flowers, she held out her arms to him, telling herself that this was the moment, this was their time.

Suspended for just a moment, she let her arms fall beside her. Although he was walking towards her, he did not look at her. His eyes seemed to stare straight over her head and her bed. What was it with this man? Was she that ugly?

'Face down,' he said suddenly, and her spirits rose.

'OK,' she smiled. 'If that's the way you want it.'

As she lay full-stretch on the bed, her eyes went to the big carved mirror that almost covered the other wall. There was a certain clarity lacking in it. The ones in the bathroom had been similar, she remembered. Then she smiled secretively. They were two-way mirrors; they had to be. Suddenly, she remembered that Alistair liked to watch. She felt like the star turn at the London Palladium. All right, if she was expected to perform, then perform she would.

With rising excitement she awaited the soothing strokes of his probing fingers. This, she told herself, was turning out even better than she'd hoped for. Of course, there was still that tingling around her love temple that needed assuaging. But now, instinctively, she knew that this blond seraphim would bring her to full satisfaction.

The towel was folded and pushed under her hips. It was a surprisingly comfortable position. Her breasts were not crushed. Briefly, she looked over her shoulder at her bottom. It was thrust slightly upwards, round, pink and gleamingly fresh from its thorough sponging. Like softly rounded hills, she thought, before closing her eyes.

Being healthy, she decided, the blood would all be running to her head and her shoulders, the first points to be massaged.

Softly she murmured, her senses poised for take-off, ready for her alone to take full advantage of this unexpected 'treatment'.

The fine fingers and oiled palms prodded new vitality into the tight muscles around her neck and down over her shoulder-blades. There was knowledge in them, an experience of touch that eased them to softness and coaxed her into relaxation.

Such was the exquisite rapture of the sensation that she hummed softly through closed lips in time with the sensuous sweep of his hands.

Long firm strokes ran down over the soft undulations of her firm flesh. Hands, sideways on, pressed into the long indentation of her spine. Her buttocks clenched then relaxed as his cool palms rolled each cheek as if kneading bread. The fingers pushed gently at each knot of tightness, spreading her cheeks to either side of their joining cleft before rounding each curve and proceeding down over her thighs.

The scent of flowers and sandalwood pervaded the air with each fresh application of oil. Her hips moved against the firmness of the towel which pressed pleasurably against the soft cushion of her pussy. A little harder, a little more pressure, and the thickness of the towel would be enough to bring about her climax.

But this was good enough, she thought. Most massages she had received before were from Ariadne who was good at it. She had of course returned the service, but according to her blonde and brazen friend, she was basically a no-hoper.

Her whole body trembled with pleasure as she was stroked, pressed and pummelled. The tight muscles of her thighs burned with new vitality as the massage continued on to her calves. She was disappointed when the hands ceased. Without being asked, she turned over and her bright-blue eyes, now infused with the electric blue of excitement, surveyed the rigid form, the face that never altered, the eyes and mouth that never smiled.

Just as she had surmised, oil was being re-anointed into those experienced palms.

Speculatively she let her gaze wander around the room; over the dark greens and dull golds of the tapestries, the dark rich wood of the furniture, until they settled on the mirror which was high and wide and edged with a vibrant carving of plump grapes and plumper naiad thighs. Well-endowed satyrs chased the running naiads just as they did on Alistair's desk. For the first time she noticed the size of the satyrs' manhoods, so large it took both hands to handle their priapic erections.

Lucky naiads, she thought to herself, and smiled knowingly at the sheet of glass. Was there someone behind the mirror at this moment in time? She guessed there was and wondered at their racing breath, their pulsing veins and their rising passion.

She stretched beneath Gregory's hands, opening her legs slightly and smiling secretively at the mirror as she did so. How did her yawning cleft and bouquet of pubic hair look to those hidden eyes? she wondered. And how did it look to Gregory?

Would he take her now? Strangely enough, she knew the answer. There would be pleasure with this man. There would be a shattering orgasm. But there was more to him than a straightforward tumble. She also guessed he had been given strict instructions, and those that had given them were safely ensconced behind the carved mirror.

Her gaze shifted and rested on the thick tuft of pubic hair that rose so defiantly from her plump mound, like fragile trees on a far-off hill. Then it travelled to her eager nipples that blushed like crushed roses at the advent of the busy hands. Penny mewed like a kitten as the fingers pulled, pummelled and pinched. All action was welcome and invoked response. Again, she closed her eyes as tension was replaced with ecstasy.

The thumbs pressed gently against her throat, the palms and fingers circled her neck. She groaned unashamedly as they travelled downwards, pressing across her collar-bone, easing the tightness away with experienced fingers.

Nothing could stop the moistness from gathering between her legs like a hidden well, and nothing could prevent her clitoris from raising its head and pushing through the matt of dark pubic hair.

With delicious pleasure, her tongue licked slowly over her quivering lips. The probing fingers were massaging her breasts, pulling at her nubs of desire that rose so prominently from their crown of pink flesh.

Slippery with oil, the hands rolled each breast between both hands. The fingers pressed around the nipples, drawing gasps of ecstasy from Penny's throat. She raised her hips as if those sweet nubs of pink were but remote controls for the rest of her body. In response, the hands progressed down over the flatness of her belly, tracing the lines of her taut stomach muscles.

As the tight thumbs pressed against the rising mound of her sex, she wriggled her hips, aware that her seeping juices were running towards the cleft between her buttocks and mingling there with the residue of oil.

Penny felt a charge of sensation wash over her as the hands gently spread her thighs then massaged in firm downward strokes, the fingers pressurising her muscles to let go of that last strain, that last stressed out tension.

Nothing could have prepared her for the surge of ecstasy that swept upwards from her throbbing sex. The hands that had massaged her thighs were now splayed upwards over her pubic hair, the thumbs lightly playing against her surging clit. A new tension gripped her, a tension that could only be released with a huge orgasm. Her breathing quickened, her hands clenched beneath her head. She wanted to open her eyes, she wanted to close them. She wanted to see this man in action, and watch the pliable hands taking her ever upwards to sexual fulfilment. But yet again, she wanted to see nothing and just to feel the exquisite sensations.

As a tumbling cascade of gratification racked her body, she arched her back and cried out. With trembling muscles she sought to drain the last tremor of climax from the knowing hands that had brought her to this apex.

Cries of delight were lost in her hair and in the sweet smells of the cotton pillowcase. Her hips writhed to and fro as throb followed throb until the final wave was spent.

Opening her eyes, and murmuring her thanks, she let her gaze wander to the mirror. She smiled.

I wonder, she thought, whether Alistair could resist that; whether his hands were busy masturbating his own cock as she was brought to stupendous heights. She hoped so. In that, there was success; and in success, there was power.

Thoughtfully she rubbed her hand over herself. Her pussy jerked, still tingling with the residue of her climax. She was satiated, in need of no more for the present time.

Gregory re-entered her thoughts.

'I'll rub you down.'

The statement was abrupt. No reply was awaited. The hands that had manipulated her to orgasm now rubbed her down. The towel was taken from beneath her hips and whisked briskly over her skin until it shone with honed perfection and glowed with healthy vitality.

'Rest,' he ordered. 'I'll unpack.'

Lovingly, as though she were a prize horse herself or an errant child, a coverlet of cool cotton was tucked around her. Surprisingly, she did rest. Her eyes closed, then opened. She took one last look at the mirror before she snuggled further down beneath the fresh-smelling cotton.

Sublime was the best way to describe how she felt. She felt renewed, invigorated and able to take on the best ... yet she also felt at ease enough to fall into a peaceful sleep.

# 4

The whiteness of her dress accentuated her honey-brown complexion, and the hint of gold around her neck added a richness to the simple cut and style. Her legs were bare, firm and bronze, the muscles of her calves well defined beneath the tightness of her skin.

Simplicity extended to her hair which she had left hanging in glossy waves of turbulent perfection. A rich mix of light shone through the art nouveau glass-shaded wall lights giving it extra sheen and colour reminiscent of old port and sleek ebony.

Zest for life and new experiences shone like white-hot diamonds in the blueness of her eyes as she surveyed the finished effect in the mirror. Her breasts were high and firm, the slight curve of her waist exaggerated by the cut of her dress. Over her hips, the dress caressed rather than clung, so that when she moved her body undulated independently of the material. Only the sound of it swishing lightly was evidence that it was there at all. And it was cool against her flesh. She wore no underwear. There was pure intimacy between the material and her skin.

Appraising her own self, her own body, she felt there was nothing she could not achieve; she could tempt anyone or try out anything.

'Fit to conquer,' she murmured, and smiled. Her teeth were like pearls against the rich pinkness of her lips and the tawny shine of her face. With pleasure and with satisfaction, she smiled to herself, to the mirror and to whoever might be on the other side. 'I hope you like how I look as much as I do,' she purred. Then she hunched her shoulders, swayed from the waist, spread her hands and ran them down over her body. It was lurid exhibitionism, more suited to Ariadne than to her.

She eyed the mirror speculatively. Who, she wondered, was on the other side at this moment. A thought occurred to her and blossomed. Her smile bordered on a laugh. The face reflected from the misty glass was not just attractive, radiant with desire, but beautiful.

Carefully, so as not to crease her favourite dress, she undid the top button which was little more than a seed pearl. After that, she let the wide straps with their cool, silk lining slip down her upper arms.

Her mouth, which was as near perfect as her teeth, flashed a more obvious and wicked smile at the mirror.

'A floor show,' she cooed to the reflected brightness, pouting her lips as though addressing a potential lover. 'A taste of things to come.'

As her dress slid slightly she cupped one breast in her hand, withdrew it from her dress and let it bide there, firmly uplifted by the rest of her bodice like a round, plump grapefruit, the areola surrounding her nipple darkly rich against the honey tone of her skin. Slowly, yet deliberately, she did the same with the other. She tossed her hair, cupped her hands beneath her precious assets and surveyed her handiwork in the mirror.

'Don't they look good like that?' she asked the mirror in her sexiest voice. 'See how firm they are, and how soft...' she murmured, running her fingers over the cool, silky flesh. Then she bent her head, pushed one breast up towards her lips, and licked her own flesh. She did the same with the other. She addressed the mirror again. 'And they taste so good and so soft, like melting sorbet. Wouldn't you like to taste them, too?'

The mirror did not reply. It didn't need to. She could see the effect for herself.

Her breasts were poised there – higher than they would usually be, and rounder – trapped like two plump pigeons, and their nubs dark pink like the stamens of a tropical orchid. Proudly they pointed directly ahead at the reflective glass.

They did look good. She congratulated herself and gently ran her fingers over her plush pink nubs that darkened to deep mauve as blood raced through her body.

Like a platter of plump fruit, she thought to herself speculatively, like the offering of a goddess, her breasts strapped high and blossoming. The effect pleased her. What man could resist these? she asked herself as she pointed them like loaded pistols at the mirror.

But what if it wasn't Alistair on the other side of the mirror?

It didn't matter. She would pretend he was there and that his own bodily desires, too, were racing along with his blood.

In every woman there is that longing to be the one who makes a man override his usual habits and routine existence. There is also the narcissist in each one, and Penny was no exception. She liked to look at her body, liked to see what it was capable of.

Teasingly, she rubbed the index finger of each hand over her willing nipples.

It felt good, it looked good, and a wetness began to invade her rapacious pussy. She took one hand from her breast and raised her skirt. In the mirror, her sex was reflected like a dark forest among white, although her creamy tan did subdue that contrast. She opened her legs and dipped one exploratory finger into her humid well of juice. As she did so, she threw back her head and moaned, yet her eyes never left the mirror.

There, once she'd tilted her hips in that expert way she had mastered with experience, she could see her welcoming haven, the pink folds of satin wetness and the jewels of juice scattering among the dark hair like tiny seed pearls as she retracted her finger.

Her breathing was quick and deep; her trapped breasts quivered as they rose and fell.

Should she finish this now or go on down to dinner and save it till later? That would be hard, of course, but then there was no knowing what encounters might arise from the dinner table, now was there?

With a sudden pang of regret she wished she had tried harder with Gregory. If only she could have got him to lie with her, to cover her and to push his hard cock into her. Thinking of him suddenly made her lose interest in the mirror, and she dropped her skirt. She would save her arousal for whatever the later hours of the evening might bring.

As though they were golden orbs for occasional viewing only, she cupped her breasts again and pushed them back inside her dress. At first she did up the undone button. Then, with a rising of her eyebrows and a careless 'So what?', she undid it again, pulled the bodice down slightly and left her cleavage free to the world.

Nadine Beaumont and Alistair, her brother, were on the other side of the mirror. Nadine's cloud-grey eyes watched and, as her mouth was wide, so, too, was her smile.

'Well, well, my pretty pussy,' she said in her low husky voice. 'You certainly are something, aren't you?'

'She's ideal.'

Nadine turned and looked down at her brother. Although he was a well-made man of average height, Nadine was exceptionally tall.

Her generous lips twitched a little in her unfeminine yet handsome face as she looked at him. Her thoughts were hidden.

They had to be. It was at times like these that she wished she could do something for him – not control his sexuality as she did now – but in that moment of release, she sometimes wished that she wasn't his sister and wasn't the woman she was.

'You find her attractive?' she asked with a cruel edge to her voice.

He hesitated before he nodded.

Nadine laughed just a short laugh. How well she enjoyed his discomfort. How much she enjoyed being in control. Her hand reached out to him. She patted then gripped at his crotch as though to confirm he was wearing his tight-fitting rubber underpants, the ones only *she* could release – even if he only wanted to relieve himself, she went with him.

'Then we will have to see, won't we?'

She saw him swallow and knew instinctively that his prick was hard and rising in his pants, and knew that only she could release it and let him have what he craved.

'Ariadne was telling the truth. She said she was ideal.'

'Yes, she did,' Nadine answered. At the same time, she checked the tightness of his waistband, running her hand around the tops of his thighs so she could also check that he couldn't even get a finger up to his throbbing tool to relieve his obvious suffering.

'How long do I have to wait?'

Nadine transferred her hand to his face. Her long, thin fingers stroked his cheek.

'Until I say so, my darling brother, Alistair; until I say so.' She sighed, and in a motherly kind of way tucked some stray wisps of hair behind his ear. 'You know that's the way you like best, my sweet dear.'

She tried to kiss his ear. He backed away. Reflexively she winced and consoled herself into thinking how much more delicious the torture would be later this evening. Yet again he would be just a spectator in the cabaret she had arranged for him. As always, she would be mistress of ceremonies.

Even Penny didn't know as yet that she would be performing and, from what Nadine had seen so far, it wasn't likely that their newest rider would object.

Ariadne had known. She had been well rewarded for setting Penny up and for keeping her mouth shut. But then, Ariadne had been a willing little bitch, ready for anything Nadine had thrown at her. Like all the rest. One year, and then away. That was the way it was, and that was the way Nadine intended it to stay. No morsel attained in order to entice her brother's passion was ever allowed to stay longer than a year.

Only those who have known each other since childhood really know each other well, Nadine mused. With a little more than sisterly affection, she glanced briefly at her brother before she spoke.

'She doesn't like to be told that she can't have something,' said Nadine. 'Ari said that. You know, the Barbie-doll type who you spent yourself with last time. That's good, my darling brother, very good. She's compliant, extremely sexual and very determined.'

The Adam's apple in Alistair's throat throbbed as if trying to escape. His gaze stayed on the mirror to the room beyond. It was empty now. Penny had gone, but his mind filled the void as he imagined what was to come.

Nadine watched him and saw the constriction in his throat. Just like his penis, she thought with perverse pleasure. How engorged it must be; swollen with need, yet unable to break free from its rubber prison, confined there until she decreed the time was right.

Nadine smiled to herself. How was Penny to know that Ariadne had indeed had sex with Alistair? How was she also to know that – powerful man as he was, always giving orders, always having people standing in awe of him – he liked his urgings controlled ... by his sister.

He had sex when *she* wanted. The rest of the time, he wore the rubber pants and was only allowed to watch and wonder whilst Nadine imagined his rising prick, trapped and unable to do anything.

And so, his passion was saved, accrued, and when he was released ...

'We'd better be off into dinner, my dear brother,' Nadine said, stretching languidly, arms above her head so her fingertips were well on their way to the ceiling.

Suddenly, Alistair grabbed hold of his sister's arm. The action took her by surprise. Eyes met eyes, and Nadine's jaw clenched squarely as he spoke. 'You know she's going to do everything in her power to get me going, don't you? She already knows these mirrors are two-way. She'd hardly have put on that exhibition otherwise now, would she?'

Nadine's smile was undeniably cruel. She raked one black-painted fingernail down over his cheek.

'Yes, brother. Ariadne knew she would. Knew she couldn't resist the wager either. If she gets you, she also gets the stallion. Sweetly, deliciously ironic, don't you think? Two stallions all in one.'

There were chandeliers in the dining-room, all starlike sparkle hanging from the high ceiling, which was predominantly Wedgwood blue but with swirls of ornamental plaster picked out in crisp gold and icy white.

The windows were like the ones Penny remembered from Alistair's office: Georgian panes set in big sash windows that left little room for walls between the high ceiling and the blue-and-gold plush pile carpet. The curtains were gold damask with heavy tie-backs that hooked to the unusually pronounced brass phalli of flying cherubs.

The walls that were left were white, their expansive iciness relieved only with a dado rail of crisp blue and spine of gold. Large paintings also relieved the white walls. The frames were gilt, the subjects' nude figures indulging in a variety of positions with more than one partner. Yet they were not piles of Titian flesh, all white and lumpy with small breasts and heavy hips. These were sleek women and well-honed and -hung men. These were today's figures, firm and supple, uninhibited in their pleasures and healthy in their bodies.

The gold, the blue, the whiteness were reflected in a myriad shades from the overhanging chandeliers and duplicated by the lead-crystal wine glasses. Some of the glasses contained red wine, dark as warm blood; others were full with white wine, the liquid softly golden.

There were four people seated at the table: Alistair, of course; another man introduced as Auberon Harding, a fellow rider, young and good-looking; and another man introduced as Sir Reginald Chrysling, who was older, but had worn well and had an instant, if predictable, old-world charm.

'Reggie,' he corrected enthusiastically, his tongue licking over thin lips in a strong face. 'My friends call me Reggie.'

'Pleased to meet you,' she said, and smiled sweetly at him as he eased himself up from his chair in an act of old-fashioned politeness whilst she took her own seat. Old-world charm had a certain attraction about it, but even if it hadn't, Sir Reggie, although his hair was white, was a well-built man who'd obviously taken care of his body, and in his youth must have been quite something to look at. He still was now. His nose was slightly hooked and his eyebrows were dark and matched his eyes. How sensuous his lips looked when they smiled. I wonder how many other lips they have kissed in his lifetime, Penny mused, or how many breasts have been sucked to distraction between his neat white teeth.

Penny beamed at them all, for no matter who looked at her and what they said, tonight she was beautiful. Tongues confirmed what eyes already said. She radiated beauty and health, and with it, sexuality.

The other person at the table was a woman who Alistair introduced as his sister, Nadine. Vaguely, Penny remembered seeing her at Alistair's side in the VIP lounges at championship events.

The two women exchanged greetings.

Penny was immediately hypnotised and discomforted by this woman. Something in Nadine's manner and the cool look in her eyes seemed to flow out from her. Whatever the nature of this strange current, it made Penny's limbs feel weak and her sex pliant.

With world-weary eyes, Nadine gazed at her with a curiously enigmatic expression and a half-smile on one side of her mouth. 'I'm very pleased to meet you,' she said slowly, elbow on table, chin supported in right hand. 'Very pleased indeed.' Her voice had a lazy buzz to it, like the idle droning of bees on a summer afternoon or the faint sound of a lawnmower.

It was not just Nadine's voice that was unusual. Her appearance was dramatic, if not eccentric. Her eyes were grey, her jaw strong, her cheekbones prominent. Her hair was very white and very short – just bristles over her skull. Her skin closely matched her hair. Her eyes were lined with kohl, her lids with dark-grey shadow.

Perhaps it was the shadow that fell across her face, but Penny had the distinct expression she was being undressed with alarming familiarity by someone she had never met, but who seemed to know her and her body very well.

'Another little jumper. Well, I shall soon put you through

your paces, my dear, you can count on that,' said Nadine. The trace of sarcasm was drowned with a sip of wine clasped in fingers whose nails were varnished black. Plush, thick lips pursed speculatively over a black cheroot. There was an exchange of looks between brother and sister that hinted at reproach.

'Quite a good one, so I hear,' Nadine added suddenly. 'You have a good body, my dear. Fit, trim; ideal for what is expected of you.' Now her smile was very wide and very warm. With the addition of more wine, her voice was deep, yet crisp as burned toffee.

'I try to excel in everything, as much as is possible,' returned Penny, unable to hide her unease that the wandering gaze inspired in her. Nadine had watched her behind one of those mirrors. She knew it instinctively. Determinedly, she declined to blush.

As she smiled at Alistair's sister, Penny took a deep breath. Her breasts struggled against the half-open bodice. It was a provocative move, one designed to suggest that she was both knowledgeable and available.

Her eyes took note of their individual reactions. Auberon merely blushed, his eyelids fluttering like frightened butterflies.

Experience and familiarity won through. Reggie licked his lips and made no attempt to stop his eyes from settling on her cleavage.

Alistair, she thought, looked uncomfortable. It was as though he wanted to stare at what was on offer, but didn't dare. There was an odd look in his eyes, a mix of desire and perpetual torment.

Only Nadine's gaze was steady, her lips smiling. There was absolute boldness in her look coupled with an odd satisfaction. Her eyes narrowed through the halo of blue smoke.

Content that she had received admiration, Penny unfolded

the crisp white napkin that smelt of fresh citrus and was stiff with starch.

Nadine was directly across from her. It is easy to study looks when the subject you are studying is facing you.

It was hard not to stare at Alistair's sister. Penny tried to look away, to concentrate on the meal, sip less slowly at the wine, but Nadine surprised her. It seemed quite amazing that someone with such white hair and angular features could possibly be related to Alistair.

Nadine caught her looking and raised her blonde eyebrows towards the cropped hair that shone like silver beneath the lights.

From a distance, Penny guessed, the short glossy spikes could almost be mistaken for her bare skull. Jet earrings jiggled gently in her ears when she laughed as she did now.

Sir Reggie had cracked a joke. Penny hadn't heard it, her mind too full of analysing these people, of surmising how they might fit into the overall picture of things.

So far since coming here, she'd learned little of timetable and other more sociable interactions; except for Gregory of course. But Gregory didn't talk much – not that such a minor problem as that detracted from his magnetism one little bit.

'I hope I haven't offended you,' said Sir Reggie suddenly, shattering the beauty and sheer sexuality of her thoughts as his hand landed on hers. 'I hope you don't mind being the butt of my little joke. I didn't really mean it, you know.'

'Not at all,' she said, smiling brightly and wondering if the wine she had been drinking had affected her hearing. 'I can take a joke any time.' Then she laughed. What he'd said about her in any joke was of no interest to her; besides, she hadn't heard him.

Her attention was drawn to Nadine whose hand reached over the table. Her palm rattled the glass and silverware as she brought it down heavily on the pure whiteness of the table-cloth.

'That's it, Penny darling. Take no notice of him. I'm sure you'll be an asset round here, darling girl. My brother appreciates perfection – in everything.'

'I won't,' she replied, her eyes catlike; her lips, glistening with the dark rich colour, slowly sipped her wine.

Their eyes met as Nadine straightened in her chair. For the first time Penny could evaluate just how tall Nadine was; six foot two at least, and clad from head to toe in black, its denseness only relieved with base metal bangles and a collar that looked to be made of dull marcasite and leather and a good two inches in depth – perhaps made for a bull mastiff rather than a woman.

'No harm in that, my dears,' chirped up Sir Reginald who Alistair had explained was a fellow director and business associate in the wide and varied group first founded by Alistair's father before the Second World War. 'Perfection is to be admired, my dears ... cosseted,' he added as his broad hand circled Penny's back. She leant forward away from the harp-shaped back of the chair. His fingers spread downwards and slid over the roundness of her buttocks. 'All perfection,' he added with a low chuckle.

He smelt of expensive aftershave and his body appeared well-looked-after beneath the expensive smoothness of his black evening suit. Being of mature age, and born with privilege and rank rather than achieving it, he was the only one truly dressed for dinner.

Alistair was not casually dressed, but not formally either. His shirt was made of grey silk that matched his eyes. He wore a tie which must have cost as much as some people would pay for a whole outfit. He looked smooth, well-groomed and as expensive as the neat gold-and-diamond cufflinks that flashed at his wrists. Smooth, she thought, sure of himself, yet strangely ill at ease; and the more he looked at her, the more ill at ease he appeared to become.

Not that he was the only one who studied her. The expressions of everyone there were symptomatic of the fantasies each one was enjoying in their minds.

All eyes relished the pertness of her nipples, which were outlined like rare etchings through the thin material of her dress.

Their eyes travelled down to her waist and over the curve of her belly. Only Reggie could see any further. His eyes alighted on her lap. His breathing was quick and hot, his hand slightly sweaty upon her thigh, but pleasant.

With daring borrowed from the heaviness of the wine, she opened her legs slightly and with one hand hitched her skirt a little higher. She heard Reggie suck in his breath as her own Black Forest came shyly into view; no more than a mass of darkness between the creamy flesh of her thighs.

Sidelong, she smiled at him, saw gratitude in his eyes and was rewarded for her efforts by his fingers edging stealthily over the soft satin of her inner thigh before tangling amongst her dusky hidden hair.

His lips were wet now. He licked them dry and smiled at her. Alistair talked to Auberon in the background, Nadine adding her more tart comments.

Yet somehow their talk was nothing more than a shadow, a mime they were going through as if to put her at her ease, to let her enjoy, to indulge and to arouse. There was more yet to come.

'I raise my glass to you,' he said with gentlemanly politeness, whilst the fingers of his right hand divided her feathered lips and touched lightly on her throbbing clit. 'I think you are a charming young woman, a great asset to this establishment and the association.'

'Association?' she queried. Her questioning tone merely disguised the moan that had escaped from her throat along with the word. She was wet, aroused and couldn't help her legs from opening wider. He took advantage of the opportunity. There was one finger now either side of her clitoris, each one folding her labia away from her innermost treasures.

He winked in a boyish way that complemented his handsome patrician features. A gold bracelet slid down his wrist as he raised his glass again.

'To you, young lady – and your association with everyone here.'

The two fingers slid towards her secret portal, dipped neatly in, retreated, then dipped again.

She was aware of her own breath quickening, her breasts rising and falling against her bodice, their curving edges peering out from the restriction of her dress like twin crescent moons. She was also aware that conversation had ceased, that she was the subject of silence and all-seeing eyes. But she didn't care. She was too far gone to care; too far along the road to a mind-shattering orgasm that she badly yearned for.

He drained his glass, she drained hers. She liked this man. Like Alistair, the power he possessed made her feel good and secure. She lifted her glass and held it to the light so the wine turned pink against the lead crystal and the light from the chandeliers. As she twirled it, rainbow colours shot through each sharp cut prism of glass and threw its beam upon her face. Like people, she thought; or, at least, like the people here. White on the surface, but composed of many colours, with many facets.

'Is she very wet, Reggie darling?' Nadine asked suddenly.

Penny gasped, glanced swiftly at Alistair's sister, then back, almost in a fit of pleading, to Reggie's face.

'Very wet, Nadine darling, very wet indeed. Just a little more effort, and this little pussy will come.'

Penny was speechless, as much from her mounting orgasm as from the sudden realisation that everyone there knew exactly what they were doing and, from the sound of it, *had* done all along.

'Then bring her off, darling. Right now!'

Like the prisms of light that had reflected so richly from the glass, the faces of those around Penny spun in a blur of colour as two fingers of Reggie's right hand pushed further into her. Never mind that everyone was watching. She was beyond caring. In an effort to capture the full impact of his fingers, she slid slightly forward on the chair so he could invade her more fully. All the while his fingers dived in, his thumb dancing over her clitoris in short, sharp flicks. Now he used his other hand to hold back her fleshy lips and the sleek black hair of her pubes. And then it came, flooding over her in a torrent of electric release. Her hips lifted against his hands and, crying out, she threw her head back, closing her eyes, her orgasm pulsing with each murmur of breath.

Reggie removed his hands and washed them in the bowl of water at the side of his fork. The bowl was dark blue. A slice of lemon floated on the surface. It was a relaxed and effective action, emphasising cleanliness, opulence and sensuality at one and the same time.

Tossing her hair and still breathless, Penny eyed those around the table.

'Splendid, darling!' exclaimed Nadine, cheroot gripped in her teeth and hands clapping. 'A splendid effort indeed. If you ride your horses like that, then you'll get no complaints from me.'

Auberon just smiled, and Reggie winked at her again, refilled his glass and raised it to her before sipping.

Alistair was staring at her, his mouth grim set and eyes glittering. She could see him swallowing consistently, and noticed that his lips were dry and that he seemed unable to say anything.

Had he not seen enough? Or, perhaps, he had seen too much; perhaps she had blotted her copybook without meaning to.

At last, he cleared his throat. Then he spoke. 'Outstanding.'

Penny flashed her eyes as she savoured the word. That one word clarified exactly what he thought. Not the word itself: there was nothing much in that, it was ordinary, just a word. But she'd detected something else in the way he said it. Deep inside it had come into existence, yet had stuck in his throat, had grated its way to the surface so that when he *did* say it, its meaning was intensified. His voice had been as low as the depths from which it had come. She knew then that he wanted her; that in time her wager would be won.

Like liquid fire she returned his stare with her own. When, she asked with her eyes, exactly when?

Alistair's gaze shifted, almost guiltily. From the centre of the table he took hold of the half-empty wine bottle – one of three that sat on there – and poured into his own glass.

But other eyes watched. Other eyes surmised and made plans for these two people.

Nadine still held the key to her brother's torment. Thoughtfully she played with the black cross that hung from her ear. It jingled playfully as she touched it. With each jingle, Penny noticed that Alistair's jaw clenched, and a nerve beneath his eye quivered.

Nadine saw her look but did not answer the question in her eyes. Nadine was taking pleasure from her brother's clenching jaw and the nerve that quivered just below his right eye. She knew what he was going through and understood how much the key, which hung behind the earring, meant to him. Only the shadow of a smile played around her mouth as she toyed with the earring and then touched the cold metal of the small key itself. Time and place was controlled by her. Nothing had changed, nothing would change. All in good time, her brother would have what he craved, and Penny would have more than she could ever have bargained for.

'More wine, Penny?'

Thoughts melted and scattered, Penny looked up into the soft, boyish face of Auberon Harding, another horse rider lucky enough to get a place under Beaumont's roof together with a wedge of his bank account.

'Yes please,' she replied. For some reason, she used her sexiest voice to answer. Perhaps it was because of the burning she felt deep inside; the need to have a real cock inside her rather than just be played with, probed and brought off purely for the benefit of other people.

She smiled her thanks to Auberon Harding, the Honourable Auberon Harding to be exact, whose family were something in the meat trade and had been for generations. Perhaps they'd been high-street butchers who were suddenly landed with the privilege of supplying Queen Victoria with pork sausages. It didn't matter. Now, he was an Honourable, and he looked it. He had a look of class about him: thick-lipped with a head-boy type of face and a hairstyle that sat firmly on the fence between fashion and conformity, yet flopped over his forehead. His clothes straddled the same fence. Not too formal, not too fashionable: white shirt; neat tie; neat jacket; neat, sharp-pleated trousers; polished black shoes. Everything about him was neat, correct, pleated and polished. Public school, she decided. She'd met others like him, men who found it impossible to shake off the residue of a rigid regime that had moulded them into a pre-set shape. It was as if they'd originally been made of jelly and now were cast in bronze.

He looked nice enough, but, although he surveyed her dark hair, her open expression and her gaping neckline, she was surprised and a mite disappointed when his eyes did not linger.

Fragments of conversation filtered into Penny's mind as she drank more wine, which was smooth on her tongue and mellow in her head. On top of that, the newness of everything, the excitement of it all and the experience of her dining-table orgasm had lightened her mind even more. Eager to learn and perhaps experience more, she continued to survey those at the table, her dark lashes sweeping her cheeks as her eyes flickered from one guest to another along with the conversation.

Sir Reginald fondled her knee each time he spoke to her. There was something strangely protective about his fondling, as though he were trying to put her at ease and to make her feel at home. She let him, and tried her best to let Alistair know that she was letting him. After all, there was still the wager to consider, though gradually she was becoming fascinated with this close group of people who had accepted her so easily and so completely.

For the moment, her massage with the blond angel was forgotten, though if nothing further came off tonight, she would need him again, if only to ease her aching libido with his flexible fingers. Though she would of course prefer his rampant cock.

But Gregory was not here. Alistair was. She caught him looking at her once or twice. It was a guilty look, as though he were a small boy and had been caught stealing from a sweet shop. So far, she thought to herself, Alistair had disappointed her.

Adopting an air of indifference to hide that disappointment, she let her eyes study the other diners whilst her mind weighed up each one.

Sir Reggie was sweet, debonair and highly attractive. She imagined that having sex with him would be a very professional experience. During his life, he would have known many women, would have indulged most readily in every conceivable practice and with every conceivable age, colour and creed of woman. Sir Reggie had been in the army. Sir Reggie had travelled.

Auberon seemed the height of politeness, the warmth between them like one old schoolmate to another whenever he included her in his conversation. There was no strange guilt in his look like there was with Alistair. His colouring and flickering eyelids came more from shyness than guilt. Of course, she still couldn't quite work out what Alistair had to be guilty about.

Nadine was the most intense watcher. Each time Penny chanced to look in her direction, Nadine was staring back at her over the top of her wineglass and, although Alistair dominated the conversation with his talk of mergers, expansion and then the world of equestrianism, she had a distinct impression his sister might be more powerful than him.

Watching and wondering about her fellow diners ignited new excitement in Penny's loins. The actions and the scenes she envisaged for each of these people were only in her mind at present, yet she knew that what could be fantasised could also be turned into fact.

As she sipped her wine, she imagined what each man's body would feel like against hers, what each cock would feel like in her as each mouth nibbled and sucked at her willing breasts.

Her eyes darted to each in turn before settling on Alistair. There was something about him that was simultaneously alluring and secretive. She was drawn to him, and everything Ariadne had said only added to her curiosity. Like getting to grips with a new horse, he was a challenge, a creature to be broken and ridden. Vaguely she knew in her mind that whatever it took, she would have him.

Ariadne had told her he was a voyeur, a spectator. Then, she decided, she would give him plenty to look at. Each and every sexual encounter she had would be within his sight so he would have to take part and would be unable to resist the depths to which debauchery and her own sexuality could take them. She drained her glass. With a smile, Auberon refilled it.

Food, wine and sparkling conversation were all in plentiful supply. As the wine poured down her throat, she began to wonder who was on offer this evening; who was there for the asking and where Alistair would be when she indulged her desire.

'Lovely meal, my dear, don't you think?' The plump-fingered hand of the errant knight squeezed her thigh, his fingers lightly touching the valley at the top of her legs.

She smiled at him, then over at Alistair. He glanced at her, almost as if he knew what was happening.

Turning to Sir Reginald, and looking into his face as though he were the lover she had always been waiting for, she opened her legs a little wider. She saw his lips get wetter, the bottom one sagging. Purposefully, she snapped her legs shut. Sir Reggie's hand retreated and his eyes flickered. He looked hurt for a moment, but only for a moment. His smile returned and he turned his face and his conversation to Alistair.

A gentle touch on her elbow made her transfer her attention to Auberon. There was a fairy lightness in his fingers, a play-fulness that betrayed the strength needed for the sport he so lovingly pursued. Reins were hard to hold on a plunging, rearing animal that weighed something near half a ton, and didn't she know it?

'It's nice to have you here. It really is so terribly nice.' She smiled at him and to herself. He even sounded like a head boy – one left over from some obscure and ancient public school.

And yet there was sincerity in his eyes and on his lips. She was aware of sudden silence. Conversation, which up until now had flowed almost unabated except when Penny had attracted their attention, had now ceased. Suddenly, she felt as though she were the centre of attention.

Briefly, she glanced towards Alistair. His eyes met hers before he leant across the table and spoke to Sir Reginald. She couldn't grasp what was said. She looked from the older man to the younger, then was aware of the eyes of Alistair's sister, Nadine. They were like pale grey pools amid the heavy black make-up. And suddenly, along with everyone else, there was lust in her eyes.

Holding Nadine's gaze and tensing her back, Penny clenched her buttocks in an effort to control the familiar ache surging between her thighs. There were opportunities here, she told herself, and though her vision was blurred and her head was light, she had no intention of missing them.

'Do you think you will like it here?' Auberon asked her.

Everyone seemed to be holding their breath for her answer. All, she guessed, needed to know how her earlier sojourn with Sir Reggie had affected her opinion.

'It's nice to be here. It really is,' she said brightly. 'Am I right in thinking you've got the room below me?' She placed her hand on his thigh, felt the iron-hard muscles tense beneath her touch.

Around the table, there was a sudden exhalation of breath, as though there had been a doubt, which was now discarded.

But Penny was only half-aware now of what was happening around her. She made no secret of what she was doing at the table, her smile wide, whilst her fingers flicked gently but determinedly at the awakening flesh just behind Auberon's zip-fastener. Here was a flower just waiting to be plucked, and she had just the vase to put it in, she thought cheerily.

He flushed as he nodded, and his eyes flitted briefly around the table. Other mouths smiled, other eyes sparkled, as though they too were experiencing what he was experiencing. Nervously his tongue licked at his lips. As his leg moved, his shaft jumped against his trousers.

And yet, there was a vulnerability about him, an innocence that seemed strangely irreconcilable with the determined sportsman she knew him to be. She retrieved her hand and smiled.

I wonder, she thought to herself, head supported on cupped hand whilst her other hand twirled the dark liquid in her glass, whether he's a bit of a cane man – even a bit gay.

'Time for bed.' Alistair got to his feet. As if it were a prescribed signal, everyone else got to theirs.

Sir Reginald coughed and yawned in disjointed unison, and Penny smiled into her wine as the shiny seat of his well-polished dinner trousers came into view.

Nadine rose in chilly black splendour like a winter's night, head and shoulders above everyone present.

She was silent, though her eyes glittered and flitted briefly from one face to another before ending up on Penny. There was no disguising the self-congratulation in her look. As though she's looking through my clothes rather than at them, thought Penny. It was as if, she reflected, weakly grasping the thought as it circled in her mind, that Nadine knew exactly what was underneath. It was then she remembered her suspicions about the mirror and also about Alistair being a man who watched, not did. There were no guesses as to who he'd be watching tonight.

'I'll be taking a stroll, if anyone wants to join me.' Sir Reginald's now bloodshot eyes searched for an offer.

No one did join him.

All the same, Penny was aware of knowing glances passing from one to the other. A curling feeling rose and fell in her stomach. Somehow she knew that no matter where she went to bed that night or what she did, someone would be watching.

Alistair bade goodnight and Nadine glared with glittering iciness at Penny and Auberon, but ignored Sir Reginald completely.

They went off in different directions, Penny holding Auberon's hand, and Sir Reginald out through the front door for his so-called walk.

Auberon and Penny went outside, too. Both wished to check on their mounts before they turned in. At least, that was what they said.

The night sky was deep indigo and scattered with stars. The air was warm, and an owl hooted from a far-off meadow.

Penny breathed deeply, threw her head back and felt the tickling of her hair against her shoulders. The cool breeze of evening lifted her skirt and wafted around her naked thighs. The muskiness of sexual secretions reached her nostrils. The memory of that orgasm tantalised the crowding nerve ends that clustered around her clitoris. Excitement re-kindled desire. There was still a need within her.

She shouldn't complain, she told herself. She'd had two superb climaxes since she'd arrived, but both had been achieved by manipulative fingers not a penetrating penis. And the need to experience such a penetration was getting stronger.

Speculatively she looked sidelong at Auberon. Perhaps, she thought to herself just a little wickedly and a little selfishly, just perhaps they could both have what they wanted – both her and the young, fresh-faced man walking beside her.

'What a beautiful night,' she murmured into her escort's ear. 'Good enough to get to know each other better.'

His smile was bashful, perhaps even vague. It irked her to see that he didn't seem particularly enthusiastic. She eyed him again, and thought of her first impression of him. Head-boy type. And he was rather pretty in a boyish kind of way. Public school, she decided, had shaped his sexual preferences. In the darkness, she grinned. Perhaps, a wicked thought said in her head, Auberon liked other things.

Gravel scrunched under their feet as they walked the path to the stables. Vague mutters born of wine and brandy drifted in the night air. Sir Reggie appeared to be wandering off towards the shining glass of the orangery.

Perhaps it was the clarity of the night air, but Penny was very aware of the odour of the man at her side, the spoor of masculine sexuality that lay in a fine film over his skin.

It was also the night air that brought the sound of other footsteps crunching on the same gravel they had walked.

Slyly she looked back along the path. Sir Reginald had stopped in his tracks; two figures had joined him.

Beaumont is a spectator, Ariadne had said. In Penny's opinion, there were others here besides Alistair who liked to watch.

As the wine cleared from her head, it occurred to her that this could well be the first chance she would have of trying her luck with Alistair; of putting on a good enough show to at least whet his appetite.

She looked at Auberon as though she could eat him. Her fingers tangled in his. He smiled at her, a little shyly. As if, she mused, he had thoughts in his head that did not quite match hers.

Never mind, she thought, we could both get what we want tonight, or at least go some way towards it. First, she decided, she must make no secret of her intentions and her willingness to cater fully to his needs.

Lightly brushing against his hip and thigh as they walked, her fingers fondled the slight rise that pushed against his fly. His gasp hung on the air between them. He gulped and cleared his throat before he spoke.

'That's terribly nice, awfully nice in fact,' he stammered.

'Just nice?' she asked, and lent an ache of disappointment to her voice as if she were feeling just a touch insulted that her adept probings had not produced a more satisfactory response.

'Very nice,' he added on the edge of a sigh.

She moved her hand, ran it around his waist, then slid it over and between the iron-hard cheeks of his behind.

Ahhh! That's better, she said to herself as his breath and a nervous cough collided into a kind of choke.

'That's delicious!' he breathed at last, his voice one or two octaves higher than it had been.

So she was right. She smiled at the night. Tonight could finish even better than it had started.

'Is that?' she asked with sudden cruelty, her nails digging into one tight buttock.

'Terribly,' he moaned.

'And that?' she asked again as her nails dug into the other buttock.

'Awfully!' he gasped. 'Ahhh!'

'That's not good enough,' she said suddenly, thanking her intuition and enjoying the unfamiliar cruelty she brought to her voice and her clawed hand. 'I'm sure you can do better than that, boy! Don't you think so?'

Beneath her nails, his flesh trembled. Her own loins quivered in sympathy.

'I . . . I . . .' His eyes glittered and she saw a bead of sweat erupt on his brow, then divide and run like melting ice towards his eyebrows.

What use did she have for his answer? She knew what he wanted, just as she knew they were being followed, and that whatever they did would be watched and enjoyed by those they had been with at dinner.

'This, I think, is what you need!' she exclaimed, her voice fierce with authority and dripping with promised discipline.

Taking careful aim, she plunged her index finger into where she judged his rectum should be.

He groaned as his cheeks tightened over her rigid finger. As much as she could, dressed as he still was in his dark and well-cut evening trousers, she pressed her finger in, deeper.

They still walked towards the stables, him almost on tiptoe, her finger guiding him like some rigid and oversize puppet to where they were going.

With undisguised curiosity, she stopped in her tracks and put her other hand on his crotch. Her fingers closed over it like the petals of a flower. There it was, the fruit of her labour, hard, erect and begging for more.

So that was what he wanted.

The footsteps behind did not cease. She looked back into the darkness before walking on; she knew they were following and also what their intention was. Well, they would see everything they were coming to see . . . and more.

If they expected a straightforward fuck, then they were going to be sadly disappointed on this occasion. Much as she might want it herself, she knew that Auberon's path to that end would be different from hers.

And they would be watching. She was sure of that, just as she was sure of the light scrunching of gravel she could hear from somewhere behind them.

'We'd better do something about this,' murmured Penny as she kissed his cheek and undid his flies.

His prick fell out, white, lean and topped with a foreskin like an unfolded toadstool. The moonlight caught it, giving it a ghostly appearance as they walked on. Like the cane of a blind man pointing the way, it jiggled from side to side as they walked. She enjoyed seeing that, and in order to maintain such an unusual sight, she pushed her finger as firmly as she could into the crack between his buttocks.

'I'm terribly excited, you know. I can't tell you how much this means to me.'

Auberon's voice held all the excitement of a small child with worn, but well-loved toys and a new friend. It was sweet, and only made Penny more curious to know what sort of a man and how much of one he was.

'Don't mention it. I'm always willing to do a man a favour.' That at least, she realised, was the honest truth.

What a picture they must present, she thought, her finger still firmly embedded in his rectum. All the time, she could feel the cheeks tensing, then relaxing, one muscled orb moving with slow deliberation against the other. The effect was arousing to her as well as to him.

Curiosity gave wing to inflamed sensations. Already she could feel the pertness of her clitoris pushing through the mat of satin hair that shielded it from the outside world. Soon it would demand its tribute, crave without pity for the height of ecstasy that was its due reward.

But, in the meantime, she would give Auberon what he wanted, and give the approaching band of spectators exactly what they deserved.

Lit only by the glow of a low moon, the stable block smelt of warm hay and the sweaty flesh of the animals it was home to. In the gloom, the beasts snickered softly and moved gently within their stables.

As his hand reached out for the light switch, she took her finger from his behind and grabbed his cock. She heard him gasp and saw him take his hand away from the switch.

'This way,' she whispered as she used his dick to lead him into the adjacent hay store.

A round window divided into four odd-shaped panes allowed moonlight to stream through and throw a silver pool on the area she had selected to give her debut performance.

She smiled to herself at the thought. Like a great celestial spotlight, outlining and accentuating everything they would be doing for their very select audience.

Beneath them the straw was warm, its scent full of the earth-iness of ripe meadows, hot summers and unbridled fertility.

'How much do you want what I am going to give you?' she asked him provocatively, one hand encompassing his hot weapon whilst the other squeezed the felt softness of his balls.

'A terrible amount!' he exclaimed. 'A truly terrible amount!'

'How much?' she asked with some sharpness.

He squealed like a pig as she squeezed his balls harder and dug her fingernails into his scrotum.

'Truly! Very. Oh please . . .'

She paused, wondering for just a moment if he might faint. Tremors of mingled emotions enveloped her. There was elation in being in control of such a situation, of having his penis so stiff, yet so vulnerable, in the palm of her hand.

She swallowed her own excitement and her own need to have him probe into her body. Auberon had definite tastes. If she was to get what she wanted, she had first to satisfy his own particular proclivities.

She let his prick drop from her hands and, although she had expected her release of him to result in temporary disappoint-ment, she certainly hadn't expected tears.

'Please . . .' he pleaded, his voice little more than a whimper. 'Please . . . anything you want you can do to me . . . anything at all.'

Now what do I do? she asked herself, her mouth slightly open, and her eyes vaguely aware of figures moving in the gloom.

Spontaneity was part of her character so it wasn't too difficult to come up with something suitable.

'Kiss me, and I will carry on. I will give you all that you desire better than you've ever been given it before.'

Ecstasy as well as moonlight lit his face.

Then he kissed her, his lips warm and soft against hers.

But Penny was very aware that such tenderness would not be enough for him.

'Dog!' she exclaimed as she slapped his face. 'I didn't tell you to kiss me like that! You can't kiss my lips. Not those anyway!'

As he rubbed his face and stared at her wide eyed, she opened her legs and lifted her skirt. Then she peed, her golden rain hot and rising like an autumn mist from the soft straw.

A whimper escaped Auberon's throat. Even in nothing more than moonlight, she could see his eyes glittered and his cock had stiffened.

'Take your clothes off first,' she told him.

He did. With fastidious precision he folded each item and laid it neatly to one side. She watched in silent fascination. How predictable he was; how moulded by his school-days.

Flesh quivering with delight rather than repugnance, he knelt before her and steadied himself by putting his hands on her thighs.

'Hands behind back!' she growled.

Like an exceptionally obedient dog, he obeyed.

She opened her legs a little wider and edged closer to his face. To accommodate her, he tilted his head backwards. Before long, his ears were against her thighs. His head was trapped. The lips of her sex kissed his mouth.

His tongue licked amongst the thick cluster of pubic hair before she opened herself for him with her own fingers. With undulating movements, she moved herself over him so she could take full advantage of his heat-seeking tongue, his chin and his nose.

He sucked at her like a hungry baby, taking the last clinging drops of golden liquid into his mouth. Then his tongue worked its way over her, prising more juice from her, but this time less salty, more sticky and resulting from desire rather than relief.

His tongue was now in her, hot, probing, like a small prick, yet more pliable.

She moaned and, as she clamped his head tightly between her thighs so he could not possibly move, she let her skirt fall over him whilst she unbuttoned her bodice and let her breasts break free.

Once they were unrestricted she rolled them in her hands, closed her eyes and felt as though she were the goddess Diana herself, bathed in moonlight and riding some creature of the night as she rocked back and forth over Auberon's open mouth and willing tongue.

Her eyes opened briefly to survey the darkness. She smiled at it. Then she took off her dress.

The moonlight streamed through the window and added an iridescent richness to the colour of her hair and an incandescent brightness to the creamy gleam of her skin.

She was a performer and she loved the part she was playing. The figures in the darkness were of no account; they were just spectators in the auditorium enjoying the show. But, like all plays, there is a first act, then there are the second, third and fourth...

A pool of erotic energy was building up around her pussy and eddying with waves of rising desire to lap against her swollen clit. Despite Auberon's best efforts, he could not make her come.

Now, she decided, is the time for the next act.

'Enough!' she shouted, and pushed his head away.

She couldn't have pushed him that hard, yet there he lay, gasping among the straw, a film of her moisture shining like silver around his lips. He looked cowed in body, yet there was an undeniable glint of desire in the bright hazel of his eyes. He was playing a part and enjoying it. Well, she'd really give him something to remember; she'd really use and abuse him for all she was worth. He yearned for it, she needed her own climax, and the watchers in the shadows expected it.

'Hands and knees!' she shouted at him. 'Get on your hands and knees!'

He rolled over and did as she ordered. She walked around him, proud in her nakedness, showing herself off for those whose eyes watched from the darkness.

If Mark could see me now, she thought to herself with a lewd smile, he'd take me and take me until we were both exhausted. But Mark wasn't there. Auberon was.

Auberon had a good body and, despite her determination to play for the crowd, she admired it. With long, sweeping strokes she smoothed her hands down his back, then smacked each cheek so that pinkness replaced the perfect whiteness. There, between his thighs, his balls hung in their soft sac. She raised her foot beneath them so they sat warm and weighty, first on her toes, then on her instep. She rolled them on her foot, enjoying the warmth, enjoying the feeling of power it gave her. She heard his breath quickening, then realised her own was racing, too. In time with the rising of his desire, hers, too, rose and waited.

'Stand up,' she ordered.

Hesitantly but with obvious subservience, he got to his feet.

'Don't hurt me,' he wheedled.

Even that, she knew, was just play-acting. Of course he wanted her to hurt him. He enjoyed being hurt, enjoyed that evolution of pain that led him to that final throb of a spent member.

'I will do as I please,' she told him, and held his prick as if it were just his handle and made of something harder than normal flesh and blood.

She bound him with items of leather harness that hung on the wall. The ends she found looped up easily into iron rings that hung from a wooden beam above his head.

She stood on bales of straw to reach the iron rings, then fastened the ends of the harness back through the pieces she'd already looped around his wrists.

His arms were raised full-stretch and the tautness of his muscles were outlined by a compliant moon. He hung there – like a sacrificial offering on some pagan altar – waiting for his moment, for his time of giving.

Surprisingly she found other matching rings in the floor. She bound him to those, too, so his legs were stretched apart, thigh and calf muscles hard and unyielding beneath the softness of her hands and the tightness of the leather.

When she had finished she stood back to survey her handiwork. She was well satisfied. He formed a near perfect 'X', his prick still proud of his body, limbs stretched to full extent, buttocks tightly clenched.

Like a preying panther she circled him, trailing her fingers over a body that was unburdened with superfluous flesh. There was only muscle, hard, primed to perfection.

Her eyes wandered over him shining with delight, and she realised suddenly just how much those other eyes in the darkness must be shining, too.

Her body trembled in anticipation as she admired the tension that rippled his muscles and quivered in hard spasms over his taut behind.

All the time she laboured, exploring with just the tips of her fingers. The more pressure she applied and the greater the sharpness of her nails, the more his penis grew.

'How does that feel?' she asked him. 'Now you're stretched to my liking.'

He groaned as she raked her nails over his stem, then groaned more when she squeezed his balls in her hand.

The sounds from his throat were unintelligible until she had released his balls.

'Glorious,' he murmured.

Even now, she knew he would appreciate her abusing him that little bit more until she judged him ready for her own purposes.

'That's not good enough!' she said, and took the final two pieces of harness from the hook on the wall.

These pieces were thin, almost thong-like. Briefly she wondered what horse they were used for – a lightweight one by the looks of it. Not that it mattered. What mattered was her performance on this most auspicious night.

She tried not to look into the darkness, yet effort was needed to concentrate her eyes and her actions on Auberon alone.

With a wicked, catlike grin, she threaded the fine strips of leather through his legs, one piece at a time so that his testes were pushed towards the centre immediately behind his cock. They bulged there, round and shiny like overblown balloons.

Auberon was in ecstasy. His head was thrown back, his eyes were closed and a series of appreciative moans escaped from his throat.

The ends of the leather she crossed over his chest, then she looped them over his shoulders so his balls and penis were bunched in one mighty mound of flesh that lunged to greater size as the man revelled in his sweet restraint. After that, she passed the end of each thong through each ring – that hung like bangles behind his balls – and fastened them securely.

Observant enough in daylight to know where everything was kept, Penny took two items from the custom-built metal shelf against the wall. One was a simple riding crop, the other a lunging whip.

Now it was easy not to look into the blackness. Everything, they say, gets easier with practice, and in this case it was certainly true.

Bondage had been something that she and Mark had got

up to when desires and emotions were too far beyond the normal level of tension. Even so, she had been enthralled by it, experiencing more powerful releases than straightforward sex could ever satisfy.

With professional efficiency, she cracked the whip then smiled with glee as she saw the reaction on Auberon's face. The fear of pain that flashed there she knew to be only pretence. Deep down, beneath that terrified facade, she knew his body was aching for pain, longing for the thin strip of leather that would raise redness over the taut hardness of his flesh.

Her eyes dropped to his trapped cock. It lurched, reared with bottled-up excitement and, just for a moment, she thought he might shoot his load before she was ready for him to do so.

There was delight in her own action. Much as this man wanted her to pleasure him, she also had her own satisfaction to think about. No matter. First, she would deal with him, whip him to a trembling mass. Then she would take him purely for her own pleasure.

His trembling loins shivered as she walked around him. She trailed her fingers from the hard shoulder muscles down to his round cheeks. She teased each one, tracing lines, each one terminating in the tight cleft between. Instinctively his buttocks squeezed like they had earlier when her finger had probed at his puckered anus.

The fingers travelled on around his pelvis to his throbbing member. She saw it rear; saw it jerk as if it could take flight if set free. But it would not be set free. It was trapped pinched between two bonds of leather.

Sharply her fingernails traced more circles around the bulbous head of his cock. Her eyes opened wide. Never could she have believed that such exquisite pain could spur one to greater things, to a greater size. With enjoyment and without protest, she entered his world and took pleasure in the sublime pain she saw fit to endow. Amid pleasurable murmurs she hissed through her clenched teeth as she drew her nails down over his stem. Surprised at her own reactions she watched with interest as the veins of his neck stood in sharp relief against his skin. A moment later he threw his head back and howled at the rafters.

This was pure delight, pure power. Thoughtfully her fingers dipped into the slippery mixture that was brimming through the length of her labia. So far this little act had been all his. She had given him a lot; he had given her little.

In time with her rapid breath her breasts heaved as power mingled with sexual excitement.

Again she cracked her whip. She heard his sharp intake of breath and sensed his apprehension as he attempted to gauge her timing.

Stretching his throat again he threw his head back and let out a yell as the fine end of the lunging whip curved over his buttocks. She saw them tense, fold one in upon the other as if he were holding something in between. She smiled. She was beginning to enjoy this, and her imagination was beginning to work overtime.

The whip rose and fell again. His cry was a rich mix of pain and delight.

Breathless, her breasts pouting to the point of ecstasy, she dropped her arm to her side, then reached out to run her hand over the quivering behind. Hot flesh trembled beneath her palm, and tight cheeks closed over the nub of her probing thumb as it dived and teased the prim ring in between. It excited her, and made her stomach tighten and her clitoris rise in rapture from its sheath of dewy petals.

'More,' she heard him breathe. 'Give me more.'

Unable to resist the lure of the stretched torso, she ran her hand from his armpit, over his ribs, and on to his hip, then across his stomach. She clenched her fist so her fingers formed a talon.

He screamed soft and low as the claw ran from navel to phallic stem, pinching at his glistening glans, before digging into the soft flesh that hung beneath.

'I'll give you more,' she growled, now unable to stop herself from entering the full spirit of the scene. 'Just wait and I'll give you more.'

The whip stung again and again across his bunched shoulders, his arched back, his round behind, the shuddering muscles of his thighs and calves.

She changed position, altered her aim so the whip fell in a long curl of leather across his heaving chest and stretched stomach, lightly kissing his jutting penis as it landed with stinging accuracy over his thighs. His knees bent slightly. Sweat glistened on the abused muscles.

But now her throat was dry and her sex soaking. Penny knew her own body well enough to know when its just desserts were due. Her aim had been strong and true, and now his flesh was glowing nicely with the searing heat of perfect pain. The sight of his cock, leaping up and down with each new dealing of sublime ecstasy, was too much for her to bear. She had to have him. At the same time, she had to satisfy his own more specialised pleasure.

The head of the lunging whip was thick, not as thick as his penis, but thick enough. Imagination rich in original thought took over as she eyed his twitching buttocks and the handle of the whip. Her mind was made up.

'Now it's my turn. There's nothing for you to do but go along with it.'

'Whatever ... whatever you want to do to me, do.' The whimper in his voice seemed more of an entreaty than a reproach.

That to her was confirmation enough that what she had in mind would delight him. At the same time it would get her what she wanted.

With the helpful rubbing of the handle against an odd piece of saddle soap, she slid it between the tight orbs of his behind. Slowly, she entered him. She heard him moan, wondering for a moment if she was doing right or if it would hurt him.

She glanced around to the front of his body at his jerking penis and smiled. It positively glowed in the semi-darkness, a pearl drop of moisture crowning its gleaming head. Auberon, she guessed, was in ecstasy.

With one hand holding on to the half-submerged handle that now stuck out from his anus, she brought the rest of the whip around the front with her, running its declining thickness through her fingers until she was facing him.

Her gaze dropped to his penis before returning to his face. Beneath half-closed eyes he watched her, his mouth open, jewels of sweat hanging from his nose and chin. She dropped down, poked out her tongue and transferred the pearl drop from tip of penis to tip of tongue.

She did not stop there, but continued her journey with the thin end of the whip until she was back where she started and could tie it round the portion of the handle that stuck obscenely out from between his cheeks. It would not fall out.

With the riding crop in one hand, she dragged a bale of straw in front of the restrained Auberon. At first she knelt on it, her eyes filled with the sight of his pulsating cock, trembling as her nails followed their previous course, leaving slight indents in the purple flesh as they went. At each dig he moaned in ecstasy and begged for more, though his moans verged on squeals of sweet pain.

She wrapped her arms around him, drawing his pelvis to her as her mouth enveloped him, the soft down of his sac caressing her chin.

As she enjoyed the sensation of her mouth drawing in then

retrieving along his entire length, her hand found the half-hidden handle and began to move that back and forth.

Above her he groaned and his knees sagged slightly. She felt his thighs tremble and his penis leap in her throat.

Not yet, she said to herself; not until I've had my reward.

She loosed him from her mouth and, with her foot, moved the bale of hay to one side, then rested that foot on it. Everything was in place for her to take what she wanted.

Breast meeting breast, she brought one hand round to the front, closed it around the imprisoned penis and readied it to guide it between her well-oiled lips and into her waiting vagina.

It slid in. She moved forward, then buried it to the hilt.

Delicious waves of pleasure spread upwards from where she gyrated on the rampant member. She mumbled her pleasure against his chest, apologising in a stupid sort of way for being unable to resist such a stout harbinger of satisfaction.

Unwilling to allow his cock to shrink from its splendid size, one hand went back to the whip handle and began to manipulate it as before, moving it gently in and out of his anus. Just to remind him who was in charge, she flicked every so often at his bare flesh with the riding crop, her strokes getting more erratic but much more virulent as her own climax began to spread from her loins.

With one leg up on the bale of hay, it was easy to manoeuvre her clitoris so it received the full impact of his thrust against her each time she pushed on the handle of the whip.

As though now going into full gallop, her movements got faster. Trickles of sweat ran between her jiggling breasts from him and her, then ran off to saturate further the slippery wetness that sucked and gulped between their thighs.

'More! More! More!' Now her tongue stuck to her mouth, her arms quivering with a current of impending explosion.

Higher and higher the current of climax ascended before tumbling down in a sparkling shower of sensitive bliss.

One, two, three, four more thrusts of the whip handle, then Auberon, too, gave all he had to give. Within her, the bunched-up and heavily engorged cock throbbed like an airlocked water-pipe as he cried his release to the high rafters and unsettled the roosting pigeons.

There was only a soft rustling in the darkness once they had finished and Auberon had licked the last vestige of her own secretions from her hot and well-used pussy.

Even so, she thought to herself, there is always someone who hopes for an additional encore or who hangs around the stage door hoping for a last word or an avid leer. She wondered only briefly who it would be, and dared not hope it would be the object of her wager. All the same, she hoped she had made a good impression.

'Nice night.'

Sir Reginald had come from somewhere behind them as they left the stables.

'Splen ... splendid,' stammered Auberon.

'Nice night for being out walking,' said Penny.

'Yes,' Sir Reggie chuckled knowingly, his dark eyes twinkling. 'Yes. Nice night for a lot of things. Very satisfactory, don't you think?' He chuckled again before wandering off along the gravel path and into the darkness.

Ears, if not eyes, tuned to the night, Penny looked into the darkness and was aware of other footfalls joining his.

# 5

'Clear round!'

The hollow echo of the loudspeaker announced her perform-ance to the crowd of pink faces that thronged around the main arena.

This was Penny's first horse show since coming to Beaumont Place and, although it was only a county show of secondary merit, she'd done well and felt pleased with herself.

Hoofs thudded beneath her and clods of earth flew out behind, lifted by the animal's iron shoes. She felt the creature's muscles between her thighs, and thought as she had so many times before, just how incredible it was that she could exert her own will over such a powerful animal.

'Well done!' There was triumph in her voice and a smile on her face as she patted the sweating neck of the rangy chestnut before exiting the arena and coming to a halt.

Beaming brightly, perhaps too conceited for her own good, she nodded at Auberon as he made ready to try his round. His hand tipped politely at his hard hat. His smile was faint and he blinked a few times.

Just for a moment, she thought she saw him blush like a nubile girl and she smiled. Was he enamoured of her, or just highly appreciative of the performance she'd made him go through the night before?

She had asked him later if he had known they were being watched. He had blushed then, too, and had stammered his answer.

'Um ... Well ... possibly ... perhaps.'

He knew, she decided. He just didn't want to admit it. Did such a thing embarrass him? Obviously. But *she* didn't feel that way. There was added excitement in performing such a delicious task when an audience was present. Just the thought of last night made her flush beneath her tight white breeches and black wool jacket.

But Auberon, sweet as he was, loved being submissive and, in all honesty, she had found the role of the dominator extremely enjoyable.

'Good round,' said the stable-lad who held her horse's head. He had dancing green eyes, copper-coloured hair and was called Stephen.

'So far so good,' she replied, her face still flushed from her ride and her breath still hurried. But she was still smiling, almost laughing. She felt good.

He helped her dismount before throwing the customary soft brown rug over her horse's steaming flanks. Her on one side of the chestnut, and him on the other, they led the horse back to the horsebox which was painted light blue with ostentatious gold lettering along the side.

'Well, here we are,' she said appreciatively, happy to have done so well, and even more happy that this particular horsebox was like a palace compared to the rattly old Bedford she had arrived in. She still had it, of course. Gregory had parked it safely until she had need of it again. Safety, she guessed, didn't even come into it. Her old horsebox just wouldn't have matched up to the Beaumont standard, whereas this long and weighty machine had six wheels with double axles.

'I could do with a shower,' she said. She'd already loosened her white silk cravat – formal and required wear when actually jumping. Now she also undid her top button. She saw him look; had meant him to.

The ride had made her glow and her flesh hanker after other things. Riding did that. Her plush sex had slid and bumped against the unyielding saddle in easy, gentle rhythm one moment, fast and furious the next.

She glanced with interest at the young man. His smile was inviting and the sprinkling of freckles over the bridge of his nose gave him a boyish, almost impish expression. His skin was creamy-white. She imagined his body being very white, as cool as milk or blue-veined like frosted ice. Like a youthful Pan, she thought, russet hair, snow-white skin and eyes the colour of a summer meadow just before sunset. Although his body was slim and not fully matured, he was poised on that threshold when the energy of youth outweighs the technique of experience. She eyed him, wondered about him, and her loins tingled.

That's not what I'm here for, she told herself. But all the same, the lad's muscles rippled like a shoal of darting fish beneath the clinging tightness of his black T-shirt. What harm was there in extending a little more than friendship and straying slightly from the path to her main objective?

His fingers curved over hers very briefly as he handed her the reins of her second mount. She thanked him.

'Need a leg-up?'

'Please.'

He looped the chestnut's reins over his arm before grasping her shin and foot and propelling her upwards to sit astride the grey, which was over sixteen hands of pure muscle. His hands lingered on her foot as he assisted her to slide it into the stirrup. Through the leather of her boot she could vaguely discern the sweaty heat of his palm. There was a questioning look in the merry glint of his eyes. She knew what the question was. She also knew the answer. Perhaps later, she told herself, and returned her concentration to the job in hand, refastening her button and retying her cravat.

'Have a good ride,' he said as she turned the grey's head towards the arena. He grinned as he said it and there was joy in his voice.

'I always do.'

She glanced at him; saw hope in his face and fever in his eyes. Perhaps it was the sheer bravado that she always felt when competing in equestrian events, or more likely the arousal caused by the friction of the saddle, but she returned his smile and let her tongue travel purposefully over her teeth. That, she judged, was enough to tell him that she too felt a high fever rising in her loins and would not be averse to a mutual quenching of it.

But, for the moment, she left him and made her way back to the showjumping arena.

Nadine glanced at her as she halted her horse in the collecting ring, the place where those about to jump or those who had already jumped waited their turn or caught their breath.

Penny nodded in greeting. Nadine's eyes left her and went back to what was happening in the arena. Nadine was a professional when it was warranted. Stopwatch in hand, she noted every timing of every competitor, every movement of hand or heel as each Beaumont rider urged their animal over the obstacles.

Even her clothes today veered towards businesslike and were, so Penny thought, vaguely reminiscent of a middle-management executive. She wore a black trouser suit, crisp white blouse, black-and-white tie and black sombrero. The latter had a thick cord hanging from behind it which normally would have fastened under the chin. The familiar cheroot was gripped tightly in the corner of her mouth, and her earrings were exactly the same pair as she had worn the day before.

Dramatic people draw curious looks, and Nadine was most definitely dramatic, even when soberly suited. Curiosity was rewarded with a cold stare. From what Penny had learnt, a cold stare was stage one. Expletives ranging from purely sarcastic to downright obscene were stage two. Stage three was not for the faint-hearted, though apparently one brave journalist at some past horse show had pressed his luck, so Penny had been told. With icy-cold stare accompanied by an equally cold smile, Nadine had grabbed at his balls. The colour had drained from his face and he'd stood on his toes, not daring to return to earth until she had let go of his family jewels. He'd scurried off clutching his groin. Nadine, he had swiftly learnt, was best left alone.

There was a roar from the crowd, followed by another unemotional announcement from the loudspeaker, and people clapped. Auberon had jumped clear, too. All eyes watched as he came cantering out of the ring.

He tipped his hat as he passed her, his face flushed now more from his energetic clearing of the fences than his memories of their night of passion.

'Good luck,' he said among his breathlessness.

Full of confidence, Penny thanked him and dug her heels into her horse's flanks. She could do no wrong today, she thought. It was almost as if she could fly.

Like a dream, the driving muscles of the grey propelled her over the first jump. With difficulty she controlled the urges that the stable-boy with the green eyes had aroused in her. More concentration was needed to ride this animal than the chestnut. Timing of take-off was imperative and had to be gauged by the rider more so than the horse.

The hoofs thudded beneath her. Just by their sound, she could judge their pace and analyse when timing was perfect.

She gathered the reins, and with the assistance of every muscle in her body, she pushed the mare on, lower legs working incessantly to take her up and over each obstacle.

All were cleared without difficulty except the last. It loomed high and wide before her, a triple-bar spread. Briefly she glanced at those watching, threw a smile in Auberon's direction – then wished to God she hadn't.

Fool! Bloody fool! She cursed that smile, cursed her own conceit.

In that one split second of relaxed concentration, she'd covered too much ground. The fence loomed up, yellow-striped and large. If she did clear it, she'd be lucky. There was also the chance of landing awkwardly. Inside, she prayed. Then she narrowed her eyes.

There was no time to draw out, to pull on the reins and head off. Whatever happened, she must land safely.

A deep moan roared from the crowd and hollow echoes of falling wood crashed behind her. Her hat fell to one side, and she lost one stirrup, but she was safe and so was the horse. Softly she swore under her breath. It was her fault. A moment's glance and she had messed up.

'Damn! Damn! Damn!' The words spilt in time with the horse's slowing gait.

As she slowed down and came to a clumsy halt, she ran the back of her hand across her brow. Her hair clung damply to her head but, despite the fact that she had not jumped clear, she was satisfied enough to sigh and strain a smile towards Nadine.

'Diabolical!'

Nadine's mouth was as straight and unyielding as a letterbox, her eyes hard.

Effort had tired Penny. She was hot, she was tired and so far she'd done pretty well. It was only one mistake. 'But I landed safely . . .'

'Inexcusable!' said Nadine coldly. 'Horse could have been injured. You could have been injured!' The usually colourless eyes were as cold as steel.

Over the top of Nadine's head, Penny could see Auberon steadily getting redder. His mouth was opening and shutting as though he were trying to tell her something.

A flush of rebellion stirred momentarily in Penny's breast. 'But they're my horses!'

'No!' exclaimed Nadine, her fingers holding Penny's knee in a vicelike grip. 'While you are here, everything is Beaumont! You will learn that!'

Penny opened her mouth meaning to deny the statement, but Nadine did not give her the chance.

'I will pass on your feelings. No doubt we will speak later about this. Punishment will be in order, I can assure you.'

Breathlessness curtailing her feelings of rebellion, Penny rose to the trot back to the shiny blue and gold horsebox. It was parked in the coolest place possible, which happened to be beneath an ancient oak at the perimeter of the show ground next to a hawthorn hedge. On the other side of the hedge was an untamed meadow and copses of scattered willow, sycamore and birch.

The oak tree dappled her hot face with cool shade, though inside she was seething and oddly confused. Why was it that Nadine made her feel like a schoolgirl? And why was it that she obeyed meekly, her rush of passionate outrage buried beneath all the reasons why she should keep her cool.

Beneath the tree her own chestnut and Auberon's other horse had been tethered. It was cooler there, and the horses plucked leisurely at the fresh green grass of the county show-ground and the longer more lush stuff sprouting through the fence from the field next door.

Stephen was sponging and brushing her chestnut. He was bare to the waist, his shoulder muscles rippling as his arm pushed the brush in wide, circular strokes over the horse's back and flanks.

His skin gleamed, a faint film of sweat lending greater definition to his moving flesh. She could smell him very faintly – pure testosterone, fresh and mingled with the pungent thickness of damp leather, sweating horse flesh and sweet summer grass.

Nadine's rebuke and talk of punishment were easily forgotten, and her attraction to Stephen remembered. As though he were a rare delicacy presented prior to a main course, she licked her lips. Like a hungry child she eyed the lean torso, the fair skin and the sweep of russet hair as it caressed his naked shoulders. Her spirits were lifted, and another wetness mingled between her legs with the fresh sweat of her riding.

'Can you manage?' he asked once he'd become aware of her presence. 'I can always help you out,' he said with obvious meaning. 'You only have to ask.'

'I always can manage,' she said with a smile. 'And I never refuse a service if I can possibly avoid it.'

The smell of damp leather and sweating flanks was strong in her nostrils as the saddle slid off the grey and into her arms.

'That's what I like to hear. A woman who can always manage.' It was no accident that his hands brushed against her breasts as he took the saddle from her.

Over the scent of leather she could smell him better now he was closer; a lingering sensation of fresh male perspiration and the earthy closeness of warm-blooded animals.

He turned his back to her and placed the saddle in the tack area of the horsebox.

Enamoured of the day and the boy before her, Penny let her senses take over from her sensibility. Stephen was one prize that she was going to have today.

'It's a beautiful day,' she said, stretching her arms once she'd taken off her hat, jacket and cravat and undid a few more buttons than she had done before. She looked up at the sky, then over the stile to the green field and clumps of trees. Her desire was strong and getting stronger. This boy was good-looking: young, of course, no more than nineteen. But she needed him. Her ego needed massaging, and he seemed just the man to do it.

'Too beautiful for working,' he replied as he turned towards her.

She saw the boldness in his eyes and the front of his jeans moving as his cock responded to what his mind was thinking and his tongue had only touched on.

'Now what else could we do on a day like this?' she asked.

His smile was knowing and the swelling in his jeans more obvious. This was no Auberon, she thought to herself. Young he might be, but he'd no doubt had his share of pussies willing to welcome his vigorous lust. She glanced downwards where his rising penis formed a curved mound as it thrust for release against his soiled jeans.

He reached out and cupped her breasts. There was desire in his eyes, and a deep hum of ecstasy escaped his lips as he bunched her breasts towards each other.

'They're so firm,' he murmured, 'so beautiful.'

'Flattery,' she told him, 'can get you anywhere.'

As her hair broke free from its net and tumbled down her back, she reached for him, touched his cheek with one hand and his neck with the other. They drew closer; both murmured unintelligible sounds of pleasure as she rubbed her body up against his. His arms wrapped around her, his hands hot against her back.

There was unfamiliar pleasure in feeling a fully-clothed body against hers, a kind of innocence as his hands travelled to press the stickiness of her blouse over the fullness of her breasts.

His lips were hot, his tongue just as experienced as she had expected. Hot skin shivered as though touched with ice beneath her searching palms as she explored each young, tight muscle.

'We can't stay here,' he said, drawing back and holding her at arms' length as though she were potentially dangerous. 'Too public. But we can go through there,' he added with a wink and a jerk of his head towards the meadow and trees beyond.

The wood of the stile was rough and dry, the grass on the other side sweet, green and cool against their hot bodies.

One pair of soiled white riding breeches and one pair of grass-stained jeans were soon lying in a single heap.

She lay beside him in the coolness of the grass, aware of the smell of wild flowers and the buzzing of insects. Her hair tumbled over her shoulders and down her back. Her eyes sparkled and her body was still except for her breathing and the slight undulations of limbs created by sexual need.

'You're beautiful,' he said, and sounded as though he meant it. Just hearing him say such things made her feel as though she were melting. Beautiful words made her feel beautiful.

'And you,' she responded, 'are quite memorable.' The words she said she meant. Her eyes drank him in from head to toe. There was a fairylike whiteness to his skin. Around his mighty member, a cluster of red hair circled like a dark-gold crown.

She was filled with a strong desire to run her fingers through that feathery nest. His eyes caught hers. They were bright and they were happy. They were also excited and eager to elicit the utmost from their experience.

They kissed and caressed. Then Penny, without any urging from him, got to her feet, and walked to a tree-trunk that had fallen amidst the clump of trees. She bent over, hands resting on the broken patches of bark. Stephen followed and came up behind her. No one could see them here, not that she'd be too worried if they could.

She felt the heat of his body as he came up behind her,

and trembled with delight as his hands traced down over her back and clasped her buttocks in the wideness of his palms.

He opened the cleft between her buttocks with his fingers, as though studying her tiniest orifice. She groaned appreciatively and wriggled against his fingers. She closed her eyes and in her mind she entered her own sensuous world where everything she received was more intense, more electrifying, than the giver of such delights could ever imagine.

As he ran his hands down between her legs and opened the more fleshy cleft of her sex, she moaned in ecstasy. His fingers went on to draw imaginary lines around her pussy and dip briefly into her burgeoning wetness.

Then against her sex she felt the warmth of his breath as he sucked at her outer lips, her inner lips, then dipped his tongue where his fingers had been.

Wanting to miss nothing of this experience, she opened her eyes and took deep breaths of fresh air, revelling in the swishing of the leaves as the breeze took them, the buzzing of the bees and the sweet smell of summer flowers.

There was a gap in the bushes and trees in front of her. From here she could look out at the mass of people milling around in the bright sunshine. And here she was, shaded in a small copse, hands on the rough bark of a tree, bottom dappled by sunlight and pubic hair rustled by a kind breeze. If this was the Garden of Eden, then she was Eve.

'Ride me,' she pleaded breathlessly, her head back, eyes closed again.

He didn't answer for a moment, as though he were thinking about it, weighing up the pros and cons of doing so. Then, with a laugh in his throat, he nuzzled her neck and sucked at her earlobe.

'You need breaking in first,' he murmured.

Then his lips went down over her behind until his tongue licked the shiny division between each rounded cheek.

She felt his body come up to cover her. His chest was warm and hairless against her back, his lips wet and soft against her neck. His hands followed his words. They pulled at her breasts, held them almost as if he were weighing them, then let them go. His fingertips tapped lightly at their pink nipples, causing them to rear with unbridled desire.

Lost in the whirling currents of her own delight, Penny murmured, moaned and purred with each sensation. She wriggled her hips and tilted her bottom, knowing that the tousled hair of her sex would be peering out at this young man from beneath the heart-shaped perfection of her arse.

'Put it back in me,' she pleaded. 'Please. Anything. Anything at all!'

Lightly, as if in answer to her pleading, she felt the silken head of his penis kiss her fleshy lips before he pulled back.

Mewing with pleasure, she felt his fingers pull back the glowing petals of her sex again, first the outer lips, then the inner ones. Like the head of a curious snake, his finger probed further, sliding along her slippery flesh, finding the hot nub of her clitoris, and teasing it to full height, before burrowing again into the torrid humidity of her widening vagina.

His finger had been only the scout. Now the head of his erect and readied penis followed, widening her lips as it followed the same course his finger had taken.

Pleas for more escaped her throat as the exploring penis continued to slide the whole length of her slit from nest of pubic hair to throbbing portal.

'Say please,' he demanded through his own gasping breath. 'Say please and I'll ram it home.'

'Please,' she gasped, her breath, her mind and her body lost in ragged whirls of pleasure. 'Please, please, please!'

The heat of his thighs met hers as his length of engorged flesh pushed its way into her welcoming sex. Possessed by desires that she had no control over, she writhed and pushed back on to it. Her dewy lips sucked noisily at the hard shaft as if it were draining it of all its strength.

How can it be, she asked herself, that something so hard can be at one and the same time so soft, so warm ... and so welcome?

There was no answer. Only the fact that it was what it was and she adored its contrasts, its mix of pleasure and pain, softness and hardness.

She let loose moans of sheer enjoyment as his balls slapped in tempo against her, his pubic hairs tickling like a mass of goose down against her silken thighs.

She wriggled on him more, determined to get the last ounce of enjoyment from the experience. Her bosoms continued to swing in time, one slapping against the other like wads of heavy silk as she moved forwards with each shove of his member. All the time her throat sang to his tempo, each breath tinged with a moan and a sigh.

The warmth and hardness of his chest rested on her back as his hands sought to restrain her swinging breasts. She howled in ecstasy as his fingers squeezed her nipples, then groaned, almost pleading, for her climax. His breath was like steam against her neck, and his breathing began to quicken, strangled gasps of joy like warm wind against her ear.

She sensed the immediacy of his release and began to panic, fearful of him leaving her unsatisfied on the pinnacle of her own sexual arousal.

Perhaps he felt her sudden tension, a tightening of her vaginal muscles around his cock. Anyway, his hand travelled over her hip to between her legs. His finger charged through and, with deft strokes, he began to manipulate the shiny wet head of passion that prodded so forcefully from her folds of flesh.

She closed her eyes, her fists clenching more tightly over the rough tree bark as ripples of orgasm spread deliciously outwards, tingling her body, flooding her mind so she barely heard his cry mingle with her own. Bodies relaxed and senses swam in floods of ecstasy before he drew himself from her.

'I much appreciate your attention to my needs,' she said softly once they were disentangled and lying on their bellies again in the sweet coolness of the meadow grass.

'I aim to please.' He reached for her, pulled her to him and hugged her to his chest. They kissed; warmth remained where a moment before there had been only the urgency to climax.

She drank in the feel and the smell of him. Then she detected another smell, then the sound of a twig snapping. She started. The faint aroma of expensive tobacco carried on the breeze.

'My, my, Stephen. You really are quite a stallion. And you, Miss Bennet, are quite a mare!' Penny, still naked except for her crumpled white blouse – which she pulled on hastily – spun round and found herself face to face with Nadine. A half-smoked cheroot hung from the corner of the tall woman's lips.

It was difficult not to blush. But Nadine had a bold look about her. There was a sneer around her mouth. The pale grey eyes stared and made no apology for so doing.

Penny glanced over at Stephen. He was already getting dressed, though not rushing it.

Penny bent down and picked up her clothes, aware at the same time of the scent of sex upon her and the glistening droplets of her own bodily secretions that clung to her nest of pubic hair. She was also aware of Nadine eyeing her naked belly and thighs. They glittered with undisguised pleasure and more than a hint of desire.

Stephen went silently, as though his service had indeed been done and there was no need for him to stay.

Nadine folded her arms across her chest. Penny reached for the rest of her clothes.

'Never mind your clothes.'

Penny froze and clutched her shirt around her. Her breeches dangled from one hand. Nervously she glanced towards the gap in the trees.

'But there are people around. What if they should . . .'

'See you . . .?' Nadine's eyebrows arched in the manner of an old-fashioned headmistress. 'It didn't worry you just then. Why should it worry you now?' Her voice was hard; hollow, even. Her sneer only half-disturbed her face.

Penny shivered. Passion induces heat, but spent passion tends to leave one feeling cold, she thought, especially if it has been spent outdoors. Goose bumps were erupting all over her body.

Penny held Nadine's gaze for just a moment of defiance before she remembered all that was at stake and lowered them. But the wager and her place with the Beaumont team was not the only reason Penny lowered her eyes. Just the fact that Nadine was here, that she had spoken, was enough to crush Penny's spirit and to make her feel as though her will was not her own and neither was her body. Strangely enough, the combination in her character of sensuality and the desire to please added an odd thrill to the experience. Even now, with Nadine eyeing her naked pussy, she wanted to show her more, wanted her to *do* more.

'I'm getting cold,' she said at last and shivered.

Nadine ignored her comment, but seemed pleased to see her suffering.

'You do not mix professional considerations with pleasure. Never!' barked Nadine. She swung a silver-headed cane against her side as she spoke. 'Do I make myself clear?'

Penny bit her lip, her eyes still studying the ground, before she got up the courage to answer. 'I'm sorry, I didn't think a little lovemaking in a wood would affect my performance. After all, I had finished my round. I know I've got a place, but the presentation isn't until four ...'

'Then you'd better get dressed.'

Penny lifted one leg to pull on her breeches.

'But first,' said Nadine suddenly, her hand gripping Penny's shoulder, 'you deserve a little punishment. Just a little tingling to remind you as you ride in the jump-off that you must concentrate. I think that would be a good idea. Don't you?'

Nadine's smile was full of teeth and stiffly held.

Penny trembled beneath Nadine's cold gaze. A rope seemed to knot in her stomach and a tingling centred in a warm spot between her legs. She knew she had no choice but to accept this punishment. Both Nadine and Penny's own yearnings required it.

Still shivering, she let her clothes drop to the ground and trembled like a flower beneath Nadine's gaze as her eyes strayed to the tangle of rich, dark pubic hair that graced the top of Penny's thighs. Nadine sucked in her breath between her teeth. She tilted her head to one side as her eyes travelled up to Penny's face then back to the clutch of curls.

'What a pretty pussy!' she said in a light and sing-song voice that hardly seemed to belong to her. 'In fact, I think it is quite the prettiest one I have ever seen.' Her eyes were half-shaded by the broad brim of her hat, but Penny knew they were devouring each nipple before sliding with intimate familiarity over each curve.

Penny glanced briefly at her own soft silky pubes gently blowing with the breeze. She didn't say anything, but a chill excitement was sending shivers of apprehension down her spine and over her skin. Nadine had power over her, and Nadine would chastise. To her own surprise, her body was responding. It was almost as though it were no longer hers, but was floating along on some never-ending stream in dreamlike fantasy. Nadine was in charge of most things at Beaumont Place. For the first time since her arrival, Penny realised that Nadine was also in charge of her.

'Lovely!' Nadine exclaimed with a sigh. 'But ripe for punishment.' With her silver-topped riding cane, Nadine pointed at the fallen tree trunk.

Adopting meekness, head bowed and her arms still wrapped around her chest, Penny walked to the tree trunk and placed her hands on the rough bark, bottom in the air, just as she had with Stephen. Her sex was tingling, her heart racing.

'No,' said Nadine sternly. 'Full-length along the log.'

'But it's rough,' Penny protested, looking up at Nadine as though she truly disbelieved what she was telling her. But Nadine was smiling; she knew it was rough. She would take pleasure from knowing that Penny's softness was lying on that coarse trunk. And Penny would take pleasure from it, too, enjoying the favour that was disguised as punishment; the pain that could so easily be pleasure.

Nadine's smile was faint and her eyes glittered. She said nothing. Again she pointed at the log. Her mouth returned to the hard line it had been before.

Penny eyed the hard, dry bark before she obeyed and lay herself full-length along the trunk. Just as she had supposed, the bark was rough against her breasts and belly. There was a knot of wood where a small branch had once been. Nadine manhandled her body as though she were made of rags, until the protruding knot of wood was pressing pleasurably between Penny's legs.

'Legs astride,' ordered Nadine in a clear, dictatorial voice.

Penny's breathing quickened as Nadine's cane tapped at

each leg then pushed in between them so they divided and fell either side of the log. Now the knot of wood was pressing a very familiar spot and that spot was reacting in a very familiar way. Penny held her breath and swallowed the moan of pleasure. A pleasurable response was something she would need to hold on to, to store and use to counteract the stinging burn she knew was to come.

Peering through her tangle of flying hair, Penny could see Nadine gloating with pleasure as her eyes and her silver-topped cane ran over her naked back and trembling buttocks. The breeze now blew unabated around her open cleft, which Nadine appeared to be studying with avid interest, prodding the cane against the soft lips and open portal. The cane tapped each buttock. Penny tensed. Then it tapped against her open portal, which was already moist with a new yearning.

'A very pretty pussy.' Nadine said the words as though she were purring them, delighting in pushing the cane close up against her vulva and between the cheeks of her bottom. 'But it won't get you off,' Nadine suddenly added sternly. 'You deserve punishment for fouling that jump, and punishment is what you will get. And I'm the one to give it to you. Am I right?'

Penny's own hair blew across her face. Her hands gripped the log.

'Yes,' she murmured, lacing her words with fear and impatience rather than the longing she really felt.

'Say it louder, pretty pussy,' said Nadine in a mocking voice, her cane tapping an arousing rhythm against Penny's damp sex.

'Yes!' Penny cried.

'Good,' said Nadine slowly. 'Good.' And the cane tapped her sex again before Nadine raised it and placed a stinging blow across Penny's buttocks.

Penny gasped. Her fingers gripped clawlike at the rough bark;

almost as if someone had pressed a button, her nipples swelled against the rough, dry wood.

Her bottom stung and burned with the kiss of the cane. Her pelvis had pushed down with the blow. Her mons had pressed harder against the knot of wood just as Nadine had reckoned. In turn, her hidden bud had burst into bloom, sensing that another orgasm could be had.

'That was just a test,' Nadine said suddenly. 'I will give you six. You will count them. Are you ready?'

'Yes,' answered Penny, a glow of tingling delight spreading upwards from her willing thighs, though her voice trembled, 'I'm ready.'

'Good,' Nadine purred. 'Then we shall begin.'

The air swished as the cane fell.

'One!' cried Penny as her buttocks clenched and stung beneath the blow. The knot of wood firmly kissed her secret rosebud, and her rosebud responded.

'One,' repeated Nadine.

The air swished again. Penny gasped again. Her bottom began to glow. The rough bark beneath her scratched her naked flesh.

'Two!' she cried. The smooth knot of wood delved more deeply against her brazen clitoris.

'Two,' Nadine repeated.

Again the cane flew threw the air. Now she was almost wishing for its stinging caress and for the pelvic movement that accompanied it. She pressed herself more firmly against the protruding knot of the tree-trunk.

Just as she had wished, it came again. Her buttocks quivered, warmed beneath the burning touch.

'Three!' she exclaimed, and felt the fires of orgasm spreading through her loins and homing in on that very sensitive spot that was pressed so tightly to the tree knot.

'Three,' Nadine repeated, then ran the coldness of her long

fingers over the burning flesh of Penny's reddening bottom. 'How hot your bottom is, my pretty pussy. How pink it is, and how it will tingle when you ride in the ring again. How it will remind you to concentrate. But I will take care of you. I will finish this punishment, then I will punish you again later. And then I will soothe your burning flesh. I will rub cream into you, soothe your aching muscles and ease your tired limbs.'

The cool hand patted each buttock as if it were a pet animal, twin pink lap-dogs that quivered at the coldness of her fingers and her voice.

Penny had held her rising need in suspension and swallowed her deep murmurs of pleasure as Nadine's hands fondled her buttocks. Now, as she heard the swish of the cane again, she let it go.

'Four!' she cried with accompanying groans. The bark of the tree held her breasts like scaly hands. The knot of wood pushed its hard, smooth head firmly against her clitoris. Her climax was rising and not far off. Her bottom quivered; it was redder and warmer now, tingling as much from sexual longing as from Nadine's cane.

But Nadine had not finished. The cane fell again through the air, and Penny moaned again.

'Five.' Her voice was shaking as the first waves started, quivering through her parted labia and causing her empty vulva to shed its moist fluid so it dripped down and on to the log.

The final blow of the cane would come now. She craved it, longed for its burning kiss on her behind so her pelvis would thrust one more time – just once more – before the flood of orgasm washed over her.

It came.

'Six!' she cried, and pressed herself tight against the wood knot, riding it in small sharp spurts until the last eruptions of her orgasm had melted away.

Laughing at her shameless exhibition, Nadine tapped rapidly at Penny's jerking buttocks until she lay supine. The goosebumps had gone. A light film of sweat covered her, and Penny's hair covered her face.

The cool hands that had caressed her earlier now caressed her again. She moaned beneath their touch, welcoming the coolness spreading over her hot buttocks, and the gentleness in Nadine's long, slim fingers.

'You enjoyed that too much, my pretty,' murmured Nadine between quick, sharp breaths. 'Much too much. I can see I will have to deal with you again; use you to everyone else's benefit so you know exactly what is expected of you. Don't you agree?'

One of Penny's tingling cheeks was gripped by long fingers and talonlike nails.

'Yes, Nadine,' said Penny.

'Say it again,' said Nadine in a cruel yet oddly affectionate way. 'Say it again and mean it.'

'Yes, Nadine. Whatever you say, Nadine. Whatever you want. I'm in your hands.' Her buttocks clenched tightly in the strong hands. She almost wanted her to do it all over again, so she could enjoy once more the mix of pleasure and pain, the contrast of hot and cold, the smoothness of her own flesh against the scratching roughness of the tree bark. But the claws released her, and she let out her breath. The hand that had tortured now patted her bottom like it had before.

'Yes, pretty pussy. That is just what I wanted to hear,' Nadine purred, and she kissed one rounded buttock. 'That's exactly what I wanted to hear,' she repeated, then kissed the other, her lips soft and gently sucking on Penny's warm flesh. 'You are in my hands,' she said before sucking at the other again. 'You are most definitely in my hands.'

# 6

When the horsebox returned to the stable yard at Beaumont Place, the sun was turning bright orange and the clouds were marbled with purple and gold.

In good-hearted mood, riders mucked in with stable-lads to get the horses groomed, fed and watered. Nadine supervised, barking her orders and aiming hefty whacks at the stable-lads if they gave her any backchat. Judging by their cheeky grins and laughing eyes, her actions were enjoyed rather than feared. They almost offered their bottoms for the slap of her long white hands, and rubbed up against her suggestively when she grabbed them by the drooping necks of their sweat-stained T-shirts. There seemed to be some sort of competition in progress as to who could goad her more, and who could get away it.

The stables were quiet once they'd all left.

'Stay here, Penny!' Nadine ordered in a harsh and demanding voice. 'We have unfinished business if you remember rightly.'

Penny stopped in her tracks and turned to face this imperious woman who seemed to have the ability to command at will and to cajole, persuade and manipulate.

She was aware of a dark sensuality invading her body. And yet, in some strange way, she recognised it as if she had briefly touched it in the most erotic of dreams.

'Yes, I remember,' Penny said softly, her eyes meeting Nadine's before she slid the bolt across the door to the grey mare's stable. She glanced only briefly at Nadine's face before looking down at the floor. Her cotton blouse now clung stained and damp to her bare breasts. She smelt of sex, and, if it hadn't been for the savage yearnings rising in her body, she would be in her bath or on her bed, with Gregory running his soapy hands and sponge over her wet body or massaging her aching muscles. She sighed and shifted her weight from one curved hip to the other and waited for Nadine to make the first move as she knew she would.

Nadine grinned rather than smiled, her teeth chillingly white, and a cheroot clutched grimly in the corner of her mouth.

Despite being in a stable where combustible materials were used and stored, Nadine still smoked, ash flying and smoke curling up towards the dark wooden rafters where pigeons nested and vermin scurried. Languidly she leant one elbow against the stable divide, the blackness of her clothes strangely out of place among the earthy yellow ochre of the straw.

'Y . . . es,' said Nadine slowly to nothing in particular as she blew smoke in corkscrew spirals. 'Y . . . es.'

A myriad nerve ends danced between Penny's legs, yet her hands trembled as she attempted to put the grooming kit away where it belonged. If the episode on the log was anything to go by, she knew more or less what to expect, and how much the degree of discomfort was outweighed by the pleasure. For the first time she wondered whether Ariadne had gone through the same punishments. Inwardly she smiled. It was more than likely. She remembered her of old. Ariadne had started young, and had no boundaries when it came to experimentation.

Yes. She knew what to expect from Nadine. She also knew to some extent what to expect from Alistair. Earlier she had discerned his look once she had left the long grass and the tree trunk behind her. With Nadine, she had returned to the box. He had been there. He'd stared at her, a wistful look in his eyes that was not entirely readable. Her eyes had met his; had sparkled enough to let him know that she'd guessed he'd watched both what she had done with Stephen and what Nadine and the tree trunk had done to her. She didn't need a crystal ball to guess that. There was mud on his boots. There was no mud in the show field, but there *was* on the field side of the stile. Clods of mud clung to his boots. Alistair had indeed seen her punishment, her lying full-length on the log. For a moment she had thought he was going to ask her something, even to reach out and touch her. This could be the moment, she had thought. But nothing had happened; and, despite her initial elation, she had once again been disappointed.

A cloud of smoke circled Penny's head, blown there deliberately by the tall female with the gaunt face. Nadine's very wide mouth smiled and her face seemed suddenly to be full of teeth, all white and large, and flashing devilishly at her.

'I'm a very fair person,' Nadine said suddenly – as if for some reason she thought Penny might have doubted it. 'I have to be strict, you see. My brother requires it of me. It's very important that everything is done in a way to suit him. He has little time to spare in his life for pleasurable pastimes, so only the very best will do, and then, only when the need is at its strongest. Everything has to be perfect. It's all a matter of self-discipline. My brother is a great believer in self-discipline.' The voice was as languorous and decadent as her pose, and dripped with the shadow of Oscar Wilde.

'I see,' replied Penny. So, she told herself, Nadine influences Alistair's life. For a moment, she wondered if there was something decidedly unhealthy in their relationship. If that was the case, then through Nadine she could actually win her wager with Ariadne. It could even be easy if those recently dormant and dark feelings that were racing through her body were anything to go by.

Nadine left where she had been leaning and came face to face with her. Penny was aware of the scent of rich tobacco as Nadine kissed her cheek.

'My brother's handsome, don't you think?'

Eyes still downcast, Penny hesitated before she nodded.

Nadine's fingers twisted in her hair, which now hung tangled and slightly damp.

'He is a very rich man, you know – and a very powerful man. Yet even powerful men have their weaknesses. Did you know that?'

Penny, uncertain about what reply to give, shrugged her shoulders and ran her tongue across her lips, but was disinclined to raise her eyes from the floor.

Nadine laughed close to her ear. Penny's submissive stance, her air of ignorance, seemed to please her no end.

'I can give him to you – if you do exactly as I say. I can arrange everything so it will suit you and suit him. What say you, my pretty pussy? Would you like me to do that for you? Would you?' Sharp fingernails traced leisurely lines over Penny's cheek. Chill thrills of excitement coursed through her veins. Her cheeks flushed in spite of herself as though she were a virgin about to lose such a state of grace for ever.

'Can you really do that?' Penny muttered, the dark feelings from within muffling the words in her throat and half-drowning the last vestiges of thought she still entertained with regard to the wager.

Nadine smiled, and a low noise issued from her throat as though she were growling or even purring. She laughed and seemed for the moment loath to answer. There was intimidation in her towering height, an icy coldness in the whiteness of her skin. The Snow Queen, thought Penny, that beautiful creature from a fairy tale who was at one and the same time both irresistible and dangerous.

Nadine's close proximity had a strangely unnerving effect. Nadine was not touching her, and yet Penny was aware that Nadine's body was only a fraction away from her own, held there in suspension. Just when she thought Nadine would cross that narrow divide, the long fingers – white as snow and cold as ice – trailed provocatively over the mounds of her breasts, then slid delicately beneath the gaping front of her blouse. Fine fingertips and long fingernails played with her rising nubs and, just as she was expected to do, she groaned with pleasure but kept her eyes on the floor.

White fingers with black-varnished nails stroked the creamy flesh of Penny's breasts before they scratched, then squeezed, her nipples. A faint cry that seemed suspended between pain and pleasure escaped from her throat.

Almost with pleading, she looked up at Nadine as her breasts rose and fell against the cold white hand. A cheroot still smouldered between the first two fingers of Nadine's right hand.

'Can you do that?' Penny repeated, thinking perhaps that Nadine had forgotten she had asked a question. 'Do you have that sort of power over him?'

Smoky breath touched her lips before the cold flesh of Nadine's mouth. Then a tongue rich in the tastes of wine, tobacco and depravity locked with hers. Surges of forgotten feelings welled up in Penny's mind. She remembered her sexual experiences with Ariadne. She had always put their fumbling lovemaking down to adolescent experimentation. This was a woman doing this, and now she was an adult. Her eyes studied the soft crown of hair as Nadine bent her head to kiss her throat and nibble at her ear. The head rose, and the pale-grey eyes, so blackly lined, met hers.

'I do have power over my brother, my pretty,' Nadine answered, her lips but a breath away from Penny's. 'With my help, and only with my help, you will have him handed to you on a plate.' Again, the head of shorn, white hair nuzzled against her, and the wide mouth enveloped her own. The large but fine hands held her shoulders, then fell to her breasts. 'Just do as I say, and my brother will be yours.'

Penny, whose arms hung useless at her sides, sighed and her nipples rose with engorged passion. Moistness spread between her legs and those dark feelings inside wrapped round her like a warm but prickly cloak.

Nadine's body was hard against hers and the smell of expensive perfume and aromatic tobacco made an odd and not unexciting assault on her nostrils. She moaned and closed her eyes as the kisses and caresses increased.

I have to do this, she told herself, the wager and her career still having some place in her mind. Then she corrected her statement. I want to do this.

There was a feeling of being on a helter-skelter as the fingers trailed onwards. Sex had the same laws as gravity. There was no way of resisting it.

She was only vaguely aware of the cheroot being thrown into the trough. It sizzled there, a last curl of smoke rising upwards like incense to an incarnate deity.

Nadine's strong arms wrapped around her and drew her closer. Penny felt surrounded by her superior height and strength, yet cosy against the hard nubs of her breasts, which were noticeably underdeveloped. She trembled in Nadine's arms, yet did not move. She waited for the orders she knew would come.

'Take your clothes off,' whispered Nadine against her ear.

Penny blinked, looked at the cool grey eyes for just a moment, then sat down on a bale of straw to pull off her boots. Her breeches followed. Then her blouse.

'What about *your* clothes? Aren't you going to get them off?' she asked Nadine.

Nadine shook her head; smiling, she ran her eyes down over Penny's creamy flesh.

'All in good time, pretty,' she said, tangling the index finger of her right hand in Penny's copious pubic curls. 'All in good time – in my time, of course.'

Strong, powerful hands pulled Penny closer before running down her back and clasping her buttocks. As Nadine bent her legs slightly, Penny felt the hard boniness of her pubic mound gyrate gently against hers, then gasped as she felt Nadine's fingers invade the deep cleft between the cheeks of her bottom.

'Don't flinch, pretty pussy. Accept it. I will do it. You will accept it.'

With the help of her new sensuality, Penny controlled her urge to cry out. All the time Nadine smiled at her, as though she were a child or a china doll playing imaginative games no one else could understand.

Once the coldness of the fingers slid between her legs, Penny knew she was lost. Her breath caught in her throat. This was another woman doing this to her, another woman who would know what each reaction to her probing would be. One who had no doubt experienced the same sensations herself.

Nadine withdrew her fingers suddenly and undid her own well-cut trousers. She wore only the trousers, blouse and boots now. Her hat and jacket had already been discarded.

'Here, put your hand here.' The voice was hushed yet firm. Penny felt her hand being guided down into Nadine's trousers and let it be so. Her fingers slid over Nadine's flat belly. There was no spare fat. Sharp pelvic bones and silky skin without blemish passed beneath her touch. Penny stayed her hand a moment as she leant and rubbed her head against Nadine's chest, her legs quivering like jelly.

Nadine's fingers were doing delicious things to her slippery sex. Sometimes they merely probed up beneath her outer lips and dipped into her wet vagina. Sometimes the fingers squeezed her outer lips together and the varnished nails dug into crisp pubic hair. Penny whimpered then groaned her compliance and complete surrender to those probing fingers that slid so tenderly and pinched with such precision over her valley of hot flesh. She sucked in her breath as her own fingers met the shorn lips of Nadine's sex. No hair. None at all. Her flesh lean – mean, even – between her open legs.

'Surprised, my pretty pussy?' said Nadine with a smile, her hot lips drowning any response Penny might have had. Nadine was not interested in negative responses. She only wanted the more positive ones. She ate them, Penny thought to herself; drank them in as anyone else might food or drink. Penny felt Nadine's silky and warm labia begin to slide under the ministrations of her fingers. As their mouths sucked deeply and kissed deep, bruising kisses, their hands became more agitated, each imitating the movements of the other, each knowing what the other was feeling. Tentatively, Penny's hand covered one small breast. The effect was sensational. She felt its firmness tremble beneath her touch, and felt the hardening erection of the pert nipple.

Eddies of pleasure spewed upwards in greater intensity as two of Nadine's fingers played with her. The thumb and the rest of her fingers created havoc among her nerve endings, stroking her inner lips and squeezing at her excited labia and jutting clitoris. Her legs trembled more. She felt as though the hand that explored between her legs was also holding her up, helping her to ride the pleasure that pulsated around her loins.

The sensations were mind-blowing, too good to keep to herself. She copied, and heard the moans of sublime ecstasy emitting in soft rushes of breath from Nadine's mouth.

In complete unison, raptures of orgasm jerked their hips, which made their arms quiver with transferred sensations. Penny cried out, unable to exercise any self-control at all as her climax washed over her, her hips jerking time after time to ride the hand beneath her. Beneath her own hand, she felt the denuded lips and the soaking sex of Nadine leap in unbridled rapture as her swollen bud yielded at last to her novice fingers.

Penny sighed, then stared wide-eyed up at the strong features, as the same hands that had given her pleasure clamped firmly to each side of her head. Intuition born of the dark feelings deep inside disposed her to think that pure pleasure was ended and might now be accompanied by pain.

'You're mine, Miss Bennet,' said Nadine in that low growly voice of hers. 'You belong to my brother, to the Beaumont estate. I'm a Beaumont, so you are mine. You might not think so, my little pussy-cat, but you are. And if you want my brother, you have to be mine – to do as I ask without question. Is that not so?'

Penny attempted to nod her head in the confines of Nadine's strong hands. 'Yes,' she murmured through pursed lips, which were pushed into that shape by Nadine's thumbs. 'Whatever you say, Nadine.'

A wide and leering smile cracked the granite hardness of Nadine's features. She bent her head and kissed Penny firmly on the lips with no pretence at affection or gentleness.

'I will help you have him, pussy-cat,' she said in a rushed and low whisper. 'On my terms. In my way.'

'Whatever you say, Nadine.'

There was a strange look of triumph in Nadine's eyes, and despite the satiation of her sex, Penny knew there was more to come, that Nadine could not possibly leave her feeling so satisfied. Nadine had to use, had to feel that only *she* had taken pleasure and inflicted only pain. The look of triumph turned to a glitter. The hands released her head.

'Then we will start as we mean to go on. We shall kiss on it,' growled Nadine.

Without hesitation, Penny kissed her mouth.

'I don't think you quite understand, my dear,' said Nadine. Strong hands landed on Penny's shoulders. She was pushed to her knees. With that, Nadine pulled her trousers down to her knees and lifted up her blouse.

There was her mons, her clit, and her de-nuded lips, which were white, almost silver, due to the sparse re-growth trying its best to poke through.

Penny was mesmerised and wondered momentarily whether her pubic hair, when left to grow wild, was as white as the bullish crop on her head. Hairy or shorn, it was difficult to tear her eyes away, wanting instead to look up questioningly at the pale-grey eyes that eyed her with all the intent of a swaying cobra.

'Kiss,' ordered Nadine.

Penny's eyes went back to the defoliated genitals. Then she dropped to her knees, smelt the musky aroma of recent sex and saw close up the glint of silver hair follicles.

As yet, Penny could neither fully recognise nor control the dark sensuality that had risen in her since coming here. All she did recognise was that the buzzing current started in some hollow between her legs and grew stronger when sexual contact was ordered rather than done purely at one's own volition.

Hands caressing the smooth, silky whiteness of Nadine's thighs, she lifted her head, pursed her willing lips and kissed the pale skin of the pure white mons.

Without being seen, a fresh sprouting of hair was already

rising through the flesh, its touch like very soft sandpaper against her mouth and chin.

Penny would have studied the white flesh further, but just the aroma of Nadine's sex, the tilting of her hips towards her lips, made her open her mouth and let her tongue loose to explore.

With her tongue and fingers, she prised the sticky lips apart and kissed Nadine's protruding clit. It was a large one and grew towards her mouth like a fledgling penis.

It didn't matter to Penny that Nadine was smiling in triumph as she writhed above her. How was Penny to know that she really had been set up for this, that Ariadne had primed Nadine with the details, and then offered her the wager. Ariadne had known Penny for a long time, since they were children, and she'd told Alistair and Nadine when they had explained to her exactly what they were looking for. Ariadne had personal knowledge of what Penny was capable of; what they had done together and also what each had seen the other do. All this information she had given to the Beaumonts. From what Nadine had seen and experienced so far, everything Ariadne had said had proved correct.

That in itself pleased Nadine. Still smiling and murmuring as she looked down at the tumbling dark hair that shone like a horse's mane between her legs, her mind worked out the path that she would force this girl to take. But for now she would enjoy, praise and punish until the time was right.

'Keep going, my pretty pussy,' she murmured, her fingers tangling in the dark hair. She smiled to herself, then chose her moment. Swiftly, before Penny could protest or withdraw, Nadine clamped Penny's head tightly against her sex, riding Penny's lips, nose and face with increasing vigour until, stretching her labia against Penny's clenched teeth, she let her orgasm break free.

Penny groaned against Nadine's sex. She was peeved; even angry. She was still aroused and in bad need of her own orgasm. Nadine's hands dragged her, protesting, to her feet.

'What about me? Please, you can't leave me like this,' she cried between demanding kisses that left Nadine's face smelling of the sex that still lingered on her lips.

She tried to force the tall woman's hand between her legs, but Nadine resisted.

'No.' Nadine said it with a smile – a cruel smile that indicated her enjoyment of Penny's obvious need.

'You must, you have to! You can't leave me like this!'

Penny herself felt lost, surprised at her own words and the terrible ferocity of the sexual need that made her labia ache and her clitoris tingle with expectation.

The hand that slapped Penny's face and made her fall into the straw was unseen and unexpected. So was Nadine's tying of her hands behind her back.

A new excitement weakened her limbs; her sex and behind tingled with anticipation. Her other cheek was slapped as Nadine, with very little effort, heaved her up and placed her so she was on her knees across the water trough. She gasped as her breasts dipped, then were completely submerged, in the cold water. Her head rested on the rim on the other side of the trough. Her hands and arms were tied very firmly behind her back.

'I promised you more punishment, and you said you deserved it and would expect it this evening. But that is only part of it. Now for some rules,' she heard Nadine say. 'You will only have sex when I say so. If you have it elsewhere I won't be pleased and you can expect to be punished. You will also provide it when I need it. Do you understand, pretty pussy?'

Penny had a need for more sex and another touch of burning on her behind. She just had to protest. 'But what if I . . .'

Just as she had hoped, there was a swishing of air before the fine tip of a leather crop landed on her behind, leaving her bare flesh tingling and clenching against the sweet sting of pain. The cane of this afternoon had been kind. *This* crop had an extra sting to it; it was thin at one end, the handle bent off to the side, and was about four inches long.

'There are no buts. Do you understand what I require of you?'

But her bottom and the new sensations inside craved satisfaction. Almost as if those sensations had total control of her vocal cords, she protested again. 'I don't know that I want to...'

The air swished again. Her bottom quivered, and she yelped and imagined the red welt that was already running across each cheek.

Nadine's eyes were glittering, her mouth slightly open and her thick tongue running along her bottom lip, delighted with the way Penny was playing along and was willing to give a performance as Ariadne had told her she would be.

'Are you sure about that?' Nadine asked, her voice as cold and cruel as she could possibly make it.

'Yes!'

The crop landed again, and sharp heat transferred from one buttock across to the other. Nadine's aim had got both cheeks that time, and Penny's sex felt as if it had turned to jelly. 'Then I will beat you until you do agree. Is that clear?'

Trembling with anticipation, Penny answered. 'It's perfectly clear. I don't care what you do. I don't care at all.'

Nadine could hardly control her delight. Just as Ariadne had foretold, here was a girl who had hidden depths, depths that Penny herself didn't know she had. She was everything that had been promised.

Wide mouth grinning, Nadine raised her arm once more

and let the crop stripe again the quivering buttocks. Three times more and Penny was whimpering.

Raising an eyebrow, Nadine stepped nearer and let the coolness of her hand run over the redness of Penny's behind. The hot flesh shivered.

'Are your breasts cold?' Nadine asked suddenly.

'Yes, they are,' Penny answered, her teeth lightly chattering, more in an effort to control her whimper than from the numbness of her erect nipples and goose-pimpled breasts which still swam in the water.

'I'll let you up from there if you agree to abide by my rules. Would you like me to do that?'

Penny lingered over her response. There was pleasure in this pain; in how it happened and how it developed.

Though her bottom burned and her breasts were cold, she didn't want it to stop; she didn't want to lose that feeling of pure envelopment of one sensation inside another.

'I have my own rules,' Penny retorted suddenly, aching for another few stings from the leather-bound crop that she knew had a silver-hooked handle.

Just as Penny had assumed, the crop resumed its course through the air and across her buttocks another six or seven times.

She cried out, wriggled against her bonds just as she was expected to. The ache between her thighs was so intense that the slightest touch would have brought her to climax. But Nadine would not do that yet. Time and patience were also part of her game. In her wide experience, she had found that anticipation inflates enjoyment both for the giver and the one who receives. The whipping ceased, and Penny could have cried.

'I will leave you to think on it now,' said Nadine with obvious pleasure, as well as authority. 'But I won't leave you without some further little reminder of me. After all, you do deserve your punishment and, at present, you are not respecting it or me as much as you should.'

Penny began to beg her to slide her hand between her legs, to rub herself until she jerked with release.

'No. Not until I say so,' Nadine replied. She began to hum merrily to herself as she slid rope around Penny's ankles and fastened them firmly to the iron rings at each side of the trough. This meant her knees, and thus her legs, were now spread wider than they had been.

Penny could hear Nadine rustling around somewhere behind her, but knew nothing about the horse collar until it was around her neck. It was a small one with jingling silver buckles and was made for a pony rather than a horse. Nadine fastened it to the anvil that sat on the side of the water trough beneath Penny's head. It was now impossible for her to move. The weight of the horse collar kept her head down and her breasts in the water. Her ankles were caught in the iron rings, her legs wide open, and her hands tied securely behind her back.

'That's cruel. How could you do this to me?'

Nadine's face came beside her, her breath hot against her ear and her teeth lightly nibbling at Penny's earlobe.

'Very easily, as I am sure you are pleased to know, you rebellious little mare. But don't worry,' she said with a long smile, 'I will leave you with a little reminder that I will return.'

Her face drew away. Nadine's hands slid down Penny's back and over her behind, fingers prising her cheeks apart, darting like sharp-nosed fishes into the puckered opening of her smallest orifice. Penny squirmed and squealed just as she was expected to. 'No,' she cried. 'You can't do that!'

'Oh yes I can, my pretty pussy. I can do exactly what I want. You told me so yourself.' Nadine laughed. Penny's buttocks burned and her sex cried out for satisfaction. She was inhibited like a horse in harness. Now she was not just Nadine's pretty pussy but her little mare, restricted in the covering yard so she could not protest at the stallion's intrusion. A slimy coldness eased between the cheeks of her behind. 'What is that?' she cried. In vain she tried to move away from the sudden intrusion.

'Just saddle soap,' cooed Nadine. 'Just to help my little reminder along a bit.'

Then Penny gasped. Something hard was being pushed into her anus, something perhaps three or four inches long, narrower at its inner end than at its stem, which still seemed to be dividing her cheeks.

'Grip it tightly, my pretty pussy. We wouldn't want it to fall out, would we?'

Nadine laughed as she smacked each of Penny's hot cheeks with the flat of her hand before walking off.

'But you can't ...' Penny began.

'I can,' Nadine retorted. 'I'll be back in ten minutes. You should be about ready by then.'

Managing to turn herself a little bit, Penny peered over her shoulder to see what object had invaded her.

With difficulty, and delight, she could see the long stiffness of the riding crop sticking up from between her cheeks like some oddly angled tail. It was the handle of the riding crop, she guessed, which was firmly embedded in the puckered hole between her taut buttocks.

The pinkness of sunset faded and the stable became darker. More than ten minutes passed. Somehow, she had half-suspected that Nadine would just leave her there to meditate on her riding faults. She closed her eyes and the effort of the day overtook her. She slept; not for long, but just long enough to know when she opened her eyes that the stable was quite a bit darker than it had been.

Horses nickered gently in their stalls. Some pawed the floor impatiently, gathering their bedding up into one gigantic heap. Others just chomped at their hay, oblivious of the delightfully tortured soul in their midst.

It might have been the rustling of straw that woke her up. There were footsteps, but she couldn't turn around to see if anyone was there. Her neck was weary – the weight of the collar seemed to have increased by a ton. Her sex was still moist, perhaps more so than before.

Hands gripped her hips, and suddenly she felt warm loins against her behind.

'Who's . . .' she tried to ask and to turn round, but the horse collar was too heavy, the stable just too dark. She cried out as a penis the size of a drum major's baton entered her.

'Ahhh!' she cried, as the penis and, with it, the crop handle pushed against her muscle walls. Both holes were filled, and the sensation made her aching clit ache a lot more.

She was trapped, in need of release yet getting none; her senses soared inexorably higher as the penis and the crop handle pleasured both orifices but left her clitoris untouched. As she cried out that she didn't think it was fair, she felt the owner of the penis reach his climax, then heard his cry of delight.

With his final spurt, he ran his hand up her back and pushed her head into the water of the trough. When the hand released her, she gasped for breath and shook her head. She tried to look over her shoulder, but whoever had taken advantage of her situation was no longer there. Only the longing for climax still remained with her, and a faint smell of maleness clung damply on her curling hairs.

If Nadine either noticed or had contrived the coupling that had just happened, she said nothing to Penny.

'Are you ready for me now, my pretty pussy?' she asked, her

voice all sweetness and honey. 'Are you willing now to follow my rules, to play my games?'

As she spoke, her long, soft fingers traced circles up and down Penny's spine before they curved around the crop and jerked it slightly so its handle jumped inside her.

'Yes, Nadine. I'm ready.' She moaned again as Nadine nudged the handle in a little further.

'You are sure of that?'

'I'm sure, Nadine. I'm sure. Please. I'm aching. Please do something.'

Nadine sighed almost regretfully, then pulled the crop from where it had been so tightly gripped. She undid the bonds as she talked, raised Penny up, then pushed her to her knees. The horse collar remained around her neck.

'Tonight,' she said, 'after dinner, you will play my first game. You will be my cabaret. Whatever and whoever is offered to you, you will take. Is that clear?'

'Yes,' Penny answered, head suitably bowed, which she felt somehow was what was expected of her. Inside she was burning with anticipation.

'Good,' Nadine replied coldly. 'Then we're agreed on that.'

With an obvious sense of purpose, Nadine unzipped her trousers and pulled them down slightly so her mons was yet again exposed.

Without urging, Penny kissed it.

# 7

Tonight her outfit was darker than her hair. The top was little more than a tube against which her breasts rebelled and showed through in blatant relief.

Black trousers matched the top. They had a sash waistband that tied at one side. Once pulled, the trousers would just drop to her ankles – soft, silky and with a distinct hush.

Tonight only gold jewellery relieved her darkness. Her earrings were gold. So was her necklace and the Celtic half-bangle on her right wrist. The metal glowed against the pale cream of her skin and the darkness of her hair. Her eyes shone like two bright sapphires which were made all the more bright by the blackness of her eyelashes. She wore gold sandals with high heels that stretched her calves and caused her buttocks and bosom to thrust in opposite directions. There was no underwear between her and the soft caress of silk against her skin.

'You look glorious, my dear.' Alistair stood alone by the open door. The others had already gone in. His jaw dropped slightly and his eyes travelled downwards over her tight bodice, her belly and thighs.

She moved a little, pirouetting on her high heels, her hips swaying. Behind her was one of the long windows that swept from ceiling to floor. Light still filtered through, and as the material of her trousers was very fine, it shone through and he could see the dark patch of hair nestling between her creamy thighs.

'How very kind of you to say so.'

He offered her his hand, though now politeness took over from appraisal. She took it anyway, and studied him as he led her into the room, left her at her chair, and went round the other side of the table to take his own.

Hair high and pulled into a ponytail, it swung as Penny took her seat. Something about tonight made her feel special. This feeling could have been the result of knowing that all eyes were upon her or may have been the residue of those dark feelings deep inside that begged for acknowledgement. She looked at each of her fellow diners in turn, and they all responded individually.

Nadine winked suggestively, her usual sardonic smile gently tilting the corners of her mouth. With difficulty, she looked away.

Alistair's glances were sporadic. When she raised her eyes to meet his, he looked guiltily away. Each time Penny was aware of a look passing between him and his sister.

Auberon had a pink face tonight. Perhaps it was the wine, or maybe it was his deepest thoughts that made him blush and stammer that way. Either way, he was looking at her, blinking and taking big gulps from his very full glass. He smiled, and his eyes glittered expectantly.

Tonight felt good and so did she. The mix of smells heightened that excitement: good food; fine wine; the smell of men and her own perfume mixed with the heavy scent of huge cut blooms in blue-and-white Chinese vases on the long sideboard. There was a breathless sensuality almost tangible in the air. Eyes glittered and voices were soft and husky like a mild sea breeze blowing over coarse sand.

'A little more wine?' asked Sir Reggie, breaking into her thoughts in that gentlemanly way of his.

'Yes please,' she answered with a smile. Her ponytail swung merrily as she turned to face him. She held up her glass and watched, almost hypnotically, as the dark-red liquid poured into the bowl of lead crystal.

After some pretty healthy eating and drinking, her top wriggled down and her breasts thrust upwards, round and shiny like balloons about to burst. Her nipples peered over her black top like two frightened eyes. As he poured the wine, Sir Reggie's eyes were fastened on them. His hand shook and the wine bottle trembled; some of the red liquid missed the glass and streamed over her gleaming mounds. She gasped as a large trickle disappeared down the cleft in between.

'Oh, my dear. I do apologise most sincerely. How clumsy of me. Allow me, my dear.' Sir Reggie covered her hand with his. 'I made the mess. Let me clear it up.'

Silence descended over those gathered as Sir Reggie lowered his mouth on to Penny's breasts. All eyes upon her and Sir Reggie's tongue lapping at her bosoms, Penny let herself become part of the atmosphere she had felt earlier. She purred with pleasure and felt herself and her senses blend as easily as coffee and cream. Sir Reggie's tongue licked long and ponderously as he savoured the bouquet and the taste on his tongue of the unusual combination of perfume, flesh and wine.

'Allow me, my dear,' he said, as courteous as only a gentleman like him could be. 'I noticed that it dribbled down through. I insist on dealing with it.'

She nodded without speaking, her breath quickening with brazen abandon as he rolled down her bodice and let her breasts spring completely free. Then, slowly, as though enjoying every diverse taste on his tongue, he licked all over her proud orbs and down her cleavage.

Gasps of pleasure broke from her throat. His tongue was hot and pleasantly wet. It had a certain rasp to its tissue, a bit like that of a cat.

Despite, or perhaps to spite, the watching eyes, she pushed

her breasts towards his mouth, and closed her eyes as his hair caressed her nipples. His tongue followed the contours of her breasts, tracing each gentle curve and valley; his tongue lapped her satin flesh around the dark halos in which her nipples sat demanding and receiving avid attention. Tenderly he sucked each one, rolled them on his tongue and neatly prodded with its tip.

When she opened her eyes, she looked over his head at each of the other dinner guests. Auberon was transfixed on what Sir Reggie was doing. Nadine's smile was wider than it had been.

'I think I've cleared all of it up,' Sir Reggie said at last with a smile. He brought his head up level with hers, and salaciously licked his lips. She had expected him then to handle her bosoms, to play to the crowd so to speak, seeing as she was so obviously tonight's cabaret. But he didn't. Instead, and to her surprise and disappointment, he pulled up her tube bodice, cupped a bosom in one hand and put it back in, then did the same to the other. He appeared to take great pleasure in doing this, as though they were priceless treasures that he had rescued from tarnish or destruction and was just gathering them in for further study later.

Penny took this in the spirit in which it was meant, though she had been enjoying his tongue.

'That's very kind of you,' she said, though inside her senses were screaming for more. 'I'm sorry to have put you to all that trouble.'

'No trouble at all, my dear. Always willing to do my duty.' She saw him exchange looks with Alistair. Tonight, like Sir Reggie, and even like Auberon, Alistair wore a dinner suit. Yet he didn't look quite so stiff as the others. There was something about him still slightly casual. It was the way, she thought, of the rich and confident. There was definitely a skill in looking formal whilst maintaining an air of casual indifference.

Penny felt almost triumphant when she saw Alistair eyeing her intensely, despite dark scowls from Nadine. His mouth was slightly open as though he were catching his breath. She saw him swallow. In that moment, she knew once more that he wanted her. But what was keeping him from attempting her seduction? What barrier did he have to overcome before he could bury his cock in her and cry his climax into her ear?

But Nadine's dark scowls seemed to get the better of him. He looked serious before he cleared his throat and began to speak.

'Nadine tells me you lost concentration this afternoon. I don't like that.' Although he was in effect chastising, his voice was even, as steady as the day he had got her to parade through the town with him. It was still gloriously deep, as if erupting from some deep fissure in the earth's crust. All the same it made her defensive, but then, of course, she felt that was what she was expected to be – something to give cause for rebuke.

'I hit the fence,' she replied hotly, her limbs already starting to tremble with apprehension. 'That's all. Four faults.' She saw Alistair raise his eyebrows. She also saw the faint nod of approval from Nadine. Obviously, she was egging him on.

The rugged features of Alistair Beaumont remained unchanged as though he were as crystal as his overhead chandeliers. In an effort to control her rising excitement, Penny looked beyond him to the windows and the reflected room and figures. It was almost as if there were two worlds, she thought; two Beaumont Places. In one of them lived real people. In the other, there were only shadows, bare reflections of the people that really existed, and those reflections were dark, muted, but could burn bright at any time just like the hidden emotions within herself.

His voice brought her back to the real room and the real people. 'So. You admit it. You lost concentration.'

'Yes.' She said it with a dismissive laugh. At her side, Sir

Reginald cleared his throat and began to fidget. She glanced at him. There was a sparkle in his eyes.

'I did lose concentration – just for a moment. I smiled at Auberon,' Penny said casually. 'Perhaps I was too pleased at having cleared all the jumps, too cocksure about clearing the last one as well.'

Smiles and low chuckles seemed suddenly to surround her.

'Or even too cock-happy?' drawled Nadine, her voice as long and drawn-out as her suck on her customary cheroot.

Despite his sister's humour, Alistair's face was unchanged but, deep in his eyes, something stirred; something as dark as it was exciting. Penny caught that look. Her eyes were locked with his. She felt as though she were diving into unknown waters – waters the more sensible would steer clear of. But she would plunge into those waters headlong. In the aftermath of the release of those dark feelings within her, the sensual had come to outweigh the sensible.

A flush of defiance and trepidation lit her face as she glanced from the self-assured paleness of Nadine to the pretty shade of pink that coloured Auberon's cheeks. She knew what they wanted, knew what was expected of her. 'My sex life is my own affair,' she retorted hotly, and eyed each of her colleagues for their response.

'Not while you are at Beaumont Place,' Alistair said grimly. 'As I am sure my sister has told you, while you are here you become part of my team. Becoming part of my team means you give yourself up, body and soul, to this place and your sport.'

For a moment she wondered if she'd gone too far. She didn't think so, but this was her first foray into the world of master, mistress and object of punishment. She reined in her words. 'I didn't mean to step out of line. I'm sorry if I offended anyone.'

'My sister tells me you took advantage of Stephen,' Alistair began, his eyes seeming to study the two silver pheasants that decorated the middle of the table. 'Oh,' he added, shaking his head when she tried to interrupt, 'I don't blame you. It's just that I thought a woman of your experience and intelligence would indulge in a higher level of sexual adventure than tumbling in the straw with a common stable-lad – a straight-forward act of copulation.'

He watched for her reaction and kept to himself the know-ledge that he and Nadine had watched nearly everything she had done since coming here. While he had watched, his cock had throbbed almost painfully against the tight rubber of his pants. But he had borne that pain, sure in the knowledge that his sex drive was becoming more powerful than that of an ordinary man. It was being conserved, saved like a bundle of electrical charges and set to explode in one almighty consum-mation when the moment was right.

But the antics of the dark-haired Penny had almost made him plead with his sister to release him from his strictures and have Penny right away. Nadine, thankfully, had refused. And of course, as usual, she had been right. A man of fibre does not give in to weakness. He saves his assets, acquires as much as possible until the time is ripe for a series of performances, not just one. Then what he had would be hers, and once its task was done, his prick would diminish and lie dormant, waiting until the next time.

In the heat of the opulent room, Penny felt her cheeks redden. She didn't like being thought of as unadventurous. Of course she was sophisticated enough to indulge in the more esoteric sexual scenarios. In the heat of the moment, the part she should play was forgotten. She rose to her feet, her fists slamming down on the table.

'The chance was there. I took it. What am I supposed to do here? Become a nun?'

She felt a warm hand caress the backs of her legs and knew

that, inadvertently, she had made the right move and spoken the right words. She looked down into the yearning expression and strong features of Sir Reginald. What a man he must have been when he was younger, she thought momentarily. He was still something to look at even now. There was a military set to his chin, a hardness to his face and body that only rigid exercise and army life could possibly have moulded.

'I believe you,' Sir Reggie said, his smile stretching the dark moustache that curled over his top lip. 'I know you indulge in other things.'

'Yes,' snapped Nadine from the other side of the table. 'She most certainly will.'

Penny fell to silence, mouth slightly open as familiar feelings grew in the moistness of her sex. She felt hands pulling at the sash that held her trousers. They dropped with a soft hush to her ankles. Her backside was bare, and her triangle of pubic hair peered shyly over the edge of the dining-table.

She tried not to moan, yet all the while her hips swayed in time to the probing of Sir Reggie's fingers. She shifted slightly and opened her legs a little wider. Where only two fingers had been, he now put his whole hand.

Leg and thigh muscles trembling, Penny rested her own hands flat upon the table in order to facilitate stronger probings. She bent forward slightly. Other eyes were upon her, glittering like hard cut diamonds. But she didn't care about them looking. As she let forth mews of delight, she lost herself in her own yearnings, in her own dark desires.

Suddenly there were no other people in the room. She was lost in her own delirium as though she were in a trance or taken by a high fever. All the while the exploring fingers of Sir Reggie tangled in her hair and pushed their way through the cleft that divided her firm buttocks.

Briefly, Penny opened her eyes and saw Nadine and Alistair

smiling at her. She opened her mouth to speak. Alistair spoke first.

'No need to say anything. Enjoy it. Just as we are enjoying it.'

She did not protest. Somehow she understood what they were saying. Through others' pleasure, those that watch take pleasure. Even through pain, they too witness an awesome presence of something more that goes beyond both, so that pleasure and pain become one and the same thing.

Wriggling with delight and pleased that those watching were sharing that delight with her, she felt the hand continue and felt the fingers sliding into her more easily as her sex responded to the situation.

On the other side of the table, Nadine leant towards her brother and whispered close to his ear. Penny, her breath audible among murmurs of delight, saw Alistair smile and nod his head. Then she saw Nadine straighten up and look directly at her.

'Reggie likes what he's doing. Do you?' Nadine asked through a cloud of expelled smoke.

Penny nodded. She tried to speak, but could only gasp. Sir Reggie's fingers were plying their way through her legs, dividing the mossy hair that covered her pudendum; her sex.

'Yes,' she replied at last in the hush of her breath. 'Yes, I do.'

As moans of ecstasy escaped her lips, her eyes met those of Alistair. His mouth was open, his nostrils were flared. Was he thinking, she wondered, of that day when she had been naked beneath a cashmere coat in the middle of the high street? There had only been the two of them on that particular day. Just asking herself that question was enough to bring her aching clitoris from out of its protective hood. As if pouncing on a reclusive creature, Sir Reggie took it between two fingers. As he squeezed it, her knees buckled slightly and deep moans erupted one after the other.

Still resting her palms on the table, she leant a little further forwards and clutched a handful of tablecloth as her fist closed over it. That way she could steady herself so Reggie could invade her more easily. It didn't matter that there were people watching her ascend towards the delicious waves of orgasm. They were just extensions of her own delight, as much victims of their own decadence as she was.

Nadine came round and placed her hand on Penny's shoulder. Falling more deeply into the abyss of her own sexuality, Penny knew that the performance had only just started.

'Your orgasm can wait a while,' Nadine said sharply. 'There are other things we wish to see before we let you have that.'

The lips that had covered hers earlier in the day now whispered just a breath away from her ear. 'Remember our bargain, my sweet pussy-cat. Remember you are due punishment, and punishment can involve pleasure as well as pain. But you know that already. Go along with all that is asked of you, exactly as I told you.'

Nadine's breath was warm and full of wine and strong smoke. Penny, still swimming upstream towards her climax, turned to look at her. She took in the square jaw and pale face of Nadine and, although she felt little more than a plaything, there was an odd security in that knowledge. For the first time in her life, she felt comfortable where she was, and with those around her.

Reminding Penny of a cat relishing a banquet of live sparrow, Nadine ran her long tongue slowly and sensually over her pale lips. Penny discerned erotic imaginings; schemes and ideas in the brightness of Nadine's eyes. Her smile was fixed, as though it was permanently painted on her face.

In one swift movement, Nadine ran her hands along Penny's back and down to her glossy behind. They were cool on Penny's warm flesh, yet she welcomed them even when each firm cheek was cupped and parted. Penny did not need to see what Nadine was doing. She knew – could feel – that her cheeks were open wide, and the dark puckered mouth of her most secret orifice was exposed. It made her gasp, it made her squeal. Nadine had offered a blatant invitation to Sir Reggie. Penny did not doubt that he would accept it.

Penny heard Sir Reggie's sharp intake of breath; felt his thumb prod excitedly between her cheeks and press fondly at the tightness of her anus.

'I think you need this, Reggie darling,' Penny heard Nadine purr.

As one buttock was released, Penny saw that same hand pass in front of her. The long fingers that she had come to know picked up a butter-knife, which Nadine dipped into the silver-edged butter-dish. Then the knife disappeared from Penny's view.

She wriggled her bottom, intent on experiencing invasion in either of her passages. Her bodice was still around her waist, her trousers were around her ankles. Everything in between was bare. On top of that, she now knew for sure that her exposed anus was about to be smeared in butter then invaded by Sir Reggie's finger or thumb. She was tonight's star – or victim. The former, she thought. That's the way I truly feel. I'm like a performer about to give the show of my life.

The butter was cold against her anus and the butter-knife obviously blunt. She felt it being spread, then the knife was held tight against her nether mouth so a portion of it was pushed inside her.

'Push it in please Reggie, darling,' she heard Nadine say.

'Glad to, my dear ... very glad to,' answered Sir Reggie.

Penny closed her eyes and gripped the tablecloth more tightly as Sir Reggie's finger, ably assisted by the butter, entered her most secret portal. She cried out more with passion than pain.

Nadine still held her cheeks firmly apart so the butter could be smeared more easily with the fingers of one hand, whilst a finger of the other hand worked its way inside her.

Penny moaned with each small thrust as the finger entered her up to the first joint. As the butter oiled its onward progress, his finger was soon buried up to the knuckle.

'I've got it right in her,' she heard Sir Reggie say excitedly. But his voice sounded distant to her. Whatever he was doing had transported her to another world. She was lost in her own pleasure, her legs were taut as she tilted her bottom to meet him, her vulva swirling with liquid desire.

Almost as if he were trying to staunch her sexual flow, Sir Reggie immersed his fingers in her pussy. Now she moaned more. This was too much. She was too full, both erogenous holes were plugged by his exploring fingers. Tingles of pleasure spread upwards and outwards from each exploration. She was plugged with desire, stuffed with fingers.

'See, Reggie,' she heard Nadine say. 'See what a lovely bottom she has. Don't you think it's the best bottom you have ever seen? See how soft the skin is, how firm the muscles, and just see how sensitive it is.'

Sharp nails scraped over Penny's skin in much the same way as Penny's own nails had scraped over Auberon's.

Penny's breath caught in her throat and she curled her fingers more tightly in the stiffness of the white linen tablecloth.

'Beautiful,' muttered the old man. 'Simply beautiful. In fact, perfect.'

'She's wet. The little mare is very wet, isn't she, Reggie?'

Penny tensed and moaned obligingly as Nadine's fingers joined Reggie's, and dipped into the fountain of fluid that seeped from her secret cavern. She opened her eyes along with her mouth now, and looked across the table. Now her gaze held Alistair's. What she saw, she liked. Although his face was still unaltered, his eyes sparkled with a multitude of different colours as if he were assessing what she was feeling and wondering exactly how far she would go.

Auberon appeared interested, yet somehow jealous.

He wishes it were him, thought Penny. He would like it to be him undergoing this treatment. The more scratching and whipping, the better pleased he would be.

'She's near climax,' drawled Nadine, her fingers mingling with Reggie's before rubbing excess fluid from Penny's juicy vulva and up through the cheeks of her bottom and around Reggie's plunging finger. 'Does she get that climax now,' Nadine went on, 'or do you have something else in mind, brother dear?'

Penny heard what she said and attempted to speak, but was powerless to do so. All her responses, all her actions, were being manipulated by others. They were using her as a puppeteer might pull on strings – and she was dancing to their tune.

She squealed as the talons of Nadine's graceful hands tangled in her pubic hair, one fingertip running delicious rings around and over her ripening bud.

'The first lesson, sister,' answered Alistair, 'is to go gentle at first. Give her what she desires. If she is as adventurous as she says she is, she will be back for more, back for the lessons yet to come.'

Penny half-opened her eyes; through her dark lashes she saw Alistair smile briefly in Reggie's direction. Only for a moment did she wonder what the look and the words meant. Her first consideration was her mounting orgasm. It took her over, felt almost as if she were rising to the crest of a giant wave that, having reached its peak, curled over and fell crashing, splattering her jerking thighs with tingling sensations and warm secretions. She cried out. Her limbs trembled and she gasped for air and fell forward on to the table, breasts pressed against the stiff starch of the very white tablecloth.

Faces beamed around her. Sighs of satisfaction filled the air as though they had shared her orgasm, and had dipped their own fingers into the warm pool of fluid that flooded Penny's open sex.

'Kneel!' ordered Nadine, her strong hands pulling her up from the table, her fingers curling in an iron grip over her shoulders. Penny, realising that they had not yet finished with her, did as ordered. Between her legs, the last sweet aches of orgasm were flowing away. She had been absorbed in them, and therefore had not expected that more would be required of her.

Reggie, face glowing with a ruddy anticipation, moved the chair she had been sitting on so she could kneel down where she was.

Alistair came round from the other side of the table and sat in the chair she had been sitting in. Again he would do nothing but watch, she thought. Again he had disappointed her.

He had a brandy balloon in one hand in which about an inch of best Armagnac swirled. He crossed one leg over the other, sipped just once, every inch the gentleman, just waiting for the performance to begin.

Auberon got up, too, and came round. He stood like a sentinel behind Alistair's chair as though in attendance on him. Both sets of eyes were glued on the kneeling Penny. Nadine stood behind her, Sir Reggie in front.

Nadine's hands stroked Penny's hair, neck and shoulders. Directly in front of Penny's face was the fly of Sir Reggie's trousers and the swelling mound immediately behind it. She froze yet watched mesmerised as his fumbling hands tugged impatiently at his zip.

Expectantly she swallowed hard and left her mouth completely empty. It needed no explanation to tell her what was intended. And yet she knew that more was expected than to pleasure the penis of the tall and well-made military man. The key to that more exquisite scenario was bound to be protest.

'I don't...'

'You will.' Nadine's fingers tangled in her hair. The roots strained in her scalp and she cried out as her head was held erect. She closed her mouth tightly. Nadine pulled her hair so her head tilted back slightly.

Unable to move her head, Penny's eyes rolled sidelong. In a bid to keep her balance and perspective, she rested her hands now on Sir Reggie's thighs which seemed to be made of iron and were covered in profuse and dark hair.

At first she continued her imitation protest and tried to draw away from the advancing penis. Then she gulped and gasped for air as Nadine pinched her nose. Before her, the white length of Reggie's cock approached her lips. Entranced by the sight, she freely looked it over, then opened her mouth wider. It was surprisingly upright and wore its mushroom dome like an imperial crown.

She closed her eyes, steeling herself for the feel of it in her mouth, the taste of it upon her tongue. Even as Sir Reggie's hands took hold of her head and guided her mouth to satisfy his needs, she wriggled in protest. Just as she had judged, his member stiffened and jerked on her lips. It danced in her mouth as her tongue traced imaginary lines over its surface, her teeth gently nibbling from its tip to its base.

With one of Nadine's hands still tangled in her hair, she gulped more cock into her mouth. It gained firmness and stature as her mouth slid up and down it, her movements controlled by his hands, which remained clamped firmly to her head.

She felt Nadine's free hand slide over her shoulder, cup her breast, then pinch fondly at a nipple. The other hand left her tangled mane and did the same to the second nipple. Now only Reggie's hands were tangled in her hair, pushing her head up and down his cock just as he pleased. Nadine's were doing other things.

No matter how much Penny had eaten that night, there was a more insatiable hunger now prevailing through her system. She raised her own hand to touch, perhaps even to control the living organ that drove so consistently in and out of her mouth.

'No!'

Nadine's orders again. Out of the corner of her eyes, Penny saw Nadine go over to the heavy curtains that hung from the windows and then undo one of the silk-rope tie-backs.

Then Nadine's long hands grabbed both of Penny's and tied them with the cool silk cords behind her back.

The man above her gasped. Her bondage had obviously pleased him, and the position of her restrained arms accentuated the thrust of her breasts beneath his busy penis. As Nadine lifted her breasts higher, Sir Reggie gasped again as the satin softness of her skin met the more feathered surface of his slapping balls.

'Perfect,' she heard Sir Reggie say between gasps of delight. 'Just perfect.'

Hot kisses rained on Penny's back as Nadine's fingers rolled her breasts and tweaked almost savagely their crowns of pink velvet.

Penny closed her eyes again. She didn't need to pretend that the man in her mouth was Alistair. It was enough to know that he was watching and even enjoying the experience. She certainly was. Anyway, Reggie was a handsome and dignified man. The years had been extraordinarily kind to his sexuality and his body which was still firm, ripe and honed to a perfection only an adventurous military man could hope to attain.

She felt she could almost swallow the eager thing that was growing to new prominence. It was as if her tongue had a life of its own as it licked around the prickly ridge of the penis and traced the deep vein that ran from tip to stem.

Reggie's hands were still clamped on either side of her head. They tightened their grip as he continued to control her head so that her mouth moved up and down his penis at his whim. Even without being able to run her finger down the throbbing vein that ran the length of his cock, Penny knew his time was near. His breathing had quickened, and so had the pushing backwards and forwards of her head along his length. In her mouth, the first juice of ejaculation settled like salt pearls upon her tongue.

'Mr Harding.'

Nadine's voice rang out. There was unmistakable demand in it.

This time, Penny could see nothing. Reggie's grip was too strong, his climax too near. The only view she had was straight ahead. She stared directly into Sir Reggie's pubic hair, aware that her own sex was wanting an extra release to the one it had received earlier.

As the hard shaft moved in and out of her mouth, she took a deep gulp of breath. Someone's fingers buried themselves in her pussy. She realised they must belong to Auberon. Like some sort of automaton, it had been Auberon who had been summoned, and Auberon who seemed to know exactly what to do without explanation. There was no barrier to their penetration, only a new wetness of excitement flooding on top of the sticky excess from her previous orgasm. Pleasure began to ripple outwards and upwards from her centre of desire. In her mouth, she felt Reggie's penis begin to vibrate with his rising climax, and was aware of her nipples responding to Nadine's teasing fingers. Both assisted the tremulous sensations erupting around her demanding clitoris, which raised its aching head towards Auberon's probing fingers.

'Is she wet?' It was Nadine's voice behind her.

'Soaking,' Auberon responded, a tremor of subdued excitement shaking the words on his tongue.

'Dirty little mare. You want it again, do you? Are you coming?'

Penny's voice was shaky, taken over by the luxurious vibrations that radiated from her inflamed centre. 'Y-Yes.'

'And you, Reggie?'

'Any second.'

To Penny, it seemed as if Nadine had given a signal. The fingers massaging her sex moved with greater dexterity and speed over her clit. Those on her nipples pinched more avidly, and rolled her breasts with greater purpose. If her mouth had been free, she would have moaned with pleasure.

Just as she reached her own peak, with her hips jerking against the hand that pleasured her, Reggie withdrew his thick cock from her mouth.

Splashes of warmth fell over her breasts, and the sticky whiteness was massaged into the satin skin by the same hands that had aroused her nipples to greater prominence. Above her, Reggie groaned, his hands releasing her head as his penis released his semen.

In white streams like weak icing, Reggie's come settled on her breasts. Nadine's hands rolled through it, massaging it over her until there was no whiteness left and only the stickiness sank into her skin. She massaged it right up into the tips of Penny's nipples so they glistened like spun silver.

The last tremors of climax shivered down her thighs and she sighed her satisfaction amid deep breaths and light moans of pleasure. At this moment, Penny felt as though she had been the centre of the universe – in this room anyway. She opened her eyes, closed them again, and savoured the last tingles of delight. When she reopened them, her eyes met those of

Alistair. Would he take her now? He stared, blinked self-consciously, then looked away. 'I think she's got the message,' he said, and rose to his feet.

Eyes still watching Alistair yet free of her bonds, Nadine massaged Penny's arms.

'Enough for tonight?' Nadine's question was aimed at her brother.

'Enough for tonight. But there's always tomorrow.'

Penny found it hard to drag her eyes away from Alistair. He looked so cool and so calmly in charge of the situation. Yet there was something in his look that expressed torment. He was like a master of ceremonies or ringmaster. He was the boss, detailing and explaining what was to be done, yet contributing nothing to it.

Nadine's lips brushing gently against her cheek distracted her. 'Do you ache very much, my darling pussy-cat?' cooed Nadine, her voice as thick and sweet as syrup.

Penny dragged her eyes from Alistair and stared directly at his sister. She blinked, thought of herself and exactly how she *did* feel. 'Yes,' she replied, 'I do ache a little – my arms especially. At this moment, I'd love Gregory to give me a massage.'

Nadine positively purred with delight. The ice-cold eyes sparkled with sweet-shop anticipation.

'Gregory should be in bed by now, my pretty. He usually is. Anyway, why disturb him, pussy-cat? I'll give you a massage.'

The smile Penny gave Nadine was sweet, but not necessarily innocent.

# 8

'I want you to massage *me*,' Nadine said, once they were back in Penny's room, where a massive flower arrangement set on a table in the middle of the room graced the air with garden-like freshness.

She didn't wait for an answer, but just pulled off what few clothes she had on and lay out face down on the bed.

Before taking the top off the oil bottle, Penny, who was already naked, glanced at the big mirror. She had no doubt that Nadine had told Alistair something more than just goodnight.

Nadine's body was snow-white against the rich red and green of the tapestry bedcover. Her body was also very long, her feet curling over the foot of the bed and the top of her head brushing the carved headboard.

Nadine moaned as Penny began to run and roll her hands over her body.

'My intention was to invigorate your muscles, pretty pussy, not for you to invigorate mine,' she purred, stretching as she said it, her hips rolling slightly against the roughness of the bedcover.

Penny stood statuesque and resolute, her skin glowing in the aftermath of the exacting session she had just endured. She watched her rolling behind, and the cheeks tight and small like a young boy's.

And how are you enjoying that? she thought, knowing that Nadine was rolling her own pert clitoris against the roughness of the bedspread.

'The more pliant your muscles, the more benefit mine will receive,' Penny said sweetly.

Nadine rested her head on folded arms whilst Penny oiled her hands again. Faint murmurs of pleasure came from Nadine's mouth and were breathed into the crisp whiteness of the pillow as Penny's hands spread and pressed at the sinuous flesh.

Nadine's flesh tensed and shivered with pleasure as Penny pushed the ball of her palms into the tight muscles of her shoulders. She probed with fingers made strong by holding in check the head of plunging horses before flying over five-foot spreads or striped cross beams.

Not without selfish intent, Penny repositioned and sat astride a rounded bottom that was soft-skinned, yet hard beneath the lingering wetness and open lips of her own sex. She murmured a little as she wriggled astride Nadine's boyish bottom. Her sex moistened and her clit erected as she felt the tight cheeks bunch compulsively beneath her.

With serious precision, she worked the muscles on either side of Nadine's spine, her thumbs following each nobble of the long indentation that lay so close to the skin. She smoothed her hands upwards, the oiled flesh glistening beneath her touch, then brought them down again, the thumbs pressing in feather-like outward strokes as she progressed downwards towards the rising mounds of Nadine's behind and the forest of her own body hair.

'Delicious,' Nadine murmured, her eyes closed to add greater perception to her other senses.

Penny studied Nadine's face as she lay supine. White lashes lay barely perceptible against the paleness of high-boned cheeks. Beneath the straight patrician nose, her mouth was wide and slightly open, exposing the strong white teeth which even now clutched resolutely at the butt of a black cheroot.

Questions circled in Penny's mind. She wanted to know more about Alistair, and more about his relationship with his sister. She also wanted to know more about herself from those questions. She wanted to find out where her new and acute sexuality had come from and what had caused its release. How much more was there to discover about this place, these people and herself? Softly, she told herself, go softly.

'Was tonight a foretaste of things to come?' she asked as her fingertips deftly rubbed the nape of Nadine's neck.

'Hmmm?' murmured the wide mouth.

'Was that a yes?'

Nadine chuckled into the pillow. 'Tonight was a mere aperitif, my pretty. It gets better. The *premier cru* is still to come.' She purred her answer, like a stroked pet craving for more of what she was already receiving.

Penny paused, and grimaced as Nadine spat the cheroot butt from her mouth. Then she studied the clusters of ornamental plasterwork on the ceiling before attempting another question. Continue the softening of the body, she reasoned, and the sharp mind will follow.

'Doesn't Alistair ever join in?'

The lashes flickered, the nostrils flared slightly. Hesitation was obvious. 'Only on special occasions – in exceptional circumstances.' The pale eyes opened and Nadine looked back at Penny over her shoulder. 'When the time is ripe,' Nadine added.

Penny slowed the massage and lowered her eyes to the white and now gleaming skin. She wondered when those special occasions would be and what the exceptional circumstances were. And when would the time be ripe and who would judge that it was so?

But she didn't ask. Not yet anyway. She altered position until she was further down Nadine's body, her legs straddling her lower thighs. Her eyes travelled over the rounded cheeks, as white as the rest of Nadine's taut flesh. The rising of her dividing cleft was marked with a solitary dimple. She leant low over Nadine's back, her thumbs on her spine, her palms and fingers spread to encompass the narrow waist. Briefly her nipples trailed over the naked flesh with no more than the touch of the lightest butterfly. A delicious shiver ran from her white shoulders to the snowy mountains of her behind. Penny, sensing the reaction Nadine was getting from the brushing of her nipples, repeated the movement, taking her own pleasure from the brief yet tingling touch before running her hands down over the hip-bones and cupping each cheek in an oily palm, her thumbs curving over the rising flesh to the cleft between.

Nadine purred again with pleasure and wriggled her hips, her bottom rising as if inviting Penny to press harder, and to probe more deeply. Now, Penny judged, the time was ripe to ask another question.

'What are these special occasions?'

Nadine's lips curled back soundlessly from her teeth before she chuckled again into the pillow.

'Patience, my little pussy-cat, patience. I know what you're getting at.' One grey eye opened and regarded Penny above a snow-white shoulder. 'Your time will come, my pretty. Your time will come.' Her voice had become a growl. Warning ran parallel in her voice with low murmurs of pleasure.

Beneath Penny's straddled thighs and moist sex, Nadine rolled over completely, the fleshy pink crowns of her small breasts pointing obscenely skywards. 'Now, oil me some more. I want you to rub my nipples first – just to get me going.'

Her eyes opened. Penny held her gaze for just a moment, then looked down again at the pure white flesh. For all the willpower she seemed to possess at this precise moment, she might just as well have been an odalisque in some Eastern harem. It seemed as though what Nadine wanted was also what she wanted. There appeared to be no dividing line between the two. By instinct, she knew what she had to do next.

Her pubic hairs brushed over Nadine's flesh as she slid up over the reclining body until she straddled her waist. She re-oiled her hands and drank in the piquant beauty of Nadine's snowy orbs, the hard nubs of dense sensitivity rising from areolae as plush as pink velvet.

Although her gaze was full of promised delights, she resisted their lure and placed her hands around Nadine's neck, pressing slightly so that a look of something resembling fear entered her grey eyes. Then they relaxed, her fingers running down the sinews, over the collar-bone to the smooth skin of Nadine's shoulders.

Nadine, reassured that Penny was as compliant as she had previously judged, closed her eyes and murmured her gratitude. Her nipples visibly pouted to be included.

Unable to resist any longer, Penny closed the tips of one finger and one thumb over each. The fine ridges of the thrusting protrusions felt strangely silky beneath her touch. She felt them rise, then grow more engorged with blood and desire as her palms rested there.

'Harder,' breathed Nadine.

Penny clasped the nipples more tightly and pulled them upwards as high as she could until the whole of the breast seemed suspended on each glaring nub of rosy tissue. The oil made them more glossy, lending a silvery shine to the trans-lucent skin. They looked succulent, too succulent to leave just to trembling fingers. Urged by waves of energy generated from within, Penny took the swollen flesh into her mouth. She closed her eyes as her lips covered them; she sucked hard and long and felt the nipple growing to an even greater proportion on her tongue. She sucked again and again, nibbling every so often as the fingers on the other hand continued to pull at its partner, then to tease and pinch it to respond better than it already had.

'Suck me harder,' Nadine's voice rasped through her lips. Her nails began to dig into Penny's back, then one hand pressed against her head, holding her fast against the swollen breast, forcing her to suck, nibble and bite exactly how and when Nadine wanted her to.

Penny managed to gulp air before the lean, yet uncommonly strong hands forced her lips on to the other breast. She repeated what she had already done, her mouth sucking long and hard, her teeth nipping gently, then more firmly, at the growing flesh. All the time, Penny's other hand pinched and pulled at the newly released nipple, which was now swollen and red from her oral treatment of it.

As the hand that held her relaxed, her mouth released its delicacy. She kissed between the breasts, her wet tongue and nipping teeth eliciting more cloudy exclamations from Nadine's throat.

Her head and her hands began to move again. She trailed low over the narrow waist, the flat stomach. Her own proud nipples brushed lightly over the skin as her hands massaged the lean hips.

She raised herself up slightly so her hands could come inwards, and her fingers and eyes could examine the prominence of the shorn mound of Nadine's sex. How naked it looked, the lips purely white and as smooth as cream, a stripe of pink showing like a delicate insert of glistening silk in between.

Nadine's legs widened. Hanging from amid the fleshy lips, Penny could see the pink frills of the inner petals and the fattening bud of Nadine's clitoris as it thrust out from its fringe of moist flesh.

Moans of pleasure accompanied the writhing of thighs, the thrusting of belly and sex before Penny's face. Penny could feel the silkiness of Nadine's flesh together with the plump sexuality of her naked labia.

She slid her fingers further, lightly teasing the gleaming frills and the springing love bud. They looked sweet, dripping with the honey of arousal. She bent lower. Her tongue tasted the smoothness of the outer lips before dipping in between, savouring the salty sweetness of another woman on her tongue.

Nadine's murmurs of pleasure were nothing to Penny now. Again, her own sex was responding to stimuli, her hips rocking gently as her fingers opened and probed more deeply, more languorously, to explore the petals and undulations of Nadine's sex.

Nothing could stop her from seeking her own climax. She swivelled round so her own pussy was above Nadine's face and she felt a shiver of delight course over her belly as the long, white hands gripped her buttocks before the wide mouth sucked at her and the long tongue teased at her clit.

Sensations of rising climax made their bodies rock in unison as their tongues dipped faster. Their teeth nipped in a sprightly fashion at each other's pink flesh, that which was usually hidden and was now so well-exposed.

Musk and sweetness spread in equal portions to cover Penny's face. She plunged faster, her fingers and mouth determined not to just imitate Nadine's actions, but to surpass her.

Their bodies fell together, their hips jerking in pulsating time as the high-crested waves of a shattering climax flowed over their entwined flesh. Buttocks plunged and breasts swayed until the last eddies of delight had shivered over their sublime bodies and faded away down their lean thighs.

'You have hidden depths, pussy-cat,' said Nadine thoughtfully, as they lay together afterwards. 'I do not believe you even knew you had such talents yourself.'

Beneath the long fingers that stroked so soothingly through her mane of dark hair – and those that traced imaginary lines over her taut rear – Penny herself pondered the same things. There was no doubt that she'd always been sexual, but these new practices to which she had only lately been introduced had never been part of that sexuality. Something had triggered them off, and now, once they'd escaped, there seemed no heights to which they did not aspire. Perhaps it was the wager, she told herself, the excitement of trying to seduce a man who so far had proved elusive. She didn't know the answer, but achieving the seduction of Alistair and the winning of her wager with Ariadne might very well be it.

The hand that had stroked her hair now stroked her face. The stark grey eyes met hers, though Nadine's look was glassy and distant. 'I shall divulge a lot before your stay here is out . . . tell you things, show you things,' she said throatily. 'So will Alistair. I hope you learn well, my dear. I hope you learn very well.'

Penny studied the sharply defined cheek-bones and the deep set of the chilly eyes before she responded.

'I'm sure I will.'

The gaze held hers. The smile was close-lipped and thoughtful, yet at the same time full of dark knowledge.

'Any and everything, pretty pussy, any and everything.' The voice was low and slow as poured treacle. Her kiss was warm and moist; again, Penny melted beneath the soothing hands of Alistair's sister.

Behind the mirror, Alistair watched. Gregory stood behind him, his eyes also caught by the scene.

'You just wait, you hot little bitch,' Alistair said grimly. 'You just wait.'

He said it almost as though he had forgotten that Gregory was there. It certainly looked that way to Gregory. Alistair's eyes were boring into the glass as though just by the heat of their desire he could make holes through it, smash it and leap through, drag Nadine off the bed and plunge his aching tool into the young showjumper.

Gregory asked himself why Alistair didn't take Penny when and where he wanted. Even though he had known her for only a short time, he certainly couldn't envisage her saying no to anything Alistair might suggest.

But he wouldn't ask Alistair why he didn't. It wasn't his place to. All he knew, as he looked at Alistair tonight, was that his jaw was clenched almost to breaking-point and his fists were balled so tight that his knuckles showed white. He couldn't believe that Alistair wasn't aroused. He certainly was. His cock was rocking against the front of his faded and over-tight, blue jeans, and beneath the blackness of his T-shirt, his heart flooded his body with rivers of passionate blood.

When Alistair did tear his eyes away from the mirror, Gregory could see droplets of sweat running down his fore-head.

'Where's Auberon?' Alistair asked somewhat curtly.

'Saying good night to his animals. He always does.'

Alistair nodded grimly before stalking off.

Gregory only glanced at him before looking back to the scene on the other side of the mirror.

He didn't care that Alistair was going to take his unrequited passion out an Auberon. He didn't care, because he knew Auberon enjoyed the sting of the whip and the abuse that Alistair would mete out to his naked body – indeed, he knew full well he would welcome it.

Gregory waited until Nadine rose from the bed, kissed the apparently sleeping Penny on the shoulder, then departed from the darkened room. He waited another ten minutes after the door had closed behind Alistair's sister before he saw Penny stir and smile sleepily towards the mirror. Even though she could not see him, he smiled back, went out the same door as Alistair had left by, and made his way down the steps that came out behind a thick green tapestry on the landing. Then he pushed down the handle of the door that opened into her room.

'Gregory,' she said in a soft and yielding voice, 'I've been longing for this.'

'So I noticed,' he replied in a hushed and expectant voice.

She laughed lightly and, in the dimness of the room now lit only by a few stray beams of moonlight, she watched as he removed his clothes, her legs gradually opening as the full beauty of his torso was revealed.

In the moonlight, he looked even more like a Greek god: the Apollo of legend, or Hector of Troy. His skin glistened and his muscles rippled. Proudly erect and rearing in expectation, his manhood stood but a hand-span from her face as Gregory paused and stood silently at the side of the bed.

Enthralled by its splendour, she lifted her head from her pillow, leant on one elbow and reached out to encircle the offering he had brought her.

'It's beautiful,' she murmured. 'Good enough to eat.'

'Then eat it.'

He tangled his fingers in her hair and brought her head closer until her lips kissed his throbbing crown. It reared in ecstasy, and, as though to calm its excitement, she flicked at it enticingly with the tip of her tongue whilst her fingers held him firmly. His flesh was as warm and soft as crushed velvet in the palm of her hand. Of course, her actions did nothing to calm his excitement. Like a live animal, it moved in her hand and leapt towards her tongue.

She opened her mouth and sucked him in until she was halfway down his mighty stem. Her hands caressed the peachy softness of his balls that hung like ripe and glorious fruit between his thighs.

'Let go,' he breathed suddenly and, to her surprise, took her hands from his cock. 'Sssh!' he added. 'Just do as I say.'

She let her hands fall and lay back on the pillow.

Thick red ropes held back the green-and-red tapestry curtains that hung from her bed. Gregory took these; as Penny writhed with rising excitement, he wound them around her wrists then tied them to the thick barley sugar twists of the wooden uprights.

He did the same to her ankles. Now the soft moonlight lit her body. She was spread-eagled against the thick bed cover.

'Now,' he said, kissing her neck and nibbling her earlobes. 'Now, don't be afraid. I am going to do everything that you need. You need only lie there and feel what I am going to do to you. It will be sheer pleasure. Is that understood?'

In the light of the moon, he saw her nod. 'Yes,' she whispered.

By the light of that same moon, she saw him smile.

'Good,' he whispered back.

From her bedside drawer he took a pair of stockings. They were black ones and, if she remembered rightly, they were trimmed at the top with black lace and red bows. But she wouldn't be wearing these, she thought to herself, not now, tied up as she was.

Raising her head from the pillow with one hand, Gregory wound one stocking around her eyes. Now she could not even see the moonlight. He tied it behind her head in a smooth and comfortable knot.

The other stocking he used around her mouth as a gag. What he did to her ears, she didn't know. Perhaps they were a pair of skiing earmuffs. All she knew was that she could neither speak, nor see, nor hear. Only one sense was left to her – that of touch.

She lay in her dark and silent world, knowing that Gregory was gazing at her helpless body. In her darkness, she tried to imagine what he was seeing and feeling.

Gregory was gazing at her. He was transfixed by the helpless beauty of her offered body. Vulnerability and the softness of moonlight had made her more beautiful than he could ever have imagined. She was naked, and her sex open to anything he cared to put into it. And that, he knew, was where he scored over Nadine. He had the ultimate weapon to put into her. Nadine did not have that. Alistair did, but seemed disinclined to act.

He put Nadine and Alistair from his mind. Now he had Penny to himself.

He ran his hands down from her shoulders and rolled her breasts in the firmness of his palms. Her back arched and her body sought to reach him.

'Patience, my beauty,' he whispered, his breath directed on her cheek. She felt that breath, but could barely hear the words upon it.

His fingers rolled her nipples before he kissed them and enjoyed the small squeal of delight that broke from beyond the nylon gag.

He lay the hardness of his chest against her absolute softness. Then he raised himself up on his hands and bent his head to nibble ruthlessly at her nipples.

Beneath him, her pelvis writhed. He understood what she was after; knew the hardness of his penis was heavy against her and that she was wet with desire.

'Not yet,' he murmured, even though she could not hear him.

Penny did, indeed, want his penis in her. His whole body was hot and hard against her, yet his penis was hotter. She wanted it badly, and in the dark world where only touch was left to her, the need for penetration was more greatly intensified.

His lips were hot as they travelled over her body and made her back arch more severely than before. She felt them linger over her belly, and felt the wetness of his tongue dive into her navel before his journey continued. Everything was feeling; it was all touch. Her very link with the world outside her darkness was touch and, because of that, her senses were sharper and her responses more intense.

Fronds of pubic hair were sucked into his mouth along with her flesh, and she rolled her hips with pleasure as his fingers opened her outer lips then furled back the delicate folds beneath.

Behind the closeness of her bonds, she whimpered. If she had not been gagged, she would have screamed for more.

Wetness erupted in her sex as his tongue flicked lightly over her clitoris. Her legs felt weak and, no matter what side she turned to, she could not escape his tongue, his lips or his hands. But then, she didn't want to.

Her body tingled, her sex was tantalised. Nothing remained in her mind except the sensations of this experience. In her dark, silent world, sex had taken over her mind, her being – her whole body. Nothing else existed: not the room, not the moonlight; not even Gregory. Sex had stolen her soul.

When at last it felt as though her sanity was under threat, he entered her. But, like everything else, it filled her being as well as her pussy.

Each sweet thrust made her nerves tingle and her body tremble. Slowly he thrust, then faster, then slower again.

Just the size of him was enough to blow her mind. She had wondered at it even before he had blindfolded her. His penis, she thought, was the one thing that bore no resemblance whatsoever to a Greek or Roman god. Like the copper statue that peed perpetually into the fountain in the courtyard, it was big and owed nothing at all to classical statuary, except perhaps its shape.

But thoughts about size, shape and what it looked like were being steadily overtaken by her imminent climax. She lifted her pelvis to meet him, the mound that enclosed her bud of passion slamming with easy precision against him.

She felt his hands cover her breasts and his fingers fondle her rising nubs and she rolled in delight. His stomach slammed hard and quick against her, and his cock, engorged with the blood of his own passion, filled her like no other had before.

Higher and higher her passion soared in her dark, silent world. She threw her head back, the only part of her body that could still truly move. Her teeth bit into her gag, and her pelvis heaved like a volcanic eruption to meet his.

It felt as if she could swallow him up whole, as though she were a very deep well around which his and her orgasm could echo till time immemorial, never-ending, always teetering on the edge of total climax.

Strongly and virulently like an explosion of dynamite, she came.

Her hips thrust again and again to meet him. She struggled against her bonds, her cries of release captured in the silky smoothness of her gag.

She felt Gregory tense above her. Then the throb of his release in gradually diminishing sensations until his orgasm was finished.

Not until he had repeated his attention twice more, and

dawn had pushed morning through the window, did he untie her.

They embraced before he left, the heat of his muscles re-igniting her passion for one last, more mutual liaison before he left her.

He had been loath to stay that bit longer, a slight nervousness entering his eyes when she had first suggested it. But once her lips were on his and her hand had captured his rising stem, his will was no longer his own.

Dawn had barely broken, but Nadine, as always, was up early. Behind the mirror she watched, grim-faced, her body still damp and naked from her early-morning shower.

'My, my,' she growled, her lips hardly parting, her teeth barely moving. She let her towel slip to the ground, and caressed one breast with her hand whilst the other folded back her shorn labia and teased her ripe bud to erection. 'But you are a disobedient little pussy, aren't you. But never mind, Nadine will do something about that. Nadine will break you in to her will.'

With that, she threw her head back and plunged her finger into her own warm depository.

# 9

Nadine was a great believer in sea water. Not that she was alone in that belief. Many in the past and present have praised its healing capacity and sworn by its ability to strengthen equine tendons as they prance and gallop through the waves.

The beach was two hours' drive away and, being that there wasn't a cloud in the sky and a warm day was forecast, lunch had been packed in generous hampers. Wine, milk, cream and butter had been safely stored in a couple of cool boxes.

Nadine seemed inordinately full of herself prior to their departure and would probably have continued in that mood for the rest of the day if Alistair had not informed her that she was to pick Sir Reggie's daughter, Clarissa, up from the airport.

Then her brightness turned to thunder.

Taking discretion as the best part of valour, and throwing herself into grooming, polishing and helping the stable lads, Penny noted the furrowed eyebrows and black looks and made an extra effort to keep out of her way. Auberon, perhaps by choice, did not.

It was only when Penny slipped into the dark humidity of the hay barn and heard the swish of a riding crop and the loud thwack of its contact with bare flesh, that she realised Nadine was taking out her bad mood on Auberon's bare buttocks.

She timed her footsteps to coincide with each stroke so the crunching of gravel or rustling of straw could not be heard as she crept towards the sound.

Auberon was on all fours, trousers around his ankles, and

Nadine was applying red stripes to his behind with all the strength at her disposal.

Nadine's usually pale face was fire red, and her steel-grey eyes blazed with light.

Penny held still and watched a while, her own breath quickening and her hips rotating as she imagined the delicious tremors of delight that Auberon was enjoying. But Nadine knew that, too.

With a look of cruel delight in her eyes, Nadine stayed her hand.

'Roll over,' she ordered.

Auberon obeyed.

Penny covered her mouth with her hand. Her eyes opened wide as she beheld Auberon's mighty member, proudly erect, a pearl drop of semen balancing on its quivering tip.

'My, my,' she heard Nadine say. 'I see you're almost there, my dear boy.'

'Y . . . es, y . . . es,' stammered Auberon as Nadine trailed the tip of the riding crop around his upright penis and over his ginger-haired balls.

'If I just tapped that one little opening of yours,' drawled Nadine, her voice laced with menace, 'that eyelet of passion, you'd come, wouldn't you, pretty boy?'

'Y . . . es,' stammered Auberon again. 'Y . . . es, y . . . es, I would.'

The cruelty of Nadine's sudden smile matched the look in her eyes.

'But I won't!' she growled. With that, she withdrew the crop and carried it upright across her shoulder as though it were a rifle.

The look of disappointment on Auberon's face was matched only by the sudden wilting of his erection.

Lightly touching her own twitching sex, Penny watched in astonished disbelief as what had been hard became soft and curled in upon itself. She saw the tears in Auberon's eyes. How cruel Nadine could be when she didn't get her own way, Penny thought to herself, and how much she must have wanted to go to the beach.

From common sense and her own knowledge of Nadine, Penny suspected something special had been planned for the occasion. What that something was she hadn't a clue, but if Nadine's treatment of Auberon was anything to go by, it must be pretty unusual and particularly special.

As she left Auberon and Nadine, she made a big effort to banish the thought that whatever plan had been scuppered today would be back another day . . . and with greater intensity.

But she forgot about Beaumont Place and Nadine once they were up in the horsebox and away.

A carefree atmosphere travelled with them to the coast. The windows were open and a warm breeze kissed her face and softly caressed her neck. Her eyes were bright, as blue as the sky, and she smelt of fresh spring flowers.

She felt cool today, shorts, T-shirt and trainers replacing the usual riding gear. Today, her long hair was plaited into a thick rope that reached just beyond her shoulder blades.

Around her, disturbed only by the breeze, was the smell of horses and leather, and the faint, but irresistible scent of well-muscled young men.

Stephen drove, Penny sat next to him, and Auberon and a beefy stable-lad with dark hair and a cleft chin named David sat next to him.

Before they had left, Penny had watched with some curiosity as Nadine had gathered the boys to her. They'd huddled in a group for a few minutes, with Nadine's long arms around their necks, drawing them to her like a clutch of this year's ducklings.

Although her curiosity had been aroused, Penny didn't let her being left out of the head-to-head worry her. It was too nice a day for that. Whatever Nadine had instructed, obviously it didn't apply to her, so she didn't even bother to ask the boys what had been said.

Today she felt elated, and once the briny freshness of the sea breeze blew through the cab of the horsebox, all thoughts of Nadine and Beaumont Place were left behind – or they would have been, if Alistair hadn't been following them.

Alistair never travelled in the horsebox. He always followed on behind in his chauffeur-driven car, a gleaming Rolls-Royce that had a sister Bentley in the garage, plus the black Porsche that Nadine drove.

The spot on the coast they headed for was private, and belonged, like a lot of other things, to Alistair Beaumont.

Steep cliffs topped with private woods of thick gorse and virgin birch surrounded the beach. A private road ran through the trees and a high gate was locked firmly behind them.

The beach formed an almost perfect crescent of yellow sand. With the sound of tumbling waves came the sound of the horses in the box behind them, nickering with excitement once they'd detected the change of air and the fact that the box had rolled to a halt.

'It's getting hotter,' said Penny, tilting her head to look up at the blue sky overhead and the fringe of steep cliffs around them, where seagulls circled and shrieked to the bright day.

'That's why we're parked here,' said Stephen with a wink, his lithe muscles swimming invitingly beneath the whiteness of his boat-necked T-shirt. 'Shady for the horses. Never mind us mere mortals.'

Penny laughed with him and tossed her plaited tail.

'But you're going to be hot,' said Alistair, his eyes raking over her peach-coloured T-shirt and matching shorts. 'You should take it all off.'

'Yes,' said Penny in an uncharacteristically clipped manner. Alistair had taken her by surprise. There was something about him today that was different. There was no furtiveness about his wandering eyes and broad smile, no perceived barrier between her and him. What was it, she asked herself, that was so different? She answered her own question: Nadine was not here.

She couldn't let this chance go. She must not; she had to take advantage of it. She pulled her T-shirt over her head. Her breasts bounced free, pink nipples responding proudly to the breezy air. Her sweat was sweet and tinged with a light floral spray.

As if the breeze had caught it and flung it their way, the two stable lads stopped what they were doing; eyes glazing over and pricks pounding against their zips, they molested her breasts with their minds.

'Not a bad idea, eh, sir?' Stephen said suddenly, his eyes looking squarely at Alistair, though sidelong glances played like the breeze over Penny's firm mounds.

Alistair stared for a moment before he answered. 'No,' he said at last in a long rush of breath. 'Not a bad idea at all.'

Penny, like the stable-lads and Auberon, took everything off. Now the breeze kissed and parted her pubic hair and cooled the warmth of her rounded behind, which had sat too long on the journey to get here.

To her disappointment Alistair did not take off his clothes, but his eyes were fixed on her. He made no bones about it, and the barest hint of a smile played around his lips as his gaze travelled from her bouncing breasts to the glossy patch of hair that nestled between her thighs.

'What about you?' she asked him as the lads bridled up the horses.

'No!' He stepped back from her reaching hands as though they might burn him if he allowed them to touch him.

She tried to read his eyes, then dropped her gaze to his pubic area. Disappointment made her frown. How could he be so different from the others? How could he not be excited by the aspect of her bare body and thrusting breasts? It didn't seem real.

She returned her gaze to his eyes. They met hers. They were bright, and his breathing seemed tight in his chest. He wanted her. She knew he did, and yet his cock gave no sign of it.

Confused and feeling slightly temperamental, she turned away from him and returned the smiles Stephen and David so willingly gave her. Even Auberon was forthright in his gaze as if his inhibitions had been thrown off with his clothes.

'Do you want a leg-up?' asked David, the burly lad with the dark hair and unusual chin. The first juices of arousal wetted his palm as he placed one hand beneath her seat to get her up on the bare back of the horse.

No saddles today. They galloped the beach bareback. Alistair was left far behind them.

The horses' legs splashed in the white froth of the rolling waves, their mouths straining against the confines of the bit.

Penny laughed. Stephen, David, and even Auberon, who had appeared a little distracted on the way here, laughed as the spray blew into their faces and white-winged, black-headed gulls cackled overhead.

The canter was fast, but the rhythm of its tempo was as steady as ever, the rolling slide and the horse's back warm, smooth and arousing against her naked pussy.

Out of the corner of her eye, Penny could see Stephen, then David, then Auberon, their cocks flipping from side to side across the horses' withers. Even so, she she knew they were stiffening as they rode; she knew the rhythm of the ride was having the same effect on them as it was having on her.

Droplets of sea water flew into her face, clung to her hair and splattered her breasts with a brisk coolness. Her nipples burst into expectant peaks, and her exposed clitoris bumped and slid along her horse's back.

All the while she laughed as she raced Auberon on one of his mounts, Stephen on another, and David on her own chestnut. She rode her grey.

At a fast gallop, they reached the end of the beach to where unassailable rocks broke jaggedly skywards and divided their private seascape from the more public areas beyond.

'We'd better turn round,' Stephen shouted breathlessly, his horse rearing as he reined it in.

Now Penny fastened her eyes on his unfettered penis which seemed to rear its head in time with the horse.

Just as he had suggested, they did turn round. This time, Penny did not lead the chase, but reined in at a slower pace behind. Responding to her own thoughts and fancies, she had an urge to study their gait, those taut buttocks and firm thighs bouncing up and down on the horses' backs as they made their way back to the horsebox and Alistair.

It was a pleasant sight to ride behind those broad shoulders and bouncing bottoms, David's being more hairy than the other two. As they bounced upwards, she could detect the faint outline of their balls hanging like ripe money bags beneath their meaty arses. As she watched, she was aware of her own arousal, and of the heat of her sex and the liquid moistness of her folds of pink flesh.

Portable tanks of fresh water had been made ready back at the horsebox by the time she got there, and David was hanging up the last of the hay nets for the horses to pull on.

She came to a halt and slid down from the back of her mount as David took the reins from her.

Penny looked around for Alistair. She couldn't see him. As if in desperation, she shielded her eyes with one hand, looked up at the cliffs, then looked out to sea towards the sparkling patch where the sun danced like diamonds on the heaving surface.

'Ahoy there! Up here!'

In the shadow of a cave where the sea had eaten the cliff, Alistair stood waving his arms. Beside him, a huge flat rock had been set with crisp linen, and the sunlight that tickled at the cave mouth made the silver cutlery and lead-crystal wine glasses sparkle so much that they shielded their eyes with their hands.

'Lunch is served!' Penny heard Alistair shout. The big beefy form of his chauffeur sauntered off in the direction of the cliff road, then he and the Rolls-Royce disappeared above the brow of the cliffs. Privacy was all theirs.

'Can't wait,' said David, with one last and covetous look at Penny's crotch as though it were the delicacy of the moment. 'I'm starving.'

'Can't wait for afters,' added Stephen, glancing mischievously at David and Auberon before looking at her. A burst of sexual apprehension made her rub the inside of one thigh. Afters, she decided, was something she, too, could look forward to.

Lemon-roasted chicken, crisp salad, fresh bread rolls and salty butter had been spread out on a low, flat rock in the middle of the cave. In a trickle of water running in mossy green bands over the rocks, stood three bottles of wine. White towels had been folded and left on top of the wicker-weave hampers in which the food and the wine had arrived, courtesy of Alistair's chauffeur.

Their bare feet having sunk into the soft warm sand, they now washed them off downstream from the lazing wine bottles, whose corks had already been removed.

'The feast is prepared,' said Alistair, spreading his arms and grinning broadly. His dark, grey-streaked hair was caught by the breeze and hurled across his forehead, and Penny perceived the faint aroma of fresh male sweat. A knot of delicious apprehension began to unwind in her empty stomach. It was a pleasant feeling, as though it were a ball of thick angora wool being slowly unravelled from its tightly bound coil.

In that sudden moment when his hand brushed his hair to one side and she breathed his maleness, Alistair's eyes held hers. He smiled, and again he looked her up and down. There was a subtle ease to the way he did it, as though he had all the time in the world to focus on her breasts and nipples which the cold spray had teased to ripe prominence. Droplets of water still ran over her tingling flesh, and her breath rose quickly and excitably in her breast.

Alistair's gaze slid over her belly and hips before settling like a homing pigeon on the burst of pubic hair that erupted from her ripe sex. This had swollen and moistened as a result of her gallop along the surf-tossed shoreline.

Visibly she responded to his look. Her breath quickened, her flesh trembled and she ran her tongue over salt-dried lips. She couldn't believe the difference in the man now his sister wasn't around. They smiled foolishly at each other, almost as if they were love-struck teenagers allowed away from home for the first time.

But Nadine had too much power. Even here, her long arm was reaching to touch both her brother and the woman she was saving him for. Yet another tableau was about to commence, and once the food was eaten and the wine well on its way to being consumed, neither Penny nor Alistair were inclined to do anything much about it. They could only be sucked into it; become part of it, like players on a stage.

'This is like an altar,' said Stephen, once the food was eaten, the dishes packed away and the crisp white cloth folded beneath the lid of the hamper.

'Fit for a sacrifice,' exclaimed David. His eyes shone brightly, almost wickedly, as they met Stephen's and Auberon's. With obvious intent, he ran his hand over the flatness of the rock.

'Fit for a virgin sacrifice,' added Auberon, his eyes glancing swiftly towards Penny before meeting those of his colleagues.

Tentatively Penny touched the rock. They could not know what she was feeling, that she was certain Nadine was here – in spirit if not in body. She stayed silent and prepared. Tentacles of abandonment reached up from somewhere deep and strangled any inhibitions she might still have.

'I don't know any,' said Alistair with a laugh, as he drained the last of the wine, glass in one hand, bottle in the other. Thankfully, his chauffeur, Broderick, was sat snoozing back at the wheel of his car having drunk nothing more powerful than a flask of instant coffee, so he was at liberty to indulge.

'Then we'll have to use the next best thing,' murmured David, his dark eyes fixed on Penny's bright-blue ones. 'An experienced woman will do.' With a sweet softness that sent shivers down Penny's spine and caused the ball of wool in her stomach to again unwind most pleasantly, he ran his fingers from her shoulder to her elbow.

Her response was immediate. Her eyes were bright and enthusiasm coloured her cheeks, making her body undulate with a rare subtlety. The wine got the blame at first until she actually admitted to herself that in reality it was *her* who was sparkling and full of hidden depths and after-taste.

Briefly she glanced over at Alistair who, by virtue of his more relaxed demeanour today, was visibly more attractive, and the sight of him was extremely arousing. Abstinence was not his creed. She could see that in his eyes. And yet, where there should have been a hard lump growing and throbbing against his flies, there was nothing discernible at all. The knowledge confused and disappointed her.

She did not protest as David and Stephen helped her up on to the flat stone. Her naked flesh tingled as much from growing desire as from the coolness of the rock. It was surprisingly smooth against her back. With a sigh, she closed her eyes. Food and drink had already been digested. Now, she told herself, she was due other things.

There was silence for a moment before she realised her hands had been clasped and pulled above her head. Hands also fastened around her ankles and prised them gently apart. It was a curiously comfortable imprisonment, especially as the third pair of hands, those belonging to Auberon, massaged her proud breasts and teased her nipples to even pinker prominence.

She moaned as she opened her eyes, and told herself that today was turning out even better than she'd expected, and so what about the wager? So what about Nadine and her whispered instructions back there in the stable yard? Everything that was happening to her she was allowing to happen. Lie back, she told herself almost hypnotically, and enjoy.

'Now what game are you playing?' she asked as shivers of apprehension and a fine film of sweat spread over her skin.

'One you'll enjoy,' replied Stephen, whose green eyes were boyish and his white flesh still attractive even though he'd caught the redness of the sun across his broad shoulders. After his lips had kissed her forehead, his thumb and fingers gently stroked her wrist as if trying to put her at her ease. Not that she really needed that. Just remembering the sight of the male riders' naked behinds and swaying penises when they had galloped back down the beach was enough to drench her sex with spicy hot fluids. He kissed her forehead again before leaning over so his tongue could trace the contours of her ear.

'Will you play with us?' he asked.

Her breasts rose and her eyes opened wide as they met his. Of course she would play with him. Stephen had a well-formed body made even harder by the strenuous work he undertook in and around the stable yard. His hardness would feel good on her softness. And yet she wanted to tease him. 'What if I say no?' she asked capriciously, turning her head away from his exploring mouth.

'Then you'll have to pay a forfeit.' His grin was cheeky, as though he already knew what her answer would be and, what's more, welcomed it.

'First things first,' David interrupted, dark eyes dancing, dark hair falling in thick waves around his neck. 'We have to take her virginity first.'

'True,' returned Stephen. 'Mr Harding. Take her hands whilst I take her virginity.'

Penny giggled and wriggled her hips suggestively. 'What virginity?'

'What cock?' responded Stephen, who, to her surprise, waved a long, smooth, phallic-shaped rock in her face. She eyed its thickness and ran her wet tongue along her dry lips. How dark it was, how cool it would feel. Her hips rose speculatively.

Obviously pleased with her reaction, Stephen's eyes glittered before he lowered his eyes and trailed the coldness of the rock down one side of her face then the other.

'Is this cool enough for you?' he asked, between hot breaths.

'Yes,' she sighed, her voice slow and just a little slurred; more so from excitement than the amount of wine she had consumed. As her imagination worked overtime and assessed just how the rock would feel, she stared at it with mounting desire and just a tinge of apprehension. It was a good width as well as a good length.

Her ankles, which were gripped in David's strong hands, were spread further apart, but the cool air that blew in from the sea did nothing to subdue the heat between her legs. Like a flood of early morning dew, the honey of her arousal moistened her and trickled like ticklish flngertips between her buttocks.

'Grip her tightly,' Stephen ordered Auberon.

She wanted to ask what for. She wasn't going anywhere and, anyway, Alistair was watching. Alistair was always watching.

Out of the corner of her eye, she could see him. He did nothing, either to stop this happening or to join in. All the same, she could see he was hypnotised by the unfolding scene, his eyes glazed and his square chin hanging like a half-open door. Occasionally, his tongue ran along the length of his drying lips.

But Alistair could watch if he wanted to. She was the centre of this thing, the sacrifice lying on the altar. Just the thought and the feel of it was giddily pleasant.

She moaned and arched her back, thrusting her breasts skywards as if meeting the body of an unseen lover.

With gently experienced fingers, Stephen opened her nether lips and started to insert the tip of the rock between the petals of her yearning flesh. She gasped, her breath caught in her throat, and she felt as if she were just a mass of senses aching to enjoy and be enjoyed. Just as she had supposed, the stone was cool – very cool – and her sex was very hot.

'Is it in?' she heard David ask.

'The first inch,' replied Stephen, threads of excitement adding extra timbre to his voice. 'I'm just going to give her a little bit at a time.'

Penny moaned dolefully and her hips rocked in expectation. Already, that one initial inch was not enough.

'Give me more,' she begged, and lifted her pelvis away from the cold surface of the altar.

'You'll get more soon,' whispered Auberon, bending his head so his mouth was against her ear. 'Be patient.' As if to reassure her, he leant further forward and kissed each of her breasts, his teeth gripping them gently at first before stretching them to their full extent, almost as if he were trying to swallow them. The wetness of her sex increased as her breasts strained upwards between his teeth. They seemed as unwilling to leave his mouth as he was to let go of her nipples.

'And now for a little more,' she heard Stephen say.

His fingers still held her outer lips and her labia apart. Another portion of the smooth stone entered her. An inch, perhaps two.

'And more,' he repeated.

She gasped as another portion pushed its hard and cold way inside her. The muscles of her vagina gripped the intruder as if they would not release it until climax had been reached and pleasure was all hers. All the time, Auberon sucked and licked her nipples, an alternate strategy of pleasure followed by pain.

'Lovely,' she heard David say. 'Let me have a look.'

As Auberon raised his head to see what his compatriots were doing, Penny could see Stephen straighten and David lean forward between her legs to study the penetrating rock and her penetrated sex more closely.

'Give her more,' David said breathlessly. 'Go on. Don't be mean, leaving her in limbo like that.'

Words totally failed Penny. She was lost in her own ecstasy. Whatever they did was entirely up to them. She was at their mercy, half-full, and there was so much rock still to go.

She saw Stephen smile at David as though there was some secret between them.

'All right,' said Stephen, still smiling.

'Keep upright,' added David, his eyes now fixed on her open outer and inner lips, 'so I can see it going in.'

Penny closed her eyes and moaned louder as she felt Stephen's fingers holding her lips open and the smooth stone being pushed in as far as it would go so its base pressed deliciously on her demanding clitoris and tingling nerve ends.

'Marvellous,' she heard from David, who, from his position holding her ankles, was leaning forward so he could see the invasion more clearly as it happened. 'Let me have a go now.'

Reluctantly, Stephen changed places with David. There was a slurping of juices as David thrust the rock more strongly into her willing cunt.

She cried out, certain that her orgasm was no more than a few thrusts away and rapidly rose her hips to meet it.

David's good-natured face smiled down at her, his dark hair clinging damply around his glistening skin. 'See how kind I am to you. I won't leave you in limbo, Penny. Would you like me to really make it feel good?'

She nodded automatically.

'I thought you might.' David grinned.

Almost in defiance at her restricted limbs, she writhed on the flat stone. The feelings that were tingling her body were snaring her voice. It was trapped in her throat, and she could do nothing – nothing at all – to let it free.

Gripping the rock with one hand, his other keeping her sex wide open, David nudged it in regular time against the dewy moistness of her clit.

'You're soaking wet,' he said, and sounded full of wonder.

She didn't answer. She was lost in a labyrinth of her own senses, her eyes closed and her will put on hold whilst the hands held her and the hard stone did its work.

'That should be about enough,' said Auberon suddenly.

His voice surprised her. Even though it was him holding on to her wrists, she had almost forgotten he was there. So had Stephen and David. Above her, they both looked across her and at him, then at each other.

For the moment, they seemed to have forgotten Alistair altogether. Penny hadn't. She was intent on knowing exactly what his reactions were. Twisting herself against the restraining hands and the hard and cold intruder, Penny peered through the crook of David's arm.

Alistair was sitting on a rock, his eyes glazed, wineglass in one hand and newly opened bottle in the other. Even from where she was, she could hear the quickness of his breathing. He was with them, but only in mind. Only his eyes was enjoying what she and the boys were experiencing. His loins were still held in check: with them, wanting to be with them, yet seemingly unable to be.

The rock was removed and Penny was helped to her feet. She began to protest. Stephen smacked her bottom in rebuke.

'Now, now. Naughty, naughty!'

'Now you have to play with us.' This was Auberon saying this, with an odd brightness in his eyes which she had never seen before. Up until now, Stephen and David had dominated the action. Now, with eyes gleaming, Auberon seemed to be taking over.

'Kneel down,' Stephen ordered. 'Mr Harding's right. It's your turn to play with us.' He grinned again, that cheeky, boyish grin that made her think whatever he had in store for her might be a lot better or a lot worse than it looked – mostly the latter.

'On this,' Auberon added, and with a consideration that she much appreciated, he placed the folded tablecloth on the rough sand. Obviously, she decided, she would be kneeling for some time.

And so she knelt, supremely aware that her climax had been just a few strokes away and that her nether lips were hot, wet with juice, and just begging for the finishing line.

The three naked young men gathered around her, their

bodies glistening with fresh sweat, their young muscles taut and well-formed beneath their unblemished skin.

Three erect penises were but inches from her face. They were all fine specimens, one sprouting from a nest of ginger hair, one from a fair and sparse covering, and David's standing strongly erect like a young oak from a bush of thick black hair. Between each set of thighs hung their precious sacs. How soft they looked, she thought, her eyes assessing each set and imagining which pair would feel like peaches, which like velvet and which like cream.

That for later, she told herself. For now, her eyes travelled irresistibly back to the three proud members, each one jerking with rising passion and determination. Each glans glistened, and on one a dewy pearl of pre-come sat like a precious diadem. In response, her tongue slid out from between her lips; her need to taste such beautiful weapons was as urgent as her need to see them.

'Take one in your mouth,' ordered Stephen, his hand gently caressing her head as though she were a child or a pet dog. 'And one in each hand,' he added, a certain hoarseness now apparent in his voice.

Even without the benefit of a mirror, Penny knew that her eyes must be shining and her face slightly flushed. Her eyes opened wide as she studied each one. It was as though three birthdays had all come at once. Three beautiful cocks were straining with anticipation, just waiting for her lips to fold around one of them and her hands to work on the others.

But this was a choice she couldn't face. She closed her eyes. 'It's hard to choose,' she said breathlessly. 'I don't want to upset anyone.'

'Soon fix that!' said Stephen. The linen towel that had earlier graced a wine bottle was bound over her eyes. It was cool, slightly damp and not unpleasant.

'This is like blind man's buff,' laughed David. 'We go round you, and when you reach out and point, that's the one for your mouth. OK?'

'OK,' she replied, glad that the decision had been taken from her.

Blindfolded, it was impossible to judge who was the first she pointed at. Whose member it was, she didn't know and didn't care. His helmet sat like a rich and tasty mushroom on her tongue. She sucked at him, drew him in, then traced all round the well-defined ridge that parted crown from stem. She had a yearning to take in more; to grab his balls with one hand and his stem with another so he could not escape.

But her hands had other tasks. Other hands guided them around firm rods which she immediately proceeded to pleasure, pummel and squeeze within her warm palm and exploring fingers. Each tip was wet, each length was hard and promising.

So here she was, knelt before them, and like the goddess Kali who she'd seen on Indian icons, her mouth and hands were full, though full with much more pleasurable demons than Kali's.

Even so, she was slightly disappointed. The first penis came fast and was closely followed by the next throbbing manhood to be placed upon her tongue.

'Enough!' she called, breathless now after two insertions and her own sex still aching with the desire aroused by the unyielding sensation of the rock.

'Enough?' she heard Stephen exclaim. 'Then that means a forfeit's in order. Now, work your hand on this a while.'

The blindfold was taken off her. Now she could see that the penis she held in her hand was David's. He tousled her hair as she rolled his stiffening cock between her hands and kissed its dewy head. Was this the one that had been omitted? She wasn't sure, especially seeing as Auberon's was still fully erect.

In a brief moment of panic, she wondered if Alistair was still watching. He was. She could see him there, still sat on the rock, glass and bottle now completely empty. He looked mesmerised but he also looked slightly angry, as though something had been stolen from or denied him. But her attention was diverted.

'I'm ready,' David said suddenly, and he lay himself out on the floor. She stared at his well-muscled body, brown and covered with dark hair on his chest, over his limbs, and thick as a forest around his upright member. It stood straight and proud from amid the cushion of dark, springy hair. Looking at it, the ache between her thighs increased in its intensity and her labia and pert clitoris felt swollen and almost painful.

David was irresistible. She had to have him. There could, of course, also be a bonus gained from this. With hope in her heart, she wondered if this little tableau would be enough to get Alistair going; to induce him to want her.

Without being told, she straddled David and held herself just an inch from his pulsating helmet. Then, slowly and surely, she lowered herself on to its rigid length.

Pleasurable sounds poured from her as she drew him in. She couldn't help but close her eyes, and even when Stephen told her to bend forward she didn't open them.

Breasts jiggling, she leant forward, palms flat on the ground. David's swollen member tightly filled her as she rode his rigid length. It felt as though her body was clamped to his; like two pieces of a stiff jigsaw puzzle, they were incapable of breaking apart.

'Take this.' Stephen's demand broke into her pleasant thoughts. Quickly she opened her eyes. His cock was just an inch from her mouth. Obligingly, she wetted her lips, opened her mouth and took him in.

Her eyes closed again once she felt his dewy-tipped and satin-smooth penis on her tongue. In the midst of intense delight, she felt fingers prising back the round hills of her buttocks, and stroking the dark cleft in between. There was a familiar touch of something slightly greasy and pleasantly cool being applied around her tightened sphincter. Perhaps it was butter again, the same as Nadine had used on her at dinner. Now her anus and its running cleft would be as shiny as her juicy lips, and both would be filled to capacity.

But this time it was not a thumb or a finger that entered her nether hole. It was Auberon, and he was using his penis.

Her gasp as Auberon penetrated her sphincter was silenced by Stephen pressing her head against his cock. His hands manoeuvred her head to suit himself. Her mouth moved at his bidding.

Burning heat radiated from her besieged anus, though shivers of delicious expectation ran in a swift current from there to her yearning sex.

At first only the tip of his penis entered her. She likened it to someone dipping one toe in a bath of hot water. Her muscles contracted at first and clenched the wouldbe invader in a vice like grip as he pushed further into her body. But then, as shivers of electric delight ran through her flesh, her muscles relaxed and allowed the intruder to travel further.

Once he felt no resistance from her, Auberon pushed in a little more length.

Now she was full as she'd never been full before. A length of penis throbbed on her tongue, another throbbed inside her, and another had entered her most secret orifice and was edging its way further in.

Sex and sensuality were smothering her senses and numbing her mind. She felt sex, she knew sex, she *was* sex, and wanted even more.

What picture, she asked herself, was she presenting to Alistair? But she could not see him. She could only hear his rapid breathing as the three penises thrust like welcome invaders into her body.

Beneath her, David shuddered and moaned ecstatically. Behind her, Auberon mewed, his fingers holding her buttocks apart whilst he manoeuvred a further portion into her tight hole. Her legs trembled, but he held her firm, pulling her hips toward him with each thrust of his pelvis.

Above her, Stephen seemed to be humming in unison to his thrusting, though not to any tune. It reminded her of the buzzing of a contented bee on a very hot day.

Stephen held her head steady, moving it up and down his stem to his own requirements. With swift, deft strokes of her flicking tongue, she followed the flood of his orgasm as it rose up the thick vein that ran up the back of his penis.

Beneath her, David's hips were slamming upwards with greater intensity. He, too, was nearing his climax. Behind her, Auberon yelled, his cry echoed by the wheeling seagulls, white triangles in a clear blue sky.

The power of her own orgasm overtook and surprised her. For the first time in her life, she had been full and her body had completely indulged itself in the experience. Her thighs shook and, as David sucked and rubbed at her swinging breasts, she slammed the last echo of orgasm from her spent and satisfied sex.

Alistair awaited the right moment. He had watched, fascinated, all afternoon as Penny had courted and submitted to what had been planned for her. He, too, had been so naive as to think that Nadine had been left behind them. Nadine was never left behind; she was always there beside him, no matter where he was. Penny would learn that, too. Did Penny know, he wondered, that some of her sexual liaisons were orchestrated by his sister for his benefit?

She couldn't of course. But sometimes he caught a look in her eye, a questioning curiosity, that made him think she might know that her friend Ariadne had recommended her, that Nadine was playing her like a concert violinist does a favourite instrument.

Now he could wait no longer. He had to ask her face to face, even though his penis would swell unbearably against the firm restraint of his rubber underwear as his eyes wandered over her body. But he had to know. So he waited, then he followed.

In late afternoon and following a dip in the sea, Penny went behind some convenient rocks to relieve herself. He smiled at that. It seemed so contradictory. After all, she had been studied most intimately by the three men who had taken her body so completely, so why choose privacy when it came to having a pee?

He watched from the shelter of a large rock as the sand dampened beneath her. She was crouching, her buttocks towards him. She'd spread her legs. It was a delightful position, he thought, as though she'd adopted it especially for him. In that position, her cheeks were spread slightly and her anus was exposed.

He could also see the dark, pink folds of her sex which hung rather delightfully, so he thought, beyond her outer lips. All in all, it was a lewd spectacle.

Although he had originally had every intention of letting her finish peeing before he stepped forwards, he judged that surprise sometimes yielded answers closer to the truth than considered replies could do.

'Miss Bennet. I want to ask you something.'

Her plait tossed girlishly and quickly to one side as she looked over her shoulder at him. She looked startled, but stayed silent. Her liquid still flowed, and the sand got damper. Now, he judged, she couldn't stop. She was in full flow, and even though she looked surprised, she appeared unwilling or unable to cease what she was doing.

She didn't say anything and couldn't run away in her present position, so he pressed on.

'I firstly want to know if you like it at Beaumont Place.'

Pert arse flesh and parted thighs went round and round in his mind.

'Yes,' Penny answered hesitantly. How was he to know that her hand was just eliciting the last tremor of a secondary orgasm from her swollen clit? Her hand continued, though her concentration was now somewhat distracted.

'You have no complaints?' he asked, his eyes dropping from her bright-blue eyes, and down over her back to her rounded bottom.

'No,' she murmured with a knowing smile and a twinkle in her eye as her fingers played on.

'Is there anything I can do for you?' he asked, edging closer. The huskiness of his voice intensified once it had struck him exactly what her fingers were doing.

Penny smiled. Here, she thought, somewhat selfishly, was her chance.

'As a matter of fact, there is.'

He didn't need her to outline what she wanted. Even though his prick pressed hard against its confines, he could not resist. He had to touch her, had to have her in any way he could.

His hand caressed her hair and her cheek then, once she had removed her hand from her straining clitoris, he let his own hand run down over her breasts as murmurs of ecstasy issued from his throat.

'You're so beautiful, Penny. So desirable.'

She closed her eyes and hoped, feeling his hand run down over her belly and his fingers tangle in her mass of pubic hair before teasing the head of her pee-soaked clit.

As if all bodily pleasures and reliefs were associated with each other, she continued to pee into the soft, yellow sand. Alistair rubbed her, then pinched her clit with two fingers so that its glistening head stood more firmly upright from its surrounding petals. Then he released it, teased it, tickled it, bringing her a delicious relief enhanced by her emptying bladder.

As she moaned, she closed her eyes and impulsively reached for his crotch. But her hand found only empty air.

Just when she thought she had him, Alistair had moved again. She frowned, opened her eyes and got to her feet.

'Why won't you let me touch you?' she asked plaintively, and cupped her pouting breasts in the palms of her hands. 'See what you can have if you want it? My breasts. Aren't they pretty? People have said so, you know. And my pussy. Look at it.' She lifted one leg and rested her foot on a two-foot-high rock. She let her breasts fall and used her fingers to pull open the lips of her sex. Pink folds of flesh blushed beneath his gaze. 'See how wet you've made my pussy. And yet you neglect it. Why is that? Please tell me.'

But Alistair could say nothing. He could only swallow hard as he stared at the pretty pink jewels she so selflessly offered him. How pretty they were, and how much would he like to get his throbbing tool into that delightful gateway.

With all the strength of purpose he possessed, he curbed the cry of anguish that lay in wait on the back of his tongue. What could he say? How could he explain? He couldn't, so he turned his back and walked swiftly away.

She stared after him. Tonight, she decided, she would console herself. Tonight before dinner, Gregory would bathe and soothe away her pains and disappointments. Tonight she would feel herself again.

# 10

Behind the deceitful reflection of the ornate mirror in Penny's bedroom, Nadine watched, her eyes glittering and unblinking, her mouth an uncompromising line. On the other side of the glass, Gregory's behind rose and fell in strict tempo and his balls slapped against Penny's upturned rear. His buttocks tensed with each forward thrust, relaxing with each backward stroke. How beautiful they are, she thought to herself, how they glisten from the oil Penny applied to them earlier, and how much better they would look criss-crossed with a welter of pink and purple stripes applied by a thin crop and the hair fine end of a riding whip!

Normally Nadine would be smiling. But today had not been a good day and, although she didn't doubt that the stable-lads and Auberon had carried out her instructions, it still peeved her that she hadn't been there at the beach to oversee things herself. She'd been annoyed that her brother had ordered her to collect that damn Clarissa, and, although he seemed genuine enough about the reasons for her doing so, she hadn't been able to avoid being suspicious. She had questioned her own self-confidence, asked herself whether he was slipping from her grasp. But, she counselled herself, she would reassert her control. Dominance was irresistible. Once its sublime sensations had been tasted, tribute flowed back to the dominatrix like the river to the sea. Today, its flow had merely been interrupted.

Normally, the scene now taking place on the other side of

the mirror would have been orchestrated by her for her brother's delight and her own egotistical satisfaction. But that wasn't true in this case. These two were acting under their own steam now, Gregory's bathing and massaging of Penny's body automatically leading to a frenzy of energetic lovemaking that Nadine was drawn to watch, but indignant that she had played no part in.

Nadine was not by nature a jealous woman. Her tastes she regarded as darkly plain, her demands simple. That was as far as it went. Simple they might be, but all-consuming, too. There was a single-mindedness in her that needed those same demands to be met in her time and on her terms. At the Beaumont stable she regarded those demands a bit like rules of the house. They were there for a purpose and the purpose was all her own.

Even though the sight in front of her annoyed her, she couldn't help her throat becoming a little dry and her eyes glazing over at the sight of Gregory's magnificent rump pumping away at the softness of Penny's pleasantly rounded arse.

She could see that Penny's eyes were closed and her mouth open in ecstasy. Her breasts swung in steady time with the tempo of Gregory's thrusts. She was leaning on her elbows so her nipples consistently brushed the rough weave of the tapestry bedspread. As they brushed the coarse material, her nipples reddened, and as they reddened, they grew in size.

Nadine, who stood naked in the small turret room on the other side of the mirror, could almost taste the ecstasy both were enjoying. Even her own hairless pussy ached and oozed with desire.

Hands clasping Penny's rear end tight against him, Gregory at last threw his head back, mouth wide and eyes shut. Penny was shaking her mass of dark hair in orgasmic frenzy. Both had reached their sexual nirvana.

Penny was insatiable and her appetite had sharpened since being at Beaumont Place. She was an apt pupil and beautiful with it. Not like Clarissa, she thought to herself. Clarissa wasn't exactly plain, but neither was she pretty. She was ordinary – perhaps even boring. What a harsh word to call anyone she thought, boring. Anything – even ugly, hideous, horrendous – was better than that. Poor Clarissa. And then she smiled. Clarissa was wanting and if she had anything to do with it, would get what she wanted, though she wasn't too sure whether she was really the virgin she insisted she was. Reggie, Clarissa's father, had promised her a special treat for her birthday and had implored Nadine to see it got done. So far, Clarissa, after a lot of false hopes and non-starters arranged mostly through her father's army connections, was still strangely unfulfilled. But Nadine would deal with that or, more accurately, Gregory would be used to deal with it. With mischief in her mind and satisfaction in her heart, Nadine smiled.

Increasingly obsessed with her own thoughts, Nadine lost interest in the scene on the other side of the mirror. She turned and looked at the outfit she had been planning to wear that evening. A nice choice, she thought, eyeing the black lace see-through kaftan which would have swept the floor but covered nothing. Nothing would have been worn underneath. But this, she decided, was perhaps not quite right for the evening she had in mind. Too soft and too pretty – and too exposing of her own body.

Instead, from the dark cupboard in the corner of the room, she got out a far more disciplined outfit, and one of her favourites. Once it was on, she surveyed herself in the full-length mirror that was strictly one-way only. Soft, clinging leather covered her body from head to toe. Black, of course, the collar was just a simple ring studded with metal spikes that caught the light when she moved. The collar was joined to the bodice with thongs of rolled leather, and in the bodice itself were two holes through which her nipples shyly peeped.

'Now, my little pretties,' she cooed as she rubbed each one between finger and thumb, 'don't be shy. Mummy wants you to come out to play.'

Dutifully, her nipples responded and stood proud of the black leather like two pink buttons. Her eyes surveyed the rest of her outfit. The legs were slashed high to her hips. A row of studs ran across her pelvis, and silver chains ran from beneath those slashed leg openings and held her thigh-high boots in place. The boots had high spiked silver heels and matching spurs.

'Very nice. Very nice indeed,' Nadine drawled with satisfaction, then held her head thoughtfully to one side. 'Perhaps one little finishing touch,' she said. Her natural sense of drama craved the unusual. From a drawer in a unit to the side of the dark wardrobe, she took a black eye patch and a silver-topped whip.

The effect was satisfying, though sinister. Smiling with menace, she placed her palms flat on either side of the mirror and leant towards it so her face was but two inches away from her own reflection.

'Oh, dark mistress,' she hissed slowly at the mirror, her breath misting the cold glass, 'go take your place in the scheme of things, and dance your dolls to the tune of your own desires.'

Satiated with sex and the smell of Gregory's maleness regrettably washed from her body, Penny dressed in a slim sheath with thin straps that she considered bordering on the virginal. It was low-cut, floaty and swept near the floor. Yet it clung to her curves and denied her rising breasts and curving hips nothing. Even the shape of her mons and belly was contoured by the soft blue material that a thousand silkworms must have beavered night and day to produce.

As she opened the door to her room, she glanced over her shoulder at her reflection and smiled. Her bottom, so recently pounded by Gregory's hot pubes, had a defiant and pert look about it. Like two pear halves, she thought, smothered by a layer of swirling blueberry syrup. Then she closed the door on the room and the reflection.

At dinner, she met Clarissa.

Clarissa's hair was cut short and vaguely fashionable. Her face was heart-shaped, but set slightly off-centre so that when she smiled her mouth looked a bit lop-sided and one eye gave the impression of being just a wee bit higher than the other.

Apart from her almond-shaped brown eyes, she was unremarkable. She was of average height, average looks and had poor taste when it came to clothes.

If what she had on was supposed to be suitable for evening, it certainly wasn't suitable for a girl of her age. Judging by the wide straps and elasticated waist, it might very likely have belonged to a middle-aged aunt of a particularly frumpy disposition.

Penny felt instantly sorry for her.

Even her constant wittering did little to endear her as a young girl on the threshold of life, but rather as a plain little sparrow never destined to be anything but easily forgotten.

The more Clarissa chattered, the more chance Penny got to study everyone else's reaction. Like her, it was obvious that whatever Clarissa waxed lyrical about was going over everyone's heads. They were commenting with negative words just for the sake of politeness but, apart from that, everyone seemed to be engrossed in their own thoughts.

But as her one glass of wine turned into two, then three, and then four, Clarissa's talk became looser, her inhibitions having been drowned in the warm bouquet of a decent bottle of Chardonnay.

So, thought Penny, beneath that drab plumage and Daddy's-little-girl image was a more exotic bird just ripe for the plucking. Later in the evening she found out Nadine was thinking very much along the same lines.

It was after dinner, when Penny had removed Reggie's hot hand from her equally hot pussy, that Nadine, her face a mass of smiles, invited Penny to leave the men to themselves and go with her and Clarissa to her apartment for what she termed a 'girly chat'.

There was something oddly Victorian and out of character about Nadine's request, but Penny went along.

Once through the heavy door that divided the more prosaic aspect of Beaumont Place from the private, Clarissa was silenced and Penny herself was overcome with the sheer opulence of the brocade coverings of the corridor walls. Vivid and obviously valuable paintings in gilt frames added to the private splendour of Nadine's very own domain, and gilt wall lights fashioned into frivolous bows and ripe heads of wheat gave reflected light to heavy mirrors and gleaming brass.

Nadine's very high heels sank silently into thick runs of blue and red Persian rugs, and the cheeks of her bare bottom swung at a sharp rate from left to right as she led the way, her cohort of Penny and Clarissa marching apprehensively behind.

Nadine paused, hand on hip in front of a pair of rich mahogany double doors. Her one uncovered eye glanced from Penny to Clarissa and back again. It was obviously done for effect, and the amused smile that played around Nadine's mouth seemed directed at the former rather than the latter.

'I've a present for you, Clarissa,' said Nadine, and, with an unusually sweeping flourish and a bright smile, she draped her long arm around Clarissa's meaty shoulders.

'For me, Nadine?' whispered the girl, her eyes as bright as a child at Christmas and her cheeks still flushed with wine. The more closely Nadine drew towards Clarissa, the more Clarissa recoiled, her fingers curling into the palms of her hands as though loath to touch the soft leather of Nadine's splendid outfit.

'For you, my darling Clarissa,' purred Nadine, gently pinching one of the girl's shiny cheeks. 'But first, you have to take your clothes off.'

'What?'

Clarissa's eyes opened wide and her face took on a deeper colour than before.

Penny raised one quizzical eyebrow and waited to see just what Nadine had in store. She half-expected Clarissa to say goodbye. But the girl, a hint of stubbornness squaring her chin, stayed put.

'Take your clothes off, little sparrow,' Nadine went on, her hands caressing a cheek before she took her chin between finger and thumb and looked deep into her eyes. 'I will help you, and Penny will take hers off, too.'

Nadine nodded at Penny. Intrigued to find out what the present was and what was behind the double doors – and knowing they wouldn't be allowed in until Nadine's orders had been obeyed – Penny let the silky dress drop from her body and fall in a swirl to the thickly carpeted floor.

Clarissa stared open-mouthed at her. Almost with reverence, her eyes skirted the creamy breasts and dark forest of pubic hair that was now exposed before her eyes.

'Come on, my little sparrow,' cooed Nadine as she undid the girl's bulky dress. 'We're all girls together, aren't we now?'

Clarissa couldn't answer. Her mouth seemed powerless to close. As Nadine stripped her of her frumpy dress, her eyes stayed glued on Penny's smooth skin. That is, until her own garments lay in a heavy heap on the floor.

Now Penny was amazed and Nadine looked amused. Beneath her dull exterior, Clarissa was wearing the smallest pair of red leather crotchless knickers she had ever seen. At the front they exposed a mass of dark-brown curly hair that burst forth from the opening like stuffing from a burst cushion.

Her bra was equally surprising. It was made of the same red leather as the knickers, but did nothing to keep her breasts in check. It simply held them in suspension, mere strips of wire and lace beneath heaving mounds of white virgin flesh. Dark-pink nipples and big areolae, stared menacingly forward.

'Why Clarissa,' laughed Nadine, 'what a surprise you are. And you still a virgin!'

Clarissa blushed visibly. 'I don't know what my father's told you, but *I* didn't say I was.'

To Penny's surprise, Nadine appeared either not to have heard what Clarissa had said or chose to ignore her. She seemed intent that all three of them entered the double doors.

'Artificial devices will never replace the real thing, my little sweetie,' said Nadine in a very matter-of-fact way. 'I think we need to rectify that matter. Penny, take her hand. I'll take the other.'

Penny did as Nadine ordered. She took one hand, Nadine the other. It was Nadine who threw the double doors open, but it was Penny who gasped more loudly than Clarissa. There, stretched out before them, was Gregory. Around his neck was a thick leather collar studded with silver. From the collar hung a chain which ran across the floor and disappeared into a half-open cupboard.

Gregory's eyes met Penny's before they drank in her naked body. His penis leapt with expectation.

Sharp nails dug into Penny's arm and Nadine's mouth whispered hoarsely against her ear. 'Now, my pretty pussy, you are only here to watch, to witness.'

Penny tore her eyes from Gregory to the cool, pale ones so near to her face. She saw triumph in those eyes. She also saw a kind of revenge. She turned her gaze back to Gregory. In his face there was no apology for responding so easily and so well to her naked body. Like Alistair, he seemed submissive before Nadine, responsive to whatever game she wished to play.

Beside her Penny was aware of Clarissa breathing more heavily than she had been. Despite herself, she felt her own sex grow heavy as her eyes followed the subtle movements of Gregory's rising stem from its glistening glans to its firm and forested root.

'Just for you, my pretty pussy,' she heard Nadine purr, whilst her cool hands caressed the nape of Penny's neck. 'This is just for you.'

Penny was so absorbed in the lounging body of Gregory, and soothed by Nadine's long fingers, that she barely felt the chain collar fastened around her neck until Nadine yanked the trailing lead attached to it. Now she was flat against the wall, breath knocked out of her.

Nadine leant on her, still murmuring in her ear, her long fingers stroking her hot flesh. Even though her eyes were drawn to the gleaming body laid out on the thick Chinese carpet, she couldn't help but respond to Nadine's soothing hands and probing fingers. Then Nadine left her side. Penny tried to move, but her hands were as firmly fastened as her neck. She had been so absorbed with the sight of Gregory's naked body and the touch of Nadine's fingers that she hadn't felt the steel clips encircle her wrists and bind her to the wall. Now she was flat against it and unable to move.

Nadine's attention had turned to Clarissa.

Clarissa was shivering, though it wasn't necessarily from fear or apprehension. Her big breasts trembled like twin jellies against the uneasy confines of her lurid bra, and the honey of her arousal added lustre to the inside of her thighs.

'Now,' said Nadine as she curved her arm around the shivering girl's shoulder, 'Gregory is here for your delight. You may do with him as you wish. Whatever you want is yours for the asking.'

Clarissa was speechless, and although Nadine was caressing her breasts – her fingers spreading in delicious sweeping movements across one then the other – Clarissa's eyes were as fixed as Penny's had been on Gregory's upright stem.

'Anything?' Clarissa asked, her words trembling as much as her breasts.

'Anything,' murmured Nadine in reply.

Penny wanted to shout out some suggestions, but her throat had grown dry and, besides, she sensed that anything she had to suggest would not be appreciated by Nadine.

Gregory glanced apologetically at Penny, before responding to the tug on his neck-chain and getting to his feet. He stood before Clarissa, nakedly available.

'Feel him,' said Nadine to Clarissa, her hand tousling the girl's shorn hair before running down over her back and sliding beneath the red leather knickers.

Clarissa's lop-sided look seemed to disappear. In absorption, she had become beautiful, or at least enraptured. Hesitantly she reached out and touched the hardness of his smooth-skinned chest.

Penny imagined the effect of that delightful touch on both Gregory and Clarissa. She clenched her hands, buried her own fingertips in her palms as though *his* flesh was burning her rather than the short and rather plump girl who stood before him now. Yet she knew Gregory was enjoying this, and knew that he was as much caught in Nadine's web as everyone else.

Clarissa, eyes bright and heavy breasts straining against what little held them in check, ran her hand over Gregory's hard chest, tight ribcage and flat stomach. It came to a halt just above the golden curls that surrounded his heaving penis like a gilt halo. Her fingertips teased haltingly at the mass of soft, springy hair as though she were making a decision. Suddenly, as though such a decision had been reached, her fingers disappeared in his crinkled pubic hair before folding tentatively around his firm cock.

Penny saw his eyes flicker, his mouth open slightly to accommodate a greater intake of air. His stomach visibly tightened as did her own. She was not Clarissa, and yet she *was* her. Each movement Clarissa made was hers, each touch, each feeling Penny experienced as though it was her own.

Penny almost willed Clarissa to make her next move. She wanted to feel his hand upon her breast, and her heartbeat quickened as she saw Gregory raise his hand and encompass one of Clarissa's swelling mounds. She heard Clarissa gasp, and felt as *she* was feeling. Clarissa's gasp was her gasp, Clarissa's murmur of joy – as his head bent to her breast and his mouth sucked at her nipple – belonged to her.

'Open your legs,' Nadine ordered. Clarissa obediently obliged. So did Penny.

'Go down,' Nadine ordered Gregory, pulling firmly on the chain that was attached to the collar around his neck. To Nadine and Penny's surprise, Clarissa snatched the chain from Nadine's hand. Her eyes were bright with excitement and her actions certainly not virginal.

Gregory almost fell to his knees, his mouth travelling from Clarissa's breasts and down over her stomach. His hands were clenched over her wide buttocks.

'Down to her pussy,' ordered Nadine, her hand pushing down on his head.

Both Clarissa and Penny opened their legs wider, although it was Clarissa who threw her head back in ecstasy as his tongue flicked between the hairy folds of her sex and cajoled her dormant clitoris into life.

Penny now only watched and waited, an unbearable tension hanging in the air. She moaned in protest that she was not a participant in this scene, only a spectator.

The soft down on Nadine's cheek rubbed against hers. Her breath and lips lightly brushed her cheek, but her voice was cruel.

'You're only here to witness, my pretty pussy,' spat Nadine, her smile half-cracking her face, and her eyes glittering with delight.

Nadine unclipped Penny from the wall, and attached a fine chain to her neck collar; pulling her to her side, she ordered Penny to her knees whilst she sat herself down in a comfortable chair. Although Penny's eyes were full of the scene before her, she was also aware of Nadine reaching out, and of the lights dimming. The room was plunged into semi-darkness. Only a pool of light stayed like an amber lake in the middle of the room to illuminate the tall, blond man and the short, dark girl.

Even though they were not truly alone, the very fact that their audience was beyond the pool of light and enveloped in shadows endowed the couple with confidence.

Clarissa, and, in her wake, Penny, gasped loudly as Gregory got to his feet and bent his mouth to Clarissa's nipples and sucked first one, then the other.

As if to remind her that she played no physical part in the scenario, Penny felt a tug on her own chain. Without words, Nadine was telling her to be quiet, and she understood the reason why. Just the sound of one syllable would be enough to destroy the fragile exploration on which the two figures were embarking.

Accompanied by more intensive breathing, Gregory pushed a yielding Clarissa back against the plush comfort of a fat sofa. He spread one leg over the back of the settee, with the other still propped on the floor. His hands ran down from her breasts until they slid inside each parted half of her crotchless pants. They hid nothing; her pubic hair and her pink inner lips were open and moist. Dutifully, and in direct response to the moistness before his eyes, Gregory circled Clarissa's clit before his finger edged into her open portal.

Penny wanted to cry out, but instead took a deep breath, almost as though it were she who smelt the heavy musk secreted by Clarissa's willing body. She wanted to cry out again when she saw Gregory's buttocks cover the yawning gap. Under cover of darkness, her own fingers dived to the moistness between her legs. But unseen hands, long and cool, intercepted her avid ministrations, gripped her wrists and held her tight.

'No,' whispered Nadine firmly.

So, with wet lips and staring eyes, Penny watched, yearning for the bucking behind to be above her hips, for the mangled cries of final climax to be hers and not the stocky girl with the military haircut and the lop-sided smile.

The pair lay sweating after, Gregory with his eyes closed, Clarissa with hers wide open. Not once did Penny see her look at Gregory's face. Her eyes were firmly locked on his prick which, although recently used, was once again rising to prominence.

Nadine's voice echoed in the darkness.

'So you've lost your flower, my little sparrow! Now,' she said, getting to her feet and dragging Penny with her, 'now I will let you see the other ways a man may use you.'

There was a deep-red hassock immediately opposite the fat sofa. Rich watermarks of heavy taffeta were picked out by the muted lights before Penny's hot flesh met the coldness of the material.

She gasped as the warmth of her breasts was cooled by the silky substance beneath her, aware of Nadine passing the chain that ran from the collar at her neck through the brass uprights of a fender which had padded velvet seats at each end and a cast-iron dog grate just beyond it. She felt her hands being hitched up behind her back and fastened with another chain to the collar around her neck. Automatically she opened her legs slightly, wanting Gregory to leave the side of the ungrateful Clarissa and slip his rising penis into her very moist passage.

Murmurs of delight caught in her throat and her hips undulated against the fingers that dipped into her cleft.

'You see,' she heard Nadine purr in that long drawn-out tone of hers. 'See how you and this man have aroused her. See how wet her pussy has become, that pretty pussy that so wants to have what *you* have had.'

Penny heard Clarissa move, wished it were Gregory, then heard the intake of breath and guessed Clarissa was responding to Nadine's invitation to inspect her damp and open nether regions.

'Will you let her have it?' she heard Clarissa say in an excited, almost reverent voice.

Nadine did not reply. Penny could visualise her smile, knew her eyes would be glittering and her teeth flashing white in her wide mouth. Instinctively, she also knew that Nadine would be shaking her head.

'Come here, my adorable angel,' she heard Nadine say.

Aroused in the knowledge that Gregory was moving towards her upended rear, Penny closed her eyes and tilted her behind just that little bit more.

'Prepare her,' she heard Nadine say. 'She's wet down here,' Nadine continued, dipping her fingers again into Penny's yearning sex. 'Transfer it to here. This is where you will penetrate.'

As Nadine's nails greased her puckered anus, Penny whimpered and writhed upon the red taffeta, her chains tinkling like fairy bells against the cold brass of the fireside fender.

Thicker fingers followed the same journey Nadine's had travelled. Gregory's fingers dipped tentatively, then more determinedly, into her willing portal.

She could not see his face, could not ascertain his responses, and yet she knew just by his breathing and the touch of his fingers that he was aroused and more than willing to fill her tightest hole.

Smears of her own fluid were spread between her buttocks, squeezed and pushed in suspended droplets into her rosebud opening. She welcomed them, clamping her halo of muscles against the intruding finger as it entered and lubricated her slim passage. Then, as it was withdrawn, she sighed and mewed with regret.

'Take her,' she heard Nadine say.

'Push it in hard,' she heard Clarissa say with rapt enthusiasm that would even, no doubt, surprise Nadine.

The warm nub of Gregory's helmet nudged gently at her wincing hole, almost as though he were asking for entry.

'*I said take her!*' she heard Nadine cry before the rushing hiss of a whip descended through the air and cracked upon Gregory's clenched behind.

As the whip landed, he burst through Penny's sphincter and parted her tightly gripping muscles.

She cried out. Nadine laughed, and Clarissa gasped.

'Pull her on to you,' Nadine said.

Gregory must have hesitated, or perhaps it was that Nadine didn't need any excuse to crease his skin yet again with the whip or crop which whispered menacingly as it cut through the air.

'Let me do it!' cried Clarissa suddenly. 'Let me whip him. I'm good at that, really I am!'

She heard Nadine laugh and felt Gregory tense against her as he pushed his prick through her tightness. His cry broke in unison with hers, but did not satisfy Clarissa.

Penny bit her lip as lash after lash sang through the air and landed on Gregory's behind. She cried out herself as the whip purposefully graced her own thighs, then slumped against the silky hassock when at last Gregory pumped his release and cried out one last and savage yell against her ear.

Penny was dragged from under Gregory before the light came on.

Outside in the corridor of thick carpets and vivid paintings, Nadine wrapped the chain tightly around her fists and pulled her close. 'No come for you, my pretty pussy. Not tonight. Just you wait. The main event will be something you'll never forget. But not tonight.'

Nadine did not allow her to dress, and the room she took her to – although round and obviously in a turret – was not her own. Terracotta walls were matched by dark and heavy silks that swept from the central point of the ceiling and ended in thick fringes around the tops of the circular walls.

There was a bed in the room of large proportions, with head- and footboards of wrought iron interspersed with gilt leaves. It was heaped with cushions covered in the same richly dark material as that draped from the ceiling.

Anticipation of what might be in store caused the leaden feeling in Penny's guts to intensify. It was further encouraged by the dull burn in her taken behind.

Nadine gagged her mouth and fastened the wristbands that she'd placed on Penny in the other room to the collar she still wore round her neck.

'Lie down on the floor at the side of the bed,' Nadine demanded.

Curious to know what was in store for her, and hoping it might alleviate the need in her loins, Penny did as ordered.

Once she was laid down, Nadine bound her ankles together with a pair of cuffs.

'Bend your knees,' she was ordered.

Penny obeyed. Her ankles were forced up behind her. A long chain ran from them, through her buttocks and up her back, and were also fastened to the collar around her neck.

Lying there, securely trussed and gagged, Penny noticed that the wrought ironwork of the head- and footboard was repeated along the side of the bed. To her surprise, Nadine lifted it and secured it with a hook to the headboard. First with her hands, and then with the toe of her boot, she pushed Penny beneath the bed. Once there, Nadine replaced the ironwork. Naked, gagged and bound, she was now beneath the bed. And yet it was not a bed. Not for her. For Penny, no matter about the sprinkling of gilt leaves that decorated the wrought iron, it was to all intents and purposes a cage.

Nadine was on all fours and laughing as she viewed her through the sweeping curls and curves of the ornamental ironwork. She poked her fingers through the ironwork, and wiggled them. She made faces like people do at the zoo. Penny felt like a trapped animal – naked, bound and mute.

'No sex for you tonight, my pretty pussy,' said Nadine with a laugh. 'From your little cage you will hear that beautiful angel, Gregory, groan as he inserts his prick into that little bore Clarissa's wet hole. You'll hear her cry out in ecstasy when his hands caress her bosom, and when he repeats with her what he did to you back there, when he fills her smallest hole with his throbbing muscle. Won't that be thrilling for you? Won't that be just delightful?'

Penny opened her eyes wide and mumbled her response. But that was all it was. Just a mumble.

Nadine tutted and laughed.

'Poor little creature. Pretty pussy,' she said, reaching her hand through the ironwork and tangling her fingernail in the clutch of hair which protruded so proudly from Penny's helpless mons now her legs were bound behind her back. 'I shall think of you lying here, neatly packaged, listening to everything they do, everything they say and not being able to do anything about it. How sweet for me. How dire for you.'

Nadine kicked the ironwork and laughed again before she left the room.

How long it was before she heard the door reopen, Penny couldn't be sure. A low light was switched on. Clarissa's voice was easily recognisable, that of Gregory seemed more obscure. Yet it shouldn't be. Wasn't his voice the most sweet she'd ever come across and the most outstanding, rich as dark brandy?

Warm words and wet kisses preceded the dipping of the mattress as the two bodies entwined above her. In her mind's eye, she imagined what they were doing and felt jealous. How hard Gregory's body would be against that of Clarissa. How soft her buttocks were, before his member divided them and nudged like a wary predator into her waiting hole. Yet, to Penny's surprise, Clarissa did not cry out.

Only once they had finished did she hear them speak more clearly.

'You gave nothing away?' said the male voice.

'Nothing, my darling. Nothing at all.'

'Did you enjoy beating Gregory?'

'It was very good, though not as good as with you, and I have to admit, I did rather enjoy seeing Penny have her bottom divided by his prick. Nadine fastened her pretty tightly whilst he did it, just like you do a mare when the stallion's about to take her. I liked that.'

Surprised and suddenly aware that the man above her with

Clarissa was not Gregory, Penny sucked in her breath and listened some more. She recognised that voice, though beneath the blurred barrier of the mattress, she couldn't quite decide who exactly it was. Yet she would. She was sure she would.

Her breathing settled as theirs settled and they slept. Three times further she was awakened by their resumed sexual Olympics during the night, the springs dipping and diving above her head together with the swish of a whip and the cries of an anguished and bound man.

It was an odd feeling, almost as though she were part of their action, yet no more than a residual part, a left-over thing whose attendance was not necessary to their enjoyment.

The day had been long and the night seemed too short: as short as the naps she managed to grab between the up and down movements of the bed.

Clarissa and the man rose at dawn and they talked about rolling in a wet meadow and him having his buttocks thoroughly chastised with a bundle of fresh young nettles.

During their absence, Nadine released her.

With aching limbs and a lessening desire in her loins, Penny made her way back to her own bed to snatch what bit of the night was left. She slept, and although the trifling niggle in her sex reminded her that it still had not received its just desserts, she curled her fingers into her palms and saved it until the time and the man were right. Gregory or Alistair. One thing she was sure of was that the man in bed with Clarissa had not been Gregory *or* Alistair.

## 11

For wet weather, three indoor arenas were available for practice, and outside three more. Those indoors had a base of ground bark and wood chippings. The others outside had sparkling green grass and were surrounded by a barrier of tall poplars whose leaves rustled lazily in the warm breeze. This latter arena was the one Penny was using now.

Consistent practice and unyielding concentration on Penny's part had combined to result in clear rounds for both the chestnut and the grey. Penny was pleased with her performance, and her body had cooled once Nadine had suggested she remove her cotton top and take the jumps bare-breasted.

The idea had amused and pleased her. She had to admit, the rush of air cooling her sweating flesh was very welcome. On top of that, the constant tapping of her bare breasts against her rib cage seemed to aid her timing. Nadine knew her job and could tell how to get the best from her charges.

Afterwards, Penny lingered with Gregory in the coolness of the stable as, in the absence of a stable-lad, he removed the tack from her rangy chestnut.

Her head was level with his shoulder as she stood beside him, aware of the masculine scent of his lightly sweating body as he reached both arms up to remove the saddle.

His muscles were obvious and inviting beneath the black of his T-shirt. Tentatively, almost as if they might melt before her very eyes, her fingertips lightly traced their hard peaks and moulded contours. As she did so, her tongue darted thirstily over her open lips. She moved closer to him and watched as the muscles in his neck tensed in response to the warmth of her breath.

He groaned as he let the saddle slide from the horse's back and into his hands. He let it slide to the floor, then cupped her face in his hands and looked down into her eyes. In response, her body moved gently against his, her bare breasts prodding, lightly skimming his hard chest muscles.

'You're incorrigible,' he said to her, and raised his eyes to heaven as if seeking help to avoid temptation. But there was nothing that could stop him falling or her catching him.

'I'm in need,' she whispered breathlessly against his ear.

'In need of what?' he responded into her hair.

'Of you.' Her hand slid down between their two bodies until it rested on the virile mound that pressed severely against the front of his faded blue jeans.

He moaned as though in pain and his breath rushed in a sudden torrent before he bent his head and kissed her. His lips were slightly salty on hers, his tongue firm and moist as it entered her mouth and met her own.

Maleness was hard, she thought to herself, and the smell of maleness was a strange mix of salt, of sweetness and the earthy aroma of a fertile field, of supple leather, of animal lust.

In unison and hand in hand, they left the stable and made their way to the most welcoming byre of all. The hay store was empty and heavy with the scent of sweet hay, and crisp yellow straw which rustled beneath their feet.

Just for a moment, she tensed and glanced apprehensively over her shoulder.

'Nadine's gone out,' said Gregory, loath to desist from kissing her lips and tweaking her nipples, but aware of the cause of her sudden hesitation. 'Once you'd finished jumping your round, she went off to town. Had arrangements to make, I heard her say to her brother. Something to do with some guy called Dominic.'

Penny sighed and shifted her hips. 'You can never be sure with her. She seems to appear when you least expect her.'

Gregory grinned and ruffled her hair with one hand. Silently he nodded, a boyish understanding, upturning one side of his mouth higher than the other. 'Up in the loft might be a good idea,' he murmured against her ear.

'There's no need if Nadine is out.'

His hands caught hers, stopping their progress down over his body. In that moment, it occurred to her that she should tell him about Clarissa, her lover and her imprisonment beneath the bed. But he kissed her, and in the warm abandonment of rising desire, she let it go. She'd tell him later.

'Change of scenery.' He smiled as he said it. The colour of his eyes, the fairness of his hair and the tight muscles of his lean body were too much for her to resist.

'Come on, then.' She led the way, moaning with pleasure when his hands cupped the cheeks of her bottom as she ascended the stairs to the hayloft.

They took off their clothes. Silently they stood eyeing each detail of the body they would shortly join with. He filled his eyes with her firm breasts, belly and strong legs, the clutch of downy hair that burst like a patch of exotic moss between her thighs. She eyed his satin-bright hair, melting brown eyes, strong jaw and powerful neck. Around his navel, she saw his stomach muscles tighten, each contour individually outlined, shamelessly accentuating the jerking muscle that rose beneath them from a bright cluster of golden hair. Behind it, his testes hung like two ripe peaches. His penis reared in abject beauty, as golden and firm as the rest of him and beckoned her fingers, mouth and the damp warm portal between her thighs.

His gaze ran over her body before settling on her black

diamond of pubic hair. With need flooding and hanging heavy from her labia, she shifted her legs slightly so her inner petals and its pert bud would peep from among the glistening curls.

He reached for the black band that held her hair and released it so it fell in a black cloud over her shoulders, breast and back. Then he lay her down, the darkness of her hair billowing out over the golden yellow of the straw. The straw scratched at her back, but was compensated by the pressure of his chest on hers, her breasts flattened by his weight and his passion.

She nuzzled his neck, revelling in his maleness, sliding her hands down his back so her fingernails could dig into the delicious hardness of his buttocks as they clenched to give his cock greater driving power.

He suckled at her breasts, his mouth and tongue drawing tantalising lines of sensation around the rich redness of her nipples and quivering flesh. His mouth moved further, his tongue flicking at her skin and dipping briefly into the hollow of her navel. When his teeth nipped at her pubic hair, she groaned and closed her eyes, raising her hips and opening her legs as his tongue darted furtively into her aching valley.

There was gentleness in the probing flesh, a sweet fragility as it flicked further, only the tip running from clitoris to vagina.

As her back arched, her hips rose more. His hands dived beneath her buttocks, clasping them tightly as he held her sex against his mouth. She moaned as his teeth nipped neatly at her mound, grinding her pubic hair as though it were crispy seaweed. He nibbled her outer lips before his tongue again flicked at her thrusting bud, then, like a small but sensitive penis, it entered her.

As if she were drowning in her own desire, her hips writhed in his hands. Just when she thought his actions would bring her to climax, he grasped her more tightly, his thumbs digging into her hipbones. He lifted her as though she had no weight at all, and turned her over on to her hands and knees.

Lips and tongue just as hot as before now travelled down her spine until they met the rise of her buttocks. His teeth nipped each round orb, making the flesh quiver and leaving pink circles on the creamy skin. She groaned, pleading with him to do more. There was an exquisite delight in such pain, a delight she welcomed. Then his tongue took over from his teeth and began to lick between her buttocks, his hands pulling each cheek apart as his tongue travelled along her glossy divide.

Mewing in a rather surprised fashion, she closed her eyes as the inquisitive tongue poked tentatively at the puckered ring of her anus, its opening like a tight mauve button that pulsated among the creaminess of her pearlike behind.

His finger took the place of his tongue, pressing inwards, overcoming the initial barrier before retreating and returning the darting wetness of his tongue to explore the tightest of her bodily orifices.

Gasping into the clean straw beneath her head, she dropped to her elbows so that her arse was tilted upwards. He held the cheeks apart as his tongue darted in and out, then sucked and licked at the puckered flesh.

She wanted him to eat her, to draw her in, chew at her most secret places as though she were some delicacy at a rich man's feast. Moaning and lost in her own hot pleasure, she raised herself from elbows to hands, unable any longer to restrain the swelling of her breast, her breath quickening as his tongue continued to explore neglected territory.

Almost with regret, he left her tightest hole and turned his attention to the fleshy lips that sucked somewhere towards his chin, their rich colour like a slash of pink silk among the black satin of her pubic curls.

His tongue curled up between the glistening flesh, diving again into her vulva, flicking in such a tantalising way over the folds of the inner lips that eddies of moaning pleasure spiralled from her throat on higher and higher octaves. She trembled at his intrusion, tingled breathlessly with the tickling pleasure of the light touch, the quickness of the action.

With one long, last flourish he took his tongue back where it had been, finally disappearing in the initial tightness of the cleft between her behind before he moved to cover her. A sigh of relief racked her body as though she had been rescued from some dire situation. She heaved a sigh, her senses dizzy from the excitement his tongue had aroused, then cooed with gratitude as he thrust into her moist cavern.

Warm and softly downed, his balls slapped in rhythm, hard yet cushioned against her smooth flesh. Penny closed her eyes and moaned her appreciation behind the tumbling mane of hair that now covered her face. Her breasts swayed back and forth as he lunged, each action knocking the breath out of her. She purred with pleasure as his hands played with her breasts, cupping them, rolling them beneath his palms, his fingers tweaking and squeezing at her yielding nipples.

Partly as a signal to him to attend to her desires, and partly because she ached for her climax, she slid her hand down over her stomach and between her legs. Her fingers probed and caressed a sex that was moist, open and yearning for expression.

His hand joined hers, cupped one upon the other. As he continued to lunge into her, their fingers entwined and rode the slippery wetness of her sex, stirring its fluid heat, searing its open lips with flames of rising climax. Her pussy was full of fingers, full of action. There was no way she could escape its intensity or its final rush of sensation. She cried out as a thundering crescendo of orgasm overcame her, soaking their hands and tightening the muscles in her throat as she gasped her climatic breath.

Tightly his golden pubes crushed against her as he throbbed his essence in final surrender. She felt him jerk, felt the seepage of her own fluid cling to her pubic curls and trickle in silent streams over her inner thighs.

Collapsed in the last throes of rapid breath and shivering orgasm, only their breathing and the movement of the horses below disturbed the silence.

With her back towards him, she curled up in the welcoming curve of his body, her back against his chest, her bottom cushioned by his now soft member and its surrounding hair. His arms clasped her to him. They were both sublimely spent. But they talked. Disjointed comments were uttered softly in hushed snatches as they gradually caught their breath and dozed in the warm security of each other's body.

He told her of the night before, of Clarissa pretending to Nadine that she was rampant to have him in her bed, then closing the door on him and telling him that she wouldn't tell Nadine if he didn't. He hadn't. He'd only told Penny.

Thoughtfully, Penny ran her hands down his back and traced the welts Clarissa's hefty beating had left on his behind. He winced.

'She lay on a few extra strokes once you were gone.'

'And you let her?'

He smiled. 'It had a most engrossing effect; one you would have approved of. A most impressive erection.' Then he sighed. 'The trouble was, it didn't impress Clarissa. I thought she was going to leave me with it. I was right. She was. Then she swore me to secrecy. Would only suck me off once I'd promised to go along with her plan.' He smiled engagingly and Penny for one knew she could never have refused him.

'What *then*?' she asked, though she already knew the answer. She just wanted to hear him say it.

He grinned. 'It was a good come.' He laughed, then kissed her.

'Then I think I'd better tell you where I spent the night and who spent it with Clarissa.'

He arched his eyebrows and looked puzzled. Somehow that pleased her. It was good to unload secrets, secrets that she didn't really want to keep. So she told him everything that had happened.

'Who was it?' he asked.

Just as she was about to tell him, straw rustled and voices mumbled in the barn below.

'What was that?' She whispered it.

'What?'

She shushed him.

'Have you really made your mind up?' asked a recognisable male voice down below them.

'Yes. Most definitely. I rather think Daddy's not going to be too pleased about it, but it is my body after all, and so it is my decision.'

The female voice was firm and obviously Clarissa's.

Gregory and Penny got to their knees and slowly crawled to the edge of the hay loft. There was a gap in the wooden casing to allow hay to be thrown down below. From here they could see what was happening without being seen.

It was definitely Clarissa. Auberon was with her, just as Penny had guessed he would be.

'Your father won't be pleased.'

Clarissa's laugh was short and blunt. 'Who cares? I know what I want. And so do you.'

'He doesn't know you very well, does he?'

'No,' she replied. 'But you do, my darling. Now, just to prove you really care, get to your knees and kiss me.'

In abject submission, Auberon did that, lifted her skirt and kissed where her pubic hair peeped out from the split in her leather panties.

'Now. Let me put this on you.'

Neither Penny or Gregory had seen the cock harness before. Silently, they watched as, once Auberon had taken off his trousers, Clarissa strapped the device around his balls and penis, pushing it forwards into one big bunch just as Penny herself had done on her first night at Beaumont Place.

Once it was in place, Clarissa took great delight in leading him around by it, his knees scraping on the straw, moans erupting from his throat, and the swish of whip rending the air when he didn't react quickly enough when ordered to pull his jersey off over his head.

Penny shoved her fingers into her mouth. Her own breath was quickening at the sight of Auberon's trapped cock, which was glistening with sweat and the first pearl drops of a white, milky essence. She was aware that, beside her, Gregory too was responding to the scene.

By the time that Clarissa had Auberon still on his knees but spreadeagled to the wall, Gregory's fingers were already re-exploring Penny's body.

Auberon's head was held fast against the wall, almost smothered by Clarissa's pelvis which firmly held him there. From where they were, they could hear the slurpings of Auberon's searching tongue as he pleasured Clarissa. In return, Clarissa was jerking like mad on the piece of leather that was attached to the cock bridle.

Knowing Auberon, it was not difficult to imagine what ecstasy he was feeling.

In turn, Gregory and Penny were experiencing their own.

Penny positioned herself on all fours over her beautiful angel, her lips sucking hungrily at his erect piston whilst her pussy hung in delicious moistness above him. As she slid her mouth up and down his cock, his fingers, thumb and mouth teased, pressed and pulled at her clit, opened her velvet folds, and dived into her welcoming vulva.

In time with the ample hips that pressed so forcibly against Auberon's mouth, Penny's tongue whisked from tip to sturdy stem, licking a tracery of lines around the swollen circumference of Gregory's prick as her head moved up and down with total abandon.

Just like before, his tongue was in her, his lips covering the velvet frills that enclosed the heart of her sex. Gregory's fingers spread her outer lips, then tangled in the mass of black curls that crowned the seat of passion.

Always the fingers moved, willing her to greater sensations as they caressed the fine skin of her inner thighs and the satin smoothness of her behind. She lunged with greater enthusiasm on to him as his finger traced again between her cleft, and ran with the juice from her seeping pussy to the tightness of the smallest orifice.

As his finger worked into her bottom-hole, Gregory's tongue continued to delight. His other hand rammed at her wet sex, juice flowing down over his knuckles.

Visions of what she had just seen fired her imagination. Her sweet ache of passion rose and flowed like lava as his thumb brought her to a shuddering climax.

Penny opened her throat, took Gregory in further, then gulped at the hot fluid that spurted in rapid succession.

Spent yet again, they listened now to the conversation below.

'Are you ready to leave now?' they heard Auberon ask.

'Yes, my darling,' Clarissa answered.

'Then we'd better be off.'

They lay undisturbed and savoured the last thrills of sensation; eyes closed, energy spent.

Penny rolled over on to her stomach, the straw crisp, yet warm against her soft belly and breasts. She rested her head upon her folded arms.

'I don't think this will go down too well.'

Thoughtfully, Gregory's hand ran casually down her back.

'Not at all. Sir Reggie won't take to her going off like that, and Nadine will be furious.'

Penny sucked on a piece of fresh straw and wriggled her hips beneath the warmth of his hand. Nadine had denied her sex the night before. Nadine had thought she had devised a sublime torture for her last night. She'd be none too pleased to know that her scheme had been ineffectual, sabotaged by Sir Reggie's daughter and Auberon. Still, nothing to be done about it now. She laughed offhandedly. 'So. Nadine will think I've been a naughty girl. And you a naughty boy.'

'Then you know what happens to naughty girls!' he said with a look of sheer mischief, a look she treated casually until he grabbed hold of her, rolled her over until she was bent over a bale of straw, then landed a few well-aimed slaps on her thrusting bottom. She squealed, wriggled, but could not get free. Her behind felt as though it were on fire, the tiny hole in between already smarting from the penetrating experience it had undergone both today and yesterday.

All the same, buoyed up that such treatment proved his affection for her, she wriggled with pleasure against her casual confinement. Her breasts slapped and rubbed against the roughness of the straw with each stroke across her behind. First he struck one cheek, then the other.

The tingling of demand tantalised her erogenous zones.

In amongst the pain he was dealing, there was pleasure – pleasure she would have more of.

'Enough! I've had enough!' she cried, although her mind was yelling the opposite.

'Who says so?' Gregory held his hand above her, waiting for her answer.

'I do!' she gasped with a wriggle of her bottom.

'I *don't*! Three more. All right? Do you agree?'

'Yes,' she sighed with a false whimper. Three more times the hand descended, stinging her flesh, reddening her creamy skin. Never had she been chastised in such a way as to make her enjoy her shame, enjoy being the opposite to the strong, dominant female modern society expected her to be – the one who always had to win and always had to be on top. When and where this change in her had occurred, she wasn't too sure of. She was just sure that nothing would ever be the same again, and nowhere could ever compare to Beaumont Place.

For the first time in a few days, Penny thought about the wager, the stallion and Alistair. The importance of the proposed seduction had lessened, yet somehow she knew that both that and the place she found herself in would ultimately be part of her life.

Now it wasn't just a case of actually winning the wager, but more one of getting to the bottom of his obvious desire for her, yet also his reluctance to take her. It had something, she knew, to do with Nadine. That was *all* she knew, however.

Nadine took a great pride in being in control. But she also gave greater insight into an individual's personal sexuality, endowing them with a more intense response to their sexual needs. As instruments of desire, Nadine knew which notes to pluck and how to pluck them.

# 12

Neither Nadine nor Alistair were very happy about Clarissa and Auberon taking off, but seemed to accept it. That was until Penny blurted out the fact to Nadine that she'd known from the day of her imprisonment beneath the bed the couple had shared. Nadine had become frozen-faced when she'd told her. Alistair was away on business, so he would not be told until later.

'He will not be amused!' snapped Nadine, venting her annoyance by lacing a whip across Penny's bottom, seeing as Auberon's was no longer available.

Penny knew better than to protest, and her wrists were tied anyway. Afterwards she enjoyed sweet compensation lying in Nadine's arms and shivering with delight as the tall woman's cool fingers soothed her burning flesh.

'My brother will not be pleased,' Nadine said against her hair. 'You have a lot to make up to him, in time. Bear that in mind. Even now his desire for you is enormous, dammed up until I judge the moment to be right; only then will he take you. He will pleasure you to distraction time and time again, and you will be breathless, saturated with sex. You must not jeopardise that.'

As the fingers stroked her hair, the image of Alistair and his potentially mighty cock filled Penny's mind. Now she knew for sure that Alistair did desire her – that he, the wager and the stallion would be hers. She was afraid to ask questions on what Nadine had said. It was almost as if one misplaced word would be enough to melt what she had just said to her. So she just snuggled down more securely and let her imagination run riot as to how much pleasure Alistair might subject her to.

To the Beaumont family, dining out did not mean pub restaurant, local amateur, and certainly not something hurried and served with chips. Dining out was something to be done with style and in the best place available. Tonight was no exception.

White linen and fine, clear glassware were the norm at a restaurant privately owned by a famous chef – by one as noted for his fiery temper as for his excellent cuisine.

Waiters hovered, all white jackets, slick hair and heavy French accents. Despite their eyes always being lowered, Penny saw the odd flicker, knew that beneath their dark lashes they discerned the outline of her naked body. There was little between her and them except for the clinging sheath of the red dress, a colour that flattered her glorious dark hair and creamy complexion, yet left nothing to the imagination.

Tonight her hair was fastened from crown to nape by a pearl-edged comb so it fell in crowning waves like a horse's mane. Although her dress was silky and very short, she wore thigh-high boots of soft red suede. She had protested to Nadine that they weren't really suitable for dining out, but Nadine, with unfamiliar humility and barely swallowed excitement, had knelt at her feet, pulling them up her legs and kissing her knees before they disappeared from view. As it turned out, the boots were well-suited to the dress. Both were red, both soft and pleasing to the touch.

Besides Alistair, Nadine, Gregory and Sir Reggie, Penny also found herself in the company of Dominic. His features were predominantly slavic; dark almond-shaped eyes – a hint of the Oriental. His hair, too, was dark and tied back in a ponytail.

Broad shoulders promised a physique well worth looking at, the sturdiness of his legs perceptible beneath the classy cut of his trousers.

Alistair introduced the man. 'An associate of mine, Dominic Torsky.'

Instinctively she knew Alistair was waiting for her reaction; a change in colour of her cheeks, an extra sparkle in her eyes. Very well. She would show him. If he wanted her to suck up to this guy, she would – and some!

'Dominic,' she enthused, smiling widely. 'How nice to meet you. Alistair has told me so much about you.' She accompanied her smile with a sudden flow of very obvious body language.

She saw the two men exchange glances. Then Dominic smiled – like a cat, intent on the bird he was about to capture or consume – yet she did not flinch.

'Has he indeed?' drawled an American accent. The eyebrows rose. The mouth widened further with amusement.

He was a man, Penny discerned, who was good-looking and knew it. To suck up to him would not be difficult at all. All the same, she cast a glance at Alistair, just to see how her attitude had affected him. His eyes glittered. Apart from that he appeared unmoved. Somehow that annoyed her. She determined to press the point a little more.

'Well, of course! Alistair is such a dear old thing. Always willing to impart friendly little asides, amusing details about his business and the people he meets from all over the world – especially from America. What part of the States are you from?'

The whole statement was a complete fabrication, but she didn't care. She wanted to goad Alistair, aimed to secure a reaction.

'La Jolla, San Diego. Not too far from the border and Tijuana.'

'Sunshine all the way, then.'

'Most of the time, honey, most of the time.' His eyes twinkled as he ran them over her body, his lips twitching around a faint smile.

Briefly Penny glanced at Alistair. He glared. His expression was unreadable.

Penny looked instead to Nadine. Nadine's expression was like fire: powerful and all-consuming. In an instant, Penny's exuberance dissolved, almost as if it had never existed. In sudden panic, her eyes fluttered around the restaurant. It was as if it had suddenly been pointed out to her that she was naked except for her flimsy dress and high boots. As her face flushed, she lowered her eyes, bent her head and studied a spot somewhere between her feet.

She stayed quiet for the rest of the evening. Though she was not invited to join the conversation, she was very often the subject of it. There were comments made about her hair, her very blue eyes and her very well-made body. To her acute embarrassment, both Nadine and Sir Reggie gave an account of the sex scenes she had been the subject of since arriving at Beaumont Place. But it was strange how her embarrassment disappeared as their words continued. There was a glowing admiration laced like toffee in their words. They spoke of using her, doing this to her, doing that; and yet, adoration and fascination danced on their tongues.

Disbelieving the compliance of someone who appeared to have a strong character, Dominic asked Nadine to prove it. Smiling, she turned her face to Penny who was looking down now at her cutlery.

'Open your legs, my pretty pussy,' said Nadine once the waiters were out of earshot. Those at the table listened. Penny did as ordered, aware that the hem of her very short dress was riding up over her thighs so her sex was completely exposed.

Nadine's hand tugged it a little higher. Her nails scraped Penny's thigh.

'Lift your bottom,' Nadine ordered.

Again, Penny complied. The dress went higher, covering her bottom, but exposing her cheeks and pussy to the coldness of the chair covering. There were sighs of satisfaction from those around the table. Napkins dabbed at the residue of wine that clung to smiling lips. In confirmation, Dominic came round to get a light from Nadine for his cigar. Inconspicuously, he moved the tablecloth and looked down into Penny's lap. Penny felt her face redden even more as he sucked in his breath. Briefly her eyes surveyed the restaurant beyond her own little party. No one looked their way. They looked ordinary, even conservative. Once he had looked his fill, Dominic ran his hand down her back and, without anyone seeing, lifted her skirt. He groaned very low and very appreciatively before he let her hem fall and went back to his seat.

'Beautiful,' murmured Dominic. 'And compliant.'

Am I really compliant? Penny asked herself. But she knew she was. She revelled in what was happening to her. In this tight circle, she was the centre of attention. She was exposed and she was theirs for the asking. When had this happened? she again asked herself. When had she become willing to bend to the will of others, and how could such a thing endow her with a greater sense of security than she had ever known?

'She still needs breaking in,' said Nadine amid a whirl of blue smoke and in a low voice that made the others smile with glee.

'Good!' exclaimed Dominic, as a waiter refilled his glass. 'Glad to hear it!'

Even Gregory, whose eyes had avoided her for most of the evening, appeared unduly excited and more involved with the others at the table than with her.

For the briefest moment her eyes caught those of the wine waiter. He was staring at her cleavage. She felt Nadine's hand run up her thigh and her fingers tangle in her pubic hair. She turned to look at Nadine. Though the order was unspoken, Penny knew instinctively what was required of her. She hugged herself as though she was cold. As she did so, her breasts kissed each other and bulged upwards. Her nipples peeked over the top of her dress.

The wine bottle shook in the young waiter's hand. He managed to finish pouring but, once he was gone, those around the table clapped and told Nadine, rather than her, what a success the action had been.

They left the warmth, dim lights and excellent service behind. Outside the night was touched with silver by the light of a glassy moon in a cloudless sky. The breeze was warm, still loyal to summer although autumn was just a month away.

Gregory had the job of driving. Alistair sat in the passenger seat beside him, Penny squeezed between Reggie and Nadine at the back, and the headlights of Dominic's hired Range Rover shone into the back window.

Street lights and buildings were soon left behind as they entered the countryside, dark blankets pierced only with the odd island of farmhouse or cottage light.

Nadine kissed her ear. Rich breath assaulted her nostrils at the same time as the long fingers circled over her bare knee and crept upwards beneath the short red dress. 'Open your legs wider, pussy-cat,' she ordered, pulling Penny's knee towards her.

Mellowed to resignation by the heady mix of old wine and soft caresses, she did as ordered. Her right knee was pulled open by Nadine's hand, her left by Reggie's. Now there was no table to hide under.

Their hands pushed under her dress, folding it upwards so

the sweet drift of her musky scent escaped to the night. Nadine's hand on the right and Reggie's on the left began to caress the soft skin of her inner thighs. The car stopped suddenly, but the caresses did not. Gregory got out of the car. Through the windscreen, she could see him unlocking a high wrought-iron gate. Stark letters on a dark sign shouted *PRIVATE. Trespassers will be prosecuted, if not shot*. They drove through. Gregory got out again and locked the gate behind them. The car began to bounce along a roughly gravelled path. At times the moon's light was intercepted by black battalions of fir and pine which stood like silent sentinels at the side of the road.

Each hand climbed higher up the soft skin of her inner thighs, which were now wide open. Hot lips mouthed at her neck and breathed moist breath against her ears. Her own arms spread along the back of the seat, and she viewed via the mirror the spark of excitement in the eyes of Alistair Beaumont. Her own eyes narrowed as whispers of blissful rapture issued freely from her lips.

As their prying fingers explored her, their free hands pulled down the bodice of her strapless dress until her breasts popped forward, exposed to the night and to their sucking mouths.

Unable to control her own delighted reactions, she moaned as the two hands prodded at her flooding pussy. Nadine's four fingers held one furry lip open, Reggie's four fingers the other. Two thumbs – one long and tipped with black nail varnish, the other, thicker and cleanly blunt – were positioned either side of her straining pink button, both squeezing towards the other.

Muffling her cries into her shoulder, she threw her head back and closed her eyes. Sir Reggie and Nadine took as much delight in watching her reactions as they did in assaulting her.

'You are so wet,' cooed Nadine close to her ear before dropping once again to suckle her hardening nipples. Her lips sucked at it, her teeth held it, pulled it hard and long to the point where

Penny wanted to scream. But she didn't scream. She bit her lip, held her voice and let whatever was happening to her happen without protest.

Alistair, too, was watching, and even from here she could hear the quickness of his breathing; she could almost taste just how much he wanted her.

Through half-closed eyes, she saw him turn in his seat. She felt the intensity of his gaze on her face before his eyes dropped to the two heads sucking at her breasts, which then dropped again. He gasped, almost in agony, as he stared at her pink nether-lips that were held so open, her sex so exposed.

Penny felt no shame in him looking at her open sex, the glistening and reddening of her clitoris as the thumbs of Nadine and Reggie squeezed it to full prominence and coaxed it out of the protection of its folded hood. She wanted him to look, wanted to please him, arouse him. How could he not be aroused when she was being so exposed, so used?

Just when she thought the sucking mouths and probing thumbs would bring her to climax, the car stopped and the action ceased.

She started to pull her bodice back up over her breasts. Alistair's trembling voice stopped her.

'No. Leave your breasts exposed. It's a warm night.'

'A very warm night,' added Nadine before nibbling one last time at one of Penny's already red and stretched nipples. 'One moment,' she ordered suddenly.

From the seat beside her, Nadine brought out a collar. Even in the dimness of the car, Penny could see it was made of leather, but covered with velvet and set with what looked like diamonds, but were more likely rhinestones.

'For you, pretty pussy,' said Nadine as she kissed Penny's cheeks and fastened the collar around her neck with a strong buckle. 'And this,' she said, 'is for me.'

A chain was fastened to the collar and attached to the thick leather bracelet that Nadine was wearing.

As usual Nadine's outfit was black, but strangely unprepossessing for her. Suddenly she took it off. Beneath it was something more to her style, similar to the sort of thing Roman gladiators or charioteers had worn, except that, over the metal breastplate, Nadine's nipples protruded, rouged bright red and very prominent.

'Follow me,' she said to Penny, whose dress was still wound down to her waist, its hem high and showing her rounded bottom and naked sex. It was nothing much more than a red band around her middle that just happened to match the high boots she wore.

The heels of her red suede boots sank into the soft ground but, once Nadine guided her to the path, her step was sure, though somewhat artificial; a bit like a ballerina going on points for the first time.

Chain tugging at her collar, her breasts, bottom and sex exposed, Penny followed Nadine, but raised her hands to cover her breasts as Dominic's car drew in behind them.

'Uncover yourself, girl,' barked Alistair. 'Nadine!' he added, turning on his sister as though she had been careless. Sudden panic registered on Nadine's face before her usual self-control returned.

'Hands on hips, my little filly!' Nadine exclaimed, and Penny wondered just for a moment why she was suddenly a 'filly' instead of the usual 'pretty pussy'. In confirmation, she felt the sting of a light riding whip across her bottom and was vaguely aware that Nadine had been wearing it at her waist. She yelped with surprise though the heat of the stroke was taken by the night breeze. But she obeyed and rested her hands on her hips. Now, what with her careful steps and her hands on her hips, she knew she was swaggering provocatively, her bottom swaying and her breasts pointing steadfastly forward, nipples raised deliciously by the night air. The night, she told herself, belonged to her no matter what might happen. And what a beautiful night it was. Crisp scents of pine, wild flowers and earthy fern acted as a natural aphrodisiac to her inborn sensuality. Silver moonlight gave sharp outlines to the nodding pines and to the figures and objects around her. It added grandeur to what was plain; magnificence to what was ordinary.

'Take your dress off,' ordered Alistair.

She hesitated, her hands hovering over her breasts and her eyes flitting between the handsome, steadfastly staring Dominic and the powerful presence of Alistair.

'Off, pretty pussy.' Nadine's hands on one side, Reggie's on the other and her dress was around her ankles, her skin translucent in the moonlight. She leant her bottom against a tree as they pulled the dress off over her feet; the roughness of the trunk scratched her soft cheeks.

Her hands hung by her sides, her fingers folding into her palms. Not wishing to ascertain her fate in their eyes, she stared down at the length of her long red boots.

She thought of Nadine not being pleased about Clarissa and Auberon; about Gregory and her. What was it she had said? You have to be broken, like a colt or a filly. Earlier, back there when they had got out of the car, she had called her a filly.

A pleasant thought came to her head and filled her with excitement. Tonight could be it. Tonight she might very well have Alistair. It had to be. If it wasn't tonight, then the time was not far off. Triumph was in sight.

'Let's walk.' Again, Alistair had taken control. Tonight, he was like a Roman emperor in charge of the games. Nadine, if her attitude and attire were anything to go by, was the ringmaster, the intermediary between those who entertained and him who was to be entertained.

The path through the trees was firm at first, then softer as high trees hid the moonlight. The ground gave slightly under her heels, and wisps of long grass tickled her thighs.

Under cover of darkness, unseen hands caressed her body as she walked. Even without the hands, the experience of walking naked except for a pair of high leather boots through a woodland in the night air caused havoc to her senses. Half with the sensation of fresh air over her skin, and half with the experience of walking naked among others still clothed, Penny's nipples thrust forward expectantly, and that familiar sweet ache arose between her legs. Whatever they might expect of her, she expected much of herself. Soon, her arousal would be undeniable. Her flesh quivered, and honey dew seeped from her sex and spread like silver threads through the darkness of her pubic bush.

The trees at last gave way to a circular clearing where the moon bathed the grass with its crystal glow.

Penny, her breasts rising with her breath, made a strong effort to focus her eyes as Nadine tugged her forward. The impression that she was entering an arena was very strong, and stronger when she espied what looked like fences around its perimeter. None of the fences were more than three feet high, low enough for a pony or even a human. And that, she realised, was what they were for. Not an equine jumper, but a human one.

'Very nice spot you've got here, Alistair old buddy,' she heard Dominic say. 'Nice fences. Cute little filly.'

'Here we go, my pretty pussy,' said a familiar voice. 'Here's your big chance.' The words were hushed.

The men had formed a half-circle in front of her, whilst Nadine placed something over Penny's head. She started, realising it was a bridle that had been fashioned for a human head. In case of protest – of which she gave no sign – Dominic's strong hands grabbed Penny's and held them behind her as Nadine strapped the bridle over her head and pushed the metal bit between her teeth. The bridle had blinkers attached to it. She could only look straight ahead.

Dominic kissed her ear. 'Steady girl. You'll be all the better for this. All the better.'

She calmed, remembering that the sort of words he was using were not dissimilar to those she used on her own horses when she had broken them in to the showjumping ring. Anyway, just the closeness of Dominic was a kind of tranquilliser. He smelt good; the richness of cloth and his maleness combined to form a natural aphrodisiac.

Her hands were bound and fastened high behind her back, then clipped to the velvet-covered rhinestone collar which was still around her neck.

The coldness of the bit was hard upon her tongue. The blinkers had ties hanging from them in case they wished to blindfold her. These were left untied. Thankfully, she could still see most of what was going on, though she was incredibly constrained, restricted by a harness more usually used on horses.

More leather with a chain hanging down the front was fastened over her shoulders, fashioned like the outline of a normal bra but having no cups. Her breasts were pushed up and forward by its circling of leather. She gasped as it was tightened beneath her breasts so that they were held obscenely high. She gasped again as the shoulder-straps were adjusted so her breasts looked rounder and thrust out even more. She watched as Nadine's supple fingers teased at her nipples, then pulled them out so they were obscenely dominant, darkly pink in the light of the moon. The chain which hung from each shoulder was left dangling. Then Nadine brought it up before Penny's eyes.

'See?' she said with delight, her usual cheroot stuck in the corner of her mouth. 'Nipple clamps.'

Penny saw. They appeared to be made of brass, like the chain. Nadine opened and closed the clamps in her fingers. They were reminiscent of bulldog clips used to grip paper together. She winced as they gripped her nipples, her cry of anguish lost in the coldness of the bit that lay so heavy on her tongue.

Something else was clipped on to the collar that encircled her neck. She couldn't see what. His eyes shining almost with reverence, she saw Gregory hand Dominic the lunging whip and knew immediately what was expected of her. In Dominic's other hand, he held the end of the lead rein that had been clipped to her collar. She would be urged to circle him, persuaded with the aid of the lunging whip. Her stomach tightened against itself and shivers of apprehension sent goose bumps over her skin.

'Walk on.' The voice was Dominic's. He stood about twelve feet away from her in the middle of the ring, a usual distance when lunging a green horse in a practice ring over jumps. The lunge whip easily reached, thick at the end where it was held in the hand and tapering to extreme thinness at the other. Its thin end tapped gently against her buttocks. It stung, and she held her breath. She walked where he directed, about ten feet in front of the first obstacle. There was no way of knowing where everyone else was, the blinkers shielded her side-view and prevented her seeing them. She could only look straight ahead and fasten her eyes upon the job in hand; the jump that came up to meet her. Now she knew how her horses felt.

'Trot.' The fine thread of the whip end laced enticingly over her behind and a cry of surprise caught in her throat. Her breasts jiggled, held tight as they were in their casing of leather.

She sprang over the first obstacle on command, the tail end of the whip assisting her concentration as it spread again over her buttocks. She stumbled a little on landing, but righted herself, glad that the boots she was wearing had such a good grip.

'Higher this time,' cried Dominic. The sting of the whip was more intense. She'd received a reprimand, and although a fine film of sweat broke out over her skin, her flesh tingled in welcome. Strangely enough, she had a pride in what she was doing, what she had achieved. She, too, could jump with or without the whip, though the whip did add a certain piquancy to the achievement.

Another fence was cleared, a higher one. This time, she made no mistake, but knew it would not matter. She tensed the cheeks of her behind waiting for the inevitable, welcoming the warmth and the admiration of her compatriots with each succeeding sting on her flesh. This time, the whip stung more, but her cry was lost in the rush of air, her tongue trapped beneath the bit. Three more jumps were all cleared, yet all were accompanied by the stinging of the whip.

How red her bottom must be by now. It was warm. That, at least, she *could* feel. Would its pinkness be easily seen in the whiteness of moonlight? Probably it would. That was really, she decided, what they were applauding, what they were admiring. Not her skill on jumping the fences, but the increasing response of her creamy flesh to the stinging rebuke of the lunging whip. She was rising to the whip as though she were throwing it off and tossing its torture aside. Applause greeted her clearing of the last jump. Hands patted her red rump, as much to feel its heat as for congratulation.

'Now. Shall we try her on drive?' Murmurs of agreement greeted Dominic's suggestion. Penny tensed, her breasts starting to rise and fall more swiftly. Did they really mean what she thought they meant? To drive a horse meant to break him to harness. For that they would need a cart or chariot. But there was nothing here. Only the jumps.

'It's folded up back in Dom's car. Can someone come and fetch it with me?' It was Nadine who ordered Gregory to accompany her.

Penny heard them return a few minutes later.

'Cover her eyes. Saves her worrying about the new harness.' Alistair said that. It seemed to be him who wanted her blindfolded. Initial panic was overridden by curiosity. How would it feel to be driven at his command, to be his beast of burden, his creature in harness? The closing of the blinkers over her eyes was all part of it. He was denying her knowledge, taking all as his enjoyment alone. And Nadine, as usual, was in charge of it all. It was her long, cool fingers that tied the blinkers together above Penny's nose. A leather belt was fastened around Penny's waist. She felt another piece dangling from it at the front, then hands pulling it through her legs.

'Open your legs, pretty pussy. Let's see what we've got.'

Penny obliged, aware that, despite her leather restraints, her sex was moist from the excesses of her own imagination. Her breath was sharp as some protrusion on the leather was pushed into her vagina. It felt solid and roughly the size of a medium erection. Despite crying out, she took it in. The leather thong continued to be pulled through her legs.

'Bend over, pussy-cat.'

A large heavy hand on her head – it could only be male – forced her head down so her rear was up. She was highly aware of the intruder in her sex, so much so that she wriggled against it, all else forgotten.

'A little oil I think.' The voice was Reggie's and brought her back to reality. She felt the fatness of his finger rubbing oil around her anus, diving in to lubricate her more fully. She groaned as he did it, her knees bending as he pushed it in, her head pushing against the hand that held her steady.

She gasped, her head firmly held as the cheeks of her bottom were divided, the leather brought up and another protrusion – smaller than the one she enjoyed in her vagina – pushed into her rear orifice. It might not have been quite as big as the other, but it was bigger than the finger that had oiled that same hole. Once both protrusions were firmly embedded in her body, then the leather strap was buckled tightly into the belt that circled her waist, her head was released and she could straighten up.

Penny groaned, and her breasts rose and fell with her quickened breathing. She could see nothing, but imagined what she looked like from the feeling her constraints gave her.

The strap that ran from her leather belt divided the fleshy lips of her sex. The muscles of her open sex and invaded anus constricted against the imitation cocks. The cheeks of her bottom were separated, made more rounded by the leather thong, which she guessed was strapped tightly into the belt around her waist.

Because she could not see what they had done, her senses were heightened. Juice flowed freely around the dildos, and against the back of her thighs. She was intrigued by the light touch of something wispy, like hair or feathers. The breeze blew it against her skin. With a blush that seemed to run from her head to her toes, she realised that the appendage that invaded her anus had a tail of long hair attached to it. To all intents and purposes, she was a mare, a mare to be broken.

There was movement at each side of the leather belt. She knew that the shafts of some small cart had been attached, and she moved slightly, feeling the rolling of wheels and the pull of something behind her – something that was attached to her.

'Keep still.' She judged the voice to be Dominic's again, and sucked through her teeth as he tapped across her belly with the whip.

'She looks a treat. Don't you think so, dear brother?' purred the dark voice of Nadine.

'So far, so good,' Penny heard him reply in a rasping way that seemed almost to crack his throat apart. He sounded entirely absorbed in what was going on; as though he were falling down a pothole and was thoroughly enjoying the experience. 'Depends on how she makes out, of course. Once Dominic's up in the driver's seat, lead her on blind. Get her used to the cart going behind her.'

This was crazy and sublime all at the same time. Here she was allowing herself to be led blindfolded and naked around this impromptu ring in the middle of the woods, harnessed like a horse to some small chariot where a driver sat, reins and whip in hand.

She felt the pressure of the reins against the bit, then a hand holding the reins next to her mouth, leading her forward.

'Walk on, pretty pussy. My brother is watching you.' The voice was low and husky and promised her much if she would only submit to what was expected of her.

Accompanied by a flick from the whip across her back, she stepped forward. The cart was light, although she was aware of there being a weight within it. She could not bend to pull it, her whole body held upright by virtue of the straps that held her to the shafts.

The strap that passed through her legs was being tightened, digging in more deeply between her pouting cheeks, and she felt the intruding rod to which the tail was attached being pushed further in. It didn't matter. The juices flowed more copiously, her legs trembling with delight in response to the mix of sensations that raced like electricity through her body.

The whip again grazed her back, the tip of it flicking across one cheek of her arse. She gasped with the pleasurable shock, her breasts thrusting out more prominently as her back straightened.

'Walk on.'

She felt herself being guided at the order, then heard the light rumbling of the wheels behind her and felt the pressure of the weight in the light vehicle.

'Very nice little filly. Very nice indeed.' The voice had to be Reggie's.

'See how they like you, my wild little filly.' She felt one of Nadine's hands pat her bottom.

'Trot on.'

At Nadine's urging and the voice and whip of Dominic, Penny did as required. Her breasts jiggled against their restricted suspension, and the friction of the two dildos embedded inside made her moan with delight despite her bondage. She was reaching the point of no return, the point when she would not be able to hold back her climax any longer.

As if sensing her imminent orgasm, Nadine grabbed her bridle, slowed her to a halt and spoke. 'The little mare's coming.'

'Stop. She's broken enough. Take off the blinkers.'

The sound of Alistair's voice made her tremble. Just before the blinkers were removed, she felt a trickle of sweat course down her cleavage and turn cold. Between her thighs, the fluid was hot and flowing unabated.

She wanted to walk on, to feel the false phalli grind themselves into her flesh. But for the moment, she was denied movement. Her senses were pushed to their height, yet sexual relief was denied.

Nadine moved away. The whip flicked across Penny's back, on to one buttock then another. She began to move forward, aware of the contraption coming along behind her. Why, she wondered, did tears of pain spring to her eyes when all she was feeling was pleasure, a gratefulness for not having to make any decision for herself, for being at someone else's beck and call?

'Even better, once she's completely broken. I'll try a trot next.'

Without waiting for the whip or any urging from Dominic, Penny broke into a trot, congratulating herself for avoiding the whip.

'Whoa!' Dominic cried out. 'Whoa!'

The reins pulled against the bit in her mouth. Her head jerked.

'I didn't tell you to go, you stupid mare.' The whip lashed across her back three or four times, flicking also against her trussed-up arms. Then, he did the same to each pearlike cheek of her bottom. Her breath was taken away with each stroke, her eyes rolled and her body quivered.

She returned to a walk, then waited for the urging she knew was to come. With the landing of the whip on her back then on each cheek, she broke into a trot.

The cart seemed amazingly light even at this pace and they must have cut quite a dash. Everyone began to clap with approval. Somehow, it made Penny feel quite proud. She lifted her knees higher and felt her nipples tremble beneath the grip of the nipple clamps.

'Well done, old sport,' cried Reggie. 'Well done.'

Sweating under the pulling of the reins, she came to a halt. The shaking was hard to stop, brought on as it was by the rubbing of the leather and the movement of the items that filled her. When would she be allowed her orgasm? she asked herself. When?

'Well done.' Hands patted her, pinched her nipples so the clamps bit more sharply. Fingers slid down the leather thong that divided her labia and the cheeks of her behind.

'And now for your oats,' said Dominic, as he came down from off the driving seat and stood beside her.

Within the shafts of the cart, she trembled with a mix of spent energy and excitement. She felt eyes upon her, though it was difficult to see who they belonged to with the blinkers still in place, even though they had now been opened. She sensed they were all waiting for Alistair to give an order. How the ache between her legs was to be cured was entirely up to him. She welcomed that. It was just another step towards impressing him, so that at some time he would have to take her, too. She wondered again whether he would take her tonight. But she'd wondered that before. Nevertheless, the prospect excited her.

'There, my pretty pussy. Not so bad, was it?'

She glared at Nadine. She tried to respond. Sounds came from her mouth, indiscernible noises fragmented by the piece of metal that still lay across her tongue. She felt her hands being untied, the shafts unfettered from the belt around her waist.

'Soaking wet,' said Nadine, sliding her hand between Penny's legs as Dominic removed the belt from around her waist, and with it the one that ran between her legs and intruded in her sex and anus. The bridle and breast halter were left in place.

She remembered the tree. They had passed it earlier. It was smooth like a silver birch, but larger, its lower branches devoid of leaves and bathed in moonlight. Each of Penny's wrists was strapped to its lower branches, one either side of its trunk. Straps were added to her ankles. She felt them being pulled apart and knew that once she was securely bound she formed an 'X' against the silver bark.

'Eyes.' That was all Alistair said.

Again, the blinkers were strapped together so she could see nothing. But she didn't need to. She knew what was to come, though who from she couldn't really tell.

'Well, my dear. How exposed you look now. How submissive the high and mighty rider who thought she could conquer all. But not everything can be conquered. Even I know that. Each of us has to have our own moment of humility; has to give a little of ourselves to the will of others. It's good to do that; good to depend on someone else for something, relying on their good judgement to enhance our own perceptions, our own lives.'

She knew it was Alistair. Deep inside, she knew exactly what he was talking about. The hidden woman who'd walked half-naked with him on a busy lunch-hour knew more now than she did then. She had found her real self and also found a place where that self could be fully released. Just the sound of his voice made her hips jerk forward. She pleaded for him to take her, to push his cock into her. Even though her words were unintelligible, he took their meaning, knew what she wanted and what he would not – in fact, could not – let her have.

'Patience, my dear Miss Bennet,' he said in a soft, gentle voice that wrapped around her like a warm blanket. 'Patience. You have given me what I desire tonight. Now I will give you your reward.'

She knew he had walked away, and she heard him and the others talking. They were discussing how prominent and white her breasts looked in the moonlight, how gleaming were her thighs with that glistening of sweat burnishing her skin. What a beautiful pink was that treasure in between, and how glossy was that patch of hair from where her humid sex pouted for individual attention!

Someone's breathing was suddenly close to her. Fingers pinched at the clips that still adorned her nipples. Small cries of pained ecstasy escaped from her throat and over the metal bit as they pinched some more. Hot lips kissed the hollow between her throat and shoulders. The flesh she felt against her was hot and naked. Chest hair tickled at her breasts and belly before the head of a hot thrusting penis tapped against her mound. Her mouth strained against the bit, longing to cry out in ecstasy as his penis parted her nether-lips, pushing them to either side like a plough turning a furrow.

Her groan was low in her throat as she felt real flesh enter where before only a hard imitation had invaded. She tilted her hips towards him, welcoming the flesh-and-blood intruder filling her from entrance to womb. She rocked as he rocked, their pubes intertwined and rasping, one thick nest against the other. His hands covered her breasts, and pushed the clips on tighter. Her nipples responded, engorged with the blood of desire, rampant extensions of the fire that was burning between her legs. This cock, she decided, belonged to either Alistair or Dominic. It had to be, though it was difficult to tell.

She felt the loins of her intruder tense, heard the breathing climb to gasping climax. Then he was rammed tight within her. He had come, and she still had not.

She wriggled as he slid out of her. It was her only sign of protest before she felt someone else against her, someone with firm smooth thighs and a hard cock that dived into her with no preliminary explorations. His chest was held away; she felt this coupling only from the waist down.

She cried out. Excitement filled her as she felt cool fingers trail deliciously over her nipples. Confused, she frowned beneath the blinkers. The loins and thighs thrust in constant tempo back and forth against her. Her breath caught in her throat, her head felt dizzy as this hardness filled her, and the tempo was strictly adhered to so her clitoris was fully rubbed and excited. This was the best so far, she told herself. It had to be Alistair.

Sensing her rising orgasm, the tempo of the lunging penis increased and the fingers pinched more determinedly at her entrapped breasts. She was beyond the point of no return and gasped in a long mutated moan against the bit as currents of release spurted like a red-hot fountain from her sex.

The body that had coupled with hers jerked in orgasm. She cried out again as the invading penis was rammed into her again and again with renewed force, each thrust making her shudder and resent it ever leaving. One last hard push, and it was all over. The body fell against her. The breath was sweet, a mixture of tobacco, rich food and good wine. The lips were warm and gentle, the teeth achingly familiar. Small breasts rubbed against hers.

'And how was that, my pretty pussy, my broken-in little filly?'

Surprise and humiliation overwhelmed her. *Nadine* had taken her in front of these people, and she had responded. Nadine wearing a false cock. How could she have been so fooled into thinking it was Alistair?

She muttered her anguish. Heard the cheers and claps from those assembled.

'She didn't know. She really didn't know,' Nadine cried, her exclamation bringing chuckles from those gathered. 'But it was good,' Nadine purred into Penny's ear before kissing the pink-ness of her cheek. 'You have to admit that. And Alistair enjoyed it,' she whispered. 'He's almost there, at his height. And when I judge he's fully there . . .'

Penny stopped wriggling and instead felt elated. She was grateful for the kiss of affection. It calmed her, and the words Nadine had whispered in her ear gave rise to other thoughts and other things. Judging by what Nadine had just whispered to her, the time was coming fast when Alistair, the wager and the stallion would all be hers.

# 13

'You are almost ready, my dear brother,' said Nadine, her finger flicking at the small key that hung just behind her earring.

'And Miss Bennet?' he asked, his eyes studying the business reports on his lap as they drove down the motorway after seeing Dominic off at Heathrow.

Nadine smiled at her brother. 'I think so. I will make certain she's completely open to you. She'll need some stamina to cope. I'll have to be sure she's got that.'

'Ariadne says she has the stamina, and from what I've see so far ...' Alistair eyed his sister almost accusingly, as though her further treatment of Penny was more for her own benefit than his.

Nadine's eyes met his at first, but did not hold him. Instead, she looked out of the car window as though the industrial fringes of London and Reading were suddenly interesting.

He smiled knowingly and turned back to the *Financial Times*. 'I won't condemn you for enjoying her body. I think she enjoys yours equally as much, even what you do to her.'

Surprised, Nadine looked back to her brother. 'Nonsense! She's putty in my hands because she's frightened of me. I am totally in control of her. Totally!'

She spat the last word as though she didn't quite believe it herself. Alistair did not answer, but the smile that dimpled the edges of his mouth was enough to tell her that he didn't believe what she said, that *his* judgement of Penny Bennet differed from her own.

'Everything will go off as before. Once you've had her we can send her packing.'

Alistair rustled his paper somewhat impatiently. 'Somehow,' he said, his eyes not leaving what he was reading, 'I don't think it will be the same as before. I perceive our Miss Bennet has deeper inclinations than we at first gave her credit for.'

This time it was Nadine who did not answer.

'You enjoyed it, pretty pussy. You can't deny it,' said a lounging Nadine. 'I can see it in your eyes.'

Penny stretched, smiling to herself and closing her eyes so she could relive the performance in the forest and keep her pleasure to herself. A while back before coming here she would never have dreamt of admitting that she liked being overpowered, humiliated and made to submit to those around her. Something had been awakened within her and, once roused, it was not likely to be dormant again.

She felt Nadine's teeth hard against her nipples, caught her breath as she sucked, pulling the flesh outwards, nibbling gently so her moans progressed to low yelps of pleasure.

'How can you say that?' she asked. 'You don't know how I felt. Only *I* know that, only *I* had that . . .'

'Pleasure? Lie back, pretty pussy,' Nadine ordered, pushing her back against the pillow. 'Lie back and remember with pleasure.'

Naked and compliant, Penny obeyed, arms stretched above her head, breasts obscenely pouting toward the ceiling. Her skin shivered with rising apprehension, her hips rose and buttocks clenched as her mind took over her senses.

Nadine kissed her, promised her pleasure, promised her Alistair. She felt the buried heat of Nadine's sex brush against her as the long legs straddled her and held her clamped at the hips. The warm palms and long fingers toyed with her breasts, teased them to grow and harden. Nadine pushed Penny's breasts together so they almost formed one mass, bulging and ripe as fresh melons. She divided them, pushed them towards Penny's face, invited her to lick them herself. With a little dexterity and bending of the neck, she did, her own skin feeling soft and silky beneath her tongue.

With the push from a gentle but firm hand, she lay back again on the pillow. Much as she wanted what Nadine was giving her, there was something else she wanted more, something she didn't have, and, because of that she wanted it all the more. That was the trouble with being a winner; you had to be a winner in everything.

'When do I get Alistair?' she moaned.

'When you have experienced everything. When you are completely at the whim of your own sexuality, your own blazing sensations. I must make sure you are ready for that.'

'When? How? Can't I get there faster?'

Nadine stiffened. Her hands tensed.

'You *are* impatient, my little pussy-cat. Much too impatient. You want to gallop before you've learnt to trot.' It was obvious she was referring to the event in the woods, when Penny had been on the receiving end of what she usually gave out.

'But I will help you get there quicker. I will help you learn.'

She felt regret when Nadine dismounted. There was a comfort in her straddling, a warm welcome in the denuded sex that sat so sublimely, so damp and warm, against her own flat stomach.

'Sit up a moment.'

Penny did as she was told. From the bedside cabinet that was decorated with carved nymphs and over-endowed satyrs, Nadine took a dog collar that Penny had noticed earlier.

'Kneel on the floor,' Nadine demanded. Her body already

warming to anything that was about to happen, Penny knelt at the side of the bed. Nadine fastened the collar around her neck, her manner changing as much as her voice.

The leather was rough against Penny's neck, the buckle cold, yet already her sexual juices were flowing and her stomach was tightening with rising excitement.

A willing participant, Penny held her arms high as Nadine wound a silk scarf around her back, bringing each end beneath her breasts. She took the ends up through her cleavage, dividing her breasts then tying the scarf at the nape of Penny's neck. Her breasts were parted, pushed up and outwards. The effect was not exactly unattractive. There was a pouting sensuality in it, a demand for bodily attention. Penny arched her back and, over the tightness of her collar, watched them leap to greater prominence.

'Stand up!' Nadine demanded.

Sensing there was more to come, and more she could not help but welcome, Penny did as ordered.

In the long, low chests of drawers that outmatched the bedside cabinet with its wealth of carvings and acrobatic couplings, Nadine seemed to have a whole collection of silk scarves.

'Over here,' she ordered. 'Now!' she shouted as Penny threw a hint of rebellion into the part she was about to play.

Nadine was pointing at the dressing-table stool which she had placed up against the wall. 'Straddle it,' she ordered.

Penny started to sit down on it, legs wide apart. 'No. Not like that; I want you stood up,' Nadine snapped.

Penny did as ordered so she was stood upright, her legs either side of the width of the stool so she could not possibly close her legs. Nadine passed from one side of her to the other, tying her legs to the stool with sheer-silk scarves. The stool was fairly wide, and so were Penny's legs; her quim balanced above the seat of the stool. Fascinated by the vulnerability of her position, Penny ran her hands over her belly and briefly touched the pink hood of her clit that stood to attention in the midst of her parted lips. She had a sudden need for a climax, yet also had an inkling that such a thing would not be allowed.

'Stop that. It's for *me* to touch, not you!'

Nadine's hands hit hers away, then caught them together and held them in her own.

'Hands above head,' she ordered, and Penny obeyed.

Her eyes followed Nadine as she went back to the drawer. There was a light tinkling of metal, like jewellery falling in folds, one chain upon another. Then Nadine was before her.

'More learning. More discipline,' said Nadine, her face near enough to Penny's to kiss. Surprisingly, she did not kiss her, and that made Penny disappointed. Instead, her quick fingers clipped fine chains to the collar around her neck. They felt cold yet light. Nadine took hold of them and threw them over Penny's shoulders so they dangled down her back.

'Lower your hands.'

Penny did so, and let her gaze sweep the floor as Nadine took her hands and forced them behind her back and fastened them there, the fine ends strong and hard around her wrists.

'Very nice,' said Nadine as she stood back a while, finger on lips, to admire her handiwork.

Penny was bound and secure, her hands immobile, her breasts pushed into the position Nadine wished to achieve. Her legs were permanently parted over the divide of the stool.

'What a sight you look, my pretty pussy,' she purred, her fingers pinching Penny's cheek before both hands dropped to her thrusting breasts.

'If you say so,' said Penny with a sigh.

'Silence!'

Nadine slapped Penny's face and she bit her lip. There was heat where Nadine's palm had landed. It wasn't unexpected. She now knew the way Nadine's games were played and knew her own part in them. She had to give rise, had to give excuses for abuse. Again, the question came into her head. Who was really the mistress? Her, or Nadine?

'You say nothing! Is that clear?' The hand slapped the other cheek, so that one burned, too.

'Yes . . . Yes.'

'Nothing!' said Nadine, slapping her again. 'Just nod. Or, better still, bow.'

Penny bowed, knowing full well that was what Nadine really wanted. Her breasts dangled alluringly as she did so. She fully expected Nadine to fall to temptation and cup them in her hands. Surprisingly she didn't. So she straightened back up, longing for Nadine to get on with what she was going to do. Her excitement was already causing her sex to become more moist and making her bud of passion break free from its hood as it sought sexual release.

While she had been bowed, Nadine had fastened another chain to the collar and attached that to the wall lamp above Penny's head. She was fixed to the spot, unable to move even if she wanted to.

Nadine ran her hand from her breasts, over her belly to the triangle of dark fur that divided her quaking thighs. Penny gulped, mindful of controlling any sound she might make. Not that she was protesting. The only sounds threatening to escape were moans of pleasure and of surprise that she should enjoy what was happening to her so much.

'Wet, my pretty,' said Nadine as her index finger played with the cluster of fleshy petals that surrounded her yearning clit. 'Very wet. Very ready. No, no, no,' she cried suddenly, waving the glistening finger in front of Penny's face. 'Not yet, my pretty pussy. Not yet. Time to contemplate. Time to think, for you, not for me.' Her teeth shone white and straight, and her eyes glinted like chips of ice.

Penny tensed as Nadine moved behind her. She shivered compulsively as the long fingers ran over her expectant flesh. Her muscles clenched as she felt the glistening finger slide between her buttocks. Nadine parted each cheek from the other. An illicit finger prodded at her anal bud, which tightened reflexively.

'Stand easy, my pretty pussy,' Nadine murmured. 'My pleasure is your pleasure. My wish is yours.'

She moved to Penny's side, her face and eyes close to her own. Penny looked at the pale complexion, the light eyes that seemed at times to be entirely devoid of colour.

'Now,' said Nadine, in a tone that made Penny think she had not quite finished with her bondage just yet. 'Complete meditation. That's what you need. I will give it to you, and you will be thankful for it.'

Penny opened her mouth, then remembered she must be silent.

'First,' said Nadine, with great aplomb and obvious enjoyment, 'silence.'

The scarf she tied around her mouth was of soft red silk.

'And', Nadine added, her tongue running over her lips with a relish that made Penny a little nervous, 'darkness.'

Penny attempted to protest, but her words were muffled by the scarf that gagged her. Nadine tied another scarf around her eyes. Complete darkness, complete bondage; her protests were silenced. This vulnerability she was being subjected to made her tremble with apprehension. Fear was one part of it, but excitement the other.

'A little rest,' Nadine whispered into her ear. 'A time for

contemplation. A few moments to think about what I will do when I come back.'

Penny wanted to ask where she was going, what she was doing. Her words were only mumbles muttered into the softness of the material. She didn't see her go, but heard the door close softly.

She tried to move. She couldn't. Her head was held firmly against the wall light by the short chain that was attached to her collar. Her hands were between her back and the wall, her legs spread and tied either side of the stool. Her sex was wide open.

Time seemed to trickle by and her legs began to ache. She strained her ears for footsteps, but only heard rustles from outside – night birds and the sound of the motorway traffic in the far distance. Her excitement subsided.

Her senses readjourned as she heard the door open, and felt a cold draught from the passageway outside. Trembling with mounting excitement, she straightened, thrust her breasts forward as if inviting a touch, however cruel or hard it might be. To have no contact, to be alone with her sexuality, was something she found hard to bear.

'Well, pussy-cat. Are you ready for more?'

Penny nodded vigorously. Her breath caught in her throat as she felt something cold being clamped over each nipple. The clamps had returned.

'How does that feel, my pretty?' said Nadine, her words purring.

Penny mumbled into her gag. Nadine took her cue, longing for a chance to chastise any hint of rebellion in her more than willing subject. It felt as though she were exerting more pressure on to the clamps with her own fingers. Penny winced, and sweat broke out in a fine sheen over her skin as Nadine pushed two fingers inside the leather collar.

'No words. Just actions. Push your pelvis forward for *yes*, move it from side to side for *no*.'

Penny thrust her pelvis forward.

'Good little pussy,' said Nadine. Like she had before, she ran her hand down over Penny's dark triangle and used her fingertip to coax Penny's clit from among its crown of flesh.

'Wet again?' Again the hands moved around to her back – tantalising her spine – and over her buttocks, that jutted at an angle from the wall by virtue of the shape of the stool.

Penny felt the finger slide down the cleft in between and wipe its wetness around her puckered orifice as if preparing it for future events.

Then there was nothing. No touch, no sound, just the slamming of the door.

She wriggled her hips, longed to get her thighs together, her hands free, so she could at least pleasure herself and ease the demands of her arousal.

It was no use. She was as firmly bound as ever, as unable to get to her inflamed sex as she had been before. Her nipples ached, reflecting the ache of her groin.

Again time trickled by. This time her ardour did not dissipate completely; the clamps on her nipples saw to that. Like two extensions to her humid sex, they throbbed with arousal, sending messages of excitement all over her body. She trembled, her state of readiness maintained at a constant level as she awaited Nadine's return.

With a sudden surge of excitement, she heard the door open.

'I'm back.' Nadine's lips were hot and moist against her ear. Her body seemed clothed, whilst Penny's was naked.

Softly, Nadine's fingers and palms trailed beneath each thrusting breast before running down over Penny's stomach to her moist sex. Penny murmured ecstatically against her gag.

It didn't matter that she couldn't see her tormentor; it was just enough to know she was there, that she had not been forgotten and left to just her fantasies.

'Just a little more exhilaration, another little toy to keep you on the boil.'

As Nadine's fingers dived into her soaking hole, Penny gasped and thrust her hips to meet it.

'Yes, my pretty pussy,' laughed Nadine. 'Yes. You like that, don't you?'

Penny thrust her hips forward again in agreement. She didn't want another slap. She wanted an intrusion into her inner sanctum. She didn't care who gave it her as long as she got it.

Tears of frustration welled up behind the blindfold as Nadine withdrew her fingers and traced them down over Penny's back as she had before. Penny felt her wetness being spread around her tight orifice; her cheeks were held firmly open.

'Just a little toy,' murmured Nadine, the delight in her actions self-evident from her voice.

Penny's hips moved forward almost of their own accord as something wet, smooth and long was pushed into her anus. Her cheeks clenched compulsively over it, holding it securely.

'That's right. Hold it in there. Enjoy its unique delight.'

Penny gasped, and found it almost impossible to relax around the foreign object. When she did, whatever was in her began to slide out. She felt Nadine's hand smack at one cheek of her behind, then the other.

'Naughty. Keep hold of it till I fix it in place.'

Penny obeyed, then felt another scarf being fastened around her waist. From that, another scarf was being drawn through her legs. Each end was tied into the belt. She gasped at its coolness and the touch of Nadine's fingers as she held back her labia then refolded them over the scarf. With the fragile softness of the scarf, the dildo in her rectum was pushed firmly back in place, the scarf tightened so it stayed immersed in her gripping channel.

'There!' said Nadine, her hands cupping Penny's bosoms once again before she made her escape. 'How pretty you look now. What a time you will have hanging around here, contemplating the gifts I have given you.'

Penny was alone again, breasts throbbing with desire, sex soaking the scarf that ran through her legs and held the stiff intruder lodged in her nether region. She moaned against her gag and peered at the blackness of her blindfold as she awaited Nadine's return. Anything she wanted, anything at all, if only she would release this flood of orgasmic demand . . .

But Nadine bade her time. She was relishing her control, lovingly acting out each chapter of her bondage to bring Penny to the very peak of desire – to the point where she would accept anything Nadine deigned to give her.

After what seemed like an eternity, she returned.

'Are you ready for me, my pretty pussy?'

In her haste for release, Penny forgot Nadine's requirement. She nodded her head.

'No!' cried Nadine, her finger shooting between Penny's buttocks, pushing the intrusion in further. Automatically Penny's hips thrust forward.

She heard a chair being dragged, then found herself unbound from the wall lamp and flung headlong across the chair. Her legs were still tied to the stool, her hands still bound firmly behind her back.

She felt Nadine loosen them, take them one by one and tie them to the chair legs. Her head was in the seat of the chair, her breasts free and swinging between the chair and the stool.

Coolness seemed to invade her great divide as the silk scarf that ran through her legs was removed. She felt Nadine's fingers retrieve whatever was in her anus before those same fingers removed the blindfold from her eyes.

'Look, my pretty pussy,' said Nadine. Her head resting sideways on the chair, Penny blinked. She noticed that Nadine was naked before she could take in exactly what it was Nadine wanted her to see.

She fully expected it to be whatever Nadine had inserted in her anus. But nothing could have prepared her for the monstrous appendage that Nadine was wearing so proudly and with such obvious intent.

Her eyes opened wide. She mumbled into the silk scarf that still bound her mouth.

Nadine laughed and wiggled her hips so that the false cock swayed in front of her. But this was no ordinary dildo. Above the main phallus was another one, slightly smaller, but not by much. It was then that Penny understood the continuous lubrication Nadine had applied to her smallest orifice and the insertion of the false penis that had been held so firmly in place by the silk scarf.

'All for you, my pretty. All for you.' Nadine's hands became entangled in her hair. She pushed the silk scarf from Penny's mouth. Penny knew what she wanted her to do. It seemed crazy to think Nadine wanted her to suck this thing. What could it do for her? This was not a real phallus. It didn't belong to a man. This was synthetic and cold. But she had no choice. Domination was Nadine's game. By using her as a man would, she would gain satisfaction from Penny's obedience.

'Get on with it. Suck my cock, hard and long as if it were real,' Nadine growled in a low gruff voice that could easily have been that of a man.

Because she hesitated, Nadine dug her fingers in her long,

thick hair, thrust her bony hips forward and nudged the larger appendage into Penny's mouth. Penny took it in, gagging on its length, the taste of plastic, the smooth obscenity of it. The extra one rubbed up and down the bridge of her nose, stiff, yet fairly flexible. It was like a reminder, an example of what was in her mouth.

'Lick the end,' Nadine ordered, smiling at the sight before her, and taking a strange pleasure that she was in the position of man, lover, husband ... or even brother!

Penny licked the end, licked the full length even down to the false balls that were harder than real ones and tasted of talcum powder.

'That one, too,' ordered Nadine, her knee bent over Penny's back as she manoeuvred the upper part of the plastic prick into Penny's open mouth.

This one was no better. Again, Penny gagged as it slid down into her throat. The lower, larger penis stroked her throat on the outside whilst the one in her mouth stroked the inner.

'Enough. I've favoured you enough,' said Nadine as she let go of Penny's hair.

Penny knew what was coming next. She opened her mouth to say something. But Nadine knew what was coming, and she would brook no protest. She'd take it all the way, have her way, and have Penny, too, in the way only a man naturally can – but both orifices at the same time.

Nadine regagged her and Penny resigned herself to what was about to happen. Whatever protests or cries she made against this double intrusion would be heard by no one. And anyway, her sex was moist and needed what was coming.

She felt Nadine's naked thighs against her own. Nadine's hands gripped her hips. Both phallic heads nudged at the holes they were destined for. Penny tensed, her legs braced as she prepared for the onslaught.

Almost ready, she thought to herself as one of Nadine's hands prepared to guide the twin pricks into the holes.

Penny moaned against her gag, then felt the anal probe break the barrier and enter as though it had every right to be there.

'I'm going to see to you good and proper,' murmured Nadine. 'I'm going to fuck you and bugger you all at the same time as you've never been done before. And you're going to love it, just love it!'

Penny didn't answer. She couldn't, but if she had been able to, she could only have agreed. But for now, her attention was absorbed by the twin penises pushing their way into her body.

The larger one met with no obstacle and, in time with the strict tempo of Nadine's movements, her hips began to move, to press back against Nadine as though inviting further invasion, more pleasurable abuse.

She braced herself more firmly, head down on the chair, legs straight and bottom up.

What a beautiful sight I must present, she thought with mounting excitement, the glossy hair of her sex spilling out beneath the silky slit of her vagina and the pink rose of her now-glossy anus.

She groaned her ecstasy as the experience progressed. Her legs trembled. Nadine's hands held her steady – one on each hip – as she pushed the sex tools in further.

Once the appendages were completely immersed, Nadine began to plunge, slowly at first, in shallow movements until she was sure that Penny's body was used to the invasion and accepted it as right. As Penny began to groan against the gag and her breasts swung faster with each pounding from Nadine's hips, Nadine herself began to groan and cry out as the fixings of the appendage rubbed deliciously against her own clit and labia.

Penny heard her cries and, knowing how she was enjoying this, could not help but respond. Nadine showed her no mercy once she knew she could take it. The lunging became fiercer and faster as her breathing increased until Nadine fell forward, her breasts hard and her nipples prominent against Penny's back. Now she was fully embedded, her hands sought Penny's breasts. She removed the clamps, replaced them with her own cruel fingers and squeezed her plump orbs in her palms as she pummelled away at Penny's ravaged holes.

'I've got you, Penny. I've got you. You're all mine!' cried Nadine as she thrust with all the power of a masculine orgasm.

Penny shoved back against her, her eyes closed as her own climax flowed over her body. Even as her climax shivered her limbs, she pushed backwards against the dildo that invaded her anus,  and downwards on the one embedded in her pussy.

Against the silk of the scarf she cried her delight. Wave after wave of trembling ecstasy ran from anus to vagina, vagina to breast and back to anus.

Nadine thrust more aggressively, seemingly lost in another orgasm as the interior of the sex toy rubbed her own clit to the height of sexual expression. They were lost in their enjoyment, smothered in climax. They fell together, sticky body against sticky body, spent, exhausted and willing to sleep till morning.

# 14

It had been a good day. In the horsebox on the way back from the Royal Forest Show, everyone laughed, joked or sang along to classic pop that blasted out from the radio. There was cause for celebration. The Beaumont team had scored the highest points of the day, and had come away with the most trophies and the best qualifiers for the next season.

Penny was equally pleased. In her mind, she saw the look in Alistair's eyes when she had carried off the biggest prize of the day. Although she had felt only the body of the horse between her legs, in that one instant, she thought she had him.

Nadine blew a kiss from the back of the Rolls-Royce as it swerved in front of the horsebox to take both her and Alistair back to Beaumont Place ahead of them.

'Cow!' muttered Alf who lived down in the village and drove part time for the family now and again.

Alf had sandy hair and matching sandy brows. He wore a flat cap on his head that seemed to lie so heavily on his hair that it burst out from underneath it and stood out all around his head like a fringe of faded thatch.

'I take it you don't like Nadine,' said Penny, though she could see the dislike well enough on Alf's features.

'Like her?' he grumbled before spitting out of the window. 'Can't stand the bloody woman. She ain't all there. She's a manip . . . manip . . ., makes you do things you don't want to do. There's a promise there, and a reward, she says, at the end – but when you get to the end, there's nothing there.'

'You're just jealous, Alf!' Gregory laughed nervously and glanced at Penny. He'd acted nervously – as though he'd let her down in some way – ever since the night in the forest, and even though she had whispered to him that she had enjoyed the experience, he still felt he was in debt to her.

'Don't worry,' she had assured him as her tongue had dipped into his ear. 'You can make it up to me.' Then she scanned her brain to think how that could be achieved.

During their sex games since she'd come to Beaumont Place, she had given into Nadine, had let her be the mistress just so she could help her get Alistair, win her wager with Ariadne and win the stallion. Now with the benefit of familiarity, Penny knew that she had all along been receiving just what she wanted. Nadine might think that she, Penny, was her slave, when in fact, the opposite was true. It seemed incredible just how well she had settled into Beaumont Place, as though she were a cork and had found just the right bottle neck to fit into.

An anxiety had arisen in her mind after it had been hinted that most riders leave after one year, that they are pleased to do so, their departure sweetened with a suitable parting gift of money, property or even horses.

She didn't particularly want to push her luck, but the anxiety she was feeling could not be ignored. When she got back, she would go straight to Nadine and ask her exactly what the position was. Deep down she knew that neither money nor anything else could replace what she had felt since coming to this place. She wanted to be part of it, to stay here for much longer than a year, perhaps even for ever. She was resolute. She would speak to Nadine.

She showered first, enjoying the warm lather that trickled in pearl-like drops from the ends of her nipples, ran over her belly and divided into a rush of tributaries that seeped through her mass of pubic hair and down her inner thighs.

By the time she was dressed, she smelt of Narcisse, and her skin felt like silk against the light-green linen of her dress. No underwear, of course, just the dress which was silk-lined and cool against her body.

Her legs were as bronzed and taut as ever, the calves attractively lengthening as she slipped her feet into the high-heeled sandals that shone with a greenish glint and matched her dress exceptionally well. She added a plain gold chain around her neck and let her hair hang free.

'Now ...' she exclaimed, addressing the beautiful woman reflected back at her from the mirror, 'now to beard the lion.'

The Beaumont private rooms were in the west side of the house, unusually sumptuous, she recalled, and unusually decadent. Alistair's office was on that side – the room she had entered on that first day when he had required her to walk near-naked through the crowded streets of the town with only a coat between her and decency. A lot of water had gone under the bridge since then, and many inhibitions had been discarded on that day along with a surplus of clothes. That day, she realised, had prepared her for what was to come. It was at that time that the dark desires hidden deep inside had escaped and could never return. Beaumont Place had teased them into flower, and in Beaumont Place they must always bloom.

'Going to the party?' Gregory looked clean, but casual. His blue jeans were bright, his shirt crisp, white and contrasting sharply with the glowing healthy tan of his skin. She ran her eyes over him and felt her stomach tighten and her sex tingle. Shining bright like a new-minted coin, his hair fell like satin from his head and tonight was caught at the nape of his neck in a piece of whip-thin black leather.

'Of course,' she replied, her eyes meeting his. She wondered just how long it would take him to breach her defences and have her throwing him up against a wall and easing his stalwart cock into her slippery sex.

'Mind if I walk with you?' he asked with something vaguely resembling reverence.

Her eyes met his again when she nodded. 'Yes,' she answered, 'I do.' Then she turned quickly away. She had a task in mind, and he, his body and her own sexuality could very easily get in the way of that. Best avoided, she decided with regret. The truth and her destiny beckoned, and so did Alistair Beaumont. 'I'd like to be alone if you don't mind.'

It was obvious he did mind. He looked hurt, and, in the briefest of moments, the longing that throbbed so positively through her veins almost persuaded her to change her mind.

But she set her jaw, looked straight ahead and pressed on regardless, adamant that she would achieve what she set out to do. 'I'm going to get a little fresh air.' She hesitated, instinctively knowing that the look on his face would accuse her of lying. 'I'll see you later.'

His silence made her feel guilty, but she'd made up her mind. Nadine was not an honest ride and truthful bedfellow, and that annoyed her. There was something more to this brother and sister relationship than met the eye, and she was determined to find out exactly what it was.

Her hand covered the brass handle of the wide double doors that opened on the Beaumont apartments. She was at the other end to where she had entered with Nadine and Clarissa. She levered it down; softly, without even a click, it opened.

The windows were similar, big, high and stretching from crisp white ceiling to polished floor.

The walls were painted terracotta in dramatic contrast with the gilt-edged paintings that hung from the walls, the brocade Louis XIV furniture and the thick-piled Persian carpets that sat in independent squares over the floor.

Not meaning to linger, but being unable to resist, she eyed the paintings. Rubens-like females of pert bosom and pendulous stomach cavorted with men whose over-defined muscles were mismatched with seriously inconsequential cocks.

She licked her lips as she studied the paintings. There were others that were not quite so classic in style, although what they portrayed could not be regarded as purely contemporary. In these, orgies were taking place, goat-footed satyrs thrusting enormous penises into wide-open female gates.

Most of the women appeared submissive, even frightened of what was happening to them, yet still they yielded, unable to resist the lure of the obscene, the animal and the bizarre. One painting above all others forced her to stop dead in her tracks.

There was a chariot, not dissimilar to the one she had been harnessed to in the middle of the woods. Like her, a woman was harnessed to its shafts, satyrs driving her on with leering faces and the flick of many whips.

There was an ecstatic yearning on the woman's features, as if she wanted to please, to do better than she already had.

Half-watching her, yet apparently enthralled with each other, was a couple. They looked alike. The eyes were the same, and they had the same leanness, the same grey eyes. Although they were fondling each other – the girl holding the man's penis in her hand, and he appearing to have his finger stuck somewhere between her legs – Penny knew instinctively that these were brother and sister and they should definitely not be doing what they were doing.

Despite the high windows, the room was getting dimmer as a cloudy afternoon folded into twilight.

Penny, the heat of desire drifting slowly down her body, forced herself to walk on.

The door at the far end opened out onto a corridor. Only a

small window of dark-blue glass let in a subdued and tinted light. A trio of wall lamps compensated for the lack of natural light, but, like the room she had left behind, the floor was covered by thick Persian and Chinese rugs.

Her feet made no sound, her heels sinking into the plush pile and rich colours of the carpets. At the faint click of what sounded like a door latch, she tried one of the doors beside her and found herself in a small room that had rows of seating like a theatre, but no screen. There was only a window; a vast sheet of glass that looked through into a room beyond it.

At first she ducked down when she saw Alistair and Nadine, until she realised that they could not see her. Engrossed in conversation, they were sat in a gangway between two rows of seats.

'Tonight, then?'

Nadine stood up suddenly and draped her long hands over her narrow hips, her face questioning. Her brother got up and began to pace up and down, hands in his pockets. He appeared thoughtful and stared mostly at his shiny black loafers and the thick red carpet of the theatre floor.

'Hmmm.'

'Well?' said Nadine with a hint of impatience.

'Yes. As long as you're sure.'

'I'm sure.'

She saw Nadine smile, a brightness in her eyes that Penny had seen so often before, but never with quite the teeth-flashing smile she adopted now.

'Tell me again,' Alistair said eagerly. He reminded Penny of a small child who's been told a story or a secret and wants to hear it all over again. Excitement caught in her belly. Somehow she knew that it was her they were talking about, that the time was ripe for her wager to be won, although winning it was no longer of such great importance.

Nadine was swaying slightly on the high heels of her black patent boots, her matching skirt barely covering the tight orbs of her snow-white bottom. She sighed as if impatient at having to repeat herself.

'Completely submissive, completely in my control. She's almost ready for you. After tonight, she'll be completely pliable. There's nothing she won't do.'

'You're sure? Are you sure it's not *you* that's hooked, rather than her?'

Nadine looked childishly petulant, and a pink flush coloured her usually pale cheeks. That made Penny smile. Even if Nadine did not accept it as fact, Penny knew it. And strangely enough, so also, it seemed, did Alistair.

'Of course I'm sure! You'll find out.'

'Good.' Alistair smiled and, as he did so, Nadine moved toward him like a child about to get a reward for being a good little girl.

'Are you pleased with me, Aly, darling?' Nadine asked in an oddly coquettish way.

Alistair's white teeth flashed, and suddenly Penny could see just how alike they really were; just how much one depended upon the other.

Penny remembered the couple in the painting, both standing to one side and watching the woman who had been harnessed to the chariot and the hoard of satyrs, clinging on behind, their overlarge cocks waving like baseball bats behind her.

'Beautiful stallion,' she heard Nadine mew. Then she laughed, throwing her head back and wrapping her arms around herself, though her eyes stayed fixed upon her brother's face. 'Ariadne was right. She'll do you fine. Miss Bennet will get one stallion more than she's bargained for! After that, it's on to the next one, my dear brother. There's always another one, isn't there?'

'At last,' breathed Alistair.

And Penny felt his excitement was tangible, but wondered again what had stayed this scenario up until now.

'Once you've finished with her, we'll let her go. There's always another one waiting for your money and more than willing to accommodate your other asset. I know she's been here less than a year, but she's indulged more keenly than anyone else we've had. It is long enough!' she finished crisply.

Nadine had said what she'd said with smiles. Her brother's response was less enthusiastic. There was a look in his eyes that did not match that of his sister. It was as though his plans were somewhat different from hers.

'Yes.' He hesitated. 'I suppose so. Though, somehow, I don't think a few months here will be enough for Miss Bennet. She's a natural at what she does, my dear sister; it's like there's something deep inside driving her on.'

'She'll have to accept it.' Nadine returned.

Alistair raised his eyebrows and gazed at his sister in a calm, even forbidding way. 'She might not.'

'So what?' Nadine shrugged her shoulders and lit up a cheroot. 'There's nothing she can do about it.'

'We'll see,' said Alistair with a smile that made Penny's lips long for his kiss and her loins for his body. 'We'll see.'

So, it was true! Once Alistair had taken her, she would be out of here. But that was stupid, she told herself, absolutely stupid. How could she ever get to the top in her sport unless she had achieved some stability? But that wasn't really the reason she wanted to stay here. Other desires had been unleashed, and Beaumont Place was where she wanted to use them; and Gregory, Alistair, even Nadine, were those she wanted to use them on.

Ariadne had got her into this, and perhaps it would be Ariadne who would get her out of it.

Penny left them there with their mutual looks and their mutual plans. Suddenly, she had plans of her own.

Flushed, she slunk back into the thickly carpeted corridor that would take her back to the more public apartments in Beaumont Place.

Had she really only been here a few months? It seemed longer, as though this were a place she had known and wanted all her life. She knew beyond doubt that she didn't want to leave, and in her mind the jumbled outlines of ad-libbed plans began to tumble into some sort of order.

She wanted to stay here. She was happy, but in order to stay here, she would have to do something drastic, and she would need help to carry out her plan. First she would phone Ariadne just to get things straight. Once she had all the facts, then she would act.

The phone rang a dozen times before Ariadne answered. She sounded breathless and Penny had the distinct feeling that her gorgeous blonde friend was not alone.

'It's me. Penny Bennet.'

'Penny?' If Ariadne was a friend, she certainly didn't sound it at the moment, thought Penny. But what the hell! She pressed on.

'It's about our wager. And it's about Alistair.'

Ariadne hesitated before she spoke. 'How are you getting on?'

'Too well. I get the impression I'm about to win our wager.'

'Already? My!' said Ariadne in a breathless rush. 'You certainly are a quick worker. Then the stallion is yours, darling.'

'Yes, I know that. But then again, he was from the start, wasn't he?'

There was silence on the other end of the phone.

'You know, then?' said Ariadne at last, her voice no more than a hushed whisper.

'That the stallion doesn't belong to you. That it belongs to Alistair.'

'How did you know?' asked Ariadne with surprise.

'I just guessed.'

Penny *had* only guessed. If Ariadne had been as bright as she was beautiful, she would have realised that Penny had led her into declaring the truth of the matter. But Ariadne wasn't bright and had fallen easily into the trap. Besides that, Penny was convinced that, though her mouth was speaking into the phone, other things were happening to other parts of Ariadne's body.

'It's like an aphrodisiac, you know,' Ariadne went on, her words suddenly fast and furious. 'He's a powerful man. He's got a lot of influence, a lot of energy. Nadine directs it, gets him to store it up in those cute rubber pants she makes him wear.'

'Yes,' returned Penny somewhat sharply. 'Really', and 'You're kidding', were the words on her tongue, but the quick, one word retort was enough to hide her ignorance of what Ariadne had just exposed to her.

'That's why she wears those big earrings; you know, those black-jet crucifixes and things – there's a key behind them that unlocks his pants. He can't get to his delicious cock without her say so. His drive's all stored up, like a dam on a river; then when it lets go ... Wow! Imagine if it got out. I wonder what his business associates would say if they knew,' Ariadne went on mindlessly. 'I bet he'd want to drop dead if anything got out about it.'

'No doubt,' Penny said slowly as the pros and cons of the situation ping-ponged around in her mind. 'No doubt he'd be mortified if anyone found out.'

'Devastated!' Ariadne exclaimed in a desperate hush.

Penny had known Ariadne long enough to surmise that some luscious hunk was licking or pushing his rod into her welcoming pussy at that very moment. Also from experience, she could imagine that Ariadne was dying to drop the phone from her mouth and stifle the words in her throat with something far more palatable.

Again, Penny pounced before Ariadne could think straight.

'He didn't ask you to stay?'

'No. I would have liked to, but he doesn't favour that. Anyway, I don't think Nadine's too keen on anyone being near her brother on a permanent basis – except perhaps herself. And besides, he made it worth my while. I've got my own stud farm now.'

'Mares and stallions?'

Ariadne gasped as though a thick member had found its mark in one or other of her most delectable orifices. Obviously, thought Penny, not her mouth. Ariadne laughed breathlessly into the telephone.

'Just me,' she cooed with undisguised pleasure, 'and a selection of fine . . . young . . . stallions . . .'

It seemed to Penny as though the telephone had slipped from her friend's grasp. An angry buzzing sounded against her ear.

But she had no more questions except in her head. So Alistair wore a pair of rubber pants. The picture that presented both intrigued and aroused her in the same instant. And Nadine controlled him by using those pants, storing up his sexual energy like an electricity generator does the power from the National Grid. Ariadne knew about it. Others probably did, too. But their silence had been bought, and they, unlike her, had been willing to accept whatever was offered to them. They hadn't found somewhere they wanted to stay like she had, where her desires and her need for security could complement each other.

Obviously, she had to do something about it. But what? The pants, Nadine . . . then the fact – the very obvious fact – came to her that the international business community would withdraw the respect they had for Alistair if they found out about his odd home life and his peculiar underwear.

The seeds of a plan started to germinate in her head. Even without her yearning to maintain stability for her equestrian career, she would still have to do this. She'd have no yearning for pastures other than those at Beaumont Place.

Ariadne had not wished to stay here; not as much as she did anyway. Ariadne had accepted her lot; Penny would not.

Beaumont Place had brought her the kind of security and pleasure she had only dreamt of in the past. Although their use of her might have appeared to other eyes as cruel or abusive, through the pleasures and pains she had endured, she had encountered status and affection.

In Nadine's long, slim hands, there was affection. In Gregory's tying her up, she had fully appreciated the sense of touch alone. All around her and along many roads, there was a loving desire to give her pleasure. And beneath Alistair's restraint, dictated to him by a pair of rubber pants and a dominant sister, there was an extraordinary passion aimed in her direction. All this was directed at her, and she was loath to lose it.

Knuckles white with determination, she took a deep breath and made herself a promise. With the help of Gregory she would not lose all this. She would keep it and stay here for as long as she wanted . . . even for ever.

# 15

They were in the private theatre that Penny had stumbled on earlier, only this time she was on the other side of the glass. Just as she had guessed, it was another two-sided mirror. Compulsively, she opened her eyes slightly wider as she glanced at it. Then she studied the rest of the room, the blush-red walls of washed silk, the deep rose of the thickly woven carpet, and the fact that the room had no windows, but was lit by square lanterns of Oriental origin which hung from gilded chains in each corner of the room.

In the middle of the room was a wooden frame that might have been mistaken for some kind of loom by the untutored eye. But Penny was not untutored. Much learning had gone into her time here and, although the details of how she would be tied to it might not yet be clear in her mind, she knew the frame was meant to be decorated with a human supplicant, a sacrifice to a man's stored-up sexual power.

'How delicious you look, my pretty pussy,' purred Nadine, her hair whiter, her eyes glinting like chips of hard glass.

Penny said nothing, nor did she acknowledge the lingering hand that slid down over her back and behind. Tension might be in her mind, but the light of excitement shone brightly in her eyes. Although exhilaration and a feeling of potential triumph whirled like dancing leaves in her stomach, she lowered her head in supplication and studied the deep redness of the carpet.

Penny had eaten little and drunk even less this evening.

Undoubtedly, there was something in the air, and that something she knew would be the making or breaking of her.

Nadine had helped her to dress in her room earlier, the costume chosen by her. Yet it was nothing, just a kaftan of black silk trimmed with jet and silver. It tied casually at the waist, but was not belted. Beneath it, Penny wore only her creamy skin which had been bathed, oiled and massaged by Gregory. Her hair hung in glossy waves melting in dark satisfaction with the black silk of her sheer garment.

There were just the two of them in the room now; Nadine and her.

'Is no one else expected?' Penny asked the question in a way that was both provocative and inquisitive.

'My brother was here earlier,' purred Nadine. 'Now it's just us, pretty pussy, just us. But he will be back.'

Nadine grinned and stretched like a loose-limbed cat. She seemed inordinately sure of herself, pleased with whatever had happened in this room earlier.

From beneath her lowered lashes, Penny saw Nadine finger a heavy jet earring, then flick at it so it jangled against the object she knew was behind it. Black earrings, black outfit and white hair. Nadine was a creature of contrasts and addicted to the dramatic. Even now her outfit was nothing more than a two-inch-wide strip of leather that started at a belt at her waist, slid between her legs and divided her boyish rear into two snowy halves. She also wore a breastplate of silver metal between her breasts. This was supported by chains which clipped to a studded collar around her neck. Her eyes were heavily lined with kohl.

Beside her, Penny felt strangely vulnerable, and almost innocently beautiful.

'Let me help you with this,' said Nadine, her long fingers undoing the loose fastening at the front of Penny's long black kaftan. Once off, Nadine flung it to one side, then led her to the wooden structure just as she'd supposed she would.

Her long fingers wound leather bands firmly around each wrist. On each band was a metal ring. Nadine fastened each of these to metal clips set into the wooden frame about a foot above Penny's head. Her ankles were fastened in a similar way beneath her. She was spread and stretched, her body forming a perfect 'X' on the custom-made frame.

Once or twice, she hesitated in what she was doing and looked at Penny a little quizzically, a half-smile playing around her broad mouth as if she couldn't quite believe just how little strength it was taking to fasten Penny in this position. Her hands were trembling.

'You are incredibly willing, my pretty pussy.' Inquisitively, she dipped one finger into Penny's wet aperture.

'My. You are ready for it, aren't you?'

Penny knew no answer was required. She didn't want to speak anyway. She wanted Alistair – more than she could ever have imagined. Furtively, she allowed her lowered eyes to look in the direction of the two-way mirror, and, as though she were playing to an unseen audience, she stretched her body and moaned in what Nadine put down to apprehension as her hips undulated.

Nadine's laugh was loud and throaty, and even more reso-nant once she'd fastened the now-familiar bridle over Penny's head and pressed the bit between her teeth.

Penny's breasts thrust forward almost impatiently, and her skin erupted with goose bumps as she watched Nadine roll back the bundle of red velvet on the table. A variety of whips and riding crops was suddenly exposed.

Nadine grinned at her as she pointed at each one. 'Shall I use this one?' she asked in a silly singsong voice that didn't suit her at all. 'No? Perhaps this one, then. What do you think?'

The question was ineffectual. Penny could not answer, so Nadine made the choice herself.

'This one, then!' she exclaimed at last.

Reflexively, Penny clenched her buttocks as Nadine trailed the tip of a bamboo-handled crop across her bare backside. She trembled again, and clamped her teeth against the metal snaffle bit that lay so cold and hard upon her tongue. She looked again toward the door where she expected Alistair to enter, then back toward the vast mirror. This was a coming-together of the two men in her life, though one of them would not know that. Not wishing Nadine to see what was in her eyes, she bent her head and stared determinedly at the floor.

Nadine laughed at her own games before her face became more serious and her eyes more intense. She turned from Penny, who was spread so deliciously on her wooden frame, opened the door, and brought Alistair in.

Thankfully this time, the blinkers attached to her bridle were not tied. She could see Alistair, could see what she was getting. He entered the room as she'd never seen him before. Gone was the Gucci business suit, Egyptian cotton shirt, silk tie and hand-made leather shoes. All he wore was some strange kind of undergarment made of shiny rubber and clipped at the sides. The device covered his body in such a way that no hint of form was detectable through it. There was no evidence of him even having a penis beneath the thick covering of latex that barricaded his sex and his desires from the outside world.

Yet, even though most of his flesh was exposed to her view for the first time, her gaze was transfixed by his eyes. Tonight, they sparkled and yet they were different. They glittered with a sublime heat as they ran over her body and surveyed what awaited him.

His breathing sounded rampant as though his lungs were guzzling air quicker than he could expel it.

'All for you,' cried Nadine as she unhitched the tiny key from behind her earring, unfastened the rubber pants and let his member expand to its full size.

The sight of it filled Penny's eyes, and her mouth hung open with surprise. It was a beautiful sight, throbbing there, jerking and rearing as though it were still wild and untameable. Just looking at it made her want its throbbing length within her, dividing her succulent labia, penetrating her most secret place and filling her whole being with its immense strength and power. Celibacy had engorged it with desire. Now it was free and determined, as resolute as she was to have it in her.

Only briefly did she glance at the viewing mirror. She licked her lips as she did it, as though savouring the sight of a gourmet meal.

Alistair's chest, which had a sprinkling of dark hair, looked as hard as his cock. His hands were out of sight. Around his neck he wore a leather collar, and it was then she realised that his hands were tied behind his back, and possibly fixed to the collar from behind.

His body was oiled, each muscle standing in stark relief from its neighbour, his skin the colour of honey, his body hair luxuriant enough to proclaim his masculinity.

A lead rein, also of leather, was attached to the collar. Nadine picked up the trailing end of it, smiling serenely as she led him towards the naked woman who was his to do with as he pleased – or so it looked.

He looked vibrant, unequivocally male, and rampant with desire.

Penny was mesmerised and electric with a current of barely suppressed excitement as she surveyed the hard body and the harder penis. It stood proudly before him, rearing as his eyes raked over her body.

Everything he'd undergone and envisaged during the time she'd been here was in those eyes. She responded to that look, writhed in welcome on the restraints that bound her. Just by looking at him she could envisage the feel of his skin against her skin, his flesh within hers.

Accompanied by loud breathing, Alistair lunged toward her, his head bent, lips hot on her breasts, teeth sharp on her nipples.

She yelped against the confines of the metal bit, yet at the same time arched her back so her breasts were more prominent, more thrusting toward his mouth.

'No! Not yet!'

As the riding crop laced a series of blows across Alistair's back, he was yanked rudely from her, his head jerking as Nadine pulled him away like a dog on a lead.

'On your knees!' Nadine ordered.

Her brother obeyed.

'Stay there!' she snapped, not that he could do otherwise. Nadine had passed the lead rein through a link on the wall and had left little room for him to manoeuvre.

She came to Penny's side.

'Now, my pretty pussy,' she murmured through her big white teeth. 'Let me just get you ready for the first part of the covering.'

Nadine adjusted the supports to which she was tied so that they slid one inside the other towards the floor. Now Penny was leaning forward, so far that she was forced to go on to her knees.

Her arms were still above her, still firmly strapped to the uprights which had now been reduced in height. Her ankles too were still restrained, only now she was on her knees, a deep 'V' between her legs still leaving her damp pussy very much exposed.

'Now, my beautiful boy, come over here and do your worst!' She said it with laughter and also with pleasure.

Nadine undid the leather from the metal ring to which she had tied him and tugged her brother to his feet. She brought him, his eyes still glazed and his breathing rapid, before Penny.

Penny gasped, her eyes big with delight as his throbbing appendage leapt with anticipation before her eyes. All the desires that had come into being after that walk through a crowded city street now reached their full potential. She badly wanted him. She moaned against the restraint of the bridle and the bit, and writhed against the bonds that held her so tightly to the frame.

How glad she was not to be blinkered. There it was before her in all its ramrod glory; soft-skinned, yet incredibly hard. All ten inches of it leapt with pleasure as its soft pink crown gently kissed her lips. It was soft, warm and begging to enter.

'Open your mouth. Take him in!' Nadine demanded.

Without hesitation, Penny obeyed. Above her, he moaned as she tilted her head to accommodate him. Sea breezes and the tang of wind-blown sand were the flavours that assaulted her taste buds. She smelt him, the hormone of his arousal filling her nostrils and her head.

Bound as she was, the rest of her body responded. Her nipples pouted and her sex wept hot tears of desire.

Gently, slowly. Back and forth. His pelvis moved; his piston retreated, then advanced. As he moved, his forest of silky soft pubic hair muffled her breath and tickled her lips.

Nadine was now out of view. Not that Penny cared. She was lost in delight and in victory. The wager was won; yet somehow, it was no longer important. With Alistair in her mouth, her eyes slid sidelong to look toward the vast expanse of mirror that almost covered one wall. Beyond that were the rows of theatre-style seats where earlier she had overheard Nadine and Alistair talking about her.

If her mouth hadn't been so full, she would have smiled. There were other things now more important than Alistair and more important than a wager. Even acquiring Ariadne's stallion was less important now.

'Take more of him, bitch! Eat some more!'

Penny winced with pleasurable pain as the riding crop lashed one cheek and then the other. Now she knew exactly where Nadine was. Obediently she took more of Alistair's cock into her mouth. Nadine was behind her and taking obvious delight in laying half a dozen whacks on each of her warming cheeks.

But the lashings were not saved for her alone.

Nadine came into view at the front now, the tight leather and metal of her outfit making more of her breasts than they really were, her naked mons strangely menacing as it curled like petals over the thin strip of leather that ran between her legs. Her face was flushed, yet her eyes were anxious. What was she seeing? Penny asked herself. Could it be that Alistair was too responsive to her mouth and her body, too carried away by a dark-haired girl whose sensuality matched, and perhaps outdid, her own?

Perhaps with passion, perhaps with fear, Nadine raised the whip and brought it across Penny's rear, then Alistair's.

'Give her more, you animal! Give her more!' Nadine snarled.

As the crop lashed his naked buttocks, Alistair shoved sharply forward.

If Penny hadn't tilted her head even more, she'd never have

accommodated any more length. But she did manage it and the crown of his penis burrowed further into her throat.

The sheer imagery of it all did not escape her. She, the captive female, receiving what she was ordered to receive. He, the reined-in stallion, told to service her, to do his duty when commanded as such. His movements increased along with Nadine's lashings. He began to cry out. 'No more! No more!'

In response, Nadine ceased her lashing, which had looked beyond stopping. Her eyes were glazed, glittering with excitement. Her mouth was slightly open. This was her domain. Sex was her weapon, and power was her game.

'Silence!'

From somewhere out of Penny's vision, Nadine fetched something that clinked, and a trail of leather touched briefly on her head before she heard what it was without actually seeing it.

'There. Now you're as silent as she is. You're both bridled!' she exclaimed, and Penny knew that Alistair now had a bit in his mouth just as she did.

But then, she didn't need his words. His thrusting was stronger, and the swelling in her mouth more apparent.

He's coming, she thought to herself. No! No! He mustn't. Not yet! He mustn't! What about me? But she couldn't say that. Her mouth was full of him.

'Take it!' Nadine ordered, her hand cupping the back of Penny's head so she would not retreat from his offering.

Warm, acrid and in a sudden flood, she felt him ejaculate over the bit and into her throat.

Tears sprang to her eyes. How could you? she wanted to scream. The throbbing of his cock lessened along with his cries of ecstasy, then died. How could you? she tried to murmur, but her words were just a mumble against the restraint of the metal bit.

'Never mind, my pretty pussy,' crooned Nadine as her hand ruffled Penny's hair. 'He's not finished yet, you know. He has a lot of catching up to do. This is a rare prize I've kept for you. A rare prize indeed. Now, let me prepare you for the next stage.'

The wooden uprights to which she was attached shot upwards again. Now she stood, arms above her head, legs wide open. Nadine fiddled with some ratchet arrangement on the machine near Penny's waist. Then the wood both her wrists and ankles were attached to moved to the parallel. Now she was laid out flat and a stool with a velvet padded top was slid beneath her hips. Two cushions were forced on top of that. She was arched, like a bow, her breasts falling toward her face, her thighs high and wide open. As she peered upwards between her breasts, she could see her tuft of pubic hair adorning her mons like a clump of fragile trees on a distant hill.

A fountain of desire ran rampant on the other side of that hill. She was wet for Alistair, avid for his penetration. She had no choice but to let him enter her. Yet she wanted no choice. Nadine had primed Alistair for this moment and, as Penny waited for his mighty rod to slide between her dripping lips, she understood just how he must feel.

Within Nadine's control was ultimate satisfaction. That was why, she told herself, she wanted to stay here, why she had asked Gregory to help her, and why she knew that ultimately Alistair would appreciate her staying.

With Nadine tugging him forwards, Alistair stepped into the 'V' formed by her open thighs. His hands were still clasped behind his back. He didn't need them. As if his phallus knew its way by heart, it prodded briefly at her glistening labia before it nosed pleasurably into her open sex.

She moaned with pleasure against the metal of the bridle bit, arched her back and brought her pussy up to meet him.

Already he was huge again, already he was pumping into her, filling her with his mighty muscle, the cast iron of his thighs strangely comforting against the satin softness of her inner thighs.

With each movement, his hanging balls beat a steady rhythm against her bunched behind. They were soft, they were firm, they were warm and mellow; velvet like peaches, yet hard as rubber.

No ordinary man could have performed like he had done in her mouth, then recovered so quickly to perform as he was doing now.

Alistair was indeed a powerful man, made all the more incredible by the restraints suggested by him and augmented by his loving sister.

Tremors of exhilaration ran through Penny's body with all the thunder of a mountain torrent. The extent of his erection seemed to reach every nerve ending in her. She bucked beneath him, pressing against the restraints of the wrist- and ankle-bands and the demeaning and curtailing bridle.

He was in her. She had him. The wager, the stallion and something more besides. Yet he wouldn't know that yet. Neither would Nadine. Only Gregory would know that, watching, waiting there on the other side of the two-way mirror.

They came together, her orgasm muffled with her lips against the restraining bit, her thighs and loins trembling until the sensations of her climax had faded to nothing more than an echo.

When Alistair's body had at last stiffened above her – his muscles screaming with tension and his tool throbbing as it unloaded its most precious cargo – she breathed a heavy sigh but did not count on her ordeal being over. If she knew Nadine that well, it would not be. If Nadine had done her job well, it most certainly had not finished yet.

Even as a smiling Nadine adjusted the ratchet again and brought Penny back to her feet, Alistair's penis, which in most men would now be dormant, was already rearing its head.

'And for our next trick . . .' said Nadine, her dark-brown husky voice bubbling with laughter as she re-adjusted the uprights of the frame.

Now Penny was down on her elbows at the front, her rear high behind her and exposed.

She heard a click and wondered if Gregory had been discovered, but Nadine explained its origins to her.

'I've released his hands,' she murmured, her voice grating almost with regret. 'Soon, it will be all over.'

Warm hands ran in softly caressing circles over Penny's upturned behind. She gasped as she felt twin thumbnails divide her pear-shaped bottom and run to the rosebud discretion of her anus to push and prod and judge reaction.

Lost in her own sensuality, Penny tensed against those hands that for so long had avoided her body. Rapture half-closed her eyes and made her moan and whimper against the bit. But she could do, and wanted to do nothing to halt the coming event.

'Her quim's soaking, Aly. Dip your fingers in there and make your entry easier,' she heard Nadine say.

Strong fingers poked salaciously into her soaking vagina, dipping, stirring and stroking the seeping fluid out of its deep pool and up and over her anal cleft, then entered her anus and pushed more of the sweet fluid around her tight little passage.

The head of Alistair's cock nudged at her puckered opening. Penny tensed her thighs, clenched her buttocks and edged slightly forwards.

Nadine, seeing her feigned reluctance, grasped her hips and held her whilst her brother penetrated.

'Are you in?' she heard Nadine ask, almost as if Penny herself wasn't there and, even if she was, the matter had nothing to do with her.

Alistair groaned in blissful reply.

His penis was still big, but, thankfully, not as big as before.

Penny groaned and moaned in alternate pangs of pain and delight as he ventured further into her most tight opening. This, she knew, would be the last penetration – at least for today.

In that knowledge, she revelled in her achievement, wriggled her bottom and pushed it against him so his shaft could travel further.

With deliberate intent, she intermittently clenched and relaxed her buttock muscles so he growled with ecstasy when she held him tight, and fell silent with regret when she let him go.

The astute Nadine assessed what she was doing, judged what Penny herself wanted, and slid her hand between Penny's open thighs.

With tumbling cries of release, Penny's body jerked against Alistair's and his tensed in throbbing rapture as their climaxes combined.

Both had got what they wanted. So, too, thought Penny to herself, had Nadine. She was still in control here at Beaumont Place, and soon Penny would see that *she* was, too.

Penny didn't wait to be summoned to Alistair's office to be told that it was time for her to go. With Gregory striding alongside her, she knocked, then barged in.

Alistair was being refitted into his rubber pants. Penny was none too sure who was the most surprised to see her – the brother or the sister.

This, she told herself, was most definitely the right time for confrontation. Both were disarmingly surprised; and even Nadine looked flustered, her mouth open and lost for words.

Without waiting for an invitation, Penny made herself comfortable in one of the leather armchairs in the room. She crossed one black-stockinged leg over the other. She did it slowly and with the optimum provocation so that at one point her bare sex flashed before the eyes of those she had come to cherish.

Yet today they felt the aura of businesslike determination that Penny felt herself. She had even dressed to play this part, this very important role on which both her future and her happiness depended.

Her suit was black with white inserts across the shoulders and a white line that cinched in her waist. It was an outfit more suited to a bank manager than a showjumper. Her shoes were plain black suede and her heels high. Her hair was fastened in a bun at the nape of her neck, though its natural bounciness edged it away from appearing severe.

Gregory stood protectively behind her chair. He had a defiant look on his face and there was triumph in his eyes.

Hands clasped loosely in her lap, Penny began to speak her well-chosen and well-rehearsed words.

'As I understand it, contracts at Beaumont Place are liable to run out at short notice once a certain criteria has been filled. This is just to tell you I will not be leaving Beaumont Place. I've decided I like it here and, anyway, it's far more worthwhile in my sport to achieve stability and likeable surroundings.'

'What are you talking about?' blustered Alistair as he struggled into a pair of sharply cut black chinos.

Penny marvelled at how vulnerable Alistair appeared without the advantage of expensive suits and handmade shirts.

'Please don't get me wrong,' she started. 'I don't have any intention of ending your disciplined regime. In fact, I quite admire it,' she finished, nodding at the rubber pants which were fast disappearing behind Alistair's zip.

Now it was Alistair blushing. Although he still looked somewhat abashed, Penny had the distinct impression that he wasn't entirely disappointed that his game was not going to end on the same note as all the others.

It was Nadine whose voice rose to anger.

'What right have you to lay down what you will or will not do? How dare you even *suggest* what you want. You'll be paid well enough for what you've done, just as your friend was.'

'Yes,' returned Penny with a curt nod. 'Just as my friend was. Like her, I was not given the benefit of knowing that. I wanted somewhere where I could be free, lead my own life, follow my own career, somewhere I could feel secure. New sensations were aroused in me. I indulged in new experiences that I am reluctant to leave behind. Now I am here, I intend to stay.'

Alistair glanced briefly at his sister before he raised his eyebrows. However, as yet, he did not smile.

Nadine still looked like thunder, though even her hard lines were beginning to break into bits.

'It's not for you to dictate!' exclaimed Nadine, her small, cold breasts quivering as she spoke.

Smiling, Penny shook her head. 'I'm staying.'

'You can't!' returned Nadine.

Alistair folded his well-formed arms across his bare, hard chest and looked from his sister to Penny in turn.

Penny took three steps toward him. In response, he came three steps nearer her. Thoughtfully, but with the barest crease of a smile on his lips, he shoved his hands into his trouser pockets. The muscles of his chest seemed to swell towards her.

'Well?' Alistair asked. 'What's the ultimatum?'

It wasn't hard to persuade him that releasing the video Gregory had taken on the other side of the two-way mirror would seriously damage his international business affairs.

At first he stared incredulously, then he laughed.

Nadine stared at him wide-eyed and open-mouthed. For once she was not smoking, which under the circumstances was just as well. In fact, it seemed to Penny that Alistair was much impressed and amused by the whole thing.

'But what about...?' began Nadine.

'Hush,' Alistair interrupted, patting unselfconsciously at the hidden underpants that served so well to heighten his sex drive and channel it from business to pleasure. He smiled now, stepped further forwards and placed his hands on Penny's shoulders. She smiled back. Even without him saying, she knew what was to come, knew what she had achieved.

'I think Penny can cope with that; and, quite frankly, I think Penny will be quite enough to suit my needs – and yours,' he added, jerking his head toward the silent Gregory who had been feeling nervous, but who now smiled. 'And you, too, my dear sister,' Alistair said over his shoulder, his teeth now flashing as whitely as hers. 'I knew there was something different from the first time we walked through the crowded streets,' he said still smiling. 'And the first time I found her bent over the trough in the stable. I couldn't resist her then, dear sister, and I can't now. But I think I'd better mend my ways. I need to truly save myself in future. If you look in the small box on my desk there, you'll find a key – a duplicate to the one you wear behind your earring. Take it. Give it to Penny. Then, whenever she wants me, I'm hers – me alone, or me with Gregory or you. Whatever. It doesn't matter.'

Penny listened bright-eyed, then opened her palm to accept the key that Nadine had got from the box on Alistair's desk.

'When did you get that copied?' she asked him.

'Never you mind,' he replied. 'But I think you'll agree that Penny will be a great asset to us. So, too, will Gregory.'

Frozen features melted as the truth of his words filtered through to Nadine's brain. 'Yes!' she exclaimed with some force, her ego and self-esteem now somewhat restored. 'I think you could well be right.'

With feline suppleness, Nadine stretched, took strides to Penny's side and wrapped the length of her hand around the nape of her neck. She smiled, her eyes almond-shaped and cat-like.

'You are probably right, my darling brother,' Nadine purred in a low growling voice. 'Why would we want other pussies when we have such a pretty little one as this?'

That night, Nadine went out to the stable-lads to search for a suitable replacement for Auberon. Penny hoped she would find one. As it was, she herself was in heaven; or rather, in her room with both Alistair and Gregory. The key, or rather Alistair's duplicate, was hanging on a silver chain and snuggled between her breasts.

Visit the Black Lace website at
**www.black-lace-books.com**

FIND OUT THE LATEST INFORMATION AND TAKE ADVANTAGE OF OUR
FANTASTIC FREE BOOK OFFER! ALSO VISIT THE SITE FOR . . .

- All Black Lace titles currently available
  and how to order online

- Great new offers

- Writers' guidelines

- Author interviews

- An erotica newsletter

- Features

- Cool links

BLACK LACE – THE LEADING IMPRINT OF
WOMEN'S SEXY FICTION

TAKING YOUR EROTIC READING PLEASURE
TO NEW HORIZONS

# LOOK OUT FOR THE BLACK LACE 15TH ANNIVERSARY SPECIAL EDITIONS. COLLECT ALL 10 TITLES IN THE SERIES!

*All books priced £7.99 in the UK. Please note publication dates apply to the UK only. For other territories, please contact your retailer.*

## Published in March 2008

**CASSANDRA'S CONFLICT**
*Fredrica Alleyn*
ISBN 978 0 352 34186 0

A house in Hampstead. Present-day. Behind a façade of cultured respectability lies a world of decadent indulgence and dark eroticism. Cassandra's sheltered life is transformed when she gets employed as governess to the Baron's children. He draws her into games where lust can feed on the erotic charge of submission. Games where only he knows the rules and where unusual pleasures can flourish.

Published in April 2008

**GEMINI HEAT**
*Portia Da Costa*
ISBN 978 0 352 34187 7

As the metropolis sizzles in the freak early summer temperatures, identical twin sisters Deana and Delia Ferraro are cooking up a heat wave of their own. Surrounded by an atmosphere of relentless humidity, Deana and Delia find themselves rivals for the attentions of Jackson de Guile – an exotic, wealthy entrepreneur and master of power dynamics – who draws them both into a web of luxurious debauchery.

Their erotic encounters become increasingly bizarre as the twins vie for the rewards that pleasuring him brings them – tainted rewards which only serve to confuse their perceptions of the limits of sexual experience.

Published in May 2008

**BLACK ORCHID**
*Roxanne Carr*
ISBN 978 0 352 34188 4

At the Black Orchid Club, adventurous women who yearn for the pleasures of exotic, even kinky sex can quench their desires in discreet and luxurious surroundings. Having tasted the fulfilment of unique and powerful lusts, one such adventurous woman learns what happens when the need for limitless indulgence becomes an addiction.

Published in June 2008

**FORBIDDEN FRUIT**
*Susie Raymond*
ISBN 978 0 352 34189 1

The last thing sexy thirty-something Beth expected was to get involved with a much younger man. But when she finds him spying on her in the dressing room at work she embarks on an erotic journey with the straining youth, teaching him and teasing him as she leads him through myriad sensuous exercises at her stylish modern home. As their lascivious games become more and more intense, Beth soon begins to realise that she is the one being awakened to a new world of desire – and that hers is the mind quickly becoming consumed with lust.

Published in July 2008

**JULIET RISING**
*Cleo Cordell*
ISBN 978 0 352 34192 1

Nothing is more important to Reynard than winning the favours of the bright and wilful Juliet, a pupil at Madame Nicol's exclusive but strict 18th-century ladies' academy. Her captivating beauty tinged with a hint of cruelty soon has Reynard willing to do anything to win her approval. But Juliet's methods have little effect on Andreas, the real object of her lustful obsessions. Unable to bend him to her will, she is forced to watch him lavish his manly talents on her fellow pupils. That is, until she agrees to change her stuck-up, stubborn ways and become an eager erotic participant.

Published in August 2008

**ODALISQUE**
*Fleur Reynolds*
ISBN 978 0 352 34193 8

Set against a backdrop of sophisticated elegance, a tale of family intrigue, forbidden passions and depraved secrets unfolds. Beautiful but scheming, successful designer Auralie plots to bring about the downfall of her virtuous cousin, Jeanine. Recently widowed, but still young and glamorous, Jeanine finds her passions being rekindled by Auralie's husband. But she is playing into Auralie's hands – vindictive hands that drag Jeanine into a world of erotic depravity. Why are the cousins locked into this sexual feud? And what is the purpose of Jeanine's mysterious Confessor, and his sordid underground sect?

To be published in October 2008

**THE DEVIL AND THE DEEP BLUE SEA**
*Cheryl Mildenhall*
ISBN 978 0 352 34200 3

When Hillary and her girlfriends rent a country house for their summer vacation, it is a pleasant surprise to find that its secretive and kinky owner – Darius Harwood – seems to be the most desirable man in the locale. That is, before Hillary meets Haldane, the blond and beautifully proportioned Norwegian sailor who works nearby. Intrigued by the sexual allure of two very different men, Hillary can't resist exploring the possibilities on offer. But these opportunities for misbehaviour quickly lead her into a tricky situation for which a diffcult decision has to be made.

To be published in November 2008

**THE NINETY DAYS OF GENEVIEVE**
*Lucinda Carrington*
ISBN 978 0 352 34201 0

A ninety-day sex contract wasn't exactly what Genevieve Loften had in mind when she began business negotiations with the arrogant and attractive James Sinclair. As a career move she wanted to go along with it; the pay-off was potentially huge.

However, she didn't imagine that he would make her the star performer in a series of increasingly kinky and exotic fantasies. Thrown into a world of sexual misadventure, Genevieve learns how to balance her high-pressure career with the twilight world of fetishism and debauchery.

To be published in December 2008

**THE GIFT OF SHAME**
*Sarah Hope-Walker*
ISBN 978 0 35234202 7

Sad, sultry Helen flies between London, Paris and the Caribbean chasing whatever physical pleasures she can get to tear her mind from a deep, deep loss. Her glamorous life style and charged sensual escapades belie a widow's grief. When she meets handsome, rich Jeffrey she is shocked and yet intrigued by his masterful, domineering behaviour. Soon, Helen is forced to confront the forbidden desires hiding within herself – and forced to undergo a startling metamorphosis from a meek and modest lady into a bristling, voracious wanton.

## ALSO LOOK OUT FOR

**THE NEW BLACK LACE BOOK OF WOMEN'S SEXUAL FANTASIES**
*Edited and compiled by Mitzi Szereto*
ISBN 978 0 352 34172 3

The second anthology of detailed sexual fantasies contributed by women from all over the world. The book is a result of a year's research by an expert on erotic writing and gives a fascinating insight into the rich diversity of the female sexual imagination.

# Black Lace Booklist

Information is correct at time of printing. To avoid disappointment, check availability before ordering. Go to www.black-lace-books.com.
All books are priced £7.99 unless another price is given.

☐ PACKING HEAT  Karina Moore     ISBN 978 0 352 33356 8    £6.99
☐ PAGAN HEAT  Monica Belle     ISBN 978 0 352 33974 4
☐ PEEP SHOW  Mathilde Madden     ISBN 978 0 352 33924 9
☐ THE POWER GAME  Carrera Devonshire     ISBN 978 0 352 33990 4
☐ THE PRIVATE UNDOING OF A PUBLIC SERVANT     ISBN 978 0 352 34066 5
    Leonie Martel

☐ RUDE AWAKENING  Pamela Kyle     ISBN 978 0 352 33036 9
☐ SAUCE FOR THE GOOSE  Mary Rose Maxwell     ISBN 978 0 352 33492 3
☐ SPLIT  Kristina Lloyd     ISBN 978 0 352 34154 9
☐ STELLA DOES HOLLYWOOD  Stella Black     ISBN 978 0 352 33588 3
☐ THE STRANGER  Portia Da Costa     ISBN 978 0 352 33211 0
☐ SUITE SEVENTEEN  Portia Da Costa     ISBN 978 0 352 34109 9
☐ TONGUE IN CHEEK  Tabitha Flyte     ISBN 978 0 352 33484 8
☐ THE TOP OF HER GAME  Emma Holly     ISBN 978 0 352 34116 7
☐ UNNATURAL SELECTION  Alaine Hood     ISBN 978 0 352 33963 8
☐ VELVET GLOVE  Emma Holly     ISBN 978 0 352 34115 0
☐ VILLAGE OF SECRETS  Mercedes Kelly     ISBN 978 0 352 33344 5
☐ WILD BY NATURE  Monica Belle     ISBN 978 0 352 33915 7    £6.99
☐ WILD CARD  Madeline Moore     ISBN 978 0 352 34038 2
☐ WING OF MADNESS  Mae Nixon     ISBN 978 0 352 34099 3

## BLACK LACE BOOKS WITH AN HISTORICAL SETTING

☐ THE BARBARIAN GEISHA  Charlotte Royal     ISBN 978 0 352 33267 7
☐ BARBARIAN PRIZE  Deanna Ashford     ISBN 978 0 352 34017 7
☐ THE CAPTIVATION  Natasha Rostova     ISBN 978 0 352 33234 9
☐ DARKER THAN LOVE  Kristina Lloyd     ISBN 978 0 352 33279 0
☐ WILD KINGDOM  Deanna Ashford     ISBN 978 0 352 33549 4
☐ DIVINE TORMENT  Janine Ashbless     ISBN 978 0 352 33719 1
☐ FRENCH MANNERS  Olivia Christie     ISBN 978 0 352 33214 1
☐ LORD WRAXALL'S FANCY  Anna Lieff Saxby     ISBN 978 0 352 33080 2
☐ NICOLE'S REVENGE  Lisette Allen     ISBN 978 0 352 32984 4
☐ THE SENSES BEJEWELLED  Cleo Cordell     ISBN 978 0 352 32904 2    £6.99
☐ THE SOCIETY OF SIN  Sian Lacey Taylder     ISBN 978 0 352 34080 1
☐ TEMPLAR PRIZE  Deanna Ashford     ISBN 978 0 352 34137 2
☐ UNDRESSING THE DEVIL  Angel Strand     ISBN 978 0 352 33938 6

**BLACK LACE BOOKS WITH A PARANORMAL THEME**

❏ BRIGHT FIRE  Maya Hess                ISBN 978 0 352 34104 4

❏ BURNING BRIGHT  Janine Ashbless       ISBN 978 0 352 34085 6

❏ CRUEL ENCHANTMENT  Janine Ashbless    ISBN 978 0 352 33483 1

❏ FLOOD  Anna Clare                     ISBN 978 0 352 34094 8

❏ GOTHIC BLUE  Portia Da Costa          ISBN 978 0 352 33075 8

❏ THE PRIDE  Edie Bingham               ISBN 978 0 352 33997 3

❏ THE SILVER COLLAR  Mathilde Madden    ISBN 978 0 352 34141 9

❏ THE TEN VISIONS  Olivia Knight        ISBN 978 0 352 34119 8


**BLACK LACE ANTHOLOGIES**

❏ BLACK LACE QUICKIES 1 Various                        ISBN 978 0 352 34126 6    £2.99

❏ BLACK LACE QUICKIES 2 Various                        ISBN 978 0 352 34127 3    £2.99

❏ BLACK LACE QUICKIES 3 Various                        ISBN 978 0 352 34128 0    £2.99

❏ BLACK LACE QUICKIES 4 Various                        ISBN 978 0 352 34129 7    £2.99

❏ BLACK LACE QUICKIES 5 Various                        ISBN 978 0 352 34130 3    £2.99

❏ BLACK LACE QUICKIES 6 Various                        ISBN 978 0 352 34133 4    £2.99

❏ BLACK LACE QUICKIES 7 Various                        ISBN 978 0 352 34146 4    £2.99

❏ BLACK LACE QUICKIES 8 Various                        ISBN 978 0 352 34147 1    £2.99

❏ BLACK LACE QUICKIES 9 Various                        ISBN 978 0 352 34155 6    £2.99

❏ MORE WICKED WORDS Various                            ISBN 978 0 352 33487 9    £6.99

❏ WICKED WORDS 3 Various                               ISBN 978 0 352 33522 7    £6.99

❏ WICKED WORDS 4 Various                               ISBN 978 0 352 33603 3    £6.99

❏ WICKED WORDS 5 Various                               ISBN 978 0 352 33642 2    £6.99

❏ WICKED WORDS 6 Various                               ISBN 978 0 352 33690 3    £6.99

❏ WICKED WORDS 7 Various                               ISBN 978 0 352 33743 6    £6.99

❏ WICKED WORDS 8 Various                               ISBN 978 0 352 33787 0    £6.99

❏ WICKED WORDS 9 Various                               ISBN 978 0 352 33860 0

❏ WICKED WORDS 10 Various                              ISBN 978 0 352 33893 8

❏ THE BEST OF BLACK LACE 2 Various                     ISBN 978 0 352 33718 4

❏ WICKED WORDS: SEX IN THE OFFICE Various              ISBN 978 0 352 33944 7

❏ WICKED WORDS: SEX AT THE SPORTS CLUB Various         ISBN 978 0 352 33991 1

❏ WICKED WORDS: SEX ON HOLIDAY Various                 ISBN 978 0 352 33961 4

❏ WICKED WORDS: SEX IN UNIFORM Various                 ISBN 978 0 352 34002 3

❏ WICKED WORDS: SEX IN THE KITCHEN Various             ISBN 978 0 352 34018 4

❏ WICKED WORDS: SEX ON THE MOVE Various                ISBN 978 0 352 34034 4

❏ WICKED WORDS: SEX AND MUSIC Various                  ISBN 978 0 352 34061 0

To find out the latest information about Black Lace titles, check out the website: www.black-lace-books.com or send for a booklist with complete synopses by writing to:

Black Lace Booklist, Virgin Books Ltd
Thames Wharf Studios
Rainville Road
London W6 9HA

Please include an SAE of decent size. Please note only British stamps are valid.

Our privacy policy
We will not disclose information you supply us to any other parties. We will not disclose any information which identifies you personally to any person without your express consent.

From time to time we may send out information about Black Lace books and special offers. Please tick here if you do not wish to receive Black Lace information. ❏

Please send me the books I have ticked above.

Name ..........................................................................................................

Address ........................................................................................................

..........................................................................................................

..........................................................................................................

..........................................................................................................

Post Code ..........................................................................................................

**Send to**: Virgin Books Cash Sales, Thames Wharf Studios, Rainville Road, London W6 9HA.

US customers: for prices and details of how to order books for delivery by mail, call 888-330-8477.

Please enclose a cheque or postal order, made payable to Virgin Books Ltd, to the value of the books you have ordered plus postage and packing costs as follows:

UK and BFPO – £1.00 for the first book, 50p for each subsequent book.

Overseas (including Republic of Ireland) – £2.00 for the first book, £1.00 for each subsequent book.

If you would prefer to pay by VISA, ACCESS/MASTERCARD, DINERS CLUB, AMEX or SWITCH, please write your card number and expiry date here:.......................................................

..........................................................................................................

Signature ..........................................................................................................

Please allow up to 28 days for delivery.